P9-BJS-643

Praise for
The Philosopher's Apprentice

"Think Vladimir Nabokov's *Lolita* meets Mary Shelley's *Frankenstein* in Aldous Huxley's *Brave New World* as written by *The Magus*'s John Fowles, and you have a small inkling of what to expect from this remarkable book."
—*Rocky Mountain News*

"James Morrow is a literary swashbuckler, his proud vessel a stalwart craft composed of rationalist thought and biological determinism, his weapons a rapier intelligence and a Swiftian gift for satire.... Morrow's intellectual fervor irradiates *The Philosopher's Apprentice*."
—*Washington Post Book World*

"Entertaining.... Fantastic images and ideas.... Morrow's inventiveness is beguiling, as are his delight in Western philosophy and his concern for the sorry state of the world."
—*New York Times Book Review*

"Morrow may not mention Diderot, but in many ways Morrow is a successor to that finest of Enlightenment thinkers, a man who believed that literature and philosophy marched hand in hand and who was not afraid to discuss serious matters in a comic tone. Enthusiastically recommended."
—*Library Journal* (starred review)

"Morrow addresses controversial topics without being heavy-handed and infuses the narrative with a wit that pragmatists and idealists alike will appreciate. A-"
—*Entertainment Weekly*

"If Plato, Kierkegaard, and Nietzsche decided to tie one on, paint the town red, and then write a novel, they might be able to come up with something like this. Morrow's tale of a sarcastic moralist and his unique protégé shocks and perplexes, while taking the reader on a marvelous adventure."
—*Seattle Post-Intelligencer*

"Morrow is as good as anybody at dramatizing the notion that ideas can both kill us and save us, and *The Philosopher's Apprentice* may well offer about as many provocative ideas per chapter as we'll see in any novel this year."
—Gary K. Wolfe, *Locus*

"Morrow's world is one where ideas matter so much they come lurching to life as intellectual Frankenstein creatures. In *The Philosopher's Apprentice*, they are wickedly hilarious—and then they can break our hearts and scare us silly."
—*Denver Post*

"This novel [is] one of Morrow's best. . . . The creative exuberances of *The Philosopher's Apprentice* are easily justified by the wisdom they support. For a wise novel, then, wittier and better proportioned than most of its predecessors, due praise." —Nick Gevers, *Locus*

"James Morrow's fiction isn't for the faint—the faint of heart, the faint of mind, or the faint of faith. Morrow roasts sacred cows, pokes holes in conventional wisdom, and raises thoughtful, if uncomfortable, questions about the nature of God and the nature of humanity." —*Wichita Eagle*

"Morrow is even more inventive than Vonnegut and has Vonnegut's willingness to milk every sacred cow in the pasture . . . but *The Philosopher's Apprentice* is not just a collection of comic gestures. It can be unexpectedly moving, with scenes of great literary ambiguity. Morrow takes on the issue of abortion in a complex, haunting sequence that could be a novel in its own right." —*Cleveland Plain Dealer*

"[A] tumultuous take on humanity, philosophy, and ethics that is as hilarious as it is outlandish. . . . [A] wildly ambitious morality play, a shrewd amalgamation of the sacred and the profane. Tips its hat with style to Mary Shelley and George Bernard Shaw." —*Kirkus Reviews*

"Morrow has produced an exemplary novel, one that explores a question central to the human understanding of self. . . . *The Philosopher's Apprentice* is thought experiment as heartbreaking drama—this is what science fiction at its best does." —*St. Louis Post-Dispatch*

"[A] hyperkinetic mishmash of horror story, sci-fi yarn, Renaissance allegory, Greek myth, and modern morality tale. . . . An ingenious riff on Mary Shelley's *Frankenstein* and Edmund Spenser's *Faerie Queene*, with ongoing commentary on antiabortion activists and satanic academic pride tossed in. . . . It's the fiction equivalent of a roller-coaster ride, where readers are meant to hold on tight and enjoy the giddy thrills of an over-the-top and overeducated plot." —Maureen Corrigan, NPR's *Fresh Air*

The
Philosopher's
Apprentice

The

Philosopher's

Apprentice

James Morrow

HARPER ⬤ PERENNIAL

NEW YORK • LONDON • TORONTO • SYDNEY • NEW DELHI • AUCKLAND

HARPER ● PERENNIAL

This book is a work of fiction. The characters, incidents, and dialogue are drawn from the author's imagination and are not to be construed as real. Any resemblance to actual events or persons, living or dead, is entirely coincidental.

A hardcover edition of this book was published in 2008 by William Morrow, an imprint of HarperCollins Publishers.

P.S.™ is a trademark of HarperCollins Publishers.

THE PHILOSOPHER'S APPRENTICE. Copyright © 2008 by James Morrow. All rights reserved. Printed in the United States of America. No part of this book may be used or reproduced in any manner whatsoever without written permission except in the case of brief quotations embodied in critical articles and reviews. For information address HarperCollins Publishers, 10 East 53rd Street, New York, NY 10022.

HarperCollins books may be purchased for educational, business, or sales promotional use. For information please write: Special Markets Department, HarperCollins Publishers, 10 East 53rd Street, New York, NY 10022.

FIRST HARPER PERENNIAL EDITION PUBLISHED 2009.

Designed by Nicola Ferguson

The Library of Congress has catalogued the hardcover edition as follows:

Morrow, James, 1947–
    The philosopher's apprentice / James Morrow. — 1st ed.
        p. cm.
    ISBN 978-0-06-135144-0
    1. Graduate students—Fiction.   2. Philosophers—
Fiction.   3. Philosophy—Fiction. I. Title
PS3563.O876P48 2006
813'.54—dc22

                                                           2007029815

ISBN 978-0-06-135145-7 (pbk.)

09 10 11 12 13 OV/RRD 10 9 8 7 6 5 4 3 2 1

To my grandson,
William Alexander Morrow,
this story of generation, procreation,
and talking iguanas

Vain is the word of a philosopher
by whom no suffering is cured.

EPICURUS (341–270 B.C.E.)

Contents

Acknowledgments

I AM BLESSED WITH A CIRCLE OF FRIENDS, relatives, and colleagues who have better things to do with their time than critiquing my novels in manuscript but who perform this service nonetheless. In the case of *The Philosopher's Apprentice,* I owe a particular debt to Joe Adamson, Shira Daemon, Sean Develin, Margaret Duda, Justin Fielding, Peter G. Hayes, Michael Kandel, Reggie Lutz, Marlin May, Christopher Morrow, Glenn Morrow, Kathleen Morrow, Emmet O'Brien, Elisabeth Rose, Vincent Singleton, James Stevens-Arce, Michael Svoboda, and Paul Youngquist.

My gratitude also goes to Jennifer Brehl and Kirsty Dunseath for their editorial acuity, to Wendy Weil and Bruce Hunter for their agenting skills, to the Peter Gould Memorial Philosophy Seminar for nurturing my perplexity, and to my wife, Kathryn Smith Morrow, for in-house research and development.

When my narrator, in defending his doctoral dissertation, wonders why God procrastinated for eons before bringing forth humankind, he is presenting an argument articulated by several estimable evolutionary thinkers, among them Frederick Crews in his remarkable *New York Review of Books* essay "Saving Us from Darwin." The

Urban Igloos of chapter 17 are derived from similar devices described in *The Interventionists: Users' Manual for the Creative Disruption of Everyday Life,* edited by Nato Thompson and Gregory Sholette. Other nonfiction influences on this novel include *Against Ethics* by John Caputo, *A Theory of Justice* by John Rawls, *Truth: A Guide* by Simon Blackburn, *Education and Mind in the Knowledge Age* by Carl Bereiter, *Cracking the Genome* by Kevin Davies, and *Darwin's Dangerous Idea* by Daniel C. Dennett. The landmass called Isla de Sangre is entirely a product of my fancy. I could not begin to specify the conditions under which even the most fecund and far-flung Florida key might come to resemble the extravagant ecosystem depicted in these pages. But fiction is, and always will be, stranger than truth.

Part I

The Sisters Sabacthani

Chapter 1

THIS BEGINS WITH A BUTTERFLY. The insect in question, a monarch, was flitting along a strand of morning glories threaded through the chain-link fence outside my first-floor apartment, systematically dipping its proboscis into the powder-blue cones. It was a warm, fecund morning in August, and I was twenty-seven years old. Contemplating the *Danaus plexippus* through a gash in my screen door, I was utterly mesmerized, transfixed by the creature's ethereal antennae and magnificent orange wings limned with black stripes as bold and stark as the leading in a stained-glass window. How numinous it must have appeared to a lesser insect: a cricket's epiphany.

Inevitably Lao-tzu's famous riddle crossed my mind—"Am I a man dreaming he is a butterfly, or a butterfly dreaming he is a man?"—and I performed a thought experiment, mentally trading places with the monarch. I don't know whether the butterfly enjoyed being an impoverished philosophy student with a particular interest in ethics, but my lepidopterous condition delighted me. The sun warmed my wings, the nectar sated my hunger, and the perfume gratified my olfactory organs, located in, of all places, my feet.

The telephone rang: a representative from my bank, recommending that I go further into debt. I slammed down the receiver and attempted to reenter my Taoist reverie, but it had evaporated. No matter. The butterfly had served its purpose. Thanks to that fragile creature, I'd finally acquired the hook on which to hang my doctoral dissertation. Mason Ambrose, embryonic ethicist, would write about the imperatives entailed in humankind's connection to *Danaus plexippus,* and to insects in general, and to everything else in the world boasting wings, legs, tentacles, talons, tusks, claws, scales, feathers, fins, fur, or flesh. With a rush of joy, I realized that this Darwinist stance would appeal neither to secular Marxists, for whom moral lessons lay exclusively within history's brute curriculum, nor to evangelical Christians, for whom a naturalist ethics was a contradiction in terms, nor to middle-class mystics, who detested any argument smacking of biological determinism. A philosophical position that could simultaneously antagonize the collectivist left, the God-besotted right, and the Aquarian fringe must, I decided, have a lot going for it.

"I've even thought of a title," I told my long-suffering adviser, Tracy Blasko, as we shared a pitcher of sangria in the Pettifog Café that afternoon.

"That's half the battle," Tracy said. In recent months she'd begun to despair that I would ever find what she called, not unfairly, "a topic sufficiently grandiose to hold your interest during the writing phase."

"I want to call it *Toward a Materialist Deontology,*" I said.

"Sounds like a goddamn doctoral dissertation," Tracy said, unsheathing her wickedest grin. She had a round, melodic face whose softness belied her gristly intellect. When the renowned deconstructionist Benoit Tourneur had visited our campus earlier that year, Tracy alone had summoned the gumption to dismantle, publicly and definitively, his ingenious apologia for Heidegger's Nazi affiliations. "But whatever you call it," she added, looking me in the eye, "the topic is eminently worth wrestling to the ground."

"Will the committee agree?" I said, all aglow.

She nodded. "I'll call in a few favors. Congratulations, Mason. You've cracked the first nut—the fruitcake can't be far behind. Shall we order another pitcher?"

"Love to, but I'm late for a class." I rose abruptly, kissed her on each cheek, and explained that in prelude to my Darwinian explorations I was auditing Ben Glockman's legendary Biology 412: Monkey Business: Sexuoeconomic Transactions in African Primate Communities.

"One more thing," Tracy said as I started out of the café. "You should call it *Ethics from the Earth*."

FOR THE NEXT TWO YEARS, I taught English at Watertown High School by day and wrote *Ethics from the Earth* by night, laboring to convert my status at Hawthorne University from ABD— which at most schools stood for "all but dissertation," though Tracy preferred "Aristotle be damned"—to genuine doctor of philosophy, and so it was that, raisin by raisin, currant by currant, the fruitcake took form, until 382 manuscript pages lay in my hard drive. And then disaster struck.

Tracy Blasko, dear Tracy who was half in love with me and I with her, poor Tracy went to pieces, checking herself into the Boston Psychiatric Center for clinical depression and alcoholism. The task of shepherding me through the final revisions fell to the innocuous Carol Eberling, a glum Hegelian who boasted none of Tracy's acid humor or affection for audacity. But for me the real catastrophe— and I'm afraid this is how graduate students construct these matters—was that the person selected to round out my committee was certain to cause me trouble. The nemesis in question was the celebrated postrationalist theologian Felix Pielmeister, newly arrived from Notre Dame.

There are certain coordinates on this planet, spatial and temporal, where one is well advised to avoid antagonizing the locals.

The Lower East Side of Manhattan at three o'clock in the morning, for example, or Fenway Park during the bottom of the ninth with the Sox trailing the Yankees by seven runs, or the philosophy department of a major university any day of the week. I never found out how Felix Pielmeister came to visit my Web site. This scholar who'd once delivered the Gifford Lectures, published eighteen books, and routinely communed with St. Augustine's shade—why would such a man waste his time picking through the dregs and dross of cyberspace? I suppose he went slumming one day, ordering his search engine to display all notices of his newest book, an anti-Darwinist screed called *The Algorithms of Immortality,* and suddenly, voilà: the blistering review I'd composed to amuse myself during the gestation of *Ethics from the Earth.*

It was Dr. Eberling who alerted me to Pielmeister's displeasure. "He's livid, you know," she said. "Really, Mason, you ought to send him an apology."

"I will not eat crow," I replied. "Nor any other bird Pielmeister would put on my platter."

What most infuriated the Augustinian, I suspected, was not my essay's sarcastic tone, savage rhetoric, or unkind cuts. My sin was that I'd caught him in a logical error. Pielmeister's argument reduced to an assertion that the acknowledged incompleteness of the evolutionary model (paradigm A) meant that divine creationism (paradigm B) must be the case. In other words, he was telling his readers that *not A* equals *B,* a lapse in rationality of a sort normally granted only to incoming freshmen and aging department heads.

It's a particularly bad idea to make academic enemies when the school in question is Hawthorne. At the turn of the millennium, our eccentric president, Gaylord Boynton, since retired, inaugurated a forum that endures to this day: dissertation defenses staged in a large auditorium and open to the general campus community. Boynton believed that such a practice would increase both the quality of the dissertations and the intellectual vigilance of the sponsoring faculty. Did this in fact occur? Hard to say. I know only that the innovation makes the average Hawthorne Ph.D. candidate feel less like he's explicating a thesis in early-twenty-first-century Boston than answering a charge of necromancy in late-seventeenth-century Salem.

So there I was, striding through the foyer of Schneider Auditorium in prelude to mounting the stage and holding forth on my *Ethics* while several dozen students and professors stared and salivated. Perhaps a heated argument would break out, complete with red faces and projectile epithets. Maybe Dr. Pielmeister would ask a question so devastating that the candidate would faint dead away. Conceivably the event would turn physical, the professors assailing each other with half-eaten doughnuts. You never knew.

My abdomen spasmed. My bowels went slack. I gritted my teeth, decorated my face with a grin, and entered the arena.

MY PASSION FOR PHILOSOPHY traces to an unlikely source. When I was ten years old, a subversive baby-sitter allowed me to stay up till midnight watching *The Egyptian* on American Movie Classics. This 1954 Cinemascope spectacle stars stolid Edmund Purdom as Sinuhe, an abandoned infant who rises to become the most famous healer of his generation, physician to the pharaoh Akhenaton. It's not a very good movie, being overlong, ponderous, and badly acted. I love it to this day.

Early in *The Egyptian,* Sinuhe's adoptive father, a master of the trepanner's art, opens up a patient's skull. "Look, this tiny splinter of bone pressing on the brain," the old man tells his son. "When I remove it, he will speak again, and walk, and live."

Young Sinuhe asks, "Why, Father? Why?"

"No one knows."

Cut to our hero, still a boy, walking beside the ancient world's most philosophical river, meditating on the mystery of it all. "From the beginning I kept to myself," Sinuhe tells us in voice-over. "I used to wander alone on the banks of the Nile, until the day came when I was ready to enter the School of Life."

Cut to civilization's would-be elite prostrating themselves before a basalt idol, among them Sinuhe, now a handsome adolescent.

"In the School of Life were trained the chosen young men of Egypt, her future scientists and philosophers, statesmen and generals," Sinuhe continues. "All the learning of Egypt lay in the keeping of the gods. For ten years I served them in the school, that I might earn the right to call myself a physician. I learned to bend my body to them, but that was all. My mind still asked a question: Why?"

From the moment I saw Edmund Purdom impersonating piety in that Egyptian academy, I was hooked. The inquiring and defiant mind thriving within a begrudgingly reverent posture—it all made sense. Bow before Isis and Horus and Thoth, perhaps even believe in them, but give them no sovereignty over your thoughts—that was the way to be in the world. Sign me up. Call me Sinuhe.

At Villanova, I took every undergraduate philosophy course I could squeeze into my schedule, and soon I'd set my sights on the doctoral program at Hawthorne. Late in my senior year, I went through a crisis of doubt when my provisional girlfriend, a willowy physics major named Morgan Piziks, informed me at the end of our fourth date that anybody seriously interested in the question "Why?" should look not to philosophy but to the physical sciences—to cosmology, quantum mechanics, molecular biology, and the periodic table of the elements.

My mind went blank. Try as I might, I could contrive no riposte. I felt instinctively that Morgan's claim enjoyed the nontrivial virtue of being true. What could I say? What counterblast was possible? By what conceivable stratagem might I send her worldview tumbling down when I couldn't even get her to sleep with me?

A few weeks later, I chanced upon a quote from Wittgenstein that renewed my faith in philosophy: "At the basis of our contemporary picture of the universe lies the illusion that the so-called laws of nature are the explanations of natural phenomena." Today that assertion strikes me as glib at best, but at the time it saved my sanity. Science could merely *describe* a phenomenon; it could never tell us the *purpose* of that phenomenon. The seminal question "Why?" still sat squarely within philosophy's domain. So I continued to think of myself as the post-Aristotelian Sinuhe, exploring the banks of the Nile, wandering and wondering and idly tossing stones into the water.

A LONG TABLE, draped in white, and five folding chairs occupied the center of the Schneider Auditorium stage, as if the audience were about to endure an avant-garde play in which the characters spent two hours sitting down and standing up and doing other minimalist things. Clutching a fresh printout of *Ethics from the Earth* to my breast, I trod across the boards, assumed my place at the table, and locked my anxious gaze on a plate of frosted doughnuts and a dewy carafe of ice water.

My committee entered from the wings, each member carrying a copy of my dissertation. One by one they shook my hand, beginning with Dr. Eberling, wearing the pessimistic countenance of a deer who knows about prions and hunting season. Then came Desmond Girard, last of the medieval scholastics, stocky, grim, reportedly in possession of a steel-trap mind, though these days he baited it not for bear but merely for the occasional logical positivist who found his way to Hawthorne. Next to greet me was Joseph Schwendeman, our Nietzschean department chair, radiating his usual air of exultant nihilism. And finally I stood face-to-face with Pielmeister, a hulking, densely bearded figure who looked prepared to defend his views via whatever forum might present itself, from philosophical colloquium to pie-eating contest.

A palpable hush settled over the auditorium as the committee, seated now, passed the carafe around and filled their tumblers. Dr. Girard asked if I, too, would like some water. I accepted his offer, lest I appear diffident on a day I was expected to exhibit tough-mindedness.

Dr. Eberling said, "Mr. Ambrose, please begin by telling us what you feel you've accomplished in *Ethics from the Earth*."

"Be happy to," I said, cringing to hear such a dumb, folksy locution escape my lips, then launched into my well-rehearsed précis. The fact that humankind now finds itself in a post-Darwinian epistemological condition, I explained, need not trouble us from an ethical perspective. Indeed, by problematizing our tendency to view ourselves as creatures apart—God's Chosen Species, discontinuous with the rest of nature—the evolutionary paradigm obliges us to address the assorted evils, from overpopulation to climate disruption to habitat destruction, that we have visited upon this, our only planet. Through a Darwinian deontology, we might at last come to know the true character of our sins, a catalog of transgressions not against heaven but against the earth and its life-forms.

Throughout the auditorium there arose mutterings of approval mingled with bursts of applause, a smattering of jeers, and several sustained moans.

"Mr. Ambrose, are you saying that your naturalist ethics supplants the other moral systems surveyed in these pages?" Dr. Girard removed his glasses and rubbed his aquiline nose. "Are you telling us to forget about Platonism, Aristotelianism, Stoicism, Epicureanism, Thomism, Kantianism, and Utilitarianism?"

Although I was prepared in principle for Girard's question, a nugget of dread congealed in my stomach. I took a slow breath, swallowed a mouthful of now-tepid water, and assumed a swaggering smile that immediately degenerated into a grimace. For the next ten minutes, I spouted convoluted and uniformly incoherent sentences, many turning to vapor before their subjects could enjoy intimacy with their verbs. Phrase by awkward phrase, I endeavored to explain why the admitted materialism underlying my dissertation was perfectly in step with the parade of ethical discourse that had tramped through human history from the ancient Greeks to the early Christians to the twentieth-century Rawlsians.

The audience grew restless. They'd come for blood, not dialectic. Only in my concluding remarks did I manage to articulate a reasonably feisty thought.

"Rather than eclipsing Kantianism or Utilitarianism," I said, "Darwinian deontology adds yet another pigment to the palette of moral philosophy."

At this juncture Felix Pielmeister slammed his copy of my *Ethics* on the table—violently, righteously, as if to crush a cockroach. From his throat came a sound suggesting a wild boar simultaneously enjoying a good joke and an important orgasm.

"As I'm sure you're aware, Mr. Ambrose," Pielmeister said, "postrationalist thought is not ipso facto at odds with the arguments of Charles Darwin. And yet I find that these fulminations of yours carry the reader far beyond the theory of natural selection, depositing him in a place devoid of all hope, meaning, and teleology. Is that in fact your position? Is transcendence an illusion? Is God dead?"

Excited murmurings wafted through the hall. This was why our audience had gotten up at nine o'clock on a Saturday morning—to watch state-of-the-art Augustinian theology stomp Mason Ambrose into the dirt.

"It depends on what you mean by transcendence," I said.

"I believe you know what I mean by transcendence," Pielmeister replied.

"Honestly, sir, I can't unpack your question."

"Stop temporizing, Mason," Dr. Schwendeman said.

I fixed on the uneaten doughnuts. A solitary fly hovered above the pile, wondering what it had done to merit such sugary grace. My dilemma was elegant in its simplicity. I needed merely to assert that evolutionary biology, like the other physical sciences, had nothing to say about God, and I was home free. I had only to insist that I had no fundamental quarrel with either Jesus Christ or Felix Pielmeister, and I could pick up my union card.

With an impertinent flourish, I seized the carafe and filled my tumbler to the brim. I sipped. The fluid that entered my mouth, however, was not Hawthorne tap water but some metaphysical beverage drawn from the Nile by Sinuhe himself. It tasted sweet. I savored the sensation, then took another swallow. Why did I want to be a doctor of philosophy anyway? Would I jump through any conceivable hoop to join that dubious fellowship whose attention I had momentarily claimed? What quantity of self-respect was I willing to lose in acquiring this most conventional of prizes?

"I believe I can best answer Dr. Pielmeister's question with a few questions of my own," I said at last. "They all begin with Sinuhe's favorite word, 'why.'"

"Sinuhe?" Dr. Girard said. "You mean from *The Egyptian*?"

"Correct," I said.

"That's not a very good movie," Dr. Girard said.

"The book was better," Dr. Schwendeman said.

"Why," I said, "do our postrationalist theologians, Dr. Pielmeister among them, expect us to prostrate ourselves before a deity who, by the Darwinian insight he claims to endorse, stands exposed as a kind of cosmic dilettante—"

"That is not the language of philosophy," interrupted Pielmeister, wagging his finger.

"—a kind of cosmic dilettante, idly tinkering plants and animals into existence only to have them go extinct from the very environmental conditions he provided for them?"

Delicate but palpable vibrations filled the stuffy air of Schneider Auditorium. The attendees shifted in their seats, delighted that the gladiator had mysteriously elected to insert his head into the lion's mouth. My committee was likewise astir, wondering what demon had possessed this outwardly rational candidate.

"Why," I continued, "was Dr. Pielmeister's presumably competent God unable to produce the contemporary biosphere through any process other than the systematic creation and equally systematic obliteration of countless species?"

Nervous laughter emerged here and there throughout the audience.

"Why," I persisted, "would this same divine serial killer have begun his career spending thirteen billion years fashioning quadrillions of needless galaxies before finally starting on his pet project: singling out a minor planet in an obscure precinct of the Milky Way and seeding it with vain bipedal vertebrates condemned to wait indefinitely for the deity in question to disclose himself?"

"Mason, this isn't going anywhere," Carol Eberling asserted.

"Right you are," I said. "The show is over. Time to close the concession stand and sweep up the peanut shells. I would rather teach front-end alignment at an auto-mechanics school in Framingham than continue to cast my lot with higher education. And so, with all humility and a deep appreciation for the effort you've expended in reading my dissertation, I withdraw my candidacy."

"Mason, no," Dr. Eberling said through gritted teeth.

"That's a terrible idea," said Dr. Girard.

"Most Nietzschean," said Dr. Schwendeman.

"Withdrawal accepted," said Dr. Pielmeister.

"Go back to your offices, good professors," I concluded. "Pick up your paychecks. See who's reviewed your latest book in the *Journal of Astonishingly Articulate Academic Discourse.* But from this moment on, Sinuhe is his own man."

I rose and, stepping toward the footlights, dipped my head in a theatrical bow. The audience members variously clapped, booed, hissed, and cheered. As I rushed down the aisle and into the foyer, a young man drew abreast of me and asked if I wanted to star in his student film about Sigmund Freud's first sexual encounter. I gave him my e-mail address, then hurried into the street.

* * *

EVERY COLLEGE CAMPUS has its beer hall, its rathskeller, its underground den of inconsequential iniquity—someplace where the philosophy majors can huddle in the corners hashing over eros and mortality while the athletes sit at the bar discussing fucking and sudden-death overtime. At Hawthorne, this favored hangout was the Shepherd's Pie, a convivial Commonwealth Avenue grotto where, according to rumor, H. P. Lovecraft had composed what is probably his worst piece of fiction, "Herbert West—Reanimator," but the theory is dubious at best, as that hidebound recluse rarely left Providence.

I skipped dinner and headed straight for the Pie, where I ordered a pitcher of Guinness, then sidled toward my favorite alcove, the very niche in which I'd once gotten my fellow Ph.D. candidate Matthew Forstchen, a card-carrying pragmatist, to admit the logical flaw in William James's assertion that refusing to believe something is itself a kind of faith. (Do I have *faith* that the moon is not made of green cheese? Must I experience a divine revelation before rejecting Ouija boards?) Although my intention was to celebrate my escape from academe, I could not summon the requisite jollity. My position at Watertown High was about to evaporate, and since I wasn't remotely qualified to teach front-end alignment in Framingham or anywhere else, I would soon be staring privation in the face. Returning to my parents in Philadelphia wasn't an option, as the law of self-preservation required me to distance myself from the slow-motion train wreck that was their marriage, nor could I imagine moving in with my sister Delia, who was barely surviving through a combination of waitressing and off-Broadway acting gigs and didn't need a grumpy unemployed little brother in her life.

I was also enduring the emotional aftermath of my meltdown in Schneider. Holding forth on the stage, I'd imagined I was participating in a venerable heroic tradition—the individual versus the system—but now I simply felt like a screwup. I vowed to send apologetic e-mails to Eberling, Schwendeman, Girard, and perhaps even

Pielmeister. Tracy Blasko also deserved a letter, a real one, the kind that reposes on paper and arrives in an envelope. I would thank her for tolerating my idiosyncrasies during the past five years, then attempt to explain why I'd jumped ship.

"Mind if I join you?" a sonorous voice inquired.

I looked up. My visitor was an owlish black man in his late forties, with a salt-and-pepper beard and eyes as dark and soft as plums.

"I'm not in a very good mood," I told him. "Have a seat."

We shook hands.

"Dawson Wilcox, paleontology department," he said. "Your notoriety precedes you. Mason Ambrose, late of the philosophy department, author of a quirky dissertation called *Ethics from the Earth*." On the nearest empty chair, he deposited a leather satchel, brown and scuffed and also bulging, as if perhaps it contained a fossil mandible. "May I buy you a beer?"

I gestured toward my pitcher of stout. "I'm fixed for the evening. Here's a question for you, Dr. Wilcox. Does this pitcher truly hold four beers, or merely four *potential* beers, each awaiting the reification that will occur upon being poured?"

Wilcox gave me a blank look. "No wonder philosophers can't get funded."

I filled my glass with stout. An ivory wave of foam frothed over the rim and cascaded onto the table. "Will you help me get to the bottom of this? The pitcher, I mean, not the ontological mystery."

Wilcox fetched a second glass from the bar, along with a bowl of miniature pretzels. I poured him a beer, grabbed a pretzel, and took a gulp of Guinness.

"I followed you here from Schneider," my drinking companion said. "Let me congratulate you on what was perhaps the liveliest dissertation defense in Hawthorne history."

"Seppuka makes a great spectator sport," I said, munching.

"I'm here to offer you a job."

"I never even played with plastic dinosaurs."

"Oh, no, not in my department, though I appreciate the kind words you put in for Mr. Darwin this afternoon."

"Let me guess. You decided to become a paleontologist when you fell madly in love with *Tyrannosaurus rex* in fourth grade."

Wilcox issued a cryptic laugh and downed some Guinness, embroidering his upper lip with a second mustache. "Ever hear of Isla de Sangre?"

"Blood Island?"

"Ringed by a rare species of red coral," he replied, nodding. "The coccyx of the Florida Keys, so far south it nudges the Tropic of Cancer. The owner's a former colleague of mine, Edwina Sabacthani, a molecular geneticist. Eccentric, capricious, smart as God—the sort of person who'll show up on the last day of an academic conference, sniff out whoever's been a particularly pompous boor all week, and start hinting that she noticed a major methodological flaw in his latest published results."

I drained my glass. The Guinness started doing what it was designed to do. "Three cheers for academic conferences," I said. The one time I'd delivered a paper at a conference, "The *Geist* in the Machine," a précis of my master's thesis on Schelling, I didn't meet any minds of Edwina Sabacthani's caliber, but I was memorably seduced by a tenured Utilitarian from Princeton named Frédérique Wintrebert, who said she'd become aroused by my use of the word "praxis."

"Here's the deal," Wilcox said. "Edwina wants me to find a tutor for her teenage daughter. I think you're our man."

"I'm a neo-Darwinian atheist, Dawson. The average American mother would rather fill the position with Humbert Humbert."

"It's not your Darwinism that caught my attention," Wilcox said. "What impressed me was your rambling but nonetheless astute overview of Western ethics. I've never met the young woman in question, but evidently she has a handicap. In Edwina's words,

Londa Sabacthani 'lacks a moral center.' You're supposed to give her one."

I poured myself a second glass. "Maybe I should print up a business card: 'Mason Ambrose. Failed Philosopher. Superegos Installed While You Wait.'"

"This is a sad and serious case," Wilcox said in a mildly reproving tone.

I gulped some stout and picked up a pretzel, orienting it so the parabolas suggested laudable breasts viewed from above. "There's a whole science to pretzels," I said as still more Guinness washed through my brain's aching capillaries. "Mathematicians can plot the twists and curves. Wittgenstein would not be impressed. Actually, I don't think anything impressed Wittgenstein, with the possible exception of Wittgenstein."

"The position pays one hundred thousand dollars for the first year. After that, you and Edwina can negotiate."

I sucked on the pretzel, enjoying the sensation of the salt crystals copulating with my taste buds. One hundred thousand dollars? Pielmeister probably made more than a hundred thousand a year, but certainly not per *student*.

"You have to realize, this is an extremely difficult decision for me. I'm broke. I'm about to lose my job. I just threw away my future. And yet, sir—and yet you have the *audacity* to imagine I would accept a small fortune for taking an undemanding sinecure in a tropical paradise."

Wilcox patted his battered satchel. "I've got the paperwork with me."

"I think I should meet the girl before I sign anything."

"A sensible precaution, but Edwina and sensible precautions haven't been on speaking terms in years." Wilcox unzipped his satchel, rooted around, and pulled out a file folder labeled SABAC-THANI. "I'm afraid you must either accept the job right now or send me off in search of another ethicist."

"One hundred thousand dollars? No fine print?"

"None required—the bold print is outrageous enough. Edwina expects you to drop everything, fly to Key West on Friday, and be prepared to give Londa her first lesson starting at ten o'clock Monday morning. On my way over here, I made your plane reservations, and my graduate assistant will sublet your apartment and forward your mail. Don't worry about your worldly possessions. We'll crate everything up and ship it to you."

"No moral center," I said. "What could that possibly mean?"

Wilcox shrugged, then set the contract on the table, taking care to avoid the liquid rings stamped by our glasses. "Your liaison in Key West will be Edwina's colleague, Vincent Charnock, another geneticist. Maybe he can answer your questions."

I retrieved a ballpoint pen from my jacket and clicked the cartridge into place. "One hundred thousand?"

"Plus room, board, and travel expenses." Wilcox ate a pretzel. "By the way, it was third grade, and it was the ankylosaur, so here I am at Hawthorne, working it all out."

Chapter 2

IN A CHARACTERISTIC DISPLAY of procrastination, I put off packing till the last minute. As dawn's embryonic light suffused my apartment, I jammed the normal necessities into my suitcase—toothbrush, electric razor, underwear, yellowed Penguin paperbacks—then topped off the jumble with a bound copy of my dissertation. I pulled on my Kierkegaard T-shirt, hurried out the door, and, by the grace of Isis, Thoth, and public transportation, caught my 8:20 A.M. flight, wafting from staid and predictable Boston to the exotic metropolis of Miami.

I found my way to the airport's ghetto district and boarded a shuttle plane, its seats designed to accommodate hobbits comfortably but not a six-foot-one beanpole like myself. Forty minutes later I touched down in the city of Key West on the island of the same name. As arranged, Edwina Sabacthani's fellow geneticist, Vincent Charnock, was waiting at the terminal, clutching a white cardboard rectangle on which he'd carefully misspelled my name with a red felt-tip marker: MASON AMBROWSE. A rotund man shaped rather like an Erlenmeyer flask, with thinning hair and eyes set so far back I wondered if he might be legally blind, Dr. Charnock displayed a sardonic smirk that evidently never left his face, while the rest of his countenance, a blobby affair, suggested a waxen Charles Laughton following a breakdown in the air-conditioning system at Madame Tussaud's.

So long had I lived in the hermetically sealed world of graduate students, where the daily demands of subsistence teaching and posturing for professors make extroverts of us all, that I was not prepared for Dr. Charnock's aloof demeanor. As we followed the usual protocols—locating the luggage carousel, retrieving my suitcase, hiring a taxi—my companion remained as taciturn as a tortoise, answering my questions in clipped phrases and uninformative grunts. Did he know my prospective pupil? Yes, he did. Had he ever observed her behave in an antisocial fashion? Yes, he had. Would he like to tell me about those episodes? No, he wouldn't. Was he glad I'd accepted the position as Londa's tutor? He wasn't sure.

Our destination proved to be the Oceanside Marina on Peninsula Avenue, where a silver-mustached Cuban expatriate waited to facilitate the next leg of our journey. The plan called for Captain López to ferry us to the island in his thirty-foot cabin cruiser, which he normally chartered, himself at the helm, to weekend fishing parties of paunchy CEOs in search of their inner Hemingways. We weighed anchor at one o'clock. The weather was wretched, the sort of chilly, fine-grained precipitation that quickly seeps from skin to ligament to core of bone, and so Charnock and I retreated belowdecks to quarters stinking of kelp and bluefish.

Our passage to the Tropic of Cancer took nearly four hours, during which interval the rain stopped, so that the thickly forested hills of Isla de Sangre presented themselves clearly to my gaze, dipping and rising like the spine of a sea serpent. We navigated the Bahía de Flores and landed at a ramshackle wooden dock, tying up between a derelict trawler and a battered sailboat. As we disembarked, Charnock deigned to initiate a conversation, explaining that the geography of Blood Island was in a class by itself, "part Florida swamp, part Mexican rain forest," and how in recent months he and Edwina had "succeeded in making the local flora and fauna more congruent with our personal tastes."

"I've heard of fixer-upper houses," I said, "but never a fixer-upper ecosystem."

Charnock frowned and informed me that he'd arranged for Edwina's staff to prepare a meal and leave it for our consumption. He hoped I liked seafood.

"I have *learned* to like it," I said. "Up Boston way, disparaging scrod is considered hate speech."

"No scrod on the menu," Charnock said, "but I think you'll enjoy our spiny lobsters."

All during our long, wordless walk through the jungle, I pondered the psychic dislocations inherent in the advent of jetliners. Ten hours earlier I'd been packing my suitcase while overhearing the chatter of Back Bay children clambering onto their school bus, and now here I was in the tropics, swatting mosquitoes, sweating profusely, and contemplating hundreds of spotted green lizards as they skittered along the tree trunks. I felt not so much like a traveler as a man on whom an operation called travel had been performed. What would modernity bring next? Might a day arrive when I would go to bed as Mason Ambrose and, courtesy of some brave new technology, wake up as someone else?

A half-hour's hike brought us within sight of Charnock's house, a weathered A-frame adjacent to the complex of Quonset huts where he conducted his biology experiments. "Five years ago I was just another molecular geneticist, collaborating with fools and groveling for funds," he told me. "Whatever impression Dr. Sabacthani makes on you tomorrow, remember that she's a person of vision. She's not afraid to ask the big questions, or to have me try to answer them. Why only four bases in a DNA molecule? Why only twenty amino acids in our proteins? What might the world look like if nature had used a bigger set of building blocks? Ever wonder about that, Ambrose?"

"Guess I'm not a person of vision."

Although its isosceles façade suggested a cramped interior, the A-frame proved spacious, complete with a screened back porch bisected by a hammock—the guest room, Charnock explained. The windows held not glass but mosquito netting, and as the gauzy fabric filtered the setting sun, I briefly fancied myself a moth trapped inside a Chinese lantern. As promised, dinner was waiting for us. The servants were nowhere to be seen, which made me feel a bit like Goldilocks about to partake of her illicit porridge. By the time I'd drunk my first cold Dos Equis, however, my unease had vanished, and I no longer imagined that the bears were about to arrive and chase us into the forest.

Resting on a bed of saffron rice and surrounded by slices of fried mango, the two indigenous spiny lobsters looked delectable, but their anatomy disturbed me. This species had never evolved the fighting claws that characterized its northern cousin, and yet our entrées boasted pincers as large as tin snips. Noting my perplexity, Charnock said, "After nine hundred trials, I managed to endow a Caribbean spiny lobster with a Maine lobster's claws."

"Impressive," I said.

"Thank you."

I smiled and said, "Of course, I'd be *more* impressed if you'd taken an ordinary Caribbean starfish and turned it into a Jewish one."

"Jewish?"

"With six points."

"Biology is not a joke, Mr. Ambrose."

We finished our dinner in silence, leaving behind two vacant lobster shells and seven empty beer bottles. Outside the house a thousand insects sang and sawed in wondrous harmony, as if a population of Buddhist homunculi now occupied the banana plants and the mangroves, ringing their little bells.

Wrapped in the beer's muzzy embrace, I shuffled to the porch and climbed into the hammock. For the next hour, I read my paperback of Walker Percy's *The Message in the Bottle,* wondering whether Londa Sabacthani might be suffering from what Percy called "the loss of the creature," the alienation that modern man has inflicted on himself by ceding the world's most valuable things—its natural wonders, artistic marvels, erotic energies, and common sense—to dubious cults of expertise. I extinguished the Coleman lantern and closed my eyes. Half awake and half asleep, half in bed and half in Xanadu, I entertained many strange fancies, eventually imagining that Charnock had experimented on me. In this reverie my hands had become leopard paws, my nose was a boar's snout, and my gums had sprouted two-inch fangs. When I went to the bathroom later that night to void the residual beer, I made a point of looking in the mirror.

BEYOND HIS WIZARDRY WITH DNA, Charnock was apparently a competent cook, for I awoke to find him preparing two complex omelets stuffed with cheese, peppers, onions, and morsels of shrimp. The meal passed without conversation. It was not yet eight o'clock, and already I was sweating. I drank two glasses of ice water. Fragrances drifted in from the jungle—sweet gardenias, dulcet hibiscus, silken magnolias. The previous night's insect musicians had returned to their burrows, and the island now belonged to the birds, filling the air with territorial caws and proprietary arpeggios.

Shortly after breakfast, a Jeep pulled up outside Charnock's A-frame, driven by a raffish, safari-jacketed Latino with a drooping black mustache and olive skin, a by-God Ramar of the Jungle pith helmet shadowing his face. He introduced himself as Javier Cotrino, Dr. Sabacthani's personal assistant, dispatched to chauffeur me to her mansion. For the next twenty minutes, Javier and I lurched and bounced along an unpaved road, descending into a verdant valley flush with hibiscus and bougainvillea, until at last we came to a high chain-link fence surmounted by spirals of barbed wire. We drove beneath a raised crossing gate, angled like a satyr's intractable erection, then continued past acacia groves and cypress stands toward the rising sun.

The mansion in question—Faustino, Javier called it—was straight out of the antebellum American South, complete with square columns and great tufts of Spanish moss drooping from the roof like a gallery of beards in a costume shop. As we climbed the steps to the veranda, Javier warned me that Dr. Sabacthani had slept badly the previous night, and I must not take her exhaustion for haughtiness. We passed through the front door, its central panel carved with a bas-relief Aztec deity who'd evidently actualized himself for the sole purpose of being unappeasable, then proceeded to a geodesic dome whose hundred hurricane-proof glass triangles served to shield a private jungle from the ravages of Gulf storms. Ferns, vines, and orchids flourished everywhere. Fumes compounded of humus and nectar filled my nostrils. The air felt like hot glue. At the center of all this Darwinian commotion, an immense mangrove tree emerged from a saltwater pond, its naked roots entwined like acrobatic pythons, its coiling limbs bearing small green fruit suggesting organic Ping-Pong balls. Beneath the tree, dressed in a white lace gown and reading an issue of the *American Journal of Human Genetics,* a woman of perhaps forty sat in a wicker chair, its fan-shaped back spreading behind her like Botticelli's scallop shell giving birth to Venus.

"Every Saturday morning," Javier told me, "you'll find two elegant and fascinating creatures in our conservatory—my friend Dr. Sabacthani, and this queen of the trees, Proserpine."

"The mangrove has a name?" I asked.

"A Christian name only," the woman replied in a sandpaper voice. Her face was a disconcerting conjunction of high-cheeked beauty and humorless ambition, as if Katharine Hepburn had been cast in her prime as Catherine de Medici. "The experiment was not sufficiently successful for me to admit Proserpine to the Sabacthani family." She flipped a pair of gold-framed polarized lenses into place over her eyeglasses, then set her book atop a wheeled cart holding a coffee urn, its shiny convex surface elongating Proserpine's reflection into an El Greco figure. "Forgive me for not rising to greet you, Mason, but I've not been well lately, and etiquette would only aggravate my condition. Call me Edwina. May I offer you some coffee?"

"The food of philosophers," I said, though a better case could be made for beer.

Javier gestured me into a second fan-back chair and, approaching the urn, released an ebony stream into a mug bearing the Odradek Pharmaceuticals logo. He passed me my coffee, filled a second Odradek mug for Edwina, and exited the dome, walking backward with the dexterity of a Hawthorne tour guide showing prospective students around the campus.

"Tell me, Mason, is sin something that Anglo-American philosophers worry about these days"—Edwina rested a bony hand on the mangrove's nearest root—"or do you leave all that to your Continental colleagues?"

"Sin?"

"No sooner had Dr. Charnock and I given Proserpine a rudimentary brain than it became clear that we had sinned."

"A brain?"

"It's gone now, most of it. Her first words—"

"Words?"

"We also gave her a tongue, a larynx, primitive lungs, and a crude circulatory system. Her first words were, 'Put me out of my misery.' Not what we expected to hear. What do you suppose she meant?"

"Are you testing me?"

Edwina smiled.

"Perhaps you'd created a kind of basket case." I sipped my beverage. It had a heady chocolate flavor, as if Charnock had induced a coffee bush to have sex with a cacao plant. "A being with an inherent desire to move its body through space but lacking any means to do so."

"Good," Edwina said, acclaiming my answer with a clap of her hands. "Dawson did not overestimate you. I told Dr. Charnock we had no choice but to amputate Proserpine's consciousness. Mercy demanded it. He said such an operation would amount to physician-assisted suicide, a practice he has always found repellent. So I took up a scalpel and performed the procedure myself. There's a lesson in all this, a parable for the neural-network community as they go about imposing self-awareness on their computers. Beware, ladies and gentlemen. To pour a free-floating intellect into a machine is to risk making an infinitely frustrated soul."

"A tormented Dr. Johnson," I mused, "eternally eager to kick a stone and thus give Berkeley's idealism the boot. But he can find no stone in his universe, nor a leg with which to kick it."

"Well said."

Just then a mild tremor passed through the mangrove's limbs and roots. Edwina and I exchanged freighted glances.

"You didn't imagine that," she said. "I couldn't excise the entire nervous system without causing death. Every so often, Proserpine shudders."

Curious, I rose and picked my way across the saltwater pond, one stepping-stone at a time, then leaned toward the mangrove's trunk. I froze. A chuffing reached my ears, low and coarse, like the sound of a passing steamboat as apprehended by an eel. Counterpointing Proserpine's breaths was a second cadence: the thump of the sap pulsing through her xylem.

"She's breathing," I said. "Her heart is beating."

"Vestigial reflexes," Edwina said. "She's no longer sentient, I promise you."

For a moment I considered reneging on my contract and going back to Boston. Yes, I needed the money, but did I really want to spend a year among people who routinely fashioned mutant lobsters and breathing trees and God knew what other sorts of biological surrealism?

"'No growth of moor or coppice,'" Edwina quoted as I returned to my seat, "'No heather-flower or vine, but bloomless buds of poppies, green grapes of Proserpine.'" She extended her arm and harvested one of the mangrove's fruits. "The world has never met with my approval."

"You're an idealist," I said.

"Or a cynic."

"The same thing."

It was a glib answer, and we both knew it. Although her polarized lenses mitigated Edwina's scowl, I still felt its impact.

"In any event," she said, "from the moment of my daughter's birth, I contrived to give her a sheltered existence, educating her entirely at home. Her father would not have assented, but he died before she was born, pancreatic cancer, a banal end for a remarkable man." She took my hand and pressed the strange fruit into my palm. "Javier calls them 'rococonuts.' Charnock prefers the term 'mummy kumquats'—'mumquats'—for they can make the consumer imagine he's immortal. Be careful where you eat your mumquat, Mason. Avoid precipices and quicksand bogs."

"Thanks for the warning," I said, nesting the fruit in my shirt pocket.

Edwina raised her hand in a halfhearted attempt to conceal a yawn. "By age six Londa was an expert swimmer. On the morning of her seventeenth birthday, she dove into a lagoon and struck her head on a rock. Javier fished her out before she could drown. Londa's first trip to the mainland occurred in a medevac chopper. The blow left no scar, but the resultant memory loss remains one of the severest in the annals of amnesia." She swallowed some coffee. "Gradually it became clear that Londa's childhood recollections weren't the only casualty—she'd also lost her ability to distinguish right from wrong. Depravity is not a diagnosis one makes lightly, but the evidence seems unequivocal."

For the next fifteen minutes, Edwina expounded upon the sorry condition of Londa's conscience. The feral adolescent had recently set fire to the rug in the east parlor, stolen cash from Javier's wallet, smashed the dinnerware on the kitchen floor, thrown rocks through the windows of Dr. Charnock's laboratory, eaten mumquats against her mother's orders—the list went on and on.

"In undertaking Londa's cure, you will have one great asset," Edwina said. "She has retained her ability to pick up any book and absorb its contents at an astonishing speed, a genetic endowment from her maternal grandfather. By devouring most of the Faustino library, she has succeeded in reorienting herself to Western civilization and its cultural norms. As for reality per se, she prefers to account for it in reference to the capricious Yahweh of prerabbinical Judaism. Not the deity I would have picked for her, but probably better than no deity at all, given her present stage of development."

A disturbing image flitted through my imagination. I was in Sinuhe's surgical theater, Londa lying before me on an operating table. I had scrolled her scalp away from her skullcap, sawed off her cranium, and exposed her brain to daylight. Now all that remained was for me to take up my knife and inscribe the Ten Commandments onto her cerebral cortex.

"I'll be honest, Edwina. I'm hesitant to intervene so radically in another person's psyche."

"Oh, but Londa *wants* you to intervene."

Just then Proserpine, for no apparent reason, began to quaver, her exposed roots vibrating like the plucked strings of an immense lyre.

"You're certain the tree has no awareness?" I asked, brushing the nearest branch.

"A complete void," Edwina said. "No qualia whatsoever. If I thought she was still suffering, I would immediately uproot her, much as I would miss her sweet fruit and cool shade and unfailing companionship. My daughter wants you to intervene, Mason, more than you can possibly imagine. She wants it with the desperation of the damned."

* * *

DRESSED NOW IN A BLUE SILK KIMONO, Javier reappeared and, taking Edwina's hand, guided her free of the chair. For an instant the two of them seemed to be dancing, and it occurred to me that Javier's duties might include appeasing Edwina's libido. I doubted that he relished these carnal obligations, not if she was as quixotic in bed as in conversation.

The three of us followed the labyrinth of shrubs and bushes to a frosted-glass door that Javier slid back to reveal a courtyard tiled with ceramic hexagons and girded by great ropy masses of jungle. A fishpond lay at the center of the patio, complete with a school of golden carp flashing through the shallow water like pennies sparkling in a fountain. Edwina led me to a round table swathed in white linen and arrayed with porcelain bowls from which rose fragrant twists of steam. Sliding into the nearest chair, I saw that we'd be dining on calamari stew, and I wondered whether before turning them over to the kitchen staff Charnock had given the little squids fins or wings or some other capricious enhancement.

"The chardonnay or the merlot?" Javier asked Edwina as she assumed her chair.

"Our guest will decide," she replied, presenting me with a blank stare. "Though personally I believe it's barbaric to consume red wine with seafood."

"The chardonnay is fine," I said, inhaling the perfume of the hibiscus.

"Londa will have the usual," Edwina informed her assistant.

As Javier passed through the patio doorway, a ginger cat with a flat, churlish face escaped from the conservatory, scurried across the tiles, and leaped into Edwina's lap.

"In making your diagnosis," she said, gesturing toward a dirt path emerging from the forest, "you must not hesitate to risk Londa's annoyance. If we spare her feelings, she'll never get well."

Branches rustled, vines swayed, a macaw took flight, and the jungle brought forth a young woman of commanding height and abundant auburn hair, flipping through a volume of the *Encyclopaedia Britannica* as if hunting up a favorite recipe in a cookbook. Was she in fact reading the thing so quickly? Comprehending it? She did not so much enter the patio as alight upon it—such was the fluidity of her tread, the delicacy of her carriage. Bronzed by the tropical sun, her arms extended from a white cotton blouse, her legs from khaki shorts. Her cheek and jaw muscles seemed atrophied, giving her a vacuous, uninhabited expression, but her eyes were as large and green as mumquats, and her lips had matured into an appealing pout. To cure this adolescent's malaise, I realized, would be to awaken a face of great beauty.

Edwina grasped her daughter's free hand, pressing it between her palms. "Darling, meet Mason Ambrose. He flew over a thousand miles to help us with our difficulties."

"Hello, Londa," I said.

She set her book on the table and, extending her arm, gave me a surprisingly vital handshake. "I am pleased to meet you, Mr. Ambrose," she said. Her voice had a hollow, ethereal timbre, as if she were speaking from the bottom of a well.

The instant Londa slid into her chair, Javier reappeared pushing a tea trolley on which rested the chardonnay and a carafe containing a mysterious ochre fluid. He filled Edwina's goblet and my own with wine. Londa received the unknown offering.

"Iced tea?" I asked.

"Coca-Cola," Londa said. "At one time its promoters favored the slogan 'Coke is it,' an assertion I find totally incoherent. Will there be pecan pie for dessert, Mother?"

"Naturally." Edwina brushed Londa's forearm. "Some people would say that by indulging my daughter I inflate her ego, but here at Faustino we have little use for received wisdom."

We proceeded to eat our stew, the silence growing increasingly conspicuous. I doubt that Edwina consumed more than a mouthful or two, although the wine occasioned no such prudence, and she eagerly drank three full glasses.

"The *Kama Sutra* catalogs seventy arts of graciousness," Londa said abruptly, staring at her half-empty bowl. "In 1859 the French daredevil Charles Blondin crossed Niagara Falls on a tightrope. The phylum Schizophyta comprises two thousand species of bacteria. Cyrus the Great, Persia's brilliant warrior and statesman, conquered Babylon in 500 B.C."

"That's very interesting," I said.

"According to Sumerian mythology, the universe was fashioned out of the primeval sea and divided into heaven and earth by Enlil, god of air and storms. All igneous rocks begin as magma. In 1972 the American swimmer Mark Spitz won seven gold medals at the Summer Olympics in Munich. The carrion-eating caracara bird has sharp hooks on its beak for tearing open animal hide."

I decided to begin my evaluation with the closest thing Western philosophy has to a sacred text, Plato's *Republic*. In Book One, Cephalus defines "justice" as speaking the truth and paying one's debts. Socrates refutes this notion by suggesting it would be wrong to repay certain debts—for example, to return a borrowed ax to its mentally imbalanced owner.

I lifted a morsel of calamari to my mouth, chewed the rubbery tissue, and said, "Londa, may I ask you a question? I would like you to imagine that a woman named Alice has borrowed an ax from her friend Jerome so she can chop a dead limb off her beech tree. When Jerome comes to reclaim his ax, he's obviously very agitated—"

"You mean he's like me?"

"Like you?"

"Insane."

"We're not insane," Edwina said.

"Alice becomes afraid that Jerome may use the ax to kill someone," I said. "So here's my question. Should Alice give it back?"

Londa closed her eyes. "In 1088 the Patzinak Turks settled

between the Danube and the Balkans. The talking drum of Nigeria's Yoruba people has strings that, when squeezed, can produce notes ranging over an octave or more."

"Please try to cooperate, dear," Edwina said.

"The question has no answer," Londa snapped.

"Many philosophers would argue that the question has a very *good* answer," I said.

"It doesn't," Londa insisted. "'Dilemma, noun, a situation in which a person must choose between two undesirable alternatives.'"

I glanced toward the nearest hibiscus. A swarm of butterflies moved among the blossoms with rapid stitching motions, as if fashioning a transparent gown with needle and thread. I fixed on Londa and said, "May I ask you a second question?"

"Another fucking dilemma?"

Edwina winced. "Londa, darling, we do not say 'fucking' at lunch."

Having failed to get anywhere with Socrates' ax, I decided to try Lawrence Kohlberg's variation on Jean Valjean stealing the loaf of bread.

"Once upon a time in Europe," I said, "a man was near death from bone cancer. The doctors thought a particular drug might save him, a radium extract that Fritz, the local pharmacist, had recently discovered. Although Fritz paid only one hundred deutsche marks for each specimen of raw radium—enough to prepare one ampoule for hypodermic injection—he priced the dose at a thousand marks. The sick man's wife, Helga, went to everyone she knew to borrow the money, but in the end she could scrape together only four hundred marks. Desperate now, Helga begged Fritz to either lower his price or let her pay the remaining six hundred marks in installments. But the pharmacist said, 'No, I discovered the extract, and I'm going to profit from it.' That very night Helga broke into Fritz's store and stole an ampoule of the drug. Now, Londa, here's the problem. Did Helga do the right thing?"

Her eyes narrowed to a livid squint. "Why would you ask me a question like that?"

"It's just a game," I said.

"It's a stupid game! You're trying to trick me! You're trying to make me even crazier than I am!"

Edwina said, "Sweetheart, we're not being fair to our teacher."

A howl erupted from deep within Londa's coltish frame, and the next thing I knew she'd tilted her bowl ninety degrees, sending the remainder of her stew slopping across the table. She bolted from her chair and, kneeling beside the fishpond, dipped the empty bowl into the water like a ladle. In a matter of seconds, she'd made a helpless carp her prisoner.

"Londa, no!" Edwina screamed, startling her misanthropic cat, who bailed out and disappeared down the jungle path. "The fish did nothing to deserve that!"

"Titanium is the ninth-most-abundant element!" Londa wailed. "In 1962, Francis Crick, Maurice Wilkins, and James Watson received the Nobel Prize in Physiology!"

Still on her knees, she upended the bowl, dumping both the captive fish and its liquid habitat onto the patio. Somehow the creature flipped from its left side to its abdomen, dorsal fin up. Inspired by its success, the carp next attempted to navigate the tiles in a pathetic mockery of swimming. It got nowhere, mired by friction and the malign indifference of the carp gods.

"The rules of the ancient Chinese game of liu-po have been lost to history! The bubonic plague of the 1340s killed nearly one-third of Europe's population!"

"Put the fish back!" Edwina shouted.

I leaped from my chair, seized the valiant carp, and heaved it into the pond.

"In 1900 the cakewalk became the most fashionable dance in the United States!"

Crouching beside Londa, I set my fingertips beneath her chin and lifted her head until our gazes met. Her nostrils quivered. Her lips grew taut. Her eyes looked desiccated, as hard and dry as ball bearings. Never had I seen such anguish in another human face, and so it was that as the warblers sang merrily and the tanagers trilled with unreflective joy, I vowed to Isis and Horus and most especially to myself that somehow, some way, I would teach my sad and sorry pupil how to weep.

AFTER LONDA TOOK LEAVE OF US, loping into the jungle with the fretful gait of a gazelle who'd lingered too long at the lions' watering hole, Edwina rose and approached the pond. She stared into its depths, counting the local population.

"Apparently this was her first carp attack," she said. "Give me your verdict, Mason. As a professional ethicist, would you say Londa is a full-blown sociopath?"

"I don't know," I said. "I'm not a professional ethicist. In my opinion, nobody is."

"Cruelty to animals is a strong predictor of future criminality," Edwina said. "Most serial killers got started by torturing their pets."

We drank a final glass of wine, then talked about my contract. Once it was clear that I understood the terms—beginning on Monday, I would tutor Londa every weekday morning over the next ten months, two hours per session—the conversation turned to my living accommodations. Although Dr. Charnock would be happy to offer me his hospitality, Edwina explained, I would instead occupy a cottage on the very lagoon where Londa had fractured her skull. I was about to contradict this assessment, noting that Charnock did not seem like a person who cherished guests—I doubted he felt comfortable hosting himself, much less intruders from the mainland—when Javier returned waving a cashier's check for twenty-five thousand dollars and explained that I could expect an identical payment every three months. I decided that I would order myself a laptop and also start sending regular grants from the Ambrose Arts Foundation to my sister Delia in New York, so she could spend more time attending auditions and less time waiting tables.

As dusk came to Isla de Sangre, Javier dropped me off at Charnock's A-frame. The biologist was nowhere to be seen. Perhaps he was in his laboratory, concocting our Jewish starfish. Beguiled by the sound of the surf, I pulled off my shoes and socks and walked down to the beach. The tide was going out. Again and again the sea threw itself upon the shore and glided away, losing ground with each cycle, a liquid Sisyphus.

"'Pale beds of blowing rushes,'" I muttered, "'where no leaf blooms or blushes, save this whereout she crushes for dead men deadly wine.'"

I took the mumquat from my shirt pocket, then knelt beside a tide pool and washed the skin clean. Rising, I popped the fruit into my mouth. The flesh fell away from the pit and melted into a thick, sweet syrup that rolled across my tongue and, trickling downward, caressed my gullet with a viscous warmth. I wrapped my tongue around the stippled stone and spit it out.

Barefoot, I waded into the surf, and as the mumquat took charge of my mind, I looked up and saw that Orion and Canis Major had left their dark niches and were now romping together across the sky. Even as the hunter and his dog gamboled through the celestial meadow, my monarch butterfly fluttered into view, and behind this regal creature flew ten thousand more, their wings beating so vigorously I could feel the wind against my cheeks. Soon every heavenly body above Isla de Sangre had transmuted into a radiant insect, flitting and floating and pollinating the night with countless new stars, and for the moment I was master of them all, an immortal being, a god who answered only to himself.

Chapter 3

PLATO HAD HIS REPUBLIC, Francis Bacon his New Atlantis, Candide his El Dorado, and I my private cottage in the jungle, an easy walk to Edwina's estate. Among the amenities of this pocket utopia, two delighted me in particular: a sturdy wooden deck overlooking the algae-coated expanse of Laguna Zafira, and a home entertainment center complete with a CD collection featuring the sorts of orchestral music that would incline even the most stringent interstellar cultural commission to rank Earth a civilized planet. On the night before I was scheduled to give my pupil her first lesson, I settled into the chaise longue, uncapped a beer, and made ready to let Ralph Vaughan Williams liberate me from the prison of my skin.

Although "Sinfonia Antarctica" sounded as sublime as ever, its pleasures were insufficient to keep me from brooding. Who was this lost young woman whose broken moral compass I was expected to repair? Would I need to teach Londa Sabacthani every ethical principle since "Don't eat of the tree," or merely help her recover certain previously assimilated rules that the amnesia had obscured? How might I follow in the footsteps of Sinuhe's father, finding and extracting the secret splinter that had paralyzed her conscience?

"Sinfonia Antarctica" yielded to the "The Lark Ascending," a composition through which Williams, during my worst bout of junior-year depression at Villanova, had single-handedly persuaded me that the world was not in fact a festering cesspool of such primordial meaninglessness that even suicide would seem like a gesture of assent. I drank one beer per movement, falling asleep in my chair.

Shortly before dawn I awoke to find my bladder distended and, less predictably, my mind ablaze with a bright idea. What Londa needed, I decided, was to participate directly and viscerally in the sorts of ethical dilemmas devised by Plato and Kohlberg. Instead of simply *pondering* morality with her intellect, she must *perform* morality with her hands and feet and organs of speech. To wit, I would turn the Riddle of the Borrowed Ax and the Fable of the Stolen Radium into drama improvisations, placing my student at the center of both crises.

Somewhere in the void, the spirit of John Dewey, America's greatest philosopher and a tireless champion of learning by doing, looked down on Laguna Zafira and smiled.

LATER THAT MORNING I jogged to the manor, flying past a dozen languid iguanas sunning themselves along the forest trail. As I mounted the steps to the veranda, Edwina came gliding toward me, her chronically disaffected ginger cat curled around her neck like a yoke. The beast hissed at me. I hissed back. Edwina explained that her daughter's rehabilitation would occur amid the estate's vast book collection, then guided me down the hall, through a set of French doors, and into the library. Scanning my new classroom, I felt a surge of optimism: the ranks of handsome hardcovers, the globe as big as a wrecking ball, the pair of corpulent armchairs by the hearth—it all seemed conducive to moral discourse of the highest order.

The one anomalous feature was a department-store mannequin,

its tawny plastic flesh dressed in the incised breastplate, morion helmet, and leather hip boots of a Spanish conquistador. Armed with sword and musket, this vigilant agent of the Inquisition stood guard beside the philosophy section, as if charged with making sure nobody checked out a work by David Hume, Baruch Spinoza, Bertrand Russell, or any other heretic.

"We call him Alonso," Edwina said. "He came with the mansion. Javier likes to make up stories about him. Evidently it was Alonso who convinced Ponce de León to quit the governorship of Puerto Rico and go seek the fabled island of Bimini and its legendary Fountain of Youth. In 1514, Ponce and Alonso stumbled upon a great landmass, which they called *Pascua Florida,* flowery Easter, because it was Easter Sunday."

Before Edwina could continue Alonso's biography, Londa floated into the room wearing white shorts and a red polo shirt. Her mother and I wished her good morning. Ignoring us, she approached the hearth and flopped into an armchair. She stared into space, saying nothing.

"Ponce and Alonso then embarked on a series of exploits," Edwina said. "Conquering the Florida Indians, quelling Taíno rebellions back in Puerto Rico, and making pathetic attempts to circumnavigate their newly discovered island, not realizing it was a peninsula." She drew me to her side and continued in a whisper. "I would say you've succeeded with Londa when she can see the irony in a gang of adventurers seeking eternal youth while leaving corpses wherever they go."

Edwina slipped out of the room, closing the French doors behind her. I settled into the vacant armchair and faced the dormant fireplace—a peculiar installation here in the tropics, as incongruous as a pinball machine in a funeral parlor.

"Mother doesn't know jack shit about Ponce de León," Londa said abruptly. "He discovered Florida in 1513, not 1514."

"I'm sure you're right," I said.

"It's in the fucking *Encyclopaedia Britannica.* And he never massacred the Indians. They kicked his Castilian ass."

"I'm sure they did. Ready for your lesson?"

"No."

"This morning we're going to try something called a theater game. You and I will play roles, like the actors and actresses you see on television."

"Mother doesn't like me to watch television, but I do it anyway. The comedians make me laugh. So do the soap operas and the tornados and the children who've fallen down mine shafts."

"Do you remember the story of Alice and Jerome and the borrowed ax?"

Londa tugged absently at her auburn hair. "How could I forget?" Issuing as they did from her infinitely absorbent brain, her words had a double meaning: the story was memorable, and she couldn't have forgotten it if she'd wanted to.

"I'll take the part of Jerome," I told her, "and you'll be Alice."

"Alice Walker is best known for *The Color Purple,* published in 1982. Mother tells me you're from Boston."

"Correct. Shall we start the game?"

"Boston is the capital of Massachusetts." From her shirt pocket she retrieved a matchbook and a blue pack of Dunhill cigarettes. "During the Boston Tea Party, the colonists dumped three hundred and forty-two crates of cargo into the harbor."

"Londa, are you listening?"

"Our planet has a solid inner core, a molten outer core, a warm rocky mantle, and a thin cool crust. On December seventeenth, 1903, the Wright Brothers made four flights in their propeller-driven glider."

"Londa, I need your attention."

With a flick of her wrist she prompted a single cigarette to emerge from the pack. "The filter tip goes in my mouth." She wrapped her lips around the cigarette and slid it free. "The other end receives the match. I'm seventeen years old, and I have many skills. I can bake a cake, drive a nail, unclog a drain, and build a castle out of sand."

"Does your mother let you smoke?"

"Yeah, but she's not too fucking wild about it." She struck a match, lit her Dunhill, and launched into a deft impersonation of Edwina. "'Sweetheart, we know that tobacco is bad for our health.'" She removed the cigarette and coughed. "I'm afraid Mother's opinions don't carry a whole lot of weight in my book. Neither do yours, as a matter of fact."

I stared at a fire poker, standing in its rack like an arrow in a quiver. During a postwar meeting of the Moral Science Club at King's College, Wittgenstein had reportedly brandished such an implement in Karl Popper's face when the latter refused to admit there were no genuine philosophical problems, only linguistic puzzles. My urge to similarly threaten Londa just then was not negligible.

"You're suffering from a serious dysfunction," I told her. "It behooves you to cooperate."

"I'm well aware of my serious dysfunction. Know something else, Socrates? I'm just as fucking moral as you. Rule one: thou shalt have no other fucking gods before me. Rule seven: thou shalt not commit fucking adultery. I can recite all ten. Can you?"

"Your mother tells me you set fire to a rug. You've thrown rocks through Dr. Charnock's windows. That doesn't sound like moral behavior to me."

"Me neither."

"On Saturday you almost killed a fish for no reason."

"If you're worried I might break your windows, I promise I won't." She parked the cigarette in her mouth and stretched out her bare arm, poking the flesh with her thumb. "It's so strange being wrapped up in this stuff." The cigarette bobbed up and down as she spoke. "Epidermis, dermis, fascia. I'm always leaking. Blood, sweat, saliva, mucus."

"But never tears."

Our eyes met. Her irises were two different shades of green. She seemed about to waft out yet another datum but instead offered a faltering smile and a snort of begrudging assent.

I climbed free of the armchair and, taking Londa's hand, led her to a mahogany reading table, where I seized a convenient duster, a bouquet of white feathers sprouting from the handle. "Let's imagine this is the ax." I waved the duster in Londa's face. "Good morning, Alice," I began in a smarmy voice. "How lovely to see you today."

Five seconds elapsed. Ten. Fifteen. Londa took a long drag on her cigarette, then flicked the ember into an inverted crab shell that evidently now functioned as an ashtray.

"Say something, Londa."

"The age of once-living matter can be determined by measuring its radioactive carbon-14."

"Say something *Alice* would say. You're Alice, remember?"

"In 1959, Los Angeles defeated Chicago to win the World Series."

"Londa, say the following: 'Good morning, Jerome. Thank you for bringing me your ax.'"

"You're not Jerome," she noted, blowing smoke through her nostrils. "You're Mason Ambrose. A mason jar has a wide mouth and an airtight screw top."

"'Good morning, Jerome.' Say it, Londa."

"The Freemasons are known for their charitable work and secret rites."

"Say it."

"Why the fuck should I?"

"Because I'm the teacher and you're the pupil. 'Good morning, Jerome.'"

Londa closed her eyes. She grunted and gritted her teeth. "Good morning, *Jerome*." She sounded like a microchip. "Thank you for bringing me your ax. This is bullshit, Mason."

"Happy to oblige, Alice. I sharpened the blade this morning—but I forget why you want to borrow it."

"I forget, too."

"Perhaps you intend to remove a dead limb from a beech tree?"

"A beech tree, sure, whatever you say, except this is the fucking tropics, and there aren't any fucking beech trees around here."

"How sad. There are plenty of beech trees back in Boston."

"Boston cream pie has chocolate icing on top and a custard filling between the layers."

"True enough, but you're wrong about the Boston Tea Party. Three hundred and forty-*one* crates went into the water, not three hundred and forty-two."

"No, three hundred forty-two."

"Sorry. Not true."

Londa cringed and sucked in a deep breath. "The *Encyclopaedia Britannica* says so."

"An ancestor of mine was *there,* Londa. He counted the crates. The encyclopedia is in error."

Her body contracted as if she were a passenger on a plummeting elevator. "You're lying!"

"Books are often in error."

"Like holy fuck they are!"

"Three hundred forty-one," I insisted.

"Forty-two!"

"Forty-one!"

Londa drifted toward Alonso and, tugging on his boot cuff, dropped her cigarette butt into the cavity. She headed for the ancient-history section. I dogged her steps, the duster tucked under my arm. She sprawled across a russet leather couch, rolled onto her back, and pulled her hair over her face like a veil.

"Was this a *favorite* beech tree of yours?" I asked, joining her on the couch. Her sandals brushed my thigh.

For an entire minute, she made no sound, then at last she swept the hair from her eyes and muttered, "You want me to *pretend* I'm Alice, is that it?"

"Uh-huh."

"Would you like to hear my poem? 'The French say *merde*. We say turd.'"

I stroked the back of her hand. "You know, Alice, I'd bet money we're talking about one of your *favorite* beech trees."

A pensive frown furrowed her brow, and she assumed a sitting position, scratching her bare ankle with the opposite toenail. "When I was a little girl in Vermont," she said slowly, precisely, "my father suspended . . . an old tire . . . from the lowest branch. I spent many a goddamn joyful hour swinging back and forth."

"Then you must do everything you can to save the tree's life." I set the feather duster in her palm and wrapped her fingers around the handle. "However, I expect you to return my ax when I need it again. Can you promise me that?"

"Sure thing," she grumbled.

"The instant I ask for my ax back, you'll give it to me."

"I fucking heard you the first time. I'll guard your fucking ax with my fucking life."

Not a breakthrough, exactly. No sea change in my nihilistic nereid. And yet my spirits rose: I could see the photon at the end of the tunnel. "Londa, you're doing great. I would even venture to say you're having fun."

"Fun? Right, Socrates. Fun on a bun." She waved the feather duster about like a pom-pom, then condescended to add, "This is slightly less barfomatic than I was expecting."

"You've got a real talent for improvisation."

"Let's just get it the fuck over with."

"Scene two," I said quickly. "One week later. Jerome has come back for his ax." Seeking to make the game as engagingly lurid as possible, I bared my teeth and presented Londa with the fierce, burning gaze of Edward Hyde transfixing a barmaid. "I need my *ax*, Alice," I snarled, "and I need it *now!*"

My savagery seemed to gratify her. "Thundering fuck, Jerome, you look *upset!*" she yelled, flourishing the duster in my face.

"My wife and I had a dreadful argument last night. With any luck I'll catch her by surprise."

"Holy shit, are you saying you intend to *kill* your wife? In Exodus, chapter twenty, God says it's *wrong* to kill!"

"It's *also* wrong to break a promise. You said you'd return the ax when I needed it. Now keep your half of the bargain."

Reveling in the crude melodrama of it all, Londa marched to the nearest window, threw open the shutters, and hurled the duster into the jungle.

"Straight to the bottom of the sea!"

"Our friendship is over, Alice!"

She pivoted toward me, her grin as wide and moist as a slice of melon. Hunching her shoulders, she released a high whistled C-note and hugged herself with palpable delight.

"Curtain," I said, dipping my head in a gesture of admiration. "Congratulations, Londa. You just saved a human life."

"Fun on a bun," she said again, in a tone that, if not exactly amicable, was nevertheless a full octave of sarcasm lower than last time.

"I'm going to reward you by ending the lesson right now. Class dismissed. See you tomorrow morning."

"Will we be doing another fucking theater game?"

"That was my plan, yes."

"Will it be more interesting than this Alice-and-Jerome shit?"

"I think you'll like it."

"I was planning to play hooky," she said, lighting a second cigarette, "but maybe I'll fucking show up after all."

* * *

ALTHOUGH IT WAS Edmund Purdom's wooden portrayal of *The Egyptian* that inspired me to study philosophy, the sensibility that underlay *Ethics from the Earth* was shaped no less by my father's unmarried and peculiar sister Clara, who lived with us until, shortly after my twelfth birthday, an ambulance took her besieged body to a Germantown hospice from whose benevolent chemical embrace she would never return. Aunt Clara was certainly no devotee of evolutionary theory—she believed wholeheartedly in the affable Creator-God of middle-class Methodist revelation—and yet for me her awed appreciation of the world's unglamorous species, its humble finches and homely toads and mundane chipmunks, was in the very best Darwinian tradition. Were I to paint the woman's portrait, I would depict her standing in our backyard, offering a squirrel peanuts with one hand while holding a bird feeder aloft with the other.

Her passing was an event on which I needn't dwell. I shall merely report that as Londa and I pursued our second lesson, an improvisation based on Kohlberg's Fable of the Stolen Radium, wrenching memories of Aunt Clara's ill-advised radiation treatments inevitably rushed back. Yet I persisted, imagining that this eccentric reincarnation of St. Francis was looking down from on high and blessing my attempt to give my pupil a robust naturalist ethics. Londa took the part of Helga Eschbach, the woman whose husband was dying of bone cancer. I cast myself as Jürgen Hammerschmidt, the police inspector who apprehends her after she breaks into Fritz's pharmacy and steals the radium extract. An empty Perrier bottle served for an ampoule of the vital drug.

"What's going on here?" I demanded.

Londa puffed on her cigarette and clutched the green bottle to her chest. "My name is Helga Eschbach, and my husband has a malignant tumor. Radium therapy might cure him."

"Well, Frau Eschbach, it appears I've caught a thief."

"Put me in jail—I don't mind." She hunched protectively over the bottle. "But first let me take this ampoule to my husband and give him a hypodermic injection."

"My duty is to uphold the law, not to facilitate the transportation of stolen goods." I snatched the Perrier bottle away and, grabbing Londa's arm, escorted her across the library toward the local prison.

"The pharmacist pays only one hundred deutsche marks for each specimen of raw radium!" she protested. "He charges a thousand for the extract!"

Halting beside the conquistador, I absently took his sword by the hilt and pulled it several inches clear of the scabbard. "A thousand marks?" I said. "A tenfold profit?"

"A thousand fucking marks," she said, twisting free of my grip.

"How terribly unfair."

"I pawned my wedding ring, sold our furniture, begged money from friends. It wasn't enough."

"I must say, Frau Eschbach, I admire your effort."

"I love my husband," Londa said.

I let the blade slide back into place. "Even if the pharmacist charged only five hundred marks, he would still be engaged in an immoral activity."

"But not an illegal activity?"

"Alas, no," I said. "Whereas you are engaged in an illegal activity—"

"But not an immoral one." Londa took a drag and flashed a triumphant smile.

"On the contrary, Frau Eschbach. What you're doing is—"

"It's pretty goddamn moral, isn't it?"

I returned the Perrier bottle to Londa's grasp. "Here. Give your husband the treatment. I never saw you tonight, and you never saw me—understood?"

"Understood."

"Herr Eschbach is fortunate to have such a wife."

She stubbed out her cigarette on the conquistador's breastplate, then dropped the butt down the barrel of his musket. "Tell me your name."

"Hammerschmidt," I said.

"I shall not forget your charity, Inspector Hammerschmidt."

"In certain contexts, Frau Eschbach, the sacredness of love counts for more than the sanctity of law."

"Why, Inspector—you're a fucking philosopher."

Much to Londa's satisfaction, I laughed spontaneously, and then, stepping completely out of character, gave her a tentative, avuncular hug. "Take your curtain call, dear. Soak up the applause. Catch the bouquets. Great job."

In a gesture that managed to be at once the soul of innocence and the quintessence of suggestiveness, Londa took my hand, led me into the biography alcove, and stamped my cheek with a moist kiss.

"I'll never forget Herr Hammerschmidt's charity, and I'll never forget *your* charity either," she told me, pursing her lips. "I hope you'll always be my teacher, Mason, even after I get my conscience back."

A BORROWED AX, a beech tree, an ampoule of radium extract. Three physical objects that had figured crucially in my efforts to rehabilitate Londa, each with a unique essence, its axness, treeness, ampoularity. But as Jean-Paul Sartre reminds us, in the case of human beings this metaphysic is reversed: a person's existence precedes his essence—he is a subject among objects. The danger, says Sartre, following Heidegger, is that he will "fall" into the world of objects, becoming ever after the prisoner of arbitrary strictures masquerading as universal principles. And so it was that I resolved to give Londa a taste of Sartrean existential freedom, confronting her with a dilemma beyond the competence of any canon.

The conundrum was one that Sartre himself had devised, con-

cerning a student whose elder brother has died in the German offensive of 1940. The student resolves to join the Free French and help
defeat the Nazi beasts who killed his brother, but his invalid mother
wants him to stay home. He is her only consolation, and she can't
adequately care for herself.

To minimize the strain on Londa's imagination, I decided
that the embittered student should be female. I cast Edwina as the
mother. Though preoccupied with packing—in twenty-four hours
she would join Charnock for a weeklong artificial-intelligence conference in Chicago, where they would implore the neural-network
community not to make basket cases of their computers—Edwina
gladly took the part, and in a matter of minutes, the two actors had
fully immersed themselves in the bedeviling scenario.

"*S'il te plaît,* Madeleine—reconsider," Edwina gasped. "We've already lost your brother. I couldn't bear to lose you as well."

"Claude would want me to avenge his death," Londa said.

"Claude would want you to look after me," Edwina insisted.

"If I stay here, I'll spend every waking minute thinking of the
Resistance." Londa grimaced and winced, as impressive an impersonation of psychic torment as I'd ever seen. "On the other hand,
if I join the Resistance, I'll spend every waking minute thinking of
you."

"Exactly my point," Edwina said. "Stay with me."

"But, oh, *Maman,* consider the implications of driving the Ger-
mans out of France! Thousands of mothers—not just you, *thousands* will get to spend their dotages with sons and daughters who
might've otherwise fallen into the Nazis' clutches!"

Edwina cupped her palms around Londa's shoulders, drawing the child so close that their noses practically touched. "Dearest
Madeleine, how can you sacrifice my happiness to this futile business of sniping at Nazis? How can you make a bargain like that?"

"I can make such a bargain because . . ."

"Yes?"

"Because . . ."

"I'm listening."

A tremulous moan broke from Londa's throat. She lurched away, rushing toward the conquistador. "Shit, Mason, you're doing it *again*! You're trying to drive me crazy!"

"Londa, that assertion gained nothing from the word 'shit,'" Edwina said.

"My head's spinning," Londa said. "I need . . ."

"A rule?" I suggested. "A binding principle? An eleventh commandment?"

Gasping like the carp she'd almost murdered, Londa slumped against Alonso. "The antimalarial drug quinine comes from the cinchona tree! In Riemann geometry a curved line is the shortest path between two points!"

"There are no rules for dealing with a dilemma like this," I said.

"An adult human skeleton contains two hundred and six bones! Galaxies can be categorized as elliptical or spiral! Joyce Kilmer wrote 'Trees'!"

"Instead of applying a rule, you need to engage all your powers of moral reasoning."

"I *hate* this fucking lesson!"

Edwina cringed. "Londa, darling, we do not say 'fucking' in school."

Approaching my pupil, I took her right hand and massaged the palm as if to heal a Christly stigma. She heaved a sigh, then relaxed.

"Let's call it quits for today, okay?" I said.

"Good idea." Londa inhaled audibly, filtering the stuffy air through her clenched teeth. "Best fucking idea I've heard all morning."

I retrieved my backpack from the reading table and pulled out *Ethics from the Earth*. "For your homework tonight, please read chapter four and write a thousand-word essay giving your personal reaction to the Stoics' worldview."

She assumed a facial expression combining forced exasperation with genuine annoyance. "Well, *that* certainly doesn't sound like much fun."

"It's not supposed to be fun."

"Haven't you read the goddamn U.S. Constitution, Mason? Cruel and unusual punishments are forbidden."

Edwina said, "Londa, sweetheart, we do not stoop to sarcasm during our lessons."

Snatching the book away, Londa announced that she intended to prepare herself "a morally degenerate lunch full of saturated fats and refined sugar," then exited the room with the punctuated jumps of a nine-year-old playing hopscotch.

Edwina and I locked gazes, and I saw that Londa's mismatched green irises were a legacy from her mother. She laid her delicate fingers against my cheek like a psychic healer performing a root canal.

"She's doing awfully well, wouldn't you say?" Edwina ventured.

"I see progress," I replied, trying not to sound too satisfied with myself. How many real philosophers, the kind with Ph.D.s, could have brought Londa so far so fast?

"She knew why Madeleine felt compelled to fight the Nazis, but she understood the mother's feelings, too. Before you came here, Londa couldn't empathize with anybody except herself. 'Progress' is an understatement. I'd say she's practically cured."

THE LONGER I STAYED ON ISLA DE SANGRE, this tropical Eden with its squawking birds, squalling monkeys, and murmuring surf, the more certain I became that my years in academia had wrought a serious imbalance in my mental ecosystem. Thanks to Hawthorne University, a kind of Aristotelian kudzu had taken root in my skull, choking out the more dynamic blooms and covering the whole terrain with a creeping carpet of rationality. It was high time for me to reclaim my natural right to entertain whimsical notions and formulate indefensible ideas.

I resolved to spend Wednesday afternoon trekking around the island, admitting to my consciousness every species of thought, no matter how grandiose. If so moved by Lady Philosophy, I would prove once and for all that humans possess *a priori* knowledge, devise an airtight case against *a priori* knowledge, and pronounce so pompously on the mystery of Being that every Heideggerian within earshot would reach for his gun. This strange vision quest, with its aim not of spiritual enlightenment but of intellectual decadence, began immediately after lunch. I donned my hiking clothes—the crate containing my earthly possessions had arrived from Boston the previous evening—stuffed my backpack with three bottles of Evian and a half dozen PowerBars, and set off for the beach, humming my favorite melodic idea from "The Lark Ascending," that passage through which Vaughan Williams arranges for the listener's soul and the Hegelian World Spirit to fall madly and eternally in love.

According to Charnock, the island had the general shape of a human kidney, and my intention was to circumnavigate the cortex before the stars came out. At first my journey proved congenial, and I continued humming "The Lark Ascending" while negotiating the range of dunes that separated the verdant rain forest and the placid Bahía de Flores. The sky was the deep blue of unoxygenated blood. The air was redolent of orchids and heliotrope. Shells of every variety covered the sand—conch, clam, oyster, scallop, mussel, snail—Darwinian artifacts that my imagination transformed into cobblestones, and I soon fancied that I was strolling the streets of eighteenth-century Königsberg, following in Kant's footsteps as he explained why the physico-theological argument for God's existence did not yield a transcendent Creator but merely a cosmic Architect at the mercy of available materials.

By the time I'd traveled perhaps three miles, I was no longer a happy hiker. Rivulets of sweat trickled down my scalp, making my brow itch and my eyes sting. Mosquitoes whined in my ears like defective hearing aids. Worst of all, an impediment now presented itself, a sheer sandstone bluff bulking out of the rain forest and jutting into the bay at the point where, if the island were indeed a kidney, the duct would emerge. For an instant I considered making an about-face and returning to my cottage with its mosquito netting and cold beer, but instead some dormant sense of adventure awoke within me, and I strode south into the jungle, the sound of the surf falling away by degrees, from boom to growl to grainy whisper.

Several miles inland, I was astonished to behold the bluff merge with a soaring concrete wall, not quite massive enough to confine a gigantic prehistoric gorilla, but of sufficient height to discourage human traffic, its moss-cloaked bulk continuing south into the jungle before dissolving in mist and shadow. Equally surprising was the taut string rising from behind the wall to join a silken kite—a golden phoenix with a flaming red tail—now lodged in a kapok tree. I stopped in my tracks. Sobs filled the air. A child was crying. Of all the explanations now flitting through my brain, I quickly discarded my initial, admittedly far-fetched hypothesis—the child was a prisoner and had launched the kite to signal for help—and settled on the obvious: distress over a lost toy.

Although athletically incompetent as a youngster, doltish at everything from softball to pitching pennies, a circumstance that provided my schoolmates with much unmerited amusement, I was always a serious tree climber. Confidently I shed my pack and, on the third attempt, leaped high enough to grab a limb. I hoisted myself into the kapok and mounted the branches until one golden wing was within my grasp. I unhooked the phoenix kite, untangled the string, and, descending several branches, inched forward until my feet dangled above the forbidden domain.

A slender little girl stared up at me, her heart-shaped face luminous with gratitude. She wore a pink pinafore fitted over a blue dress daubed with tomboy blotches of mud and moss, and she clutched a wooden spindle around which was coiled the surplus kite string.

"I believe you lost this," I told my beaming admirer, lowering the toy into her outstretched arms.

"Thank you *so* much!"

She held the kite against her body like a shield, the vertical axis extending all the way to her forehead. I moved to the bottommost branch and, after hanging briefly like a sloth, uncurled my legs, relaxed my grip, and dropped to the ground. No sooner had I recovered my balance than a large and lithe Doberman pinscher appeared from out of nowhere, his amber eyes glowing through his black-on-brown bandit's mask as he patiently awaited the child's command to pounce on the intruder and extract his throat.

"My name's Donya," she said, stroking her guardian's broad, rocky skull. "And this is Omar." The dog had been spared the modifications to which breeders commonly subjected his kind—bobbed tail, ears forced erect by scar tissue—but he looked plenty scary without them. "What's *your* name?"

"Mason," I said, cautiously extending my hand, palm down, toward the Doberman. "Hi there, Omar." The dog sniffed my fleshy offering, then issued a semantically complex snort. I was not to be entirely trusted, but at least I'd followed the proper protocol.

Surveying my surroundings, I saw that Donya's intention to launch her kite that afternoon was not unreasonable, for we were standing on a windswept scrubland broken only by distant ranks of cypress trees and the occasional lone acacia. To have a successful kite-flying experience here, one need merely avoid the concrete wall and the forest beyond.

"I'm five years old, and I'm having a tea party with Rupert and Henry and Deedee," Donya said, starting away. "Would you like to come, too?"

"Sure."

Crossing the scrub, Donya at my side, I looked in all directions, hoping to spot an adult. Apparently the child was playing unsupervised. What sort of dumb-ass, irresponsible parents would abandon their preschooler to the perils of an island wilderness? Was Omar really equal to any threat that might arise?

My hostess guided me toward a banyan tree as vast and sprawling as its Indian cousins, the naked roots arcing from trunk to earth like ropes anchoring a circus tent. Cradled within its branches was a clapboard cottage, white with yellow shutters, scaled to Donya's proportions. The child deposited her kite at the base of the trunk, told her dog she'd be back soon, and directed me up a zigzagging wooden staircase to the porch, where the other guests awaited. Donya made the introductions. Rupert was a velveteen giraffe boasting red fur covered with yellow polka dots, Henry a stuffed koala bear dressed in a Come to Queensland T-shirt, and Deedee a plush chimpanzee wearing a Florida Marlins baseball cap.

Stooping, I entered Donya's diminutive domain. The raw materials of a tea party—four white china cups and saucers, a small silver pot, a stack of peanut-butter sandwiches, a plate holding chocolate-chip cookies and vanilla wafers—covered a table adorned with Ernest Shepard's classic drawing of Christopher Robin descending the stairs dragging Edward Bear behind him, bump, bump, bump. Donya brought Rupert, Henry, and Deedee in from the porch, propping them up in their little cane chairs, then installed herself at the head of the table. Given the frailty of the chairs, sitting was not an option for me. I crouched in the corner.

"Might I infer you're here on vacation—or are you a local resident?" In my efforts to avoid condescending to children, I commonly burden them with my most tortured diction, but Donya nevertheless understood me.

"I live here," she said, offering me a cherubic smile. Freckles decorated her cheeks like sprinkles of cinnamon.

"With your mother and father?"

"Just my mother. I don't have a father. Henry and Brock visit every day." Donya upended the silver pot, poured out a measure of red liquid, and set the teacup before her stuffed chimp. "The *other* Henry, I mean. Henry Cushing, not Henry Koala."

"Is Henry Cushing a person?"

"Of *course* he's a person. He gives me my lessons. Brock does, too."

How strange to think I wasn't the only tutor on Isla de Sangre. I wondered how many of us there were, and whether we all worked for Edwina.

While my hostess filled two more teacups, passing one to Henry Koala, keeping the other for herself, I increased my crouch ten degrees and peered out the window. A grand and garish edifice met my gaze, a kind of ancient Spanish villa secluded by cypresses, each tower capped by a conical roof covered in tiles suggesting fish scales. Thick, swarthy vines crisscrossed the dark stone walls like twine securing a brown paper package.

"Tell me your full name," I said. "Is it Donya Jones maybe? Donya Smith?"

"Donya Sabacthani." Puckering her lips, my hostess whistled "Pop Goes the Weasel" as she filled the remaining teacup and held it out to me.

"Shouldn't this be for Rupert?" I asked, staring into Donya's eyes. Her irises, like Edwina's and Londa's, were two different shades of green.

"Giraffes don't like Hawaiian Punch."

"Donya, do you know your mother's first name? Does she call herself something like Judy or Carol or Edwina?"

"I call her Mommy. She's the best mommy in the whole world. She built the wall just for me."

"Could her name be Edwina?"

"I don't know, but I can show you her *picture*!"

Donya reached under the table and obtained a blue lacquered music box. She lifted the lid, unleashing a tinny rendition of "Lara's Theme" from *Doctor Zhivago*. The green velvet interior held several pieces of costume jewelry, a compact mirror, and a snapshot of Edwina wearing a grin as artificial as a paper carnation.

"My mother's very pretty, isn't she?" Donya said.

"Very pretty," I echoed. In a rainy-day, Blanche DuBois sort of way. "I'm a friend of hers."

"Are you a molecular geneticist, too?"

"No, I'm a teacher, like Henry and Brock. My student is your sister Londa. She's seventeen years old."

"I don't have a sister Londa. Mommy says I'm a lonely child."

"An *only* child?"

"That's what I meant. *Only* children are lucky. They get their mommies all to themselves. What makes you think I have a sister Londa?"

I took my first swallow of Hawaiian Punch. It tasted vaguely like watered-down mumquat nectar. Something extremely odd was happening on this end of the archipelago. If the March Hare suddenly appeared at the present festivity, I would not be entirely surprised.

"My student's name is Londa Sabacthani," I said.

"Well, she can call herself that if she wants to," Donya said, "but that doesn't mean she's allowed to be my sister." She picked up the snack plate and addressed the chimp. "Would you like a cookie, Deedee?"

I affected a falsetto and dubbed in Deedee's voice. "I would *love* a cookie."

"What kind?"

"Vanilla wafer."

My hostess served her chimp a vanilla wafer and said, "I invited Mommy to the party, but she's in Chicago this week."

"I know," I said. "An artificial-intelligence conference."

"That's right. She's teaching people to be nice to their computers."

I sipped more punch. Sinuhe's favorite question rattled around in my skull. Why hadn't Edwina told me about this second child? Why had she bisected the island with a wall? Why did her daughters need separate estates? I wondered whether the woman in the photograph might actually be Edwina's twin sister, likewise a molecular geneticist and likewise attending an artificial intelligence conference in Chicago—a fanciful theory, but not unimaginable.

I drained my Hawaiian Punch. "Donya, I have to say something. This is important. If you ask me, a five-year-old girl should not be out flying a kite by herself."

"Mommy says that as long as I stay inside the wall, nothing bad will ever happen to me."

"I believe that an adult should be watching over you at all times."

Donya gestured toward the rear window. "Henry's looking at me right now."

My opinion of parenting standards at Donya's villa improved considerably as my gaze alighted on the highest tower. A bulky human figure, backlit by the descending sun, scrutinized the scrub through a brass telescope. The instrument seemed focused directly on me. I wondered if it was powerful enough to show Henry my perplexed expression.

"Would you like to know the name of my house?" Donya asked. "My real house, I mean, not my tree house. It's Casa de los Huesos. That means the House of Bones."

"What sorts of things do Henry and Brock teach you?"

She bit into Deedee's vanilla wafer. "You ask a lot of questions, Mason. It's getting on my nerves."

"That's not a very nice thing to say, Donya."

Instantly her brow and cheeks turned red, and I braced myself for a squall of tears, but instead she took a deep breath. "I'm . . . I'm *sorry*."

"I accept your apology."

"I'm so sorry."

"It's all right."

"I say bad things like that because I don't have my rectitude yet."

"'Rectitude.' That's an awfully big word."

"Like the time I smashed Mommy's cell phone and said I didn't, and that other time when I threw Chen Lee's watch in the bay, and once I dug up all of Mommy's hyacinths. Henry and Brock are teaching me the three R's. Reading, writing, and rectitude."

"I see."

"After I get my rectitude, I won't dig up any more hyacinths. Are you teaching Londa her rectitude, too?"

"That's one way to put it."

Over the next half-hour, I consumed three additional cups of punch, two peanut-butter sandwiches, and four cookies like nobody's grandmother used to make: disks of impossibly moist cake studded with scrumptious chunks of chocolate. When not eating, Donya and I played Candy Land, sang nursery rhymes, and discussed whether Christopher Robin might have found a more considerate way to transport Winnie-the-Pooh downstairs. It would be a better world, I decided, if tree-house tea parties occurred with greater frequency.

At four o'clock Donya announced that Henry and Brock expected her to be home soon, so we descended to the scrub. Omar sniffed my knees, thighs, and ankles, quickly deciding I'd acquired no unacceptable aromas since his previous inspection. Donya made me promise to visit her again. I scrambled back into the kapok tree. As I returned to the jungle and retrieved my pack, I wondered whether Edwina, by applying her considerable monetary and material resources to Donya's domain, had indeed made it a completely safe haven. Quite possibly I was living on the wrong side of the concrete wall, and if I moved into Casa de los Huesos, nothing bad would ever happen to me.

Chapter 4

A PARTICULARLY BAROQUE PRODUCT of Charnock's genetic engineering skills greeted me when I entered the library the next morning, a winged and feathered iguana boasting the same talent for uncomprehending repetition found also in parrots and poststructuralists. The creature was perched on Londa's shoulder, swathed in her luxurious hair, his forked tongue flicking wildly as he peeked out from behind her tresses like a theater manager counting the house.

"Does he have a name?" I asked.

"Quetzie," Londa replied, feeding the iguana a handful of dried ants. Her bright yellow sundress gave her the appearance of a gendered banana. "After Quetzalcoatl, the Aztec feathered-serpent god."

"Quetzie is a handsome devil," the iguana said. His plumage was indeed astonishing, a red-and-gold raiment flowing behind him like an emperor's robe.

"Quite so," I told him.

"Quetzie is a handsome devil," he said again.

"Indeed."

"Quetzie is a handsome devil."

"There's no disputing it."

"Quetzie is a handsome devil."

"That will do," Londa said, and Quetzie apparently understood her—at any rate, he dropped the subject.

"I'd like to see your homework," I said.

Londa sighed and rubbed up against the conquistador's breast-plate like a house cat alerting its owner to the menace of an empty food dish. "Your chapter on the Stoics—I'm not sure how to put this—it simply *amazed* me. My pathetic essay doesn't even *begin* to convey what it's like to meet a mind like yours."

"Chapter four isn't about my ideas. It's about the Stoics' ideas."

Quetzie hopped from Londa's shoulder to the conquistador's helmet. "Mason is a genius," the iguana announced from his new perch.

I furrowed my brow and groaned. "Did you *teach* him that dubious proposition," I asked Londa, "or is it merely something he overheard?"

She smiled coyly, then approached a massive writing desk, ornately carved with flowering creepers—I imagined some mad Caribbean poet at work there, scribbling the national epic of Isla de Sangre, a phantasmagoria of mutant lobsters, sentient mangroves, talking iguanas, greedy conquistadors, and mysterious concrete walls—and retrieved a printout from the top drawer. Retracing her steps, she transferred Quetzie back to her shoulder and presented me with an essay titled "In Praise of Adversity."

"While you were slaving away on this, I had something of an adventure," I told her. "I was hiking along the beach and suddenly found myself facing a high concrete wall. Do you know about it?"

She pursed her lips and shook her head.

"Evidently it runs far into the jungle. I climbed over—"

"I thought it was high."

"I used a tree. And you'll never guess what I discovered."

"The Fountain of Youth?"

"A large house—big as Faustino. Bigger, even. A villa."

"How strange."

"A little girl lives there. She calls herself Donya. Is that name familiar to you?"

"I don't think so. Donya?"

"That's right."

"Since I hit my head"—Londa gulped loudly, as if swallowing a horse pill—"I've forgotten so many things."

"Is it possible you have a little sister named Donya?"

She blinked in slow motion. "Mother says I'm an only child. What makes you think this Donya person is my sister?"

Londa's morality teacher now proceeded to lie to her. "A wild hunch. I shouldn't have mentioned it."

"Shit, I *hate* it when the amnesia takes somebody away from me. I goddamn fucking *hate* it."

"For what it's worth, I believe you've never met the child in question."

"Know something, Socrates? I'm not enjoying this fucking conversation one little bit."

"Mason is a genius," the iguana said.

"Shut the fuck up," Londa said.

Quetzie took flight and landed atop the globe, perching on the North Pole like a gigantic vulture about to devour the rotting carcass of planet Earth. I apologized to Londa for introducing such a painful topic, promised never to do so again, then suggested that while I negotiated "In Praise of Adversity," she should amuse herself with a book of her own choosing. She ambled to the fiction collection, plucking out *Pride and Prejudice,* and we sat down together at the reading table.

I was barely two sentences into Londa's essay before realizing that she was uncommonly skilled at articulating her thoughts on paper: not a complete surprise, given the many acres of text she'd

["

soaked up of late—though, God knows, my Watertown High students had rarely made the leap from reading lucid prose to writing it. Her last paragraph struck me as downright eloquent.

> Above all, the Stoics sought wisdom, a condition that I myself hope to achieve after I stop wrecking and burning things. While I can't claim to understand this philosophy, despite Mason's dazzling overview, I imagine there must be great rewards in living one's life by Stoic principles. Am I equal to the challenge? There's only one way to find out.

During the ten minutes I spent with her essay, Londa reached the midpoint of *Pride and Prejudice*.

"You're a good writer," I told her.

"You think so?" she asked. "How good?"

"Very good. Excellent, really."

"I'm not as good as this woman," she said, tapping her novel. "Jane Austen makes me believe that Elizabeth Bennet is fucking alive."

"A pithy tribute, Londa, but how about curbing the profanity?"

"Okay. Jane Austen *doesn't* make me believe that Elizabeth Bennet is fucking alive."

I rolled my eyes and snorted. "You clearly got a lot out of my Stoicism chapter. But there's a small problem. From these pages it almost sounds as if you intend to *become* a Stoic."

"Of course I do."

"Stoicism died out fifteen centuries ago."

"Quetzie is a handsome devil," the iguana said.

"As a matter of fact, the experiment has already started," Londa said with a disconcerting grin. "Yesterday at lunch I had a smaller piece of pecan pie than usual, and I passed up the scoop of vanilla ice cream entirely. It's like I said in my essay. 'Just as nature abhors a vacuum, a Stoic abhors satiety.' What's more, as you may have noticed, I've stopped smoking."

"But not swearing."

"I'm working on it."

"And how long do you plan to pursue this project?"

"Long as I can. The hardest part will be to stop masturbating."

"I see."

"I'm rather well informed about sex," she told me, as if I'd said she wasn't. "I've read all the books. *Fanny Hill. Justine. Lady Chatterley's Lover.* I know there's a positive side to fucking, but on the whole it's messy and dangerous, wouldn't you say?"

I swiped my tongue across the roof of my mouth, as if to detach a popcorn husk. "Messy. Dangerous. Yes."

"A person could get a venereal disease."

"This is true."

"Do you have a girlfriend, Mason?"

"Not right now."

"What about in the past?"

"Several girlfriends. You wrote a marvelous essay."

"Did you fuck them?"

"We're drifting away from the topic."

She snickered and said, "Stoicism: putting pleasure in its place. The Stoics believed that in bearing pain without complaint, a mortal might transcend the mundane world and enter the eternal matrix of divine thought—so that's part of my experiment, too."

"What is?"

"Pain."

"I don't understand."

"Pain is part of my experiment."

Several harsh and foreign chemicals flooded into my stomach. "Pain has nothing to teach you, Londa."

"Not according to chapter four."

"The Stoics did not deliberately hurt themselves."

"I intend to build on their work."

The chemicals roiled around, interacting with the native acids.

"Listen to me, Londa. You will not, under any conditions, you will *not* hurt yourself."

"Last night I snuffed out a candle with my hand."

She held up her left palm. A shudder of alarm passed through me. At the juncture of her head line and fate line, the very spot I'd massaged twenty-four hours earlier, lay a stark white blister.

"Fuck," I said, frightened and confused but mostly angry.

"A useful word, huh?"

"I don't believe this."

"I moaned and whimpered, but I didn't shriek. I also did stuff with a rose thorn." She extended her right thumb. An angry red welt was blooming beneath the nail.

"Christ, Londa, I think it's *infected*!"

"It hurts like hell." She sounded pleased. "Later today I'm going to sit in the conservatory and push a sewing needle through my tongue and open my heart to the divine matrix."

I clasped Londa's shoulders and shook her, rhythmically, emphatically, as if I might dislodge her fantasies as I would a quarter stolen by a vending machine. "You will *not* push a needle through your tongue! Not today or any other day! You have to promise me that!"

"This is really important to you, isn't it, Mason?"

"*Promise* me."

"All right, if that's what you want, I promise." She approached the world-eating iguana and gently stroked his tail feathers. "But I don't see how I'm supposed to get cured if I can't take my lessons seriously."

WE PASSED THE REST OF THE MORNING in a heated and unhappy conversation, during which I tried convincing Londa that a person could comprehend a moral principle without becoming obligated to act on it. After a two-hour debate, she finally conceded that self-mutilation was not essential to the pursuit of ethics, but her words sprang more from acquiescence than assent. Before our next meeting, I told her, she must reread chapter four, searching for the nuances she'd missed the first time around, the better to benefit from our upcoming Stoicism role-playing exercise.

I did not so much leave Faustino that afternoon as flee it, seeking the buoyant company of Donya and the Edenic serenity of her tree house. Jogging frantically along the beach, I vowed to begin Friday's lesson by inspecting Londa's tongue and every other part of her that lent itself to scrutiny. If I saw the slightest evidence of violence, I would probably conclude that I was out of my depth, return to Boston, and send Edwina an e-mail advising her to replace me with some fuck-the-Enlightenment Lyotard disciple from Vassar.

By the time I reached the concrete wall, a storm had broken over Blood Island, not quite a Gulf hurricane but still fearsome, with lashing winds and sheets of rain, and I was not surprised, after scaling the rampart and surveying the banyan tree, to find Donya's little elevated cottage empty. I proceeded to the villa. The doorknocker was a brass quoit fixed in the jaws of the same Aztec god who decorated the portal to Faustino. I banged the ring forcefully, thereby setting Donya's Doberman to barking.

"Omar, be quiet!" came a man's voice, chirping through the loudspeaker above my head.

"It's Mason Ambrose. I'm a friend of Donya's."

"Your reputation precedes you."

Omar kept on barking. The door swung back to reveal the frantic dog, bouncing up and down, bellowing madly, not far from canine hysterics. Holding Omar's collar was a portly middle-aged man who introduced himself as Henry Cushing. His beard was white, his brow sunburned, his manner genial: a Santa Claus for adults, I mused, bringing tax refunds and nonaddictive hallucinogens to good grown-ups everywhere. Whatever explanation this fellow might offer for Edwina's schizoid approach to parenthood, I would take it at face value.

At last recognizing my scent, Omar grew calm.

"When I saw Donya escorting you to the tree house, my impulse was to run over and check you out," Henry said. "But she and Omar had obviously found you acceptable"—he released the dog's collar—"and they're both excellent judges of character, so I decided not to intrude."

"She charmed me off my feet." I staggered into the foyer, carrying with me a condensed edition of the outside storm, the rain spouting from the sleeves of my anorak to form puddles on the stone floor.

"Preschool children," Henry said, "they're one of the *better* things in the world—wouldn't you agree?—like red wine and *New Yorker* cartoons and Christina Rossetti. 'When I am dead, my dearest, sing no sad songs for me. Plant thou no roses at my head, nor shady cypress-tree.'"

I peeled off my soggy jacket and hung it on the coatrack. "You left out George Gershwin."

"Don't tell Brock. He'd never forgive me."

"My lips are sealed."

"'Be the green grass above me with showers and dewdrops wet. And if thou wilt, remember. And if thou wilt, forget.'"

Omar returned to his post, settling down on the rug before the door. Henry led me into a Gothic parlor, its fluted pillars ascending to a vaulted ceiling, its stained-glass windows thrusting ever heavenward like rectangles who'd found Jesus. Dressed in an oilcloth smock and gripping a paintbrush, Donya stood before an artist's easel, staring at a half-finished watercolor of Deedee the chimpanzee. Her subject sat two feet away on a Windsor chair, self-possessed as only a professional model or a stuffed animal could be.

"Donya, look who's here," Henry said.

"Mason!" She dashed across the room and threw her arms around me as if I were Edward Bear himself, dropping by for a game of Candy Land. "I'm so glad to see you! I told Henry and Brock all about our tea party!"

"The social event of the season," I said.

"Look what Brock's building for me!"

She led me to the far corner, where a man in his early forties, handsome as Dorian Gray, was methodically adding tiny trees to a miniature amusement park spread across a plywood platform. This raucous and frenetic marvel, as lovingly detailed as the Lionel O-gauge electric train set I'd inherited from my grandfather, featured a Ferris wheel spinning in place like a vertical phonograph record, a six-horse carousel rotating to the tune of "The Washington Post March," and a roller coaster subjecting a dozen diminutive passengers to its scale-model vicissitudes. As I gaped in appreciation, the tree planter introduced himself as Brock Hawes, "the sensitive half of the relationship, Henry being in charge of dental appointments and balancing the checkbook."

"Donya, will you excuse us, darling?" Henry said. "The adults need to talk."

"I want to stay here," Donya said.

"Sorry, tomato," Henry said.

"You can't *make* me go."

"Donya . . ."

"If you try to *make* me go, I'll tell Mommy you were mean to me, and I'll do other stuff you won't like either—with matches, maybe, or scissors."

"Know what, Donya?" Brock said. "I'll bet you a million dollars there's something yummy in the fridge, second shelf down on the right."

"You can't *make* me do anything. What's in the fridge?"

"I forget exactly," Brock said, "but there's some major yumminess involved, I promise you."

Donya pirouetted toward the kitchen, moving so gracefully I

wondered whether Henry and Brock's curriculum might include ballet lessons. Omar, stretching, rose from his rug and followed his mistress out of the room.

"The person who hired you—she claims to be Donya's mother, right?" I asked.

"Edwina Sabacthani," Henry said, nodding.

"Edwina," I muttered. So much for my theory that Donya's mother was Edwina's twin sister. I could imagine a Monty Python routine about twins with the same first name, but I doubted that the practice flourished on Isla de Sangre. "I'm working for her, too."

"We know," Brock said. "Donya told us."

"Are you by any chance a connoisseur of children's television?" Henry asked. "*Professor Oolong's Oompah-pah Zoo?*"

I shook my head.

"For six years running, I was Professor Oolong on Nickelodeon, but then the ratings went south, and I became plain old Henry Cushing, unemployed actor. This job has been a gift from heaven. Edwina's nephew used to enjoy my antics every Saturday morning, and that was recommendation enough."

"I was hired to tutor an adolescent named Londa," I said.

"Londa Sabacthani," said Brock. "Seventeen years old. Donya's got a fabulous memory. She showed you a photograph of her mother."

"Who looks exactly like Londa's mother," I said. "Apparently our students are sisters—half sisters at least."

"Are you merely *tutoring* Londa," Brock asked, "or would it be more accurate to say you're *rehabilitating* her?"

"Rehabilitating, yes," I said. "A diving accident resulting in cerebral trauma. The symptoms include severe amnesia plus—"

"Let me guess," Henry said. "Alienation, anomie, and sociopathic behavior."

I frowned and nodded.

"In other words, Londa woke up without a conscience," Brock said. "Donya has the same deficit."

"So I hear," I said. "No rectitude. What a strange coincidence."

"I don't think it's a *coincidence* at all," Henry said. "It appears that Edwina has been playing games with our heads, and her children's heads, too, and maybe her own head as well."

"Did Donya also have a diving accident?" I asked.

"Supposedly she fell off her bicycle," Brock said.

"Londa has inherited her maternal grandfather's gift for speed-reading," I informed my new friends. "And Donya?"

Henry hummed in corroboration. "Yesterday she got through *Heidi* in fifteen minutes. This morning she devoured *The Secret Garden* in ten."

"Did Edwina ever mention a second daughter?" I asked.

Henry and Brock shook their heads in tandem.

"When I had tea with Donya, she told me she's an only child," I said. "Londa believes the same about herself. Evidently Edwina makes a point of it."

"Curiouser and curiouser," Henry said.

For the next half-hour, we attempted to construct a coherent narrative that would account for the bizarre domestic arrangements on Isla de Sangre, but far from dissolving the mystery, we only deepened it. Our employer's nomadism had us especially confused. Just as I'd assumed that Edwina resided exclusively with Londa at the moldering estate called Faustino, so did Henry and Brock believe she was permanently ensconced with Donya at Casa de los Huesos.

"Apparently she spends much of her time on the move, a peculiar lifestyle for a person allegedly in poor health." Henry flipped back the top of the carousel and removed the mini-CD. "Proposition, Mason. While the cat's away in Chicago, why don't we mice spend Saturday afternoon exploring the island?" Receiving my nod, he smiled approvingly, then inserted a disc labeled "Being for the Benefit of Mr. Kite" into the carousel. "I can't speak for you or Brock, but I won't rest until I've figured out precisely how many daughters Edwina has, and who their fathers are, and why the hell the children aren't supposed to know about each other."

DURING THE INTERVAL since my last encounter with the mutant iguana, a new sentence had coalesced in his cold-blooded brain. When I walked into the library on Friday morning, Quetzie stared at me from his perch atop the conquistador's helmet and proclaimed, "All you need is love."

"That's a matter of some controversy," I said.

"All you need is love," Quetzie insisted.

Just then Londa stepped into the room, dressed distractingly in blue denim cutoffs and an orange halter top, clutching her copy of *Ethics from the Earth*. As she approached Quetzie, he hopped from the conquistador to her head, so that she now wore an Aztec princess's feathered crown.

"Stick out your tongue," I instructed her.

"I didn't mutilate it."

"All you need is love," the iguana said.

"Stick out your tongue," I repeated.

Londa stuck out her tongue. It looked entirely healthy.

"Show me your hands."

She did as instructed. The inflamed skin beneath her thumbnail seemed to be healing, likewise the blister on her palm, and I saw no evidence that she'd manually snuffed another candle. I inspected her shoulders. No aberrations. I glanced at her knees and calves. The skin seemed intact.

"I'm still a Stoic," she explained, "but from now on I won't *behave* like one, since it makes you so fucking unhappy, though your fellow educator Jean Piaget believes that a developing child constructs her world through action."

"Your teacher this morning is Mason Ambrose, not Jean Piaget. Did you reread chapter four?"

"Twice."

"Mason is a genius," Quetzie said.

"Here's the setup," I said. "Imagine you're an artist living in a contemporary version of the Stoics' fabled City of Zeus. Your name is Sybil Bright, and you believe that personal integrity is the highest virtue."

"Let me get this straight," Londa said. "I'm allowed to *play* at Stoicism, but I'm not allowed to *practice* it."

"What you're not allowed to do is burn your palm or puncture your thumb or any such crap," I said curtly. "A man named Alvarez has come to your studio. He works for a bank. Ready?"

"Whatever you say."

I rapped my knuckles on the reading table to simulate Mr. Alvarez knocking on Sybil Bright's door.

"Could I have a minute of your time, young woman?"

Londa pulled a colorfully packaged piece of bubble gum from her hip pocket. "My newest vice," she said, unwrapping the pink lozenge. "It helps me overcome the urge for a cig."

I cleared my throat. "Could I have a minute of your time?" I said again.

She shrugged and popped the gum into her mouth. "Would you like to buy a painting?"

I pantomimed a banker entering Sybil's studio. "Casper Alvarez of the Seaboard Bank and Trust Company. I'm here to offer you a credit card. No annual fee, a stunning five-point-eight percent APR, and you get to accumulate a hundred and fifty thousand dollars in debt before we bat an eye, assuming you keep up the minimum monthly payments."

"I don't need a credit card."

"Sure you do."

"Why?"

"To buy things."

"What things?"

"A recreational vehicle, a snowmobile, a sailboat, a home theater."

"Will they make me a better person?" she asked.

"They won't make you *better,*" I said, "but they'll afford you countless hours of enjoyment."

"We Stoics distrust enjoyment. My life is a quest for divine wisdom."

"Don't be self-righteous, Sybil. When you experience intimations of the numinous, this gives you a rush of satisfaction."

"True enough, but it's the wisdom I value, not the rush."

A crackerjack retort, I thought. Perhaps I was a better teacher than I knew.

Our conversation went on for another twenty minutes, an interval during which Mr. Alvarez failed to make Sybil stray even one centimeter from her personal code with its imperatives of integrity, forbearance, and openness to epiphany.

"Curtain," I said, resting an affirming hand on Londa's bare shoulder. "You were terrific."

"Was I?"

"Absolutely sensational. For Monday's class, I want you to study the next chapter, all about Epicurus, then write out a two-page conversation between an Epicurean and an anti-Epicurean."

She set her hand atop mine, pressing down until I felt the bone beneath her flesh. "The Epicureans believed pleasure was a virtue, didn't they?"

"True enough," I said, retrieving my hand.

"You won't allow me to experiment with pain. Am I supposed to run screaming from pleasure, too?"

"Depends on what you mean by pleasure. An Epicurean would be the first to argue that hedonism is both degrading and dangerous."

Londa blew a bubble that looked like a pink cantaloupe. She let it pop, returned the strands to her mouth, and smiled. "I've got the whole fucking weekend ahead of me. There's no telling *what* I might do."

* * *

ON SATURDAY MORNING I filled my backpack with trail mix and juice boxes, then hiked to Casa de los Huesos, where I found everyone assembled on the lawn for croquet—Donya, her tutors, plus a rangy Asian man and a ruddy, zaftig woman, whom Henry introduced as, respectively, Chen Lee, "a cook with Szechuan credentials," and Rosita Corona, "a gardener with a green thumb on each hand." Omar sat on his haunches just beyond the midfield stake, ready to referee. Donya offered me the blue-striped mallet— me, the washout at soccer, badminton, volleyball, kick the can, and every other athletic activity save tree climbing. I told her I'd rather watch.

The game was barely ten minutes under way when I realized that the four adults were arranging for Donya to win. They deliberately missed wickets, allowed her to retake bobbled shots, and declined to roquet her ball even when that was the only rational tactic. I wondered how this pathetic charade was supposed to further her moral education. Did Henry and Brock really believe that a sham victory would help give Donya a superego?

When at last the contest reached its predictable conclusion, Donya the winner and still champion, Henry shouldered his own backpack, bulging with luncheon delicacies secured in Tupperware containers, then announced that he and I were about to go rambling around the island in imitation of Robinson Crusoe.

"I want to come, too!" Donya shouted.

"Sorry, cupcake," Henry said.

Storm clouds gathered above the child's head. She screwed her features into a cameo of disgust and hurled her croquet mallet onto the grass. "You never let me do *anything*!"

"Guess what, pumpkin?" Brock said, strolling nonchalantly up to Donya. "A special package came yesterday."

"What special package?" she demanded shrilly. "What was in it?"

"*Indoor* voice, Donya," Brock admonished her, "*indoor* voice."

"But we're *outdoors*."

"Let's say we go open that special package," Brock suggested, stooping into a leapfrog position. Donya jumped onto his shoulders, swinging her legs around his neck. He rose, grasped her ankles, and started toward the villa. "I think it might be the bumper cars for our amusement park."

"Giddyap!" Donya cried. "Giddyap! Giddyap!"

As I followed Henry across the croquet field, barely resisting the temptation to hook my instep under the wickets and loft them into the air, he informed me that in fact the narrative of Robinson Crusoe was much on his mind these days. He'd recently hit on a concept for a children's show, *Uncle Rumpus's Magic Island,* centered on a castaway who spends his days combing the beach for whatever flotsam and jetsam might help him to survive. Being part of a larger artifact, each piece of junk he finds proves perplexing—table leg, bicycle chain, umbrella frame, clock face—and so Rumpus enlists his young viewers in interpreting each treasure, thus presumably enhancing their powers of inference.

"I think the Nickelodeon people will go ape," he said. "I just need to show them a couple of spec scripts."

Breaching the rain forest, we headed south along the wall, the ground beneath our feet dissolving in muck and marsh, the air thickening with bird cries, primate calls, and peppery swarms of gnats. The farther inland we ventured, the more Isla de Sangre revealed itself as a world of great beauty and abiding strangeness. We gobbled trail mix under the watchful eyes of an alligator clan whose title to the surrounding swamp we were not about to dispute, drank cranberry juice by an amber waterfall cascading down a series of ridges like ale spilling from an ogre's keg, and consumed our lunch near a quicksand bog ringed by astonishing conical blossoms as large and golden as French horns.

"Do you always let Donya cheat at croquet?" I asked, eating the last red grape.

"The first time we played, she lost and became instantly hysterical," Henry replied. "She ran into the kitchen screaming, 'I'm no good! I'm no good!' If Chen hadn't intervened, she would've cut off her little finger with a bread knife."

"Jesus."

"She's a far more troubled child than she appears. For the immediate future, we're wiring the game in her favor."

"On the day I first met Londa, she tried to kill a carp," I said in a commiserating tone. I approached the nearest blossom and inhaled its perfume, a heady scent suggesting pumpkin pie topped with mumquat nectar. "We've spent the past week acting out ethical dilemmas. I think it's helping."

Henry joined me by the flower, savoring its fragrance. "Oddly enough, the therapy that seems to work for Donya is DVDs of moralistic TV programs."

"You mean like *Professor Oolong's Oompah-pah Zoo*?"

"Professor Oolong rarely addressed matters of right and wrong. We started her out on *Mister Rogers' Neighborhood*, and we've just added that family-values superhero thing from the Jubilation Channel, *The Kindness Crusaders*. Sure, they're grinding the usual salvation ax, but the ratio of ethical signal to evangelical noise is much better than you'd expect. Be gentle, be generous, think of someone besides yourself—who can argue with that?"

"And you've seen progress?"

Henry raised his eyebrows and dipped his head. "Before the month is out, I believe that Donya will come to us and say, 'I know you've been letting me win at croquet, and I want you to stop it.'"

We resumed our trek, eventually reaching the island's ragged, craggy spine. Here the wall met a second such concrete barrier, angling off abruptly to the right, the juncture reinforced by a sandstone pillar as white and coarse as the saline remains of Lot's wife. Henry suggested that we had "nothing to gain by staying inside the box," and I agreed. It took us only a minute to locate an overhanging kapok limb. We availed ourselves of this natural bridge—despite his bulk, my companion was quite agile—crossing over the rampart without mishap and dropping safely to the ground.

The pillar, we now saw, lay at the hub of three discrete walls. Supplementing the familiar north-to-south barrier were two others, one running southwest along the ridge, its twin coursing southeast into the forest, both stretching past the limits of our vision but seemingly destined for the sea, an arrangement that evidently divided Isla de Sangre into three equal regions. From a frigate bird's perspective, Henry and I were standing in the cusp of an immense slingshot. We proceeded due south, along the trajectory of an imaginary flung stone, improvising a downward path through a dense and fecund wedge of jungle.

By midafternoon the forest had turned to scrub, and then a ribbon of gravel appeared, perpendicular to our path. To be sure, we were inclined to follow this unexpected road—it might teach us something important about the island, and its pursuit was unlikely to involve alligators or quicksand—but we decided it was probably an enticement, built by Edwina to lure her more inquisitive employees away from places she didn't want them to see. We crossed the road and continued our journey, descending toward a line of cypress trees, and in time the guttural hiss of the incoming tide reached our ears.

Beyond the cypress windbreak, another surprise awaited us, a Spanish fortress lying in ruins like a sand castle demolished by a wave. Only the central keep remained, emerging from a rocky spit surrounded by a turbulent green bay. The longer I stared at that looming tower, the more ominous it seemed—a twin to Kafka's castle, perhaps, or an Auschwitz chimney, or a nuclear-tipped missile. Stoicism was an admirable philosophy, and Epicureanism had much to recommend it, but no Greek school would ever equip Londa to comprehend and critique the bombs and rockets of modernity. We must advance to the Enlightenment as soon as possible.

Having come so far without misadventure, Henry and I blithely decided to inspect the woebegone stronghold. We approached slowly, moving among lone acacias and solitary boulders, until at last we reached sea level. A gazebo appeared before us, a bamboo construction as large as a village bandstand, its funnel-shaped roof shading two human figures, one slender and birdlike, the other squat and sluggish.

Anger rushed through me like a hit of grappa. Edwina had lied to us. She and Charnock were not in Chicago any more than Henry and I were in Istanbul.

"Rubbish," my employer was saying. "Pure twaddle." She stepped toward the gazebo bench, on which rested a glass container the size and shape of a fire hydrant. "You need a vacation, that's all."

Henry and I ducked behind the nearest acacia.

"This isn't fatigue," Charnock said.

"Who's the troll?" Henry whispered.

"Biologist named Charnock," I replied. "Operates a genetic-engineering lab near Faustino. Overstrung, irritable, probably a little nuts."

"Coming soon to a theater near you," Henry muttered, *The Mad Doctor of Blood Island*."

"Indeed."

"That's a real movie."

"No doubt."

Scrutinizing the glass object, I realized it was a huge beaker to which various devices—pump, compressor, oxygen tank—had been retrofitted, presumably to sustain whatever being inhabited the foggy interior.

"I'm experiencing—what should I call it?—a crisis of conscience," Charnock said. "During this past month, I've extinguished forty-three embryos."

"Naturally you heard their pathetic little screams." Edwina made no effort to purge her voice of scorn.

"Some screams are silent," Charnock said.

"Since you so enjoy crying crocodile tears over dead embryos, perhaps you should join a community of like-minded mourners," Edwina said. "The Roman Catholic Church, for example, or the Republican Party."

"I had imagined our having a serious discussion."

Edwina offered no response but instead sat down beside the beaker and contemplated its misty reaches. "You do beautiful work," she said at last, her tone now free of sarcasm—tender, in fact, almost reverent. "The painter has his pigments, the sculptor his stone, and you have your medium, too."

"My medium, right," Charnock said. "Bald egotism combined with rampant ambition and galloping self-deception." He settled his gelatinous frame onto the bench and heaved a sigh. "Maybe you're right. Maybe I need a vacation."

"Then take one, for Christ's sake." Edwina gestured toward the tower. "We can bring everything to fruition as early as . . . when? Tomorrow afternoon?"

"God rested on Sunday. I intend to do the same."

"Monday night?"

Charnock grunted in assent.

"And then we'll send you to the Bahamas," Edwina said.

"I would prefer Hawaii."

"Excellent choice. You'll have a splendid time. I picture you on Waikiki Beach, drinking mai tais and diddling the native girls."

"I thought I might get around to reading *War and Peace*," Charnock said.

At that instant the vapor in the beaker lifted, and I saw a sleek, fishlike something immersed in a translucent fluid. Briefly Charnock and Edwina contemplated the creature, and then the fog rolled in again.

"She'll be the best of the lot," Charnock said.

"Do you hear the man, Yolly?" Edwina said. "You're the best.

And don't worry about living up to your potential. There are people around here who will do that for you."

NEEDLESS TO SAY—a phrase that any language-obsessed, word-bewitched, Wittgenstein-haunted philosopher like myself uses only with great reluctance—needless to say, Edwina's duplicity was the principal topic of conversation as Henry and I headed back to Casa de los Huesos. At first, he sought to explain away her presence in the gazebo. Perhaps the artificial-intelligence conference had been canceled. Maybe Edwina and Charnock had given their presentation and flown directly home. But the tension in Henry's voice suggested that he, too, felt betrayed, and by the time we reached the sandstone pillar, he was imagining how we might deceive Edwina in kind.

"I'll spare her my incredulity but not my curiosity," he said. "Come Monday night, when she and Charnock do whatever the hell they're planning to do, I'm going to be there, hiding in the shadows. Might I persuade you to join me?"

I responded at once, without consulting the more prudent and self-protective areas of my brain—"You bet, Uncle Rumpus, I'm your man"—and so we agreed to become uninvited visitors to the crumbling tower, spying on our employer and her majordomo as they performed their alchemical mischief.

On Monday morning I left the cottage promptly at nine-thirty and headed for Faustino with the aim of tutoring Londa in Epicureanism. Suddenly, with an almost predatory pounce, she burst from the jungle and, landing on her feet, stationed herself directly in my path. Her attire was as minimalist as a knock-knock joke: a yellow spandex tube top revealing regions of skin both tanned and untanned—apparently she favored one-piece bathing suits—plus pink flip-flops and a white towel slung around her waist like a sarong.

"Hardly the proper outfit for a philosophy lesson," I admonished her. "You'll have plenty of time to go swimming this afternoon, but right now your business is chapter five."

"You asked me to make up a conversation between an Epicurean and an anti-Epicurean," she said, opening her shoulder bag and taking out a manuscript of perhaps a dozen pages. "Before I knew it, I'd written a one-act play."

"That's swell," I said mordantly. "Now go change into something that bespeaks the life of the mind. I'll read your play in the meantime."

"I call it *Coral Idolatry*," she persisted, depositing the pages in my hands. "I've given you the part of Thales, a fictional Greek Epicurean. I'm playing Sythia, a sea nymph seeking to fulfill her destiny. The setting is my secret beach. Follow me."

Although Londa's interpretation of the assignment struck me as too clever by half, I decided that such creativity was to be encouraged, so I allowed her to lead me along a path I'd never taken before. In time the trees and bushes yielded to dunes as white as refined sugar, a pristine canvas that, as we continued our walk, the incoming tide painted in agreeable shades of beige and brown. A quarter mile out to sea, a mound of crimson coral rose from the reef like a buoy, and the instant Londa told me the formation's name, the Red Witch, I knew exactly what she meant, for it indeed resembled a crone wearing a conical hat.

"Don't worry, I'm not about to bore you with a thousand facts about witches," Londa said.

Spontaneously I removed my socks and sandals, allowing my toes to savor the sand. Directly before us lay a piece of driftwood that suggested the horned head of a Cretan bull, and Londa now instructed me to sit between the prongs and wait for the curtain to rise. I declined, explaining that the sun was too hot for a pale philosopher from Boston, and if I stayed out here much longer, I'd be broiled alive. Londa responded by retrieving a bottle of sunscreen from her bag and spraying my bare arms.

"Close your eyes," she demanded.

I did so. A vivid bloodscape filled my field of vision. Londa lacquered my brow, jaw, nose, and neck, rubbing the juice into my pores with two contiguous fingertips.

"Your cue occurs halfway down the page," she said. "'Will the man I see before me grant my wish?'"

She unhitched the towel from her waist, letting it drop in a heap on the sand. Her bikini bottom matched her tube top in color and audacity. She headed toward the Red Witch, wading into the bay until it reached her hips. She took a breath and disappeared. Evidently her diving accident had not left her with an indiscriminate fear of water. I sat on the driftwood and glanced at the script. The setting was a Greek island called Sérifos. According to the stage directions, the undine Sythia would now abandon her home beneath the waves and approach Thales as he relaxed on the shore thinking rarefied Epicurean thoughts.

"Action!" I called in Londa's direction.

Slowly, elegantly, she rose from her aquatic abode, the foam spilling from her hair, cascading down her tube top, trickling along her thighs. She strode toward me through the surf, each step an emphatic splash.

"'An undine lives with one purpose in her heart,'" she declaimed, as that was indeed Sythia's first line. "'She seeks a mortal who will love her, betroth her, and lavish his body upon her, for in this manner alone might she acquire a soul.'" Gaining the beach, she took a dozen steps forward and stood over Thales, dripping seawater on his script. "'Two hundred days have I followed the submarine currents, seeking the legendary Isle of Sérifos, whose pleasure-loving Hedonists never hesitate to avail themselves of succulent nymphs and willing sylphs. Could it be that my search has finally ended? Might the man I see before me grant my wish?'"

"'Forgive me for gaping, but I'm astonished to find myself a mere stone's throw from a creature of your kind,'" I said. "'Until now I've observed undines only from afar. Whenever I take ship, I stand on the deck and stare out to sea, hoping to glimpse a nymph sporting with the dolphins.'"

"'My name is Sythia. Are you a Hedonist?'"

"'Call me Thales, disciple of Epicurus.'"

"'Epicurus? Then I must surmise that for you the essence of pleasure is the removal of pain.'"

"'True, fair Sythia. Once pain is gone, pleasure admits of variation but not of increase. I'm equally at odds with the self-indulgent Hedonists and the life-denying Stoics. An Epicurean pursues the quiet virtues. Friendship, conversation, tranquillity.'"

"'So for you the nubility of an undine is no more pleasurable than the nobility of an idea?'"

"'Quite so.'"

"'Could you direct me to the nearest Hedonist?'"

"'Alas, there are none on this isle.'"

"'I'd heard that Sérifos is swarming with profligates.'"

"'You were misinformed.'"

It was at this point that I had the good sense to skim the next three pages, and what I encountered was so appalling I had no choice but to shut down the production on the spot.

"Well, Londa," I said, lurching free of the driftwood and stepping out of character, "you certainly know your Epicureans. I especially enjoyed your wordplay: nubility, nobility. Wonderful. For your next assignment, I'd like you to—"

"We aren't finished."

"I glanced ahead," I told her. "The script requires you to kiss me on the lips."

"No, the script requires Sythia to kiss Thales on the lips. And for Thales to kiss her back, and before you know it, they're following their pagan impulses."

"Only last Thursday, you described that sort of behavior as messy and dangerous. An Epicurean eschews all pleasures that have potentially painful consequences. Bacchanals, binges, fornication."

"But that's what makes the play *interesting*," Londa insisted, running a hooked finger along her thigh to remove a furl in her bikini bottom. Her nipples had molded the yellow spandex into lemon drops of such magnificence they would have confounded any passing postmodernist bearing theories of gender as a social construction. "Thales is torn in two. He can't decide between his desire for the undine and his loyalty to Epicureanism."

"Your assignment for tomorrow is to read my chapter on Aristotle's *Nicomachean Ethics*," I said. "We'll sit in the library and discuss it wearing street clothes."

"Of course, after Sythia and Thales have their roll in the clover, he realizes that pleasure *does* come in degrees." Londa took hold of her beach towel, spreading it across the sand as if fitting a sheet to a mattress. "And once Thales realizes that Epicureanism is flawed, he no longer hesitates to bend its rules."

This was not an unprecedented situation. Such circumstances had arisen before. Young teacher, moonstruck student, sufficient privacy. On numerous occasions throughout human history, these very factors had come into conjunction.

"I'm not going to kiss you," I said.

"Once you give me a conscience," she replied, setting her rump on the towel, "I'll become a completely honest person, won't I?"

"No one's completely honest."

"But it's an ideal worth striving for, right?"

"Indeed."

"Do you want to kiss me, Mason? Tell me honestly."

Saying nothing, I resumed my driftwood seat and pulled my socks back on without bothering to shake out the sand. I restored my sandals, the straps and buckles vibrating in my hands. Londa stayed on her towel, smiling broadly as she arranged herself in a lotus position.

"The Aristotle chapter is one of my better efforts," I said. "Study it thoroughly."

"Don't you want to fuck me?" she asked.

"Pay particular attention to the notion that virtue consists in avoiding extremes. When Aristotle speaks of the optimum response to a stimulus, he's not endorsing mediocrity. He's celebrating harmony."

"Mother is still in Chicago. Dr. Charnock never comes here. We could fuck until our eyes fell out, and nobody would know."

My stomach seemed to break free of its moorings and, ascending, collide with my heart. An erotic lava gushed through my veins. "This sunscreen isn't working very well," I said, starting into the jungle. "I'm getting burned."

"What did you think of my play?" she called after me.

"B-plus at the very least, perhaps an A-minus!" I shouted over my shoulder. "Class dismissed!" I cried, running toward my cottage as fast as my conscience could carry me.

A SIMPLE CONCRETE WALL, an unremarkable rampart of sand and cement—but as Henry and I followed its southerly course that evening, our path lit by moonbeams and the glow of our Coleman lanterns, I felt as if the thing had replicated itself, again and again and again, so that we were negotiating a maze as complex as the one Daedalus had designed to confine the Minotaur. I suspected that Edwina and Charnock counted Daedalus among their heroes, for that audacious artificer was arguably the world's first genetic engineer, having supervised the synthesis of a beast as chimeric and unnatural as Proserpine. If I'd correctly interpreted the conversation in the gazebo, tonight Henry and I would witness the birth of a biological contrivance called Yolly, though I could not imagine whether its lineage would be piscean, reptilian, amphibian, mammalian, or some profane amalgam of all four.

"Londa tried to seduce me this morning," I said as we approached the sandstone pillar.

"Tell me more," Henry said. "I'll try to keep an open mind."

"There's nothing more to tell, I'm happy to say. I ran away before things got out of hand."

"A wise policy. Stick to it."

We vaulted the wall, advanced to the scrub, and, fearful of encountering some armed sentry with a damaged superego, jogged all the way to the cypress windbreak. By the time we reached sea level, the heavens were rumbling with the kettledrum cadence of an incipient thunderstorm. Moments later the deluge arrived. We took refuge in the gazebo long enough to catch our breath and shake off the rainwater. Staring through the downpour, I beheld a trellis of lightning flash behind the Spanish fortress like puppet strings affixed to a cosmic marionette. The tower was dark but for the uppermost window, which emitted a luminous white shaft as bright as a lighthouse beacon.

We abandoned the gazebo, negotiated the ragged spit, and followed the span of a lowered drawbridge extending from the keep like an impertinent tongue, then crossed the frothy channel spawned by the restless bay. Although Henry had thought to bring along what he called his "Official Professor Oolong Breaking-and-Entering Kit"—a satchel packed with a crowbar, a sledgehammer, and a coil of rope—it proved superfluous, for to breach the keep one needed merely to push open a squat wooden door that nobody had bothered to lock.

Cleaving to the shadows and shedding raindrops, we made our way along the perimeter of the great hall, a pristine and convivial space, clearly intended for human habitation: new furniture, linen drapes, oriental carpets. We crept up the main staircase, a stone helix winding ever upward like the rifling in a gun barrel, until we gained the topmost landing, where a steel door presented itself. Henry twisted the knob. The door pivoted quietly on well-oiled hinges, and so we slipped unnoticed into the room beyond, hiding behind a freestanding glass cabinet jammed with surgical instruments, perhaps including the very scalpel Edwina had used to rid Proserpine of her brain.

The laboratory proper was a sunken affair resembling a theater-in-the-round, harshly illuminated by halogen lamps and dominated by a worktable on which rested the mysterious beaker with its retro-fitted pump, compressor, and oxygen tank. Dressed in black rubber aprons and neoprene gloves, Edwina and Dr. Charnock peered into the vessel's mouth. I stifled a gasp. Sitting amid the whorls of mist was a female human fetus—eyes closed, lips sealed with silver tape, body immersed in a clear fluid. A newborn? Doubtful, for it could not yet breathe on its own, or so I surmised from the pair of delicate plastic tubes connecting the nostrils to the air supply.

At the far end of the worktable rose a steel gantry culminating in a pulley from which hung a nylon cord that, before reaching the beaker, split into two strands that looped around the fetus's upper arms, giving the creature the appearance of a Christmas-pageant angel bound for the rafters of a small-town church. No sooner had I absorbed this weird tableau than Edwina drew near the gantry and began cranking the winch, slowly, carefully, clockwise, raveling up the cord and lifting the fetus from its amniotic bath. I glanced at the ceiling. An array of plasma computer monitors lined the dome, each screen displaying a sea of shivering gray static. The fetus continued its ascent, beaker fluid trickling from its miniature fingers and toes.

Now Edwina pivoted the gantry, so that the fetus traveled horizontally across the laboratory until it dangled above the sealed hatch of a cobalt-blue metallic chamber that, with its spherical shape, riveted plates, and bellyband of portholes, suggested nothing so much as an antique diving bell. Charnock locked his gaze on four glass tanks stacked like aquariums in a pet store, each holding a vivid liquid—gold, crimson, violet, turquoise—and connected to the diving bell via a mesh of translucent corrugated hoses. Approaching a console bristling with valves and regulators, he proceeded to turn the handles in tiny increments, thus controlling the force and generosity with which the tanks delivered their contents to the riveted sphere. In less than fifteen minutes, the chamber had acquired a dark seething soup in which millions of bubbles cavorted like fireflies speckling a summer night.

Charnock threw a lever on the console, causing the chamber hatch to groan and creak and finally flip back like a cranium yielding to Sinuhe's fingers. Coils of steam rose from the vat, plus a nauseating fragrance redolent of burning hair. A burst of lightning filled the laboratory with a sudden radiance, turning the suspended fetus as white as a christening gown, and an instant later the thunder boomed.

Edwina worked the gantry winch, counterclockwise this time, and the fetus began its descent, soon disappearing into the broth, oxygen tubes trailing behind it like filaments from a silkworm. Henry and I fixed on the nearest porthole, peering into the milky fluid in hopes of learning the creature's fate. Briefly I entertained the darkest of all possible notions—the scientists were dissolving the nascent baby in a caustic fluid, sacrificing it to some god to whom only Daedalus and Edwina and Charnock prayed—but then I realized that a different phenomenon was unfolding. The fetus was growing, its flesh and bones pressing ever outward in an image evoking a set of Russian nested dolls being packed safely away, each hollow soul subsumed by its ancestors.

For a full hour, as the thunder crashed and the lightning ornamented the sky with quicksilver stitchery, the fetus continued to undergo its hyperbolic maturation, steadily progressing from the tender flesh of infancy to the pliant lines of childhood to the supple contours of preadolescence.

"Finished!" Charnock cried.

Henry and I exchanged horrified glances. In recent years I'd seen Max Crippen's sculpture of the Crucifixion rendered entirely in LEGOs, Valerio Caparelli's Norman Rockwell–style painting of

God inseminating the Virgin Mary on their first date, and Leonard Steele's rock opera set in the Vatican's luxury suite for retired pedophile priests, but what Edwina and Charnock had achieved was sacrilege of a wholly different order, blasphemy beyond the meaning of the word.

Edwina rotated the winch. The girl rose from the diving bell, oscillating like a criminal in a gibbet, the dark fluid sluicing down her limbs and along her oxygen tubes, her flesh glistening under the halogen lamps.

Now came the final flourish, the last ingredient in the stew of her nativity. From a black box embedded in the dome, a gleaming inverted bowl descended on a golden thread. Bristling with bright nubs and silvery nodes, the device resembled a motorcycle helmet customized by a schizophrenic bent on receiving messages from Alpha Centauri. Even as the strange gear settled over the girl's damp hair, snugging against her cranium, the computer monitors flared to life, their static yielding to frenetic montages. Trees, plants, flowers, insects, birds, fish, snakes, lizards, turtles, toads, rodents, and ruminants paraded across the screens—kind after kind, beast upon beast— soon yielding to pots, pans, lightbulbs, hammers, saws, hats, gloves, guns, eyeglasses, automobiles, and ten thousand other artifacts, and then came a cavalcade of kings, queens, emperors, empresses, caliphs, pharaohs, rajas, shahs, dictators, prime ministers, and presidents, followed by those mathematical signs denoting addition, subtraction, multiplication, division, ratios, percentages, and square roots. The child learned of shoes and ships and sealing wax, of cabbages and still more kings, each input registering for a fraction of a second, like pips on playing cards being shuffled by a manic croupier.

Edwina and Charnock approached the diving bell and cast their gazes upward.

"Yolly, this is your mother," Charnock said.

"Welcome to the world," Lady Daedalus said, "my dearest, sweetest darling."

Yolly's lids flickered open. Her eyes, mismatched emeralds, glowed and pulsed in her skull like luminous moons orbiting her cerebrum. She raised one hand and tore the silver tape from her lips. She clucked her tongue and coughed, but it was only when she released a howl compounded of fear, shock, and dismay that I grew certain of her lineage. The creature suspended before Henry and me was Londa's newborn sister, and Donya's sister, too, bereft of ethics, barren in experience, and condemned to live whatever facsimile of a life Edwina had designed for her.

Chapter 5

MANTLES AGLOW LIKE LUMINOUS MUMQUATS, our Coleman lanterns lit the way as Henry and I doubled back through the jungle, every leaf and branch dripping with the residue of the recent storm. The surrounding darkness colluded with my fevered imagination to populate Isla de Sangre with monsters—misbegotten beasts spawned by Edwina's ambition and Charnock's art. I saw a colony of shaggy primates, half-man, half-ape, sucking up water from the swamp. An immense spider spinning a web whose jagged geometry suggested a windshield bashed by a mailed fist. A python coiled around an acacia, its tubular body studded with a hundred eyeballs, so that not only could the creature see in all directions, it could see itself seeing in all directions.

Throughout our return to the island's saner shore, Henry and I discussed the conception, quickening, and forced maturation of Yolly Sabacthani, trying without success to persuade ourselves that Londa and Donya had not arisen from this same unseemly science. We decided that in each case Edwina must have donated the essential ovum, and we further hypothesized that, once this egg had been fertilized by some Nobel laureate's sperm, she'd been unable or unwilling to gestate the subsequent zygote. A rational scenario. So far, so good. But why then subject the embryo to that infernal diving bell when dozens of financially desperate women would have gladly leased their natural reproductive apparatus to Edwina? And what did Lady Daedalus hope to accomplish by dumping reams of data into the brains of Yolly and her sisters—yes, it seemed logical to assume that Donya and Londa had been similarly programmed—when conventional schooling would have surely served them better?

Without particularly meaning to, I ended up escorting Henry all the way to his beachfront bungalow, a stout cinderblock structure set on concrete piles as a defense against the ubiquitous hurricanes. Vibrant paintings of the local monkeys, macaws, flamingos, and toucans decorated the place, each signed with Brock's filigreed initials, a serene and soothing gallery that soon drove the ape-men and their brethren from my mind. The artist himself had fallen asleep in his armchair, snoring softly before an unfinished canvas of a cone-hatted sorcerer, bent with age and weary with wisdom, staring into a mirror and seeing his youthful self stare back, doubtless a gift for little Donya. Before parting company, Henry and I exchanged cellphone numbers, agreeing that whoever first sighted Edwina would tell her we'd witnessed what passed for procreation on Isla de Sangre, and therefore a candid conversation among Lady Daedalus and her employees would be in order.

"I wonder, from now on will we bring some subtle prejudice to our dealings with Donya and Londa?" I asked.

Henry moaned knowingly. "I'll get up each morning, and I'll tell myself that Donya is completely human, but then a sardonic voice will whisper in my ear, 'What ugly epithet shall we invent for her today? Shall we call Donya a beaker freak? A chamber maid?'"

"A vatling," I suggested.

"Petri doll," Henry said.

"Bouillababy."

"Gumbo girl."

"Tureen queen."

"Shame on us," Henry said.

"Shame on us," I agreed.

TEN HOURS LATER I entered the Faustino library in thrall to a despair whose utter Aristotelian reasonableness—only a fool or a madman would have reacted otherwise to the previous night's Daedalusian circus—did nothing to lessen its intensity, and so I felt especially grateful when Londa, standing crestfallen beside the conquistador, apologized for attempting to seduce me, calling her scheme "sneaky and snaky."

"Those are two good words for it," I said.

"I guess I'm still basically crazy, huh, Mason?"

"Of course not. You're coming along fine. A few rough edges, but the prince of philosophers will smooth them off for you."

"You *are* a prince, Mason."

"I meant Aristotle."

"Snakiness aside, I'd like to know whether you find me—what's the word?—attractive."

"Aristotle is commonly regarded as antiquity's most brilliant mind. Let's try to find out why."

"Sometimes I think I'm terribly ugly."

"You're not ugly, Londa. Once you're in college, you'll have dozens of boyfriends."

"None of them as interesting as my morality teacher."

"Every time I read the *Nicomachean Ethics,* I find something new."

We spent the rest of the lesson on the venerable Greek's doctrine of the mean—the virtuous man does not burden himself with inhibitions, but neither does he permit his impulses to reign unchecked—and I must admit that this principle now struck me as superficial in the extreme, unlikely to have netted Aristotle a master's degree from Parsons, much less a Ph.D. from Hawthorne. All through the lesson, I pondered Henry's astute and disturbing question. Were we now fated to perceive our charges as creatures not quite human? Evidently Londa had been made in a cauldron, like a wizard's elixir or a witch's brew. Quite probably she could summon no preadolescent memories for the breathtakingly bizarre reason that she'd had no preadolescence. I still knew her as my pupil, my mentee, my eminently worthy mission—but now she was also my vatling.

On Wednesday we mulled over Aristotle's answer to a paradox first identified by Socrates. How can a human being know what is right and yet do what is wrong? But because neither of us found this puzzle compelling—it seemed a nonproblem, really—we couldn't get excited by the solution: anger or desire may momentarily compromise a person's philosophical commitment to virtue. The following day we wrestled with the great man's notion of justice, and within an hour we'd become so bored with the usual dreary Aristotelian dichotomies—universal justice versus particular justice, distributive justice versus rectificatory justice, household justice versus political justice, natural justice versus legal justice—that we turned our energies to teaching Quetzie the phrase "Hedonism, anyone?" By the time Friday rolled around, Londa and I were heartily sick of Aristotle, and so instead of analyzing his excruciating consideration of pleasure, complete with the usual paean to temperance, we sat down at the chessboard. During the first game, Londa succumbed to my skill with the knight, inadvertently allowing me to fork her queen and her queen's rook. She learned from her mistake, however, and in game two I barely played her to a draw.

I passed all of Saturday morning lazing around the cottage, drinking too much coffee and reading too much Gadamer. At noon my cell phone rang. It was Henry, bearing the news that he'd just stumbled upon Edwina, performing Liszt on the villa's Steinway. She'd stopped playing long enough to announce that she and Dr. Charnock had returned from Chicago the previous evening. "No, you didn't," Henry had insisted, then proceeded to explain how he knew this, and so Edwina agreed to meet with him, also Brock and myself, three hours hence in the Faustino conservatory.

"I imagine she wasn't too thrilled to hear we'd witnessed Yolly's birth," I said.

"She avoided the subject," Henry said, "but when she went back to playing Liszt, she switched from the Concerto in D to an aggressive rendition of *Totentanz*. If music could kill, Mason, I'd be a dead man."

BEFORE WE THREE UNHAPPY TUTORS entered the conservatory that afternoon, I warned Henry and Brock about the sentient tree, lest Proserpine's unnerving habits distract them from the matter at hand. A wise precaution, for throughout our conversation with Edwina the mangrove's branches quavered, her lungs chuffed, and the sap throbbed audibly in her trunk.

Lady Daedalus occupied her customary wicker chair, the spiteful ginger cat socketed in her lap. The rest of us were accorded fanback furniture as well, so that our meeting resembled a gathering of wilting southern aristocrats in some recently unearthed and best forgotten Tennessee Williams play.

"Had you not already established nourishing relationships with my daughters," Edwina began, "I would dismiss the three of you as spies and traitors."

"Unless we quit first," I noted.

"Your prerogative," she said.

"Our prerogative," Henry agreed.

Edwina heaved a sigh, stroked her cat, and contemplated her anamorphic reflection in the silver coffee urn. As usual she had dressed elegantly, her white lace gown accessorized by a rope of lustrous pearls. "Hear my confession," she said at last. "If you find my actions unconscionable"—whatever remorse her tone contained failed to conceal the sarcasm—"I'll put on sackcloth, stuff my mouth with ashes, and otherwise mortify myself."

"We'll settle for severance pay," Henry said.

She began by admitting that our pupils owed their existence less to sexual reproduction than to scientific contrivance. By repeatedly fusing her cumulus-cell DNA with anonymous denucleated donor eggs, nurturing the resulting zygotes in petri dishes, transferring the surviving blastocysts to glass wombs, injecting the three most auspicious embryos with pituitary hormone, allowing them to reach fetushood, and, finally, inserting each genetic twin into Dr. Charnock's titanium chamber, his RXL-313 ontogenerator, its arcane broth carefully brewed to stimulate the child's glands, Edwina had brought Londa, Donya, and Yolly into the world.

"Names that, as you may have noticed, meld rather musically into 'Yolonda,'" she said.

By Edwina's account, Londa possessed the body of a woman in late adolescence, yet she'd been on the planet barely eight weeks. Although she appeared no younger than five years of age, Donya was only six weeks out of the vat. And while Yolly's growth had been accelerated until she'd come to resemble an eleven-year-old, she was in fact, as Henry and I knew all too well, a newborn.

The headgear through which the girls' brains had been flooded with facts, programmed with purpose, and marinated in mores was quite possibly the most complex machine-human interface on the planet. Its inventor, Vincent Charnock, had dubbed the thing a DUNCE cap: Data Upload for Normal Cognitive Efficacy. As Edwina proceeded to describe in detail the ontogenerator and its concomitant DUNCE cap, I soon realized that her enthusiasm for this technology bordered on fetishism, and I found myself rejecting her claim that, alienation and anomie notwithstanding, Londa, Donya, and Yolly had all left the laboratory as whole and healthy persons. Even the lesions in her children's superegos gave Edwina no genuine pause. After all, this pathology could evidently be circumvented by a competent professional—Yolly's tutor, a female psychologist from Baltimore named Jordan Frazier, would arrive before the week was out—and so there was no reason to doubt that her progeny would enjoy normal and happy lives.

"And has your sick little enterprise run its course," Henry asked, "or are you building up to a lacrosse team?"

"Yolly is the last," Edwina said. "From your long faces and low comedy, gentlemen, I surmise that you find my project unsavory."

The three of us nodded in unison.

"Unsavory, unseemly, and self-centered," Henry said.

"Your children aren't the only ones around here with an ethics problem," Brock noted.

"Question, Edwina," I said. "When you told me Londa's father died of pancreatic cancer, was that a total falsehood, or did you in fact once have a husband?"

"For ten years I was married to a plastic surgeon named Francis Ulmer," she replied. "Our union was without issue. At last report he'd moved his practice to New York City and committed himself to helping Park Avenue matrons stay off the mortality track." She took a long sip of mumquat-enhanced coffee. "If only you could comprehend the depth of a woman's need to have children. But such empathy is probably beyond the male imagination."

"No, Edwina," I said, cheeks burning with anger, "I can comprehend it just fine. What I can't grasp is a woman bringing three duplicates of herself into the world without their consent."

"We *all* come into the world without our consent," she noted.

Henry issued an indignant snort. "As *babies,* Edwina, as *babies,* not as morally impaired doppelgängers who've been told they're amnesiacs. I can respect your desire to have children, but I can hardly condone the way you've denied Donya her infancy and Yolly her childhood and Londa her preadolescence."

"You've stolen *years* from the lives of those girls," Brock added, "and given them only books and toys and tutors in return."

Edwina raised a hand to her collar, nervously manipulating her pearls like a merchant working an abacus. "True enough," she said, slowly and without affect. "But it happens that I shall never have the luxury of watching a child of mine pursue a conventional developmental path. In a year, give or take two months, I shall be dead. I might even die before Christmas."

Decades after Edwina's abrupt announcement, I still remember how it stunned and disoriented and—yes—infuriated me. The woman was terminally ill. Most lamentable. The Reaper had her on his radar. What a shame. And yet her attempt to redeem her imminent oblivion through this recombinant-DNA carnival, this genomic jamboree, seemed utterly deranged to me, narcissism promoted to a psychosis, vanity evolved into pornography.

"My disease is so rare the hematologists need three Latin words to name it," she continued. "Gradually but relentlessly, my blood is turning to water. Happily for Yolonda, the etiology is not genetic but traces to certain toxins I encountered during my years at Odradek Pharmaceuticals."

"How sad that you have such a knack for bending nature to your will," I said, "and yet you can't cure yourself." A cruel remark, but sparing Lady Daedalus's feelings wasn't my top priority just then.

"The irony is not lost on me," Edwina said. "But at least, thanks to Yolonda, I'll get to experience the totality of motherhood before I die."

Against my expectations she now became buoyant and effervescent, as if immersed in some inverse ontogenerator that caused its occupants to grow younger. In the months that remained to her, Edwina said, eyes sparkling, fingers dancing as if scurrying along her piano keyboard, she would know the pleasures of nurturing a preschooler. She would likewise experience the delights of amusing, and being amused by, a preadolescent, even as she tackled the challenging but rewarding business of ushering a young woman into adulthood.

"And then, when the end comes, I will have my daughter to comfort me."

"And who will comfort *them*?" Brock asked, curling his lip.

Edwina turned suddenly defensive, haughtily asserting that she'd "put more thought into Yolonda's future" than we could possibly imagine. The patents she held on various genetically engineered seeds, foodstuffs, and antivirus drugs were "worth several fortunes," and each sister would inherit a sum sufficient for her to hire whatever caregivers, teachers, and legal advocates she might require.

"If you would like to remain on the island after my death and continue to instruct your charges, that can be arranged," she told us. "But please don't begrudge me the satisfactions that the coming year promises to bring."

Before the month was out, we now learned, as soon as Yolly had acquired a rudimentary conscience, Edwina would throw herself into the project, alternately imparting maternal wisdom to the children and lavishing them with love. During any given week, she would circulate among the three domains—Faustino, Casa de los Huesos, and the renovated Spanish fortress on the Bahía de Matecumba—according each daughter at least two days of her undivided attention. She hoped we would allow the girls to continue ascribing their memory gaps to amnesia, and she entreated us to keep them ignorant of one another, so that their energies and affections would stay focused on their mother.

Their "mother." Edwina kept using that word. This woman was no more a mother than her pearls were her father's eyes.

"So that is my story, gentlemen," she said. "And now it's your turn to hold forth. Go ahead. Be honest. What do you think of me?"

Without hesitation I said, "I think you're the woman Nietzsche would've wanted for a mother. I think you're the Übermom."

"I shall take that as a compliment," Edwina said. "And what is your opinion, Henry? Do you find anything in my project beyond Nietzschean bravado?"

"Here's my promise to you, Edwina," he replied. "Once Yolly has grown up and moved out of her tower by the sea, I'm going to hire a mob of peasants with torches to wreck your damn laboratory."

"I'll be leading the attack," Brock said, "and by the time we're finished with Charnock's ontogenerator, it won't be good for making a bowl of buttered popcorn, much less a human being."

"Are you saying you wish to resign?" Edwina asked.

"I would *love* to resign," Brock replied. "But that wouldn't be fair to Donya."

"I feel more loyalty to this mangrove tree than I do to you," Henry said. "I won't desert my post, though, not before Donya's cured."

"What about you, Mason?" Edwina asked. "Can Londa count on your continued tutelage, or do you plan to walk out the door?"

I reached toward Proserpine's nearest branch, curling my fingers around the pulsing bark. Could Londa count on me? An excellent question. The best question I'd heard all day.

"I must say that Brock's reasoning makes sense to me," I began. "He and Henry have an obligation to Donya, and they intend to honor it. And I can easily imagine Yolly's tutor hearing the whole story and still deciding to go ahead with it. But my case—that is, Londa's case—is rather different."

I plucked a mumquat, inhaled the consoling scent, and regarded Edwina with quintessential contempt. Londa, I explained, had entered the world burdened with the flesh and physiology of a seventeen-year-old, and yet, before I took her under my wing, her psyche had been a blank slate—a literal blank slate, not John Locke's hypothetical tabula rasa. It was still largely a blank slate. Apart from our role-playing exercises, she'd had absolutely no experience with confronting ethical dilemmas or making moral choices.

"Don't you see the evil in this, Edwina? Chronological age, seventeen. Deontological age, zero. Don't you see the disconnect? You didn't hire me to *shape* Londa's soul—you hired me to *make* her soul. What right does a mere mortal have to do that?"

"A scintillating distinction, Mason, but you haven't answered my question," Edwina said. "Are you going to walk out the door or not?"

CALL IT MY SIN, DEAR READER. My fall from grace, my plunge into presumption, my seduction by pride. I did not walk out the door that afternoon. Instead this mere mortal fixed Edwina with an incandescent eye and said, "If I don't finish my work with Londa, you'll simply hire another philosopher, somebody who doesn't know Epicurus from ipecac."

"Good decision," Edwina said.

"God help me," I said.

"God help us all," Henry said.

During the remainder of this fractious gathering, we three teachers struck a bargain with our woefully ill and possibly insane employer. Professional ethics, we insisted, forbade us to sit back and watch her deceive yet another member of our fellowship. We fully intended to give Jordan Frazier of Baltimore a complete account of Yolly's genesis, making it clear that, for better or worse, Jordan would not merely be tutoring the girl but crafting her moral essence, and if Edwina contradicted us on any point, we would gleefully tell the children that they each had two sisters—three, counting Edwina. For our part, we would allow Londa and Donya to continue believing they were amnesiacs bereft of siblings, and we would prevail upon Jordan to nurture the same illusion in Yolly.

My colleagues persuaded me to spend the rest of the afternoon in their bungalow, sampling beers imported from various Miami microbreweries and attending what Henry called "the first official meeting of the faculty of Hubris Academy." I wasn't sure to whose hubris he was referring, ours or Edwina's, but the name fit in either case. As our colloquy progressed, we gradually convinced ourselves to adopt a more generous attitude toward Lady Daedalus's scheming, something between acquiescence and acceptance. After all, beyond their deontological difficulties, both Londa and Donya seemed fairly well adjusted, and Yolly was probably equally sound of mind and body. True, Edwina meant to exploit them, but it so happened that this exploitation looked a great deal like love.

"I'm afraid our efforts to help the children may prove even trickier than we imagine," I confessed, sipping my coconut ale.

"I don't want to hear this," Henry said.

"Martin Heidegger," I said.

"Heidegger was a Nazi," Brock said.

"A Nazi, a nitpicker, and the worst sort of pedant, but I still have to respect his concept of *Geworfenheit*," I said.

"Sounds like a character out of the Brothers Grimm," Henry said, sampling his mango lager. "'Geworfenheit and the Enchanted Lederhosen.'"

"*Geworfenheit*, thrownness, the paramount fact of the human condition," I said. "Every person is hurled into a world, a culture, a set of immediate circumstances not of his own choosing. The authentic life is a quest to comprehend one's status as a mortal *Dasein*, a self-conscious subject, an entity for whom the riddle of situated existence—being there, inhabiting the given—is a central problem, if not *the* central problem."

"I don't know what the fuck you're talking about," Henry said irritably, an attitude I attributed to his enthusiastic beer consumption.

"But if the average person is *thrown* into the world," I continued, "then Edwina's offspring have been *shot* into the world, like a circus performer getting blasted out of a cannon. For most of us, pondering the mystery of *Dasein* leads to anxiety. For Londa and Donya and Yolly . . . well, I shudder to imagine what they might be facing down the road. Exponential despair. Angst to the nth. But there's reason for hope. According to Heidegger, a *Dasein* can ameliorate its encounter with nothingness by adopting a nurturing attitude toward other beings."

"And according to me, a *Dasein* can ameliorate its encounter with nothingness by not reading Heidegger," Henry said.

"I'm feeling pretty anxious myself right now, but it has very little to do with my thrownness," Brock said, taking a long swallow of velvet cream porter. "I keep thinking about that ontogenerator thing. I'm jealous of it."

"You're jealous of a *machine*?" Henry said.

"It got to Donya before we did," Brock explained, "filling her brain with whatever crap Edwina and Charnock thought she'd need to survive. I feel like—this sounds strange, but I feel like *I* should've been Donya's first tutor, not that damn DUNCE cap. I want to go to Edwina and say, 'The next time you ask Henry and me to forge somebody's soul, invite us in sooner, and leave technology out of it.'"

"I'll tell you what's got *me* rattled," Henry said. "It's not that Edwina decided to make three copies of herself. It's that she insists on collapsing them into a single person."

"*E pluribus unum,*" Brock said, nodding.

"Exactly," I said.

Henry said, "So now all Edwina has to do is exile good old-fashioned linear time from Isla de Sangre—a simple enough trick if you're the Übermom—and she gets to nurture her precious Yolonda in a grand spasm of maternal self-actualization."

"*E pluribus unum,*" Brock repeated. "And Jesus H. Christ."

"Jesus H. Christ," I echoed, lifting the coconut lager to my lips. "A man who, if you subscribe to the Western world's most popular theology"—I took a final sip—"was likewise three persons in one."

SUNDAY AFTERNOON FOUND ME browsing through the Faustino library, searching for whatever Heidegger works might be in residence. I'd decided that the more deeply I plumbed his notions of *Dasein* and *Geworfenheit,* the more effective I might be in treating Londa's nascent despair. I didn't expect to come across *Being and*

Time, that Mount Everest of philosophy tomes, but the collection did boast *What Is Metaphysics?* sandwiched alphabetically between Hegel's *Aesthetics* and Husserl's *Logical Investigations.* I abducted the book from beneath the conquistador's vigilant gaze, returned to my cottage, climbed into bed, and got to work.

My initial perusal of *What Is Metaphysics?* yielded no insights into Londa's situation, but my efforts were nevertheless rewarded. "Only because the Nothing is revealed in the very basis of our *Dasein* is it possible for the utter strangeness of what-is to dawn on us. Only when the strangeness of what-is forces itself upon us does it awaken and invite our wonder. Only because of wonder, that is to say, the revelation of the Nothing, does the 'Why?' spring to our lips." Where else but in Heidegger could a person find such exhilarating obscurity? This wasn't the Food Channel. This wasn't *Chicken Soup for the Credulous.* This wasn't Jesus on a stick. This was philosophy, by God, red in tooth and claw, Sinuhe wandering the banks of the Nile, asking the great "Why?" question until Isis and Horus and even wise Thoth himself were sick of hearing it.

A frenzied pounding interrupted my idyll. Reluctantly I abandoned Heidegger and stumbled to the door. My visitor was Edwina, breathlessly announcing that Londa was in trouble.

"An ark full of assholes has run aground in the cove," she elaborated. "They're driving her crazy, which speaks well of her ethical development, but she could use our help."

"Huh?"

"Get dressed."

As always, I bristled at the Übermom's presumptuous manner, but if Londa indeed needed me, then my obligation was clear. I buckled on my sandals, then joined Edwina as, huffing and puffing, she made her way down to the Bahía de Flores.

Our three intruders, beefy men in Bermuda shorts and strident Hawaiian shirts, had recently enjoyed a picnic supper on the dunes, or so I guessed from the smoldering cooking fire and the trail of trash strewn between the campsite and their beached dinghy, a procession of beer bottles, soft drink cans, empty Kraft marshmallow bags, hot-dog wrappers, white plastic utensils, and paper plates streaked with grease. In the middle of the bay, a sleek fiberglass cabin cruiser, the *Phyllis II* according to her stern, lay jammed against the coral reef. Not only had the intruders despoiled the beach, they were also polluting the water. A profane halo of full-spectrum, iridescent petroleum surrounded the yacht's hull, spreading outward like the rainbow through which Satan had sealed his covenant with Exxon in Genesis 9:13.

Londa was wandering around the picnic site, conscientiously picking up the trash and placing it in a burlap sack. The intruders showed no inclination to assist her, being content to play Frisbee in the gathering dusk, killing time while waiting for the rising tide to free their yacht.

Upon spotting her mother and me, Londa halted her bagging operation and strode toward us wearing an expression of supreme dismay.

"This is a private island, not a public dump," Edwina informed the nearest sailor, a bearish man with a Hapsburg jaw. "Kindly dispose of your crap."

The yachtsman raised his hand, nonchalantly intercepted the Frisbee in midflight, and offered Edwina a deferential nod. "Of course, ma'am, you're absolutely right." To judge from his headgear, a captain's cap embroidered with an anchor, he was the skipper of the *Phyllis II*. "If there's one thing I respect, it's private property."

"I'm not surprised to hear that," Edwina said dryly.

"Ralph Gittikac, CEO of Gittikac's Getaway Adventures," the captain said, as if we were dying to know how assholes earned their living these days. "That's my brother Brandon with the major sunburn."

"And I'm Mike the Spike," said the third intruder, his neck hung with gold chains, "king of the investment brokers."

"Well, I'm Edwina Sabacthani, queen of Isla de Sangre."

"Queen, huh?" The captain set the Frisbee spinning on his index finger and shouted to his friends. "You heard Her Majesty! Hop to it! In five minutes I want this beach looking as neat and tidy as Buckingham Palace!"

Resentful grunts arose from the other two Frisbee players, but they proceeded to obey their captain's orders. While brother Brandon held Londa's burlap sack wide open, Mike the Spike combed the beach, gathering up armloads of debris and dumping them into the cluttered cavity.

"Your Majesty's resemblance to this exquisite creature"—Ralph tipped his cap toward Londa—"tells me I'm in the presence of a mother and her daughter."

"Quite so," said Edwina, ever eager to cultivate her favorite falsehood.

"And the way you rammed your boat into the reef tells me *I'm* in the presence of a piss-poor pilot," I said. "Your ineptitude has caused an oil spill."

Mike the Spike halted his beachcombing long enough to say, "No, sirree, she's been dripping like that ever since we left Sugarloaf Key. We'll try to fix the leak later today."

"You'll *try* to fix it?" Edwina said, aghast.

"With all due respect, ma'am, oil spills aren't the unmitigated disaster certain Marxoid squid kissers make them out to be," Mike replied. "Aquatic bacteria gobble the stuff right down. I'm giving you basic biology here."

"You're giving us basic horse manure," I said.

Ralph shot me a poisonous glance. "Who *is* this person?" he asked Edwina. "Your court jester?"

"My daughter's tutor. His specialty is moral philosophy. Let me suggest that you hire him yourself."

"He's absolutely brilliant," Londa said, her first comment of the afternoon.

"Ma'am, I can see we've caused you grief," Ralph said, bowing before Edwina, "for which I'm truly sorry, so let me make it up to you." From his wallet he retrieved a business card, pressing it into her palm. "Just send me an e-mail mentioning that you're the feisty lady with the private island and the lovely daughter, and I'll see to it your whole family and all its philosophy tutors receive a special gift—like, for example, first-class tickets on the *Titanic Redux* when she steams out of Southampton in maybe ten years from now."

"Ralph knows how to think big," brother Brandon noted.

"You're building a new *Titanic*?" I said, at once intrigued and appalled.

"Project *Titanic* Ascendant," Ralph said, beaming. "We're re-creating the grand old Ship of Dreams right down to her last frigging rivet, keel to crow's nest, poop to prow." He pointed in the general direction of Greenland. "There's a whole raft of demons out there, Your Majesty—all those imps, devils, and angels of catastrophe who haunted the North Atlantic on the fateful night of April fifteenth, 1912. We're going to exorcise the lot of them. And once we've sent all those wicked spirits back to hell, presto chango, the way will be clear again for the sort of entrepreneurial derring-do that gave birth to the first *Titanic*. Brandon here knows the Latin word for it. What's that word of yours, Brandon?"

"Catharsis," Brandon said.

"Catharsis," Ralph said. "Our plan is to take the whole catastrophe and give it a by-God catharsis."

"The word is Greek," I noted.

"I've never heard a more arrogant idea in my life," Edwina said.

"I have," I said, casting a cold eye on my employer. She bristled and frowned.

"There are lots of ways of being arrogant, ma'am," Ralph said. "Some people would say it's arrogant to practice extortion on our country's most creative sector and call it progressive taxation. Some people would say it's arrogant to pay welfare mothers for spreading their legs."

Before Ralph could further develop this subtle line of thought, the metallic shriek of a Klaxon horn echoed across the bay. The captain pivoted toward the *Phyllis II*, frantically waving his arms. "We hear you, Billy!"

"Looks like we're afloat," said Mike.

"Don't you worry about the leak," Brandon told Edwina. "The bugs'll take care of it. Gobble, gobble, gobble."

Moving with the confident swagger of the congenitally privileged, our visitors loaded their bagged trash into the dinghy, scrambled aboard, and rowed toward the damaged reef. As the three sailors climbed into their vessel, Londa made her second remark of the day.

"*Phyllis II,*" she said, pointing toward the yacht. "I guess that means they're boorish materialists—you know, Phyllistines!"

"Very witty, sweetheart," said Edwina.

"A clever name," I said. "But let's remember"—I touched Londa's forearm—"it's easier to label our enemies than to forgive them, and easier to forgive them than to love them."

"Love our enemies?" Londa said. "We haven't gotten to that lesson yet, have we, Mason?"

"I've been saving the worst for last."

"Someday I'll have more enemies than I can count," Londa said, "the better to propagate my love."

THE FOLLOWING MORNING we continued our voyage through *Ethics from the Earth*. Had Londa and I dropped anchor at the next scheduled port of call—chapter seven, "From Parable to Parousia"—we would have ended up exploring that vast moral continent first reconnoitered by the same Jesus Christ who'd exhorted us to love our enemies. But I sensed that she was not yet ready for such heady terrain, so we sailed on, circumnavigating the Dark Ages, cruising past the medieval era, and skirting the Renaissance, until at last we disembarked in the Enlightenment, subject of chapter twelve, "From Revelation to Reason."

My pupil was profoundly impressed by Immanuel Kant's notion of the categorical imperative—doing the right thing because it is right—versus the hypothetical imperative—doing the right thing to get what you want. Indeed, Herr Kant's imperially rational construct was in her words "the perfect way to keep Ralph Gittikac and his fellow Phyllistines from gaining the upper hand." But she balked at Kant's claim that the "moral law within" amounted to a proof of God's existence.

"Do you prefer some *other* proof of God's existence?" I asked.

"I guess you haven't heard the news," she replied. "I'm going to stop believing in God."

"You're going to *stop*?"

"If it's all the same to you."

"It's all the same to *me,* but it's hardly the same to *most* people. The leap into disbelief is not a step one takes lightly. It will put you at odds with the rest of the world."

"I'm *already* at odds with the rest of the world." She picked up my dissertation, squeezing it against her chest as tightly as Donya embracing Deedee the chimp. "I know that the God hypothesis has its partisans, but, oh, what a *boring* idea. Where did the universe come from? *He* did it. How do we account for rivers and rocks and ringtailed lemurs? *He* made them. Ho-hum."

"You've been reading ahead."

She smiled coyly. "Your chapter on Darwin took my breath away."

I studied my reflection in the conquistador's breastplate, which suddenly seemed to me a kind of crystal ball or scrying glass. Darwin had taken Londa's breath away, even as her mother and Vincent Charnock were busily taking Darwin's breath away. The bright metal showed me the convex shape of things to come, a future in which humankind, tired of being mere *Homo sapiens sapiens* and en-amored of the RXL-313, had elected to plunge headlong into a per-ilous age of cottage eugenics and do-it-yourself evolution. At the mirror's glittering center stood the forbidding figure of Charnock, leaning over his titanium cauldron and pulling out confection after confection, each wet, slippery neonate stronger and swifter and smarter than the last.

A terrible pounding arose in my skull. Nausea unfurled its cold, quivering wings in my stomach.

"You look sick," Londa said, joining me by the conquistador.

"Hedonism, anyone?" Quetzie said.

"Homo sapiens sapiens sapiens sapiens," I said.

"If you'd like to go home and take a nap," Londa said, "that'd be all right with me."

I was tempted to accept her offer, but instead we continued our conversation. With admirable coherence and startling confidence, she argued that the Kantian "moral law within" did not necessar-ily imply the existence of a benign, omnipotent deity who spent his waking hours supervising human affairs. The God who'd planted a conscience in his creatures might instead be the *deus absconditus* of Enlightenment skepticism, winding up the universe like a clock, going home for lunch, and never coming back. This Unmoved Mover was no more a continuing presence on the planet, argued Londa the teenage atheist, than was that long-dead Uncle Max who'd willed you his stamp collection.

On Tuesday we left God on his Enlightenment lunch break and took up the next topic in my book. Chapter thirteen, "The Square Root of Happiness," featured my attempt to explicate Utilitarian-ism, that imperially pragmatic—indeed mathematical—system de-vised by Jeremy Bentham in his quest for an ethics unencumbered by values, ideals, and other squishy sentiments. It soon became ap-parent that Londa had grasped neither my critique of Bentham nor the refinements in Utilitarianism wrought by John Stuart Mill and G. E. Moore, but as we parted company, she agreed to revisit the chapter and prepare a paper or project—anything but a one-act play—proving that she'd wrestled chapter thirteen to the ground.

Although Londa was twenty minutes late for class the next morning, she arrived bearing the promised demonstration: the prototype of Largesse, a Monopoly-like game of her own design, complete with tokens, chits, chance cards, a spinner, and a posterboard rectangle on which she'd drawn the continent of Benthamia. Largesse could be enjoyed by two, three, or four players, each of whom assumed the role of a benevolent dictator ruling his own nation-state of nine million citizens. During any given round, the participant made a well-informed and charitable decision that he believed would promote the famous Utilitarian goal of "the greatest good for the greatest number." A typical winning ratio: 8,999,985 happy citizens, fifteen unhappy citizens. Another normally successful combination: 8,999,990 happy citizens, ten unhappy citizens. Any monarch who could ultimately claim 8,999,999 happy citizens and one unhappy citizen automatically won the game.

"Haven't you left out an important possibility?"

"Nine million happy citizens on the nose?" Londa replied.

"Indeed."

"Ah, but you see, in the universe of Largesse, there must *always* be at least one innocent victim. You might say that's the whole point."

We traded acerbic grins. Londa continued to summarize the rules. As the game progressed, each Largesse player-king acquired a hand of cards that specified exactly what those citizens identified as "unhappy" were enduring just then. A person who ended up on the wrong side of charity in a Benthamian nation-state might be a mother lacking the wherewithal to have her son treated for leukemia—or the sick child himself—or a starving alcoholic living in a cardboard box under a bridge—or a slave with an iron manacle around his neck and an overseer's whip on his back—or a five-year-old girl whose parents had locked her in a freezing woodshed and fed her nothing but sawdust and dog shit. Londa had written one hundred and thirty such scenarios.

"So, Mason, do I understand your critique of Bentham or don't I?" she asked.

"I think you understand it better than I do."

"Hedonism, anyone?" Quetzie said.

"I got the freezing child from Dostoyevsky," Londa said.

It occurred to me that, ruthless and unprincipled as the universe of Largesse might be, Edwina had failed to attain even that impoverished plane of morality. The greatest good for the greatest number? Edwina's demented dream had required for its realization four genetically identical sisters of four different ages, and yet she'd sought the greatest good for only one of those *Dasein*, herself. As any serious Utilitarian would tell her, it simply didn't compute.

Chapter 6

ON SATURDAY AFTERNOON Henry appeared at Laguna Zafira driving the most pathetic automobile I'd ever seen this side of a junk-yard, its chassis as pocked as Swiss cheese, its engine clattering like a garbage disposal devouring a fork. Evidently it had been a Volvo at one time. Brock lounged in the backseat, reading the *Key Largo Times*. The miserable vehicle, Henry informed me, was on loan from Edwina, and I immediately recalled an observation once made by my sociology professor at Villanova. In America the transcendently wealthy, the out-of-sight aristocracy—a population to which Edwina clearly belonged—didn't give a damn what sorts of broken-down cars they drove.

"You might say our new recruit is on loan from Edwina, too," Henry said, indicating his other passenger, a slender, fortyish, woman of African descent with sculpted features and café-au-lait skin. She flashed me a warm croissant of a smile. Henry elaborated that he and Edwina had been waiting on the pier when Captain López's cabin cruiser sailed into the Bahía de Flores two hours earlier. Before Jordan Frazier could disembark, Henry had announced that no serious discussion would occur between Edwina and

Yolly's prospective tutor until the latter had spoken with us—unless, of course, Edwina wanted Donya and Londa to learn that their mother was really their twin sister. Edwina had then accused Henry of blackmail, and Henry had replied that blackmail was a very good word for it.

I welcomed Jordan to my humble cottage, supplied everyone with Mexican beer and Nyonnaise olives, then led the way to the rear deck with its expansive view of the lagoon. The air was stifling and muggy, as if the entire island were suffering from a low-grade fever. Two chubby green frogs responded to our intrusion by croaking indignantly and jumping into the water.

The more Jordan spoke about herself, the more obvious it became that Edwina could hardly have picked a better mentor for Yolly. A Montreal-born educator with a master's degree in child development, Jordan had been variously employed as a guidance counselor at a middle school in Alexandria, a riding instructor at a day camp in Silver Spring, and the associate editor of a classy but short-lived "parenting skills" magazine called *Wonderkids*. She hoped one day to acquire a Ph.D. in "knowledge building," a discipline that "doesn't quite exist yet" but whose founding father was her intellectual hero and fellow Canadian, Dr. Carl Bereiter, from whom she'd learned that "whatever the human mind is, it's not a container."

For the next hour, Henry and Brock unspooled the story of Yolly Sabacthani: her passionless conception, mechanized gestation, hothouse education, tabula rasa conscience. Throughout the presentation I scrutinized Jordan's ever-shifting facial expressions. To judge from her gaping mouth and furrowed brow, the chances of her joining our dubious company lay somewhere between abysmal and nonexistent.

"So there you have it," Henry said, squeezing Jordan's hand. *"Nancy Drew and the Secret of Blood Island.* What do you think, lovely lady?"

"What do I *think*?" Jordan said, narrowing her eyes. "I think your Dr. Sabacthani is a lunatic."

"You'll get no argument from me," Brock said.

"I also think I should take the first boat home," Jordan said.

"We've all had the same impulse," Henry said.

"Hubris Academy, where angels fear to teach," I said.

"But I *still* wish we could talk you into staying," Brock said.

"No way," she said.

"None at all?" I said.

"None." Jordan grinned obliquely and offered us a sly wink. "However, there's a distinct possibility *I* can talk me into staying."

I laughed and said, "You seem like a very persuasive person."

"I'll bet you could convince Vlad the Impaler to take up knitting," Brock said.

"Point one, you folks seem like my kind of oddballs," Jordan said. "Point two, the city girl is enchanted by these tropical surroundings. Point three, if I were to back out now, Edwina would probably replace me with an incompetent."

"An utter doofus," Henry said.

"A complete chowderhead," Brock added.

"Yolly deserves better," I said.

"Okay, gentlemen, deal me in," Jordan said. "I'll take the whole damn package. The health plan, the stock options, the Hubris Academy sweatshirt." She sighed expansively. "The responsibility."

"What about the duplicity?" I said.

"For the time being, I'll take that, too," Jordan said. "Yolly's an amnesiac? Sure, Mom, you're paying the piper. She doesn't have any sisters? Fine, Edwina, if that's how you want it."

"You won't regret this," Henry said. "Or, rather, you *will* regret it, but you'll be among friends when the pain starts."

"What matters is that we never forget ... you know," Jordan said.

"How *weird* all this is?" Henry ventured.

Jordan nodded and said, "It would appear that Edwina's invented a brand-new sin. God's still trying to figure out a name for it."

"She insists that any woman with the right technological resources would have done the same thing in her place," I said. "Being men, Henry and Brock and I can't understand her urge to experience motherhood."

A skeptical grunt escaped Jordan's lips. "In my opinion, women don't need to be mothers any more than they need to be trapeze artists." She cracked the knuckles of her graceful hands. "So what sort of curriculum do we use around here?"

For the remainder of the afternoon, as the setting sun turned the lagoon into an immense bowl of gazpacho, we described the lessons that had proved effective so far: Kohlbergian drama improvisations for Londa, a steady diet of *Mister Rogers' Neighborhood* and *The Kindness Crusaders* for Donya. Jordan said she would probably amalgamate the two strategies, Yolly being "old enough to do role-playing exercises without getting bored, and young enough to watch *The Kindness Crusaders* without becoming embarrassed," though she intended to point out that the series was basically "just another opiate of the bourgeoisie."

"I'd like to see Edwina's face when she realizes you've turned her daughter into not only a moral being but a moral *Marxist,*" Henry said.

Jordan smirked and, furling her tongue, launched an olive pit into the lagoon. "Unless I miss my guess, Yolly is about to become obsessed with horses. It's practically a stage on Piaget's developmental profile. Do you suppose Edwina might be willing to get Yolly a horse?"

"If I know Edwina, she'll get Yolly a *herd,*" Henry replied.

"A toast," Brock said, raising his Dos Equis high. "To the beautiful children of Isla de Sangre."

"To the bewildered faculty of Hubris Academy," Henry said.

"To trapeze artists," I said.

Our four bottles came together in perfect synchrony. The glassy clatter echoed across the lagoon and decayed in the dusk.

"Now take me to the kid," Jordan said.

THE MOST DRAMATIC SCENE in *The Egyptian* occurs when Sinuhe, recently returned from self-imposed exile among the Hittites and now enjoying a lucrative private practice in Thebes, is sought out by his old nemesis, the Babylonian courtesan Nefer, whose machinations once prompted him to lose his ideals and betray his adoptive parents. Formerly wealthy, glamorous, and proud, Nefer now creeps through the city like a vision of death, veiled and shrouded. Upon finding Sinuhe, she opens her robe and bares her breast, and he confirms her self-diagnosis: cancer. He proposes to excise the malignancy. "I can save your life," the physician tells his old enemy, "but I can't restore your beauty—the trouble has eaten too far for that," though the expression on Sinuhe's face suggests that her condition is in fact terminal. As you might imagine, this moment fell upon my preteen sensibility with astonishing impact. I was terrified by the gnawing tumor, appalled by the paradox of a breast that wasn't beautiful, and moved by the dignity with which the doomed Nefer accepted her fate.

In the weeks that followed Edwina's revelations in the conservatory, I gradually and with mixed emotions came to see her as a contemporary equivalent of Nefer. Edwina, too, was under a sentence of death, yet she maintained her regal bearing, head held high, determined to make the best of it. Her devotion to her daughters—and, yes, we'd all acquiesced to that misnomer, daughters—was absolute. Every Monday and Thursday, Lady Daedalus traveled to the Spanish keep, Torre de la Carne, where Yolly was now in residence, and proceeded to favor the newborn eleven-year-old with unqualified adoration. On Tuesdays and Saturdays, it was Donya who became the object of Edwina's maternal drive. Wednesdays and Fridays belonged to Londa, which meant I was now seeing my pupil only three mornings a week. Given the robust condition of her soul, however, the moral compass she'd acquired by withholding borrowed axes, stealing cancer drugs, and embracing Immanuel Kant, I didn't regard the abridgement of our studies with alarm. As for Sundays, Edwina had wisely set this day aside for whichever girl seemed most in need of her—normally little Donya, of course, though sometimes the inchoate Yolly received the extra session, and sometimes our moody adolescent.

Sundays also proved the ideal time for the Hubris Academy faculty to meet and trade notes, usually on my deck, occasionally on the terrace of Jordan's beach house or the screened porch of Henry and Brock's bungalow. Donya had made substantive progress of late, even to the point of insisting, as Henry had predicted she might, that the grown-ups stop rigging the croquet games. As for Yolly, after some inevitable experimentation—smashing windows, mutilating furniture, setting fire to drapes, plundering Jordan's wallet, learning how to make "fuck" function as every part of speech— she now possessed a flourishing conscience. A person would never know she was playing ethical catch-up, so well had she responded to Jordan's presentations of Kohlbergian dilemmas leavened with *The Kindness Crusaders*. In short, it seemed that everyone's superego was developing normally, and so far the children's *Geworfenheit,* their thrownness, had not plunged them into a nihilistic vortex or sent them wandering through Dante's dark wood. Instead of dwelling on deontology, we tutors were now free to discuss the topic that most interested us, our employer's ostensibly praiseworthy campaign to give her daughters every blessing within her power.

By Henry's report, Edwina was having little difficulty connecting with Donya, who always articulated her wish of the moment loudly and unambiguously—cupcake, cookie, hide-and-seek, bedtime story set in Faerie Land or Camelot—subsequently showering a delectable affection on whomever took the trouble to fulfill it. Under Donya's guidance Edwina had become an expert teller of folktales, a competent flier of phoenix kites, and a welcome guest at tea parties. After a few failed attempts, Edwina had even projected herself into the rarefied world of Donya's miniature amusement park, learning how to make tiny plastic heroes outwit their pocket-sized enemies, who were forever plotting to derail the roller coaster, turn the Ferris wheel into a giant scythe clearing the way for shopping malls, and replace the merry-go-round horses with fiendish robots who routinely abducted their helpless riders and imprisoned them in an evil sorcerer's castle.

Yolly, meanwhile, was just now entering the stage at which many parents would like to arrest their daughters' growth, that interval between ten and twelve when sophistication has not yet allied itself with cynicism. True to Jordan's prediction, Yolly had become enamored of all things equine, though she was equally enthused about cultivating orchids, reading dopey fantasy novels, and taking music lessons from an itinerant teacher, Pandora Duval, formerly a flautist with the Baroque Ensemble in Seattle, now an alcoholic with the Hog's Breath Saloon in Key West. Edwina responded to Yolly's horse obsession not only by giving her dozens of horse books, horse tchotchkes, and horse DVDs, everything from the smarmy *My Friend Flicka* to the splendid *Black Stallion,* but also—as we knew she would—by presenting the child with a living, breathing exemplar of the species, a Chincoteague pony. Thanks to Jordan, Yolly learned to saddle and mount the spirited Oyster in a matter of hours, ride him in a matter of days, and ride him skillfully before the month was out.

Adept with a digital camera, Jordan recorded her pupil's growth through a series of beautifully composed snapshots, periodically displaying them to the rest of the faculty via her laptop. Each image bore a pithy caption, composed by Jordan. "A Whiff of Heaven" (Yolly smelling an orchid). "Goodness, How Delicious" (Yolly eating a mango). "Morning Swim" (Yolly and Edwina floating on their backs in the Bahía de Matecumba). "Racing the Wind" (Yolly on her pony). "Vivaldi's Spring" (Yolly playing her flute). "Sun Worshippers of Blood Island" (Yolly and Edwina napping on the beach, dressed in identical green spandex bathing suits). "Harvesting the Tide" (Yolly and Edwina standing on the point, surrounded by a plume of surf). Far from occasioning anxiety, the child's thrownness had evidently made her a connoisseur of every imaginable sensory delight. I could only hope that her devotion to the pleasure principle did not portend a disastrous encounter with Dr. Heidegger's nothingness.

"Whatever you're doing with that child, it's obviously working," I told Jordan. "My hat goes off to you."

Not surprisingly, it was her eldest daughter with whom Edwina had the most trouble connecting. Like the rest of the civilized world's seventeen-year-olds, Londa had recently discovered that her prime nurturing parent was not in fact a brilliant and omnicompetent demiurge who could do no wrong, but rather just another dreary adult member of the species *Homo sapiens*. And like the rest of the civilized world's seventeen-year-olds, she had grown indignant at this discovery—so indignant, in fact, that a visiting Martian would never have guessed that Londa was herself in danger of one day becoming an adult *Homo sapiens*.

Edwina, to her credit, refused to be daunted by the billowing black thundercloud that hovered perpetually above Londa's head, and in time Londa came to realize that she could have drawn a far worse parent in the great *Geworfenheit* lottery. By Londa's admission their regular Wednesday and Friday luncheons boasted a reasonable facsimile of rapport enhanced by incandescent flashes of candor. Particularly gratifying to Londa was her mother's willingness to give her a plenary sex education. It was one thing merely to read about such bewildering matters as menstrual cramps, yeast infections, the G-spot, birth control pills, STDs, and condoms, quite another to receive such information from a blood relation who by all indices loved you without condition.

Being older, cannier, and better informed than her sisters, Londa did not for a minute imagine she was living a remotely normal existence on Isla de Sangre. Although Edwina had denied Londa the Internet, she did permit her to receive *Up!,* a lurid and almost comically materialistic magazine targeted at female adolescents, every issue of which implicitly informed Londa that the gap between Faustino and the outside world was very large indeed. Above all, *Up!* bespoke a civilization filled to bursting with hip clothing, mesmerizing jewelry, alchemical cosmetics, transformative body-care products, and innocuously transgressive music, and before long Londa had developed a keen interest in the loot that the Western industrialized nation-states and their Asian equivalents were prepared to distribute, for a price, to a demographic apparently willing to remain permanently incurious about the hidden human cost of any particular prize. Every sane young woman wanted her share of the goods, wanted it desperately, and so Londa, always eager to have her mental health corroborated, decided that she must, simply must, become a consumer.

Edwina satisfied her daughter's yearning for conventional treasures in the simplest manner imaginable, by having them delivered to the door. Sweaters, jeans, boots, sneakers, lipstick, fingernail polish, eyeliner, blush, perfume, hair spray, lotions, bracelets, necklaces, and CDs started appearing at Faustino like gifts left by elves in a Hans Christian Andersen story, though the bearer was in fact FedEx. Day and night, the halls of the mansion reverberated with the apocalyptic chords of Shoot the Works, Distressed Leather, Et Tu Brute, and other bands specializing in commodified nihilism. Wherever Londa went, the cloying aroma of her *parfum du jour* trailed behind her, an invisible cloak of fragrance, even as her bracelets clanked and jangled like a night watchman's keys.

In her maternal wisdom, the Übermom understood that without a social context this cavalcade of artifacts would afford Londa only limited amusement. Edwina solved this problem—brilliantly,

I must say—through the clever expedient of turning Faustino into a residential haven for Florida adolescents in need of summer employment. The job seekers arrived variously by catamaran, houseboat, trawler, yacht, and cabin cruiser, and with the exceptions of a female heroin addict from Coral Gables and a wild-eyed Key Largo lad hooked on Grave Robbers II, a stupefyingly violent computer game, Edwina hired them all. There was lanky Julio, who promised Edwina that by summer's end he would single-handedly build a stone wall circumscribing the patio; meticulous Brittany, who contracted with Edwina to reorganize the library; industrious Nick, who undertook to repair the dock on the Bahía de Flores; cheerful Charlotte, who assumed the role of Javier's girl Friday; ethereal Shana, who agreed to cultivate the manor's flower gardens; and a brooding fellow named Armand, who apprenticed himself to Charnock—the Mad Doctor of Blood Island had just returned from Honolulu, skin tanned, misanthropy intact—and in consequence spent his days catching geckos and iguanas for some experiment whose purpose I preferred not to know.

And then there was Gavin Ackerman. There had to be a Gavin Ackerman, the handsome, muscular, nincompoop drummer in Savage Rabbit, a high school garage band that had recently released its fourth home-brew CD, *Spur of the Moment*. Although Edwina had ostensibly engaged Gavin to repair gutters and pick figs, it was obvious that his real function was to develop a requited crush on Londa. From Edwina's viewpoint this was a no-lose situation. If her daughter neglected to fall in love with Gavin, then Edwina would have occasion to praise Londa, extolling her for not allowing mere hunkiness to merit her admiration. Should Gavin greet Londa's apathy with passion, Edwina could then play the teacher, advising her daughter how to let a suitor down gently. In the event that it was Londa who became smitten while Gavin remained unmoved, Edwina would be right there at her daughter's side, recounting the time that she, too, had nearly died of a broken heart. Finally, scenario number four: Romeo and Juliet in the Florida Keys—sexually conceived Montague and genetically engineered Capulet, savoring the joys of puppy love and goatish lust. Naturally Edwina would monitor the relationship through every twist and turn, sharing vicariously in Londa's happiness and commiserating with her when September arrived and Gavin had to return to the mainland.

For better or worse, the two youngsters and their hormones performed as anticipated, and it soon became impossible to run into Londa without simultaneously encountering Gavin, and to glimpse either adolescent alone would be as momentous as seeing a sea serpent poke its snout above the Bahía de Flores. They held hands constantly, necked conspicuously, and bragged about each other to anyone who would listen. The figs that Gavin had been engaged to pick stayed on their trees, though I came to suspect that as the torrid Florida days rolled by and the sultry tropical nights elapsed, swain and maid were reaping their own succulent harvest.

So complete was Londa's infatuation that at least once per tutorial the topic would shift from the conundrum of justice—we were devoting the summer to my chapter on John Rawls—to the protocols of desire. Londa wanted to know exactly what went on in men's minds, and whether their seeming enslavement to their penises made them despise women without knowing it. I addressed her confusion as best I could, explicating various theories that indeed posited an unconscious male animus toward the female, though at some point in each disquisition I insisted that we return to Professor Rawls and his ingenious idea that a truly just society would be founded behind a "veil of ignorance," each architect totally unaware of where in the socioeconomic hierarchy he might end up. The fact was, however, that I found these digressions therapeutic. By tuning in to Londa's romantic life, listening patiently as she waxed rhapsodic over Gavin's scorched-earth politics and off-the-shelf alienation, I managed to convince myself that she was really just another bubbleheaded *Up!* subscriber, and this assessment, inaccurate though it was, proved crucial to my conclusion that, on the whole, all things considered, certain indications to the contrary, I was not madly in love with her.

Thanks to the benign hedonism of Faustino's youthful work corps, the estate soon came to resemble an American-International beach party movie from the mid-1960s. On the dunes of Isla de Sangre, our imported teenagers staged barbecues, dance marathons, sand-castle competitions, and volleyball tournaments. It occurred to me that, like the vast majority of Western adolescents, they believed themselves immortal—mumquats would have been a superfluous addition to their diets—though I myself had no difficulty picturing their various appointments in Samarra. Occasionally, prompted by self-pity combined with too much beer, I would wander down to the bay and superimpose my depression on their rites, beholding limber zombies tossing horseshoes, agile corpses riding surfboards, and frisky cadavers burying each other in the sand. *Beach Blanket Geworfenheit.*

While Londa was the putative hostess of these celebrations, Edwina did most of the planning and supervising, and during the festivities themselves my student and her boyfriend stayed noticeably aloof. As "Medusa's Mirror" or "Redneck Serenade" or some similarly dance-friendly Distressed Leather hit poured from the boom box, and the teens shook, rattled, and rolled accordingly, Londa and Gavin would linger in the shadows, sparking everyone's resentment through this seeming assertion of a superior sensibility.

A curious situation. Now that Londa finally had a social life, she apparently didn't want it—unless, of course, the vacuous Gavin satisfied her need for companionship, which I doubted profoundly. When I apprised my fellow teachers of this paradox, Jordan revealed that every time she proposed to ferry her prepubescent stepsister from Tampa to Torre de la Carne, Yolly replied that she wouldn't have any idea how to entertain such a visitor, nor did she want to learn. Henry told a similar story about Donya. On numerous occasions he'd announced that he would happily fly to Houston, collect both his nieces, and bring them back to Casa de los Huesos. Invariably Donya had responded that she wanted as her playmates only Edwina, Henry, Brock, her dog, and "that man called Mason who talks so funny."

"The loneliness of a vatling must be dreadful," Brock said.

"They aren't just stuck on an island—they're marooned in their skulls," Jordan said.

"And so they pass their days in solitude," Henry said, "waiting for each other."

WHILE EDWINA HAD DONE A REASONABLE JOB of scripting her eldest daughter's adolescence, she'd evidently failed to anticipate the most obvious crisis of all. At some point in the courtship, the boy was certain to ask Londa about her past—and what was she supposed to do then? Hem and haw? Change the subject? Perhaps Edwina actually imagined Londa telling Gavin she was an amnesiac, in which case someone would have to inform Lady Daedalus that the average teenage girl would rather spend eighteen hours a day manicuring a golf course with nail scissors than risk being thought a clueless, vapid, brain-damaged dork.

It happened that Londa herself had not only foreseen this problem, she'd attempted a solution. Upon realizing that her every waking thought invariably circled back to Gavin, she went rooting through her mother's desk, found a blank leather-bound journal, and spent the next six hours inventing a life for herself. She titled her project *The Book of Londa,* and upon its completion she talked me into taking the thing home for the weekend.

The Book of Londa told of a seven-year-old girl, born and raised in Boston, whose mother, the stellar molecular geneticist Edwina Sabacthani, had one day vanished without a trace. The father of this hypothetical Londa—the equally hypothetical David Sabacthani, a writer of bestselling murder mysteries—soon decided that his beloved Edwina was gone for good. He arranged for his wife to be declared legally dead, then married his most ardent fan, a disturbed dental hygienist named Gretchen Coldwell.

The fictionalized Londa's fortunes now went from bad to worse. Two days after her eighth birthday, her father died in a sailing accident off Cape Cod. When Gretchen Sabacthani née Coldwell undertook to raise Londa single-handedly, the woman's latent depravity emerged from the swamp that was her soul. With a nod to the sadistic parents who figured in Largesse, her Utilitarian board game, Londa imagined Gretchen feeding her stepdaughter on worms and dirt, beating her with a bicycle chain, and locking her in the basement for weeks at a time.

This monstrous state of affairs persisted for five years, and then one glorious day Edwina escaped from her abductors, an anarchist cabal that had been forcing her to design biological weapons in the Canary Islands. Arriving home, Edwina lost no time deposing her dead husband's wife, rebonding with Londa, and assisting the CIA in tracking down the anarchists, after which mother and daughter fled to Isla de Sangre to start a new life together.

The Book of Londa did not end there. Years later, Gretchen was kidnapped by a mysterious woman called the Crimson Kantian—a swashbuckling vigilante, masked and cloaked like Zorro—then taken to a secret grotto on the southern shore of Isla de Sangre. After threatening Gretchen with a thumbscrew and menacing her with a torture rack, the Crimson Kantian abruptly switched strategies and introduced her prisoner not only to the categorical imperative but also to Stoic self-denial, Epicurean self-restraint, and Rawlsian fairness. These mandatory tutorials took hold, and Gretchen eventually became a model citizen who dedicated her remaining years to organizing food banks and running soup kitchens.

"So what do you think of my life?" Londa asked shortly after the start of Monday's lesson. I had just given her the fundamental Rawlsian thought problem: specify the limits—both to wealth and to privation—that you would impose on an embryonic human community, knowing that you yourself could be cast into any of the circumstances you allow, from the lowest to the highest.

"You want my honest reaction?" I replied.

"Uh-huh."

"Gavin won't buy any of it."

"The ending *is* rather fanciful," she said in an abashed tone.

"I won't mince words, Londa. The ending is ridiculous."

"Perhaps the Crimson Kantian shouldn't wear a mask. That's a bit much, huh?"

"I meant *psychologically* ridiculous. This Gretchen character wouldn't mend her ways just from hearing about Stoicism or Epicureanism."

"But isn't that what happened to *me*?"

I exhaled wearily and returned the journal. "I don't know *what* happened to you, Londa." Our gazes met. Her mismatched green eyes had never looked lovelier. "I wish I did, but I don't."

We proceeded to give her a more credible childhood, one spent largely on Isla de Sangre under her widowed mother's tender care, with occasional trips to the mainland. From *The Book of Londa* we took only the idea of a father who'd died while sailing. For the balance of her manufactured memories, we cracked the spine of my own life and riffled through its bland but plausible anecdotes. Romping with a German shepherd named Kip, collecting postcards from around the world, falling under the spell of *The Little Prince,* staging amateur fireworks displays for my cousins on the Fourth of July, improvising a stink bomb using the antique but functional Gilbert chemistry set I'd acquired at a flea market—it all entered Londa's trove of nonexistent recollections.

"Gavin was especially impressed with the fireworks," she told me later that week. "He wants me to add skyrockets to the Savage Rabbit concerts."

"Skyrockets? That's insane."

"The *outdoor* concerts. I told him I'd forgotten all that stuff, but my tutor could probably help."

"Tell him your tutor has forgotten, too."

"There's a cut on *Spur of the Moment* called 'My Country, Right or Wrong.' A satire on mindless Phyllistine patriotism."

"How subversive."

"Did you know that the man who wrote 'The Star-Spangled Banner' was related to Roger Taney, the Supreme Court justice responsible for the Dred Scott decision? Pretty astonishing, huh? Francis Scott Key goes all gushy about the land of the free and the home of the brave, and forty-three years later his brother-in-law rules that black people belong to an inferior biological order. All Gavin wants is a bunch of computer-launched rockets turning into flaming pinwheels when the lead vocalist sings about the racists' red glare."

"I wouldn't know where to begin. Tell your boyfriend that good music doesn't require pyrotechnics."

It was at this juncture in our uneasy conversation that Londa issued the first negative remark I'd ever heard her make about Gavin. "Listen to any Savage Rabbit CD," she told me, a wry smile curling her lips, "and you'll decide they need the goddamn Chicago Fire."

ALTHOUGH THE BOOK OF LONDA was in theory a moot text, its preposterous thumbscrew-wielding vigilante at best peripheral to our work, the wretched thing continued to trouble me. Why had she cultivated in these pages so dark an alter ego, this Crimson Kantian as nearly cruel as the stepmother she'd sought to rehabilitate? Could it be that Londa had merely learned to *mimic* a Stoic love of integrity, an Epicurean taste for virtue, an Enlightenment sense of duty, and a Rawlsian commitment to fairness? At the end of the day, was she still the ambulatory moral vacuum with whom Edwina had first presented me?

From these unhappy thoughts flowed my fateful decision to transport Londa and myself to ancient Judea, circa A.D. 30. Our itinerary had us following the rising terrain as it resolved into that Jerusalem mount made immortal by the Gospel According to St. Matthew. Continuing upward, we reached the summit and met the prince of paradox himself, delivering his famously counterintuitive sermon.

Londa's first reading of the Beatitudes and their surrounding text left her utterly perplexed, so she decided that, having previously benefited from role-playing exercises, we should apply this same approach to Christian ethics. We began by enacting the story of the Good Samaritan, Londa portraying the title character while I sprawled on the floor as the robbed and beaten wayfarer. She ministered to my imaginary wounds with surpassing kindness. The following morning I repeatedly pantomimed the action of slapping Londa's cheek. After every such assault, she confounded her assailant by inviting him to strike again. Later that week we staged the famous story of the vengeful mob chasing after the woman taken in adultery. Our teenage librarian, Brittany, played the slattern, I was the mob's leader, and Londa became the Nazarene. I can still hear her saying, in her sensually husky voice, "Let him among you who is without sin cast the first stone."

Picture two freight trains meeting in a head-on collision, or a tornado corkscrewing through a trailer park, hurtling gas grills and crates of Budweiser every which way, and you will understand the impact that Londa's repeated readings of the Sermon on the Mount had on her psyche. In retrospect it all seems inevitable. Here was a young woman whose encounter with Stoicism had inspired her to burn her palm. The Beatitudes were bound to loosen a few screws as well. But what really got under Londa's skin, I soon learned, was not the Messiah's sermon per se but the discontinuity between its sublime directives and the ignominious course of Western history, a spectacle that, the more we thought about it, increasingly struck

Londa and me as largely a fancy-dress *danse macabre, Titus Andron-icus* on a hemispheric and ultimately global scale, though I hastened to point out that the chronicles of other civilizations were likewise awash in blood. What had gone wrong? she wanted to know. When and why had the teachings of Jesus Christ become an optional component of Christianity?

"I'm not the right person to answer that question," I said. "Try an anthropologist, maybe a religious-studies professor."

"You know what the world needs, Mason?" she asked. "It needs a Second Coming."

"I'd say one was quite enough."

"Not of Christ. Of Christianity. I'm going to make it happen."

"That's not a very good idea."

"Well, *somebody* has to arrange for the merciful and the meek and the peacemakers to take over. The Phyllistines can't remain in charge *forever.*"

"Beatitudes by fiat—right, Londa, sure, that's just the ticket," I said, rolling my eyes. "May I be frank, my dear? You don't want to become a Christian. You want Christianity to become *you.* That way lies madness."

On certain days my pupil's hungering and thirsting after righteousness seemed so intense that I half expected her to flagellate herself, put on a hair shirt, or walk barefoot on broken glass, but she settled for a less florid saintliness, persuading Javier to become an organ donor, Dr. Charnock to join Amnesty International, her morality teacher to send his parents a smarmy e-mail ("You sacrificed so much for my benefit . . ."), and Edwina to write a million-dollar check to the Heifer Project, a nondenominational Christian foundation providing domestic animals to families in impoverished countries. Poor Gavin Ackerman, he didn't stand a chance. He thought he'd been blessed with a dreamy and eccentric but eminently desirable girlfriend, and suddenly he had a hyperventilating, whack-job Joan of Arc on his hands. It all came to a boil when

Gavin mentioned that his mother used to drag him to Lutheran services in Orlando. From that moment on, there was no stopping Londa. She simply *had* to know whether he'd taken the Beatitudes to heart.

"I asked him to imagine that Savage Rabbit had become an overnight sensation," she told me. "Would he be willing to give his newfound fortune to the poor, after which we'd run off together and start an AIDS hospice in Nigeria? You'll never guess what he said. He said that if he *kept* his money, we'd find it a lot easier to start an AIDS hospice in Nigeria."

"I can follow his logic."

"Then I told him to imagine he'd turned Savage Rabbit into a success only by making enemies. Might he see his way clear to *loving* those enemies instead of hating them?"

"A provocative question," I said, suppressing a smirk. "What did he say?"

"He said I was getting on his nerves, and he didn't know how he felt about me anymore, and then he confessed he was thinking of dating Brittany, which I said was fine by me, but I would appreciate it if he didn't fuck her in the same places we'd used, and he said he would fuck her wherever he felt like, and then we got into a big fight, and then we broke up."

"I'm sorry, Londa."

"Don't be. He's really a very immature person."

At Londa's request we spent the rest of the morning talking about Jesus's cryptic concept of the Kingdom, and whether it was earthly or ethereal, but my thoughts kept drifting to the schism between Londa and Gavin. This was probably not the first time the Sermon on the Mount had wrecked an adolescent romance, but I was disturbed by the vehemence with which she'd forced the issue. Love me, love my Beatitudes. The Crimson Kantian had much to answer for, but this new version of Londa, this *belle dame avec trop de merci,* this Purple Pietist, was hardly an improvement. The sooner we left first-century Judea, fleeing across the Mediterranean like the Trois Maries of Provençal legend, the better.

FOR THE REST OF THE SUMMER, Londa and Gavin engaged in an elaborate dance of mutual avoidance, until it came time for our youthful roustabouts to scramble aboard their vessels and go home. The kids had acquitted themselves well. A sturdy sandstone wall now encircled the patio, a magnificent new dock jutted into the Bahía de Flores, the Dewey decimal system had wrought its rationality upon our previously chaotic library, and the manor gardens boasted a vitality that would have sent Edwina's beloved Swinburne retreating pell-mell into his gaunt and glamorous wasteland. Being a romantic at heart, I imagined a last-minute rapprochement between Londa and Gavin, but when I asked her about his departure, she reported, with magisterial indifference, that he'd sailed off without saying good-bye.

As September came to Isla de Sangre, Londa and I took a much-needed imaginary cruise to the Galápagos Islands and thence into the luminous heart of Darwinism. Just as I'd hoped, the core chapters of my *Ethics,* with their argument that a universal and robust morality lay dormant within the theory of natural selection, seemed to bring Londa to her senses. Whenever we talked about our planet's vast ecological tapestry with its innumerable species pursuing their interconnected existences, and how the Phyllistine megamachine with its insatiable appetite for forests and wetlands and other fragile habitats—Gittikac's Getaway Apocalypse—was tearing that tapestry to pieces, she would occasionally spice the conversation with a Beatitude or two. But she had evidently abandoned, or at least postponed, her ambition to supervise the Second Coming of Christianity. Just as the Crimson Kantian had deferred to the Purple Pietist, so was the Purple Pietist now yielding to a thoughtful and humble Scarlet Darwinist.

"I think I'm almost cured," she told me. "I feel like a lizard who's had his tail cut off, and now the thing's growing back. I'm ashamed of the person I used to be. Setting fires. Killing fish. The old Londa makes me want to puke."

"We're *all* ashamed of the person we used to be," I said.

As for Donya and Yolly, their tutors were convinced that both girls had finally conquered the void to which their ontogenerated flesh was heir. For a while Henry and Brock considered celebrating Donya's breakthrough by giving her some objective correlative of a conscience, a statuette of a Kindness Crusader, perhaps, or a heart-shaped clock like the one Professor Marvel awarded the Tin Man. Jordan likewise imagined presenting her pupil with a trophy, and Brock, our resident artist, soon hit upon a concept we liked: a Lucite slab in which was suspended a shiny blue sphere representing the human soul. But in the end my colleagues decided that any such material prize would trivialize their students' accomplishment.

Despite our apparent success in providing each Sister Sabacthani with a moral compass, Jordan argued that we still had work to do. In her view we were now obliged to give our charges what educators of her epistemological persuasion called "conceptual artifacts," so that the ultimate fruit of the girls' DUNCE cap programming and subsequent consumption of book after book after book would be "minds enlivened by knowledge, as opposed to brains anesthetized by data." Her pitch made sense to the rest of us, and so we all set about enriching the Hubris Academy curriculum. Our lesson plans boasted a theatricality that I believe fell short of gimmickry. To give Donya an experience in cartography, Brock buried a box filled with costume jewelry behind Casa de los Huesos, drew a pirate map on a crumpled sheet of coffee-stained paper, and cheered his pupil on as she moved, chart in one hand, spade in the other, from the patio to an oleander bush to a garden gnome and finally to the rock beneath which the treasure lay. To introduce a unit on astronomy, Jordan had Yolly study the night sky, thread the stars into novel constellations, and then invent her own myths accounting for these sparkling beasts and glimmering gods. To help Londa grasp the poetry of mathematics, I invited her to recapitulate the steps, so elegant, so exquisite, by which Euclid had proved the Pythagorean theorem.

"He didn't need algebra at all," I noted as we bent over my diagrams. "Look, he brings it off entirely with geometry. His stroke of genius was to frame the right triangle with three perfect squares, so that the proof becomes a matter of—"

"A matter of showing that the big square is the same size as the two smaller squares combined!"

"Shazam!"

So Hubris Academy was a lively place, with nearly every lesson occasioning an intellectual epiphany, a eureka moment, a flash of rational revelation. We were all taken aback, therefore, when a strange malaise descended upon the Sisters Sabacthani, a condition that had them nodding off in class and moving about the island with the lethargic gait of deep-sea divers shuffling along the ocean floor. By monitoring the girls' sleeping habits, we soon cleared up the mystery. In the middle of the night, Londa would rise from her bed, wander down to the Bahía de Flores, and spend hours staring at the rollers as they crashed against the rocks. Yolly's nocturnal anxiety prompted her to saddle up Oyster and go galloping through the surf like a banshee making a house call. Even little Donya's nights were plagued. At the godforsaken hour of 4:00 A.M., she would come suddenly awake, possessed by a phantasm, thrashing and writhing and tearing the sheets until she broke free of its clawed and scaly clutches.

Upon learning of her daughters' insomnia, Edwina decided to give Yolly and Londa sleeping remedies from her personal store, a therapy that proved generally effective, though Jordan complained that Edwina was treating the symptoms and not the cause. The Übermom's approach to Donya's disquiet was less mechanistic. She installed an extra bed in the child's room, so that at the earliest sign of distress, whoever was on duty—Henry, Brock, Chen Lee, Edwina herself—could hug Donya reassuringly and tell her, over and over, that she wasn't really sinking in quicksand or fleeing from hornets or climbing the branches of a burning tree.

In theorizing about the children's demons, Brock seized upon Henry's remark of the previous summer—"And so they pass their days in solitude, waiting for each other"—and speculated that each girl had somehow intuited the existence of her doppelgängers. These nebulous presences, these intimations of a second self, and a third self after that, were haunting our charges night and day. My own theory was that *Geworfenheit* had started catching up with the girls. Their thrownness was sending them over the edge. The least elaborate and, as it turned out, most accurate explanation came from Jordan, who noted that Edwina's failing health was no longer something she could hide. Her death was now encoded all over her body, and the children had deciphered the woeful text.

Oddly enough, it was little Donya who first put her fear into words, taking Henry and Brock aside and describing her mother's skin, whose mottled brown surface she compared to the peel of an overripe banana. Her tutors told her the analogy was astute, but they said no more. Yolly spoke up next, mentioning with feigned casualness that Edwina seemed to have difficulty drawing her next breath. Jordan admitted that she'd observed the same phenomenon. Only Londa remained silent concerning her mother's symptoms, exhibiting instead a preoccupation with death in the abstract. This development would not have surprised Heidegger. The more clearly the *Dasein* recognizes its thrownness, the more intense its encounter with nothingness.

"Which alternative is worse, I wonder?" she said. "To deny death and thus risk never being wholly alive, or to face oblivion squarely and risk paralysis by dread?"

"Nobody knows," I said. "It's ambiguous."

"If I ever get to be God," she said, unleashing the grin of the person who'd invented Largesse, "my first act will be to make ambiguity illegal."

Much to the faculty's dismay, Edwina declined to be honest with her daughters, answering with weasel words and outright lies their questions about her blotchy skin, sunken eyes, and chronic exhaustion. Usually she told the girls she looked haggard merely because she'd been working too hard. Sometimes she mentioned an experimental drug guaranteed to restore her vitality. I could not exactly accuse Edwina of being in denial: privately she still spoke freely of her disease, noble Nefer baring her breast to Sinuhe. But by leaving to us the task of preparing the children for her death, she confirmed my suspicion that this whole byzantine scenario, with its interlaced deceptions and impacted mendacity, was being performed solely to appease her voracious egotism, and the children's ultimate welfare be damned.

"My mother's dying, isn't she?" Londa said abruptly as we sat down to discuss social Darwinism, Mengelism, and other dark episodes in the Galápagos revolution. "Tell me the truth."

"She's dying. Yes. I'm sorry."

"I knew it. Fuck. Will she die soon?"

I squeezed her hand between my palms. "Sooner rather than later. I'm so sorry."

"When I was in love with Gavin, I used to have horrible dreams." With her free hand Londa wiped away her tears. "Once we went swimming, and he drowned in the bay. Another time Alonso shot him with his musket, and the next thing I knew, Gavin was lying in a coffin." Approaching the conquistador, she grasped the hilt of his sword. "I crouched over him, trying to push his eyes open with one of his drumsticks, but they were frozen shut." Abruptly she pulled the sword from its scabbard, sending a harsh clang through the air like the resonance of a diabolical tuning fork. She held the weapon upright, its blade corroded with rust and tinged with dubious battle.

"I would say that my life is underpopulated, wouldn't you? Gavin's gone. My father's gone. Mother's dying. I'm not a happy person, Mason. You'll always be my friend, won't you?"

"Of course."

"Maybe someday I'll learn how to use a sword," she said, sheathing the weapon. "A woman should be ready to take the offensive at a moment's notice."

Chapter 7

ON THE FIRST DAY OF SPRING, Edwina staged a birthday party for Donya at Casa de los Huesos. The child was now ostensibly seven. I didn't doubt she'd been winched from the vat on that date, and giving her advent the name "birthday" was by no means the most dishonest game Edwina had ever played with the English language, but the whole affair still struck me as pathetic and false.

All the guests brought gifts. Chen Lee gave Donya a pair of cuckoo clocks, suggesting that she mount them on opposite sides of her room, so that once an hour the birds would enter into a spirited conversation concerning the time of day. Dr. Charnock presented her with one of his biological contrivances, a colony of twelve sea horses from whose customized bodies sprouted delicate membranous wings. My own contribution was a new addition to Donya's stuffed-animal collection, Septimus Squid, whom I'd crafted from odds and ends found around Faustino—a silk pillow for the body, discarded vacuum-cleaner hoses for the tentacles, tennis balls for the eyes. But the most extravagant offering came from Henry and Brock, the Stargazer Deluxe, a portable planetarium they'd obtained two months earlier during a trip to Orlando. You inflated the plastic dome with a bicycle pump, thereby creating a cavity large enough for the projector and several amateur astronomers. After everyone squeezed inside, you threw the switch, then watched in awe as dozens of constellations materialized on the walls.

It may have been Donya's party, but it was Edwina's celebration. The Übermom was everywhere at once that afternoon, distributing conical hats and plastic noisemakers, supervising rounds of Pin the Horn on the Unicorn, leading the guests in a rousing chorus of "Happy Birthday to You," and serving the chocolate cake she'd meticulously baked and frosted. From start to finish the event delighted Donya, though occasionally I saw her cast a worried eye on her mother's forearms, the blue veins rising from Edwina's skin like earthworms dispossessed by a rainstorm.

In the name of physical fitness and metaphysical prowess—I was still taking every opportunity to weed my brain of its Aristotelian dandelions—I had jogged to Casa de los Huesos. But being bloated now with chocolate cake and cherry-vanilla ice cream, I was disinclined to repeat the regimen, and so I gladly accepted Charnock's offer of a lift home in his Land Rover.

"I would like your perspective on a philosophical problem," he said as the villa's silhouette receded in the rearview mirror.

"What sort of philosophical problem?" I asked, cringing. While I was always eager to dally with Lady Philosophy, Charnock was among the last people with whom I could imagine having a substantive discussion about Plato's cave or Heidegger's abyss.

"Ethical."

My cringe entered the realm of contortion. "I see."

"I'm impressed by how much you've helped Londa," Charnock said. "Being the oldest of the three, she was doubtless the hardest to civilize."

"Civilizing her was a walk in the park. The challenge will be to decivilize her, so she can function in the real world."

A soft rain descended on the Land Rover and the surrounding scrub. Charnock activated the wipers, thus compounding the visibility problem by smearing grime across the windshield.

"Am I a murderer, Ambrose?" he asked abruptly. "Do I have blood on my hands?"

"I'm not following you," I said, though in fact I was, his conversation with Edwina in the gazebo having alerted me to his protective attitude toward microscopic beings.

At the press of a button, Charnock caused dual jets of cleaning fluid to intersect the path of the windshield wipers. Three strokes, and the glass was clean again.

Among the steps required to satisfy Edwina's "unfathomable passion," he explained, "her unhealthy need to create iterations of herself," was a technique he found repulsive. Yolly's advent had entailed the sacrifice of forty-three embryos. Donya had come into the world at the cost of sixty-eight. Behind Londa lay ninety-seven canceled lives. "Every one of those creatures, placed in the RXL-313, would've become a person. Naturally we always had a *reason* for throwing it away. Spina bifida, dysfunctional heart, malformed kidneys. But in seven cases—I remember them all—in seven cases Edwina asked me to discard the thing merely because she didn't feel right about it. 'This one isn't my daughter. This one won't do.'"

Absently I fiddled with the favor I'd borne away from Donya's party, a noisemaker capped by a coiled paper tube. "I can hear Edwina saying that."

"So why did I obey her? I'm not sure. When it came to our mutant mangrove, I wouldn't do the dirty work—I made Edwina extract the cerebrum on her own—but with those embryos I lost my bearings. I dumped them into the Bahía de Matecumba and let the salt water destroy them."

The road from Casa de los Huesos now brought us to the soaring façade of the southwest wall, its spiky iron gate padlocked shut so that Donya's life would never accidentally spill into Yolly's. Charnock had the key, and thus we passed without incident into the principality of Torre de la Carne.

"I'm afraid Western philosophy can't answer your question," I said. "Aristotle never told us what basket to put our eggs in. Is a zygote a human being, an insensate speck, or something else? For once in his life, he neglected to categorize something."

"I can feel the blood," Charnock said. "Coagulating on my fingertips, crusting under my nails."

A mile beyond the gate, the road split, one branch running southeast toward the Spanish fortress, the other becoming the east-west gravel strip that Henry and I had encountered during our explorations. Had Charnock and I followed the lower fork, we might have seen Yolly—Yolly and her Chincoteague pony and her forty-three phantom sisters—but we logically took the alternative, heading for the wall demarking Londa's domain with its ninety-seven ghostly blastocysts.

"Western philosophy can't help you," I told Charnock, "but maybe I can. I think you're being too hard on yourself. It's all very well to become an antiabortion activist and spend every waking hour fetishizing fetuses, but those seven discarded embryos belong to a different class altogether."

"Let's not call them fetishists," he admonished me. "Let's not stoop to caricature."

I blushed profusely, a crimson chagrin made even redder by my anger at Charnock. Yes, I'd maligned the embryophiles, unfairly for all I knew, but I hated being scolded about it by this creepy curmudgeon. "My point is that when most people speak of the rights of the unborn, they're simply expressing a hope that every existing pregnancy will come to term. They don't mean that all conceivable souls must immediately achieve *Dasein*. Otherwise their motto would be 'Fuck now.'"

Charnock laughed—probably not for the first time in his life, though I couldn't be sure. "'Fuck now.' Not a slogan you're likely to find on Father O'Malley's rear bumper."

I placed the noisemaker to my lips and blew, producing a festive toot. "If Father O'Malley came upon the schematics for your RXL-313, would he set about building one of his own, so he could pass his evenings manufacturing children in his basement? I think not. Most likely he'd burn the schematics on the spot."

"A beaker is not a uterine wall," Charnock said haughtily. "An ontogenerator is not a womb. I knew that before we began this conversation." He lifted his hand level with his face, studying the pudgy digits. "No solvent can remove this stain. Not soap, not turpentine, not sulfuric acid."

I offered him a commiserating grunt, saying I was sorry that I hadn't relieved his guilt.

"I didn't expect you would." He restored his tainted hand to the steering wheel. "Nevertheless, I found our exchange fruitful. Having heard your incoherent thoughts on embryos, I realize what I should do with my life. Edwina has—what?—two months to live. After she passes away, I'll shut down my laboratory, forsake molecular genetics, and devote myself to a different domain."

"Sounds like a plan."

"The spiritual realm."

"Ah, yes, the spiritual realm." In those days "spiritual" was my least favorite word. It still is.

Charnock firmed his grip on the wheel, squeezing until his fingers turned white. "'This one is not my daughter. This one won't do.' Seven different times she said it, and then she gave me the beaker, and I made my decision, the vat or the bay? In each case I would swish the fluid around and watch the embryo swimming in its little universe. I always flushed the creature away. I'm not sure whether I still believe in God, Ambrose, but I know I no longer believe in biology."

* * *

EDWINA DECIDED TO ACCOMPLISH HER DYING where she'd done so much of her living, in the Faustino conservatory with its damp, coagulated air and Mesozoic fragrances. Somehow Javier had maneuvered her bed, a wide gurney hedged with satin pillows, through the labyrinth of ferns and vines, bringing it to rest alongside Proserpine's salt pond. Instead of obeying God's banishment decree, this Eve would stand her ground and die in the Garden, prostrate before the Tree of Knowledge.

Two male nurses from Miami, solemn Hector and jovial Sebastian, supervised the requisite technology—no votive candles for Edwina, no smoking censers or hovering priests—an array that included a cardiac monitor, a liquid-nutrient fount, and a computerized morphine dispenser, this last machine deployed to guarantee that in the end she could elect to trade lucidity for lack of pain. With their immaculate white jackets and equally immaculate trousers, Hector and Sebastian looked less like medical personnel than stewards on a cruise ship—and the conservatory had indeed become such a vessel, the sleek and seaworthy *Lady Daedalus,* bearing Edwina to that distant keep where even the wealthiest woman is beyond the reach of ransom.

Not surprisingly, the Übermom had written an endgame scenario that would enable her to continue regarding Donya, Londa, and Yolly as a single individual occupying three distinct space-time domains. The plan called for each child to pay her mother a separate farewell visit, so Edwina would feel she was experiencing a succession of adieus from the same daughter. Only after she was dead might we teachers escort our pupils out of the conservatory, introduce them to one another, and help them weather the hurricane of cognitive dissonance that was certain to follow.

While Henry, Brock, and I all thought it was a bad idea for Donya to attend Edwina's passing, Jordan took the opposite view. She did not recommend that Donya be present when Edwina actually drew her last breath, but she insisted that the child join the vigil, lest she spend the rest of her life vaguely anticipating her mother's return. A logical argument, and it soon gained everyone's assent, though it seemed to me that if we didn't whisk Donya away in time, she might spend that same life trying to forget her mother's death throes.

Shortly after dawn on the first Friday in June, as golden spokes of sunlight filled the eastern sky, and the toucans and parrots loudly proclaimed the acoustic borders of their territories, Javier telephoned to say that within the hour Henry, Brock, and Donya would arrive at Faustino and proceed to the geodesic dome. Londa and I, meanwhile, should go to the library, where we must wait until summoned, even as Jordan and Yolly bided their time in the drawing room.

Twenty minutes later Londa and I settled into the russet leather couch before the ancient-history section, her head pressed against my shoulder in a posture recalling one of Jordan's best digital photos: Oyster nuzzling Yolly, captioned "I Love You, Now How About Some Oats?" Evidently aware that something was amiss, Quetzie fluttered around the room in erratic ellipses. A soft staccato wheezing rose from deep within Londa's frame, a kind of anticipatory dirge. Part of me wanted to reveal that her mother's death would not be the most disorienting of the day's events, but having kept my promise to Edwina all these months, I wasn't about to break it now.

The morose Hector appeared and announced that Edwina required a sponge bath, after which she would receive her beloved daughter, "sponge bath" no doubt being a code term for Donya's visit to the deathbed. There was little conviction in the man's voice—I hoped he was better at nursing than deceit—but Londa seemed to accept his story. As Hector slipped out of the library, Quetzie landed on the conquistador's helmet and squawked out his newest sentence, *"Cogito ergo sum,"* which Londa had taught him the previous month by way of commemorating, as she'd put it, "the first anniversary of that fateful meeting between a Boston philosopher and a crazy teenager without a conscience."

A cry of grief slashed through the glutinous air. I knew its source immediately. Little Donya's scream contained a greater measure of cosmic despair than I thought a seven-year-old's soul could hold.

"That sounded like a child," Londa said.

"It did," I muttered. "It was," I added.

A second cry, same voice, penetrated the library.

"What child?" demanded Londa. "Do you know her?"

Now that Donya had revealed herself to Londa, should I continue cleaving to Edwina's script? I felt no such duty. Given this turn of events, the charade was surely beyond salvation.

"I've eaten cookies in her tree house," I said.

"Who is she?"

A third shriek. The iguana, frightened, hopped from the conquistador to Londa's shoulder. Without a moment's hesitation, Londa strode through the French doors and scanned the hallway. *"Cogito ergo sum,"* Quetzie repeated with inimitable reptilian dismay.

"Remember the day I theorized that you might have a sister named Donya?" I said, drawing abreast of Londa. "In point of fact, the person making those sounds—"

"She's my *sister*?"

"Your sister Donya."

"I don't understand."

"This way."

I took Londa's hand and guided her toward the conservatory, all the while attempting to explicate the strange procreative ecology of Isla de Sangre. A petri dish instead of a marriage bed. A beaker instead of a womb. A catalyst instead of a childhood. Amnesia that wasn't amnesia but something far stranger. Three genetically identical sisters—and a fourth, progenitor sister bent on representing herself as the first three girls' mother.

"You're not making much sense," Londa said.

Donya's next scream inspired us to break into a run. Quetzie abandoned Londa's shoulder but stayed with us, gliding directly above his mistress's head. We rounded the corner and veered into the conservatory. Edwina lay on her back, wrapped in a green smock and sleeping soundly. Donya, sobbing and quivering, had flung herself across her mother's chest. Henry stood over his pupil, a guardian tree as faithful and protective as Proserpine.

Our arrival prompted Donya to lift her head and glance toward the doorway. Tears stained her cheeks. Her eyes were as red as radishes.

"Hello, sweetheart," I said.

"Mason . . ." Donya stepped toward me, then changed her mind and, retreating, hugged her mother more tightly than before, a shipwreck survivor clinging to a floating spar.

The two nurses fidgeted near the cardiac monitor, a noisy black box the size of a microwave oven, its cathode-ray tube displaying a dancing sine wave, its sound chip bleeping in high-pitched counterpoint to Edwina's heartbeats. Brock leaned against the sentient mangrove like Ulysses bound to the mainmast of his ship. Upon noticing Proserpine, Quetzie judged her an ideal perch and soared to the highest branch.

I rushed to Donya's side, and together Henry and I looped our arms around her quavering body, squeezing her tight until she stopped crying.

"Mommy's not going to get better," she gasped. "Not ever."

"I know," I said.

"Isn't that *terrible*?"

"It's terrible."

Donya jabbed an accusing finger toward Londa. "Who are *you*?"

"This woman's daughter."

As Londa set her hand on Edwina's shoulder, the patient opened her eyes, then rotated her head far enough to determine that the worst had happened: her youngest daughter and her oldest were occupying the same spatiotemporal location, and they looked conspicuously like two different people.

"No, she's *my* mommy," Donya protested. "She's *mine.*"

"We're sisters," Londa told Donya.

"It's true, Donya," Henry said.

"No, that's *wrong*," Donya said. "I don't *want* a sister."

At last Edwina spoke, her voice bloodless and far away. "You must stop this, dear child. Stop coming apart."

Now Yolly raced into the conservatory, doubtless drawn by Donya's cries, wearing the expression of a stranded traveler watching the last bus leave the station, and behind her came an equally bewildered Jordan. I'd not seen the middle Sister Sabacthani since her nativity. Sharp, bright, and skillfully composed as they were, Jordan's snapshots hadn't done Yolly justice. She was a glorious child with radiant skin and shining eyes, her hair as vibrant and summery as a crown of laurels.

"Are you the person Jordan says you are?" Yolly asked, pointing at Londa. "Are you my sister?"

"Probably."

"Londa, right?"

"Right."

"I'm Yolly, and I don't like *any* of this."

"Me neither," Londa replied.

"Me neither," Donya said.

"My teacher says I'm really only thirteen months old," Yolly said.

"Mine insists I've been around just two years," Londa said.

Yolly circumnavigated the gurney, soon entering Edwina's field of vision. "My wonderful mother."

"You're not supposed to be here yet." Edwina sounded like a lost ghost asking directions to a séance.

"But I *want* to be here," Yolly said.

Edwina closed her eyes, and for a few moments the air was free of human voices. The only sounds were the caws of jungle birds and the bleeping of the cardiac monitor.

Stretching an arm toward Donya, Yolly ran her palm along the child's hair. I imagined she brought a similarly unqualified affection to the act of stroking Oyster's mane.

"Little sister?" Yolly said.

"I'm *not* your sister." Donya began weeping again.

"Donya, it's *great* having a big sister, and now you've got *two,*" Henry said.

Tears streamed down Donya's cheeks like raindrops on a windowpane. "But who's going to take *care* of me?"

"I will," Henry said. "Brock will."

"You bet," Brock said.

"And I'll take care of you, too," Yolly said.

Donya's sobs grew softer. The monitor kept bleeping. Edwina opened her eyes.

"This is not acceptable behavior, Yolonda," she said in a thick whisper. "I forbid you to break apart."

"Mommy, can't we have just one more tea party?" Donya said.

This proved too much for Yolly, who started weeping as prolifically as her little sister. She wrapped her arms around herself, then slumped against the IV dispenser, shivering and whimpering, her face hatched by tears.

"I was a good mother, wasn't I?" Edwina said to no daughter in particular.

"You're the best mommy in the *whole world*!" Donya exclaimed.

Yolly uncurled one arm and pulled her sleeve across her nose and mouth, gathering up a mass of mucus, spittle, and tears. "Thank you for everything, Mother," she said, staggering toward the gurney. She kissed Edwina's pale, thin lips. "Thank you for Jordan and Oyster and the flute lessons. I'm the luckiest girl alive."

"Mommeee!" wailed Donya.

Londa now shifted her gaze from her doomed mother to her bemused morality teacher. We locked eyes. She glowered. This Gorgon would not settle for turning her victims to ordinary stone: only New Hampshire granite would suffice, or diamond-grade carbon. "Mason, damn it, you should've *told* me about this! You *liar*!"

I grimaced but remained silent.

"Londa, dear, your mother needs a kind word from you," Jordan said.

"*You're* a liar, too!" Londa wailed, lurching toward Jordan. "You made Yolly think I didn't exist!" She extended her index finger, aiming it first at Henry, then Brock. "And *you* two did the same thing to Donya! But I *do* exist!"

I wanted to tell Londa there were five liars in the room, not four, most conspicuously the patient on the gurney, but I simply said, "Jordan is right. You owe your mother something. Blessed are the comforters."

There was no such Beatitude, and Londa knew it, but rather than correcting me, she stepped toward Edwina and grasped her limp, wrinkled hand. "I love you, Mother. Whatever this crazy thing is you've done, I love you."

I assumed that Edwina would now smile. I expected her to acquire a seraphic face, aglow with peace and maternal fulfillment, but instead an arcane, almost preternatural force seized her body. Her teeth chattered. Her lips quivered. Her limbs trembled so violently that I feared her ligaments might rip free of her bones.

Without exchanging a word, the tutors moved to shelter their charges from Edwina's terminal spasms. Henry took one of Donya's hands, Brock the other, and together they propelled her toward the patio. Jordan approached the gurney, curled an arm around Yolly's shoulder, and escorted her behind the cardiac monitor. Londa did not resist when I set my palm against the small of her back and guided her into Proserpine's fecund shade.

"Stop splitting!" Edwina suddenly cried. "Stay together!"

Donya released a shrill moan. Londa slouched beneath the breathing tree and wept.

"Quetzie is a handsome devil!" squawked the iguana.

"Together!" Edwina demanded.

The cardiac monitor played a few final measures of reassuring bleeps, and then the cadence disintegrated into random chitters.

"Cogito ergo sum," Quetzie averred, but his insight was lost on Edwina, who had entered a realm where cogitation does not occur.

ALTHOUGH THE TWO NURSES had proved only marginally useful during Edwina's final days, they certainly earned their salaries after she was gone. Seizing upon a hidden potential of the IV dispenser, Hector and Sebastian filled her veins with a small quantity of embalming fluid, just enough to counter the spoilage threatened by the Florida heat. They ordered a steel casket, signed the death certificate, and ran interference with a health inspector from Key West who'd long ago deduced that biological events on Isla de Sangre rarely fell within the norm. They even interred the body, digging a grave at the axis of Edwina's empire, in the shadow of the sandstone pillar where the three concrete walls converged, then setting the casket in its moist groove and shoveling back the soil.

Shortly before the funeral, Londa composed an epitaph, which Brock, master of all media, succeeded in etching onto a bronze tablet the size of a sandwich board. After everyone had assembled by Edwina's resting place—children, tutors, chefs, servants, groundskeepers—we propped the tablet against the burial mound, so that the grave acquired a door: a brazen gate opening onto the Nothing, much as the ontogenerator was a titanium portal into *Dasein*.

IN LOVING MEMORY OF
EDWINA SABACTHANI
*

Servant of Science
*

Seeker of Wisdom
*

Eternal Protector of
Three Devoted Daughters

Donya read the words aloud, slowly, haltingly, then began to cry, partly from her frustration over not understanding them, partly from her realization that those same words, comprehended, would have broken her heart. Henry deftly led her away from the knot of mourners toward a commodious clearing ringed by ferns. From his backpack he withdrew a bag of figs, a bunch of bananas, and a flask of Hawaiian Punch, immediately convening a jungle picnic for Donya and himself, leaving the rest of us to continue the ceremony on our own.

For the next hour, we eulogized Edwina with anecdotes. Brock described her touching attempts to enter the universe of Donya's miniature amusement park. Javier praised Edwina's financial generosity, most especially her insistence on paying for his father's bypass surgery. Chen Lee recalled the time he'd carelessly allowed thirty pounds of fish to go bad and how his boss had unhesitatingly absolved him. Charnock offered his opinion that Edwina's brief but productive career with GenoText, Inc., would eventually lead to effective germ-line therapies for cystic fibrosis and muscular dystrophy. Yolly spoke of how she and her mother had wept openly during their screening of *The Black Stallion*. Londa noted that her mother was "always there when I needed her," then added, under her breath, "as long as I needed her on Wednesday and Friday." Paralyzed by ambivalence, Jordan and I said nothing.

Later that week, two attorneys from the classy Miami law firm of Acosta, Rambal, and Salazar descended upon the island. While their ostensible intention was to apprise the girls of certain postmortem arrangements, it was obvious that Rex Fermoyle and Martha Carrington were primarily looking to score slices of the walloping financial pie Edwina had left behind. Watching them sift through their late client's private papers, I thought of those proud corps of airport dogs employed to detect heroin, explosives, and illegal foodstuffs, though Fermoyle and Carrington's specialty was sniffing out obscure stock options, neglected government bonds, and misfiled life-insurance policies.

When it came to the legal dimensions of her death, Edwina had obviously been willing to regard Yolonda as three distinct entities, for Fermoyle and Carrington began their presentation by noting that each girl had inherited her own billion-dollar trust fund. Moreover, by scrutinizing every twig and burl of the Sabacthani family tree, Edwina had located three blood relations willing to become the girls' legal guardians, though in her prescience she'd also included a provision whereby we tutors might take custody of our charges. For Londa, Edwina had found a dullard first cousin whose life revolved around his marginally profitable Milwaukee hotel, for Yolly a dotty female second cousin who every Halloween turned her Baltimore mansion into a Poe-themed haunted house, for Donya a gifted great-aunt still employed as a cellist by the Pittsburgh Symphony Orchestra. I was not surprised when Henry and Brock announced their intention to adopt Donya, nor was I taken aback when Jordan said she would make Yolly her ward, for despite her protestations concerning motherhood and trapeze artists, it was obvious that Yolly's advent had simultaneously diagnosed and treated a void in Jordan's life. I myself did not address the guardianship issue that day, but the following morning I confided to Fermoyle that I'd be just as happy to let the Milwaukee hotel manager worry about Londa for a while, even as I admitted to myself that this decision was unlikely to free me of her sticky charisma.

In the months following the funeral, the Sisters Sabacthani came remarkably close to fulfilling their mother's dream of a unified Yolonda. They laughed together, cried together, ate, slept, gossiped, sang, danced, swam, sailed, windsurfed, flew kites, played croquet, built sand castles, and—once Jordan had imported a mare named Guinevere for Londa and a Welsh pony named Crackers for Donya—rode across the scrubland together. And of course they also drove one another batty, for only a sister has that special talent for breaking your last bottle of perfume, spilling grape juice on your best sweater, dropping your curling iron into a sink full of soapy water, losing your favorite Distressed Leather CD, borrowing your bicycle and then blowing out the tires, and cutting you to pieces by criticizing your taste in music or clothes or movies or anything.

But such lapses were rare. On balance the children were companionable as littermates and compatible as Dumas's musketeers, with Londa and Yolly entering into an amicable rivalry over who could be the better big sister. They nursed Donya through an episode of chicken pox and an encounter with a poison sumac plant, presented her with abridged versions of Londa's colorful answers to Yolly's incessant questions about sex, and despite their own sorrow ministered diligently to Donya's grief, suggesting that she and Edwina might one day be reunited in some transcendent realm, though they declined to call it heaven, paradise, or any name implying geographic actuality.

It was Jordan's idea for the sisters to explore the upper reaches of Torre de la Carne, a domain that, prior to Edwina's death, Yolly had been forbidden to visit as strictly as Bluebeard's new bride had been barred from the room in which her pickled predecessors hung. Jordan invited the other tutors along, Charnock as well, and so we were a party of eight who ascended the tower that afternoon, following the spiral staircase ever upward.

Stepping into the laboratory, I inhaled a gulp of mummified air and immediately began to cough. Dust covered everything—ontogenerator, control console, enzyme tanks, DUNCE cap—like a stratum of newly fallen snow. The spiders had been industrious in Edwina's absence, so that the place suggested the atelier of an architect who was forever modeling avant-garde suspension bridges. Londa went instinctively to the great riveted sphere that had variously functioned as her placenta, bassinet, cradle, and playpen. She selected a porthole and peered inside, and soon Yolly and Donya did the same, so that the sisters formed a tableau evoking my favorite New England Aquarium poster: three children standing before a fish tank, faces aglow with curiosity, ichthyologists in the making.

Charnock now improvised a lecture concerning the rarefied procedure by which he'd taken five hundred anonymous donor eggs, stripped away their DNA, and injected each hollowed-out oocyte with cumulus cells harvested from Edwina's ovaries. A subtle electric jolt was sufficient to transform the majority of these chimerical zygotes into blastocysts, scores of which survived to become full-blown embryos. With consummate care Edwina and Charnock had nurtured each nascent life. In three particular cases, the experiment yielded auspicious specimens—the budding Londa, the blossoming Donya, the burgeoning Yolly—all of whom were allowed to enter fetushood. The biologist exuded an understandable pride while describing the hormone shots he'd given each sister shortly before her transfer to the RXL-313, explaining how these injections had interacted with the vat's unprecedented enzymes to radically accelerate first Londa's maturation, then Donya's, and finally Yolly's.

Throughout Charnock's lecture I studied the sisters' faces, soon concluding that nobody was remotely interested in what he had to say, and I realized that if they were to truly comprehend their situation—their passionless conceptions, ultramarine infancies, lateral kinship with Edwina—they must spend some time alone in this place. When I suggested in a cheery but emphatic tone that "our young charges would probably like a few moments of privacy," the girls all released spontaneous sighs of relief.

Ten years later, when Londa and I were no longer tutor and pupil but partners in a considerably more convoluted relationship, she told me what had happened that afternoon once the adults left the laboratory. By fiddling with the knobs on the control console, the girls managed to flip back the hatch on the ontogenerator. Without a single word passing among them, they removed their clothing, climbed the exterior rungs, and, heedless of the amniotic residue clinging to the inside surfaces, descended into the chamber. The cool, sharp scent of the titanium was oddly soothing. Its hardness made their whispers resonate. For well over an hour, the girls huddled in the dark, talking and then not talking, fused like Siamese triplets, arms linked, hip pressing hip, until it was apparent that they'd made peace with the late Edwina Sabacthani in her many guises—mother, sister, progenitor, confidante, nemesis—and so they returned to the outside world, laughing and joking and eager for a swim in the Bahía de Matecumba.

DOZENS OF AMERICAN UNIVERSITIES would have been pleased to count Londa among their first-year students, but she would consider only her mother's alma mater. She intended to follow in Edwina's footsteps, pursuing her undergraduate studies at Johns Hopkins, obtaining a Ph.D. in molecular biology from that same institution, and subsequently joining the cutting edge of medical research. My vatling was determined to master all existing techniques—bone-marrow infusions, liver resections, domesticated retroviruses, artificial chromosomes—for delivering healthy genes to patients who'd drawn losing tickets in the great DNA sweepstakes, and then invent a few such vehicles as well. But unlike her mother,

Londa assured me, she would never succumb to the allure of self-replication.

Initially the Hopkins admissions committee raised a collective eyebrow at Londa's inability to produce anything resembling a high-school transcript. They weren't sure whether to believe her claim that she'd read her way through the largest private library in the Florida Keys, likewise her curious assertion that she'd received "a rigorous education in ontology from an independent scholar whose unpublished thesis, *Ethics from the Earth,* will one day set philosophy on its ear." But then they noted her stratospheric SAT scores, her sterling performance on the biology and mathematics achievement tests, and her cashier's check for one year's tuition in advance, whereupon their skepticism evaporated like alcohol in a petri dish.

It turned out that Yolly, too, would be leaving on Labor Day. Jordan had accepted a job running the Department of Human Development at Merrimack Academy, a tony private school in Haverhill, Massachusetts, and she'd lost no time arranging for her ward to join the freshman class. One campus visit was enough to persuade Yolly that Merrimack would make her happy. It had an equestrian program, after all, including a stable that Oyster would likely find congenial, not to mention an orchestra, a state-of-the-art computer lab, a theater modeled on the Globe, and a low teacher-student ratio. When I first heard of Yolly's imminent departure, my instincts told me she was making a mistake, for the middle Sister Sabacthani had thus far failed to concoct a convincing personal history, a plausible *Book of Yolly,* and I worried that the other Merrimack students, realizing they had a naïf in their midst, would torment her mercilessly. I presented my troubling prediction to Jordan, and against my expectations she managed to allay my fears with a single cogent remark.

"Yolly's practically my *daughter,* for Christ's sake," she told me. "I'll be looking out for her twenty-four hours a day, which is a better deal than most kids get from their parents, teachers, or guardian angels."

As for Donya, both Henry and Brock wanted to continue educating her on the island, though they admitted to enjoying little objectivity in the matter, as neither could imagine a better place for pursuing his pet passion—in Henry's case, a cycle of speculative scripts for *Uncle Rumpus's Magic Island,* in Brock's, a magnum opus: ten huge canvases that would ultimately form a 360-degree cyclorama of Isla de Sangre as refracted through his surrealist's sensibility. It was Jordan who settled the question, arguing that several additional years of idyllic isolation would do Donya more good than harm. Sometime around her sixteenth birthday, she should be given the same choice as Yolly—another season in Eden, pumpkin, or a leap into the larger world?—but for now it made sense to cultivate her innocence.

On the same day that Yolly received her acceptance letter from Merrimack, Javier informed me that Vincent Charnock, having completed his last experiment and removed his equipment from the Quonset-hut complex, was no longer in residence. Shortly after sunrise the father of ontogeneration had strolled down to the Bahía de Flores, boarded Captain López's cabin cruiser, and left for Key West without telling a soul. I was hardly surprised. Charnock had gotten what he wanted from me—corroboration of his suspicion that philosophers couldn't think straight about embryos—and he obviously had nothing more to say to the Sisters Sabacthani, no bits of avuncular wisdom, no nuggets of godfatherly advice.

"Now that Edwina and Dr. Charnock are gone, I can do a forbidden thing," Javier told me one night as we savored Cuba libres on my deck. "I speak now of our poor, miserable Proserpine."

"Let me guess," I said. "You're going to gobble down a dozen ro-coconuts and mud-wrestle an alligator."

Smiling, he sipped rum and shook his head. "I want to end her suffering. Edwina wouldn't allow it—she always said Proserpine doesn't feel anything—and Dr. Charnock, he was just as stubborn, but for different reasons. Whatever Proserpine's quality of life, he said, we've got no right to commit euthanasia."

"So you're going to uproot her?"

"The tree will bless us for it."

Two days later, Javier gathered together Henry, Brock, Londa, and myself, fed us a hearty lunch of calamari stew in the Faustino dining hall, and guided us into the conservatory. We stripped Proserpine of her fruits. The harvest fit into two hundred king-size Ziploc bags, which we stored in the manor's largest freezer. Having never experienced the unique inebriation afforded by mumquat nectar, Henry and Brock briefly considered sharing a rococonut, but they decided to abstain, knowing that the day's task would require a clear head and steady hands.

We returned to the conservatory and, after three hours of hard labor with picks and shovels, extracted Proserpine from her brackish habitat. As we carried the mangrove to the Quonset huts, her breathing became softer, her heartbeats slower, her trembling imperceptible. Charnock's Faustino laboratory was even larger than his workshop atop Torre de la Carne, but Proserpine's roots and branches still jammed the place to its corrugated walls. Under Londa's direction we inserted the tubers in buckets of morphine and, once convinced that the tree was insensate, incised her trunk with a chain saw and got to work. Our efforts continued from midafternoon to dusk, until at last all traces of the biologists' interventions were gone, every chunk of lung, scrap of heart, and curd of neural tissue.

Shortly after dark we hauled the vegetable cadaver down to the beach, stopping near the site of Ralph Gittikac's prodigal picnic. A full moon rose over the Bahía de Flores, painting the waters with streaks of such silvery beauty that they suggested some benevolent inverse of an oil spill—a slick of angel's tears or dolphin's milk. We filled the mangrove's dredged trunk with kerosene, then set it on fire. For nearly an hour, the five of us stood on the shore, chatting idly as sparks swarmed around the flaming tree. Javier was the first to leave, saying he needed to work on his résumé. Henry and Brock departed next, explaining that Chen had done more than his share of baby-sitting that day.

Dressed in ragged chinos and a white T-shirt, Londa looked exquisite by firelight. The flames bronzed her cheeks and burnished her brow. She told me that earlier in the week she and Yolly had brought Donya to this very spot. The three girls had baked clams and played Frisbee, and when the stars came out, they'd sprawled on the beach and wriggled their toes in the sand, "playing footsie with the planet," while scanning the dome of heaven. Thanks to her Stargazer Deluxe, Donya had quickly identified Orion, the Pleiades, the Big Dipper, and a half dozen other constellations. Seeking to stimulate her youngest sister's sense of wonder while expanding her other sister's intellect, Londa had speculated aloud that the night sky was an illusion—a projected vista of bright bodies and black voids generated by an immense planetarium located on Platonia, an invisible world in orbit between Earth and Venus.

"I trust your siblings were amused," I said.

She answered with characteristic Sabacthani solemnity. "They giggled idiotically. Humor was not my intention. I wanted them to imagine that Platonia and the Platonians really exist."

"Sisters can be so annoying."

"You call us sisters, which is more or less correct—but I'll bet our teachers call us other things behind our backs. Be honest, Socrates. Are we kettle kittens? Chowder chicks? Bisque bitches?"

"Vatlings, actually."

"Vatlings?" Londa laughed, pleased with herself. She'd smoked us out. "Very funny. What else?"

"Beaker freaks, gumbo girls, and tureen queens."

"Any more?"

"Well, yes."

"What?"

"Bouillababies."

"And?"

"And petri dolls and chamber maids. That's all."

"I like gumbo girls best."

"Me, too."

She hooked her thumbs through the belt loops of her chinos. "Mr. Fermoyle tells me you don't want to be my guardian."

"I wouldn't put it that way."

"You stuck me with some chucklehead cousin. I don't mind, really—not as long as you'll keep on being my auxiliary conscience." She gestured toward Sagittarius, as if signaling the centaur to release his arrow. "Hey, Mason, you want to hear something interesting about the Platonians' projection? It isn't just a sky map. It's also a blueprint."

"A blueprint," I echoed evenly.

"A blueprint for a city."

"A city. Right."

"See how it shines? Streetlamps, lighted windows, mooring beacons for zeppelins—all glittering like Donya's sea horses."

"I love those sea horses. They're all I know of God."

"The Platonians fully intend to build it one day, a perfect city, a haven for the misbegotten."

"The misbegotten deserve no less," I said dryly.

"Once the Platonians get an idea in their heads, there's no stopping them."

"Be careful, Londa. Even Jesus failed to bring heaven to earth."

"Jesus didn't have a trust fund." She lifted a stone from the beach and tossed it into the fire, breeding a new generation of sparks. "For a while I was committed to the name 'Zeus City,' in honor of the

Stoics' utopia, but then I decided 'Themisopolis' was a better choice, you know, after the goddess with the sword and the blindfold and the balance scales."

"I applaud your ambition."

"Don't patronize me."

"The last thing on my mind."

"Themisopolis, the City of Justice. And with the help of my auxiliary conscience, I'm going to make it happen."

"Your auxiliary conscience has other plans," I said. True enough: I was planning to have nothing to do with Themisopolis.

"You'll miss all the fun," she said.

"Fun on a bun," I said.

A vibration passed through my bones, as if I were the late Proserpine enduring a vestigial fit. When Londa installed herself as monarch over her trust-fund utopia, which of her personae would be ascendant? Even if the benign Scarlet Darwinist proved dominant at first, the Crimson Kantian and the Purple Pietist would be lurking in the shadows, waiting to seize power.

"Question, my dear," I said. "What will happen when the Platonians switch off their planetarium?"

"Isn't it obvious? The heavens will vanish, every last star, and then we'll finally see what lies beyond. It promises to be impossibly magnificent and utterly incomprehensible."

"That's the difference between you and me, dear. I don't want to be there when the stars blink out."

"Whereas I would try to get a front-row seat."

She took two steps forward, kissed me squarely on the lips, and, pivoting abruptly like a weather vane in a gale, melted into the night.

"Your gumbo girl will build a city!" she called out of the darkness. "You don't believe her, but she'll do it! The Phyllistines will curse every brick! The downtrodden will cheer!"

I shifted my eyes from Londa's retreating form to the flaming tree and then to the bright speckled vault. For a full minute, I stood on the beach and studied the luminous City of Justice. Slowly, one by one, the lamps, windows, and mooring beacons floated free and transmuted into stars again, so I lowered my gaze and turned from the sea and walked into the forest.

Part II
Londa Unbound

Chapter 8

NO, LADIES AND GENTLEMEN, I did not unscrew her skull-cap, insert her brain into its white vault, and knit her medulla to her spinal cord: someone else performed that operation. Still, I was her creator. I did not take gouts of dripping tissue in my hands and sculpt them around her bones, feeding the scraps to the dog who ate God's homework: a different person shaped her flesh. She was nevertheless my creature. I did not install her beating heart in its thoracic cavity, lodge her eyeballs in their sockets, or tap her teeth into place with a steel mallet tempered in the Pierian Spring: those duties fell to another. And yet I am responsible for what she became.

Yes, ladies and gentlemen, my detractors speak the truth. For nearly ten years following my departure from the Florida Keys, I pretended to the outside world that I'd played no part in the construction of Londa Sabacthani's increasingly conspicuous soul. Every time her press secretary, the indefatigable Pauline Chilton, dispatched yet another reporter to my abode, deliriously eager to hear about the Isla de Sangre curriculum and maybe learn what made Londa tick, I would tell the invader that while I had indeed served briefly as Dr. Sabacthani's private tutor in certain abstruse deontological matters, my influence on her ethical development had been negligible.

I am still haunted by the case of Emily Seldes, who tearfully begged me to grant her an hour of my time lest she lose her job at the *Hartford Courant*. When I turned her down, Miss Seldes proceeded to fabricate and publish a story, "Sabacthani's Mentor Recalls His 'Moral Prodigy,'" subsequently receiving the boot and descending into clinical depression after the article was exposed as a fraud. An unfortunate episode, but I was immune to regret in those days. Nor could I be moved by avarice. The producers of *The Roscoe Fisher Show* offered me fifteen thousand dollars for a ten-minute interview. I told them I would appear on condition that we talked about nothing but Heidegger's concept of *Dasein*. The powers behind *Cordelia Drake Live* raised the stakes to twenty thousand dollars. I responded that I was ill-disposed to revisit a closed chapter in my life, but I'd be pleased to tell Cordelia's viewers why Darwinian materialism offered a more exalted view of humankind than did the Book of Genesis.

Londa herself had no better luck getting my attention. I recycled her letters unopened, erased her phone messages without listening to them, slammed doors in the faces of her envoys, and deleted her e-mails with alacrity. *Subject:* Mason, I Need You. *Subject:* Calling All Consciences. *Subject:* Please, Socrates. *Subject:* Win a Free Trip to Themisopolis. *Subject:* Desperately Seeking Superego. *Subject:* Gumbo Girl on the Verge of a Nervous Breakdown. *Subject:* For God's Sake. *Subject:* I'm Not Kidding. *Subject:* Jesus Christ! *Subject:* Fuck You!

What sense was there in my self-imposed exile? By what lights would a reasonable man dissent from the Sabacthani miracle? Who but the crustiest curmudgeon would disdain the omnibenevolent community that Londa and Yolly had seeded in the rural environs of Bel Air, Maryland? Who but the sourest sophist would gainsay the splendid projects administered within the walls of that Susquehanna River utopia? One thinks immediately of the Mary Wollstonecraft

Fund, providing contraceptives and small-business loans to women in underdeveloped countries, not to mention the Susan B. Anthony Trust, running to earth the architects of various international prostitution rings—sexual slavery, the sisters called it with a characteristic contempt for euphemism—as well as the Elizabeth Cady Stanton Foundation, tirelessly lobbying against the user-friendly fascism, feel-good theocracy, and creeping Phyllistinism that now dominated the American political landscape. O come, all ye faithful. Come ye to Themisopolis. Come and behold the Institute for Advanced Biological Investigations, dedicated to eradicating the female cancers. Tour the Vision Syndicate and chat with its idealistic engineers, fiercely determined to inaugurate a postcarbon age in which fossil-fueled power plants will have gone the way of workhouses and witch trials. Drop by the Artemis Clinic, offering free medical services, including abortions, to pregnant women. Visit Arcadia House, sheltering hundreds of runaway wives, battered girlfriends, pregnant teenagers, abused children, and unadoptable orphans.

But you see, ladies and gentlemen, despite Londa's munificence, or maybe because of it, there was never a moment when she did not seem monstrous in my eyes, beauty and beast in a single skin. The woman frightened me. She scared me to death. Whenever I started to compose an e-mail to my vatling, images of her stigmata flooded my brain—the burn scar on her palm, the thorn under her thumbnail—and I shut down the computer. Each time I picked up the phone to call her, the vindictive Crimson Kantian from *The Book of Londa* rose in my imagination, and I returned the handset to its cradle, knowing that for the sake of my sanity, and perhaps hers as well, I must continue to banish her from my life.

And so it happens that these pages contain a dearth of inside dope concerning Londa's ascent from biology major to celebrity saint. You will find herein nothing to supplement the standard narrative—how a beautiful and brilliant molecular geneticist from Johns Hopkins burst one day upon the clinical-research scene, perfecting a therapeutic technique whereby specially designed patches of healthy DNA were knitted into the chromosomes of patients suffering from malign mutations; how this same prodigy ultimately turned her back on avant-garde chimeraplasty and announced that she intended to pursue an even grander agenda; how she then joined forces with her younger sister, Yolly, her personal manager, Dagmar Röhrig, and her eternal inspiration, the Good Samaritan, to bring a substantial tract of paradise to earth, in time earning the sobriquet Dame Quixote. No gossip today, ladies and gentlemen. No jaw-dropping disclosures. If you want to learn about the Golden Age of Themisopolis, rent the PBS documentary *She Walked Among Us*. Read Sandra Granger's runaway bestseller, *Weltanschauung Woman*. Hunt out back issues of that old Marvel Comics series *The League of Londa*, the first of which currently commands a $350 minimum bid on eBay. Collect the trading cards. Play the board game. Fondle the action figure.

So extreme was my wariness that it extended even to Londa's youngest sister back on the island. Every time Donya invited me to Casa de los Huesos, I invented a pretext for staying put—poor health, low spirits, a deadline for delivering a revision of *Ethics from the Earth* to a prospective publisher—though I did agree to exchange e-mails and Christmas cards with her. When Omar the Doberman went to the Elysium of Endless Bones at the ripe old age of fifteen, I composed a five-stanza elegy, "I Just Got a Postcard from My Dog," that, as Henry put it, "helped us move our favorite little girl from mourning to remembrance."

By Donya's account, all was well on Isla de Sangre. Henry had written a half-dozen scripts for *Uncle Rumpus's Magic Island,* "and they're really, really funny," she assured me. Brock's emerging surrealist cyclorama "makes you feel like your eyeballs have fallen out and gone rolling around on a Day-Glo pool table," which I took to be a recommendation. As for Donya herself, while her hand-crafted conscience was probably no less extravagant than Londa's or Yolly's, her messages betrayed little of the unbounded swash-bucklery that had made her older sisters the decade's most beloved and vilified women. When not marking the Bahía de Flores with signs imploring passing yachtsmen to keep their refuse out of the water, she was protecting newly laid sea-turtle eggs from predatory egrets and petitioning the federal government to designate the island a National Wildlife Refuge. I imagined that Donya might one day redirect these pastoral passions, scaling her ambitions upward from her local ecosystem to planet Earth, but just then, for better or worse—better, I felt—she seemed happy to circumscribe her dreams.

Had I been utterly determined to keep Londa from crossing my path, of course, I would have moved as far from Maryland as possible—to San Francisco, maybe, or London. But instead I returned to Boston—to my old haunts, in fact, Hawthorne University and environs. My goal was not to engage in further tussles with Felix Pielmeister, nor was it to resurrect my Ph.D. candidacy. What drove me was my craving for philosophical discourse, the desire that Sinuhe's riverside ruminations had sparked in me at such an impressionable age. I needed to hear sentences ornamented with "categorical imperative," "Cartesian dualism," "Hegelian idealism," and "the encounter with nothingness" the way a believing Sabacthanite needed the latest issue of *The League of Londa*.

My bright idea was to open a used-book store, an amenity to be found nowhere within a six-block radius of the campus. A solid nut of one hundred thousand dollars remained from my Isla de Sangre salary, and this proved sufficient for me to attract a business partner, easygoing Dexter Padula, a member of that ubiquitous academic breed, the professional graduate student, forever revising his dissertation while eyeing external reality with the anxious demeanor of a nursing infant struggling to imagine life beyond the tit. Dexter stood out from his fellows on four counts. He was not on antidepressants; he knew how to groom himself;

he had a plan for finishing his book—*Overlapping Intersubjectivities in "The Canterbury Tales"*—before the year was up; and he'd inherited a bundle from his father, though apparently the bundle would have been bigger had Dexter decided to become a lawyer instead of a Chaucerian. In a matter of weeks, we'd secured a two-year lease on 1,924 square feet of the Pequot Building, an easy and picturesque walk from campus, and we'd also acquired the private libraries of four bibliophiles whose ability to enjoy their collections had been compromised by, respectively, illness, impoverishment, blindness, and death. After making these moves, we still had sufficient funds for several part-time employees and a hand-carved sign reading PIECES OF MIND: USED BOOKS, FRESH COFFEE, LIVELY CONVERSATION.

Neither Dexter nor I knew the first thing about running a small business. We were entrepreneurs the way Abbott and Costello were watercolorists. And so naturally it came to pass that Pieces of Mind was a hands-down, thumbs-up, flat-out success. Was it possible that those Egyptian gods to whom Sinuhe had declined to defer—royal Isis, valiant Horus, wise Thoth, and the rest—were not only real but sending their smiles our way? I liked to think so, though when we did the math, it appeared that the decisive factor was not divine intervention but the espresso machine in the back of the store, tirelessly transforming brown beans into black ink.

We'd been in business barely three months when another stroke of luck augmented my bank account. After collecting a dozen rejection letters, I somehow persuaded Bellerophon Books to publish an abridged version of *Ethics from the Earth*. Defying expectations, my opinionated opus soon earned out its thousand-dollar advance, and then the biannual royalties began to arrive. Sometimes the payment would be as much as two hundred dollars, more than enough to cover our combined cream, sugar, and toilet-paper budget for a month.

Although we were thriving in the material realm, my grander

vision for Pieces of Mind never came to pass. My dream was that while Daphne and Forrest and our other student employees attended to the tedious tasks—shelving the merchandise, working the cash register, posting inventory on the Internet—I would sashay through the coffee bar, inviting myself into whatever fascinating discussions caught my ear. A foolish notion. A delusion on stilts. For one thing, the owner of a used-book store does not sashay. He runs around putting out fires—the irate customer, the overdue phone bill, the crashed computer, the housewife from Chelsea who's just shown up expecting a hundred dollars for her worthless carton of Reader's Digest Condensed Books. Furthermore, even if I'd had time to mingle, I wouldn't have enjoyed it, for what emerged from my customers' mouths was not so much conversation as a litany of complaint. The undergraduates lamented the high price of textbooks and the equally outrageous fact that they were expected to read them. The graduate students bemoaned their small stipends and large workloads. The professors apportioned their spleen among the graduate students, the administrators, and one another. Indeed, during the store's entire life span, I never encountered a single spontaneous seminar concerning Foucault or Derrida, though I learned more than I wanted to about tenure. Sad to say, the one time I heard the delectable question "How, then, should we live?" within the walls of Pieces of Mind, the speaker turned out to be Felix Pielmeister. I instantly made an about-face and retreated to the children's section.

If my little haven was no agora, there were compensations nonetheless. It became my habit, after closing up for the evening, to pour myself a glass of cabernet sauvignon, sprawl on the couch, and think, taking incalculable delight in what I'd wrought, this bibliographic cornucopia, this box seat in God's brain. Then, too, there was the happy fact that managing a bookstore is a terrific way to meet women. Fair are the daughters of men, and fairest are those who read. Is there any creature more desirable than a damsel in intellectual distress? I see you're a Joseph Heller aficionada—allow me to argue that *Something Happened* is a greater achievement than *Catch-22*. No, we don't have *A Prayer for Owen Meany,* but in my opinion *The Cider House Rules* is a much better novel.

Throughout this period, Pieces of Mind netted me dozens of dates and several unexpected seductions. I suffered three broken hearts and inflicted as many such casualties in turn. Then one day the woman of my dreams walked into the store, and my life was changed forever.

LIKE DANTE CATCHING his fateful glimpse of Beatrice, I first spied her from afar—or, rather, from above. I was standing on the stepladder, shelving a near-mint collection of Heinlein juveniles in the topmost loft of our science-fiction and fantasy section, when a female voice called out from the precincts of J. R. R. Tolkien below.

"Excuse me. I'm looking for a hardcover *Faerie Queene.* Is there such a thing?"

I glanced downward, and my eyes met the upturned face of a goddess with generous lips, endearing dimples, and the sort of large, intelligent eyes behind which, if I was any sort of judge, elegant thoughts were routinely entertained.

"It's not with the poetry," she continued, "and I tried literature, too, so maybe somebody shelved it with your wizards and elves?"

As luck would have it, two days earlier a retiring professor of British literature had dropped off a complete run of those lavishly illustrated, out-of-print marvels known as the Erlanger House Classics, including a slipcased incarnation of *The Faerie Queene,* so I could assess their condition and make him an offer. "There's a rare three-volume set on the premises, but I haven't priced it yet," I told my adorable Spenserian, then carelessly followed up with a question that a retailer must never, under any circumstances, ask a customer. "How much are you willing to pay?"

"Anything," she said. "Three hundred dollars."

Assuming it was in good shape, I would happily give the professor four hundred dollars for his *Faerie Queene,* which would probably fetch seven hundred on the Internet. "You can have it for two hundred and fifty," I told her. "Meet me at the cash register."

Leaving my heart aloft, I descended to earth and floated into the back room, where I unsheathed all three volumes and leafed through them in search of underlinings and dog-ears. The books seemed free of blemishes. I considered lowering the price to two hundred dollars, then decided that if my goddess ever found out what this edition was really worth, she would think me an idiot.

"We don't get many Spenserians in here," I said, approaching the sales counter.

"I'm sure," she said.

As if Isis and Horus hadn't already done enough for me, the object of my infatuation wrote the store a personal check, and thus I learned not only her alliterative name, Natalie Novak, but also her address and phone number.

I probed, I pried, I snooped, I sleuthed, and by the end of the month the salient facts were mine. An ABD in the English department, Natalie divided her time between writing her dissertation, something about the function of Providence in Emily Brontë, and teaching a panoply of courses ranging from Elizabethan Tragedy to the Twentieth-Century Novel. On agreeable spring days, she was not embarrassed to escort her Victorian Poetry class down to the Charles and recite "The Lady of Shalott" aloud while the students imagined the hapless maiden drifting past on her funeral barge. But the surest route to Natalie's heart doubtless lay in Spenser's Faerie Land, and so I undertook a journey to that extravagant realm.

For six full weeks, I immersed myself in the epic, keeping company with its valiant knights, foul witches, beautiful shepherdesses, lustful giants, virtuous adventurers, and depraved magicians. I accomplished this feat even though *The Faerie Queene* suffers from the defect of not being very good, or such was my reaction to its stone-obvious moralizing, in-your-face allegory, and retrograde political dogma. It wasn't easy working up affection for this god-awful masterpiece, but somehow I suspended my revulsion long enough to start appreciating its positive aspects: the occasional neat plot twist, the intermittent linguistic felicity. "Sleep after toil, port after stormy seas, / Ease after war, death after life does greatly please." A fine couplet, no question. "Her angel's face / As the great eye of heaven shined bright, / And made a sunshine in the shady place." Well done, sir. "Her birth was of the womb of morning dew." I had no idea what that meant, but I liked it.

One golden April afternoon, I decided to bring my project to fruition. I left Dexter in charge of the store, rode my bike to the river, and hid behind a forsythia bush. Right on schedule Natalie appeared, her fifteen Shakespeare 101 students trailing behind her like imprinted ducklings. For the next forty-five minutes, she lectured on *Antony and Cleopatra,* arguing that it was at once the most cerebral and the most emotional of the tragedies. She fielded some questions, answered them astutely, then bade her ducklings scatter. Time for me to make my move.

"Hello again." A good opening gambit, I felt. Precise but non-threatening.

"Have we met?"

"I'm the guy who runs Pieces of Mind. I'll be honest, Natalie. When you bought that pricey *Faerie Queene,* I was so dazzled I lost the power of speech, and before I'd untied my tongue, you were out the door. At long last, I told myself. At long last—a kindred spirit!"

"We're not communicating."

"'Her birth was of the womb of morning dew.' It doesn't get any better than that."

"It doesn't?"

"I'll wager that of all the people down by the river today, only you and I fully appreciate that astonishing moment when Duessa stands exposed as a filthy, scabby hag, not to mention Error showering the Red Cross Knight with her vomitus of books."

"I really love your store."

"Thank you."

"I'm afraid I can't say the same for *The Faerie Queene*."

"Come again?"

"To tell you the truth, I think Spenser is the most pompous twit ever to molest the English language. Sorry. Really. Art is so subjective."

All my muscles contracted, a whole-body wince. "I see," I mumbled. "So that's how it is."

"I know the man has his partisans. He also has his virulent anti-Catholicism, his bigotry toward Saracens, his contempt for democracy, and his treacly notions of piety. Pieces of Mind is a great gift to our community. May I buy you a beer?"

"If you can't stand Spenser, why did you spend two hundred and fifty dollars on that Erlanger House edition?"

"A college graduation present for my brother. Verbal filigree and ersatz medievalism never had a bigger fan. You and Jerry should get together. I'm serious about the beer."

"What sorts of books *do* you like?"

"Lately I've been reading a lot of nonfiction, looking into the impact of science on philosophy. I just finished a thing called *Virtue from the Dirt*. No, that's not it. *Ethics from the Earth,* by somebody named Ambrose. I think he lives around here. Breathtaking book. Do you know it?"

TWO DAYS LATER NATALIE MOVED out of her cramped, cluttered, second-floor apartment on Cummington Street and into my cramped, cluttered, third-floor apartment on Sherborn Street, and we joyfully set about our objective of living happily ever after. For the better part of a year, our relationship flourished. Having previously transformed Londa into the restless and obsessive Dame Quixote, I had no ambition to make any woman, vatling or otherwise, into a putatively better version of herself, and I willingly endured Natalie's habits of scrawling illegible messages on the kitchen calendar and stashing unpaid bills in her handbag. Natalie, for her part, announced that she would not battle my various defects—my illiterate understanding of laundry, my tendency to deface the bathroom sink with blobs of toothpaste—until I was her eager and unresentful ally. In short, we allowed one another to be terrible roommates, a forbearance that doubtless figured crucially in our becoming great friends.

But there was a serpent in the garden, a worm in the apple of our idyll. Natalie's symptoms were not particularly disturbing in and of themselves—intermittent pelvic pains, numbness in her legs and feet—yet in this case they pointed to a serious condition: blood clots. Once the diagnosis was confirmed, we listened in dismay as a team of specialists argued not only for putting her on a regimen of Coumadin injections but also for equipping her circulatory system with plastic screens designed to trap errant embolisms before they could lodge in her lungs. This plenary approach was no cure, as clots could easily form upstream from the Greenfield filters. It was better than doing nothing, however, and so despite her chariness toward orthodox medicine, Natalie submitted to the technique. There were no complications, and within a few weeks she was back at work, reciting Tennyson in full throat as the waters of the Charles lapped against the shore. Truth be told, she handled the situation much better than I, for whom this sword of Damocles seemed especially heavy, its thread singularly thin. Many were the nights I trolled cyberspace searching out the latest sonic, surgical, and pharmaceutical approaches to blood clots—once I even visited the Web site of Londa's avant-garde Institute for Advanced Biological Investigations—but I failed to unearth any breakthroughs.

Among the consequences of Natalie's quasi-Luddite worldview

was a commitment to what she called "pagan birth control," which boiled down to a combination of fertility charts, herbal contraceptives, and wishful thinking. I was skeptical but willing to gamble, especially since for Natalie the natural correlate of pagan birth control was pagan lovemaking. Under cover of night, we shed our garments in woods and dells. We connected in sacred spaces, calling each a Bower of Bliss—for a couple of anti-Spenserians, we were peculiarly ready to appropriate his diction—most memorably the shallows of Walden Pond, the stacks of Widener Library, and those cryptic New Hampshire megaliths known as America's Stonehenge.

Despite our prophylactic intentions, we soon learned that one likely outcome of conjoining pagan birth control to pagan lovemaking is a pagan pregnancy.

"I *knew* this was going to happen!" I wailed when Natalie told me the news. "I goddamn fucking *knew* it!"

"No birth control method is foolproof," she said.

"We didn't practice birth control. We practiced druid superstition."

"This is not your finest hour, Mason. You're behaving abominably."

"I'm behaving abominably," I agreed, and then I continued behaving abominably for the rest of the afternoon, accusing Natalie of "self-delusion masquerading as shamanism" and "flakiness posturing as subversion." Natalie, to her credit, accepted delivery on none of these indictments. By sundown we were calm again, assuming demeanors more appropriate to our circumstances: two civilized adults facing questions for which neither civilization nor adulthood furnished palatable answers.

As any good Darwinist will tell you, ontogeny does not recapitulate phylogeny. In noting the transient gill slits of a developing human fetus, one must avoid the temptation to regard the creature as an adult fish. And yet, as that same good Darwinist will tell you, there is something astonishing about a fetus's gills, an intimation of the epic through which algae became Aristotle and the cucumber turned into you, for these wispy slits resoundingly echo the corresponding features in an embryonic fish. And so it happened that as Natalie's pregnancy progressed, I found myself wondering whether the mite in her womb had yet embraced its piscean ancestry, and when it might take title to its reptilian estate. As long as the thing had not claimed its mammalian heritage, I would endorse whatever decision Natalie made.

Over the next three weeks, we consulted a quartet of health professionals, and they were unanimous in their view that Natalie's pregnancy would aggravate the propensity of her blood to form rogue clots. "The danger is serious but not grave," said Dr. Millard, her primary-care physician, a remark that struck us as a distinction without a difference. The gynecologist was equally unhelpful. "If you elect to bring the fetus to term," Dr. Harris told Natalie, "I'll do everything possible to keep you out of the danger zone." Hematologist number one, Dr. Protter, offered a more upbeat verdict—"Although I can't make any promises, this impresses me as a low-level risk"—but her optimism was canceled by the unequivocal gloom of hematologist number two. "In your shoes," Dr. Shumkas informed us, "I would terminate the pregnancy."

The human mind, I learned that month, had not yet evolved sufficiently to wrap itself around this sort of issue. My thoughts were a stroboscopic muddle of flashes and voids, every second burst showing me a vignette from the life of my provisional son, my hypothetical daughter, a Donya Sabacthani sort of childhood, abrim with tree houses and toy planetariums, but it was the interlaced images, the glimpses of mourners and pallbearers, that stayed with me. Two days after our consultation with Dr. Shumkas, I told Natalie I thought she should get an abortion.

"I don't want an abortion."

"You want a baby, then?"

"Not that either."

"What *do* you want?"

"I want the pregnancy to go away."

At the end of the week, we drove to Mass General and withdrew our contribution to posterity. It was the simplest of procedures, a routine outpatient dilation and curettage. My root canal had been more complicated. We decided not to ask about the gender of the extinguished fetus. On the way out of the hospital, we stopped by the pharmacy and obtained the prescribed antibiotics. We went home, split a bottle of Chianti, and crawled beneath the blankets, sobbing in each other's arms.

I awoke near dawn with a foul, metallic taste in my mouth, as if I'd been licking a spigot. Leaning toward my drowsy friend, I kissed the nape of her neck. I shuffled to the bathroom, appeased my bladder, and, upon returning to bed, endured a long and distressing Isla de Sangre dream. I was snorkeling in the Bahía de Flores, gliding above a clamshell the size of a hatbox, which suddenly opened to reveal, besides the expected clam, a sodden copy of *The Book of Londa*. Applying some amorphous appendage, the clam turned back the cover, whereupon I read, "My mother conceived me, my godfather gestated me, my sisters nourished me, but it was Mason who made me the monster I am."

IN THE WEEKS FOLLOWING her D and C, Natalie grew increasingly sad, until it seemed she was in thrall to that wan and manipulative troglodyte from Book One, Canto IX, whom Spenser had with characteristic subtlety named Despair. Nothing helped. When I recommended that we get a cat, she reminded me about her allergies. When I proposed that we fly to the Bahamas for the weekend, she pointed to a stack of ungraded papers. When I suggested she might be a candidate for Prozac, she accused me of wanting her to be "somebody else, anybody else, so long as she isn't Natalie Novak." We had sex infrequently and indifferently, keeping further embryos at bay with condoms. Neither of us was surprised when I reverted to my old habit of staying in the store after hours, Mason the Gutenberg ascetic, the hermeneutical hermit, immured by other people's wisdom.

With our romance withering, our affection wilting, and our rapport a thing of the past, we did what any rational couple would do under the circumstances. We got married. The ceremony occurred at the home of Natalie's geeky medievalist brother, Jerry. We decided that no depressing people could attend, which ruled out our parents and most of our relatives. Besides Jerry, our audience was limited to Dexter Padula, my sister Delia—then in the process of transplanting her nonexistent acting career from New York to L.A.—and three of Natalie's friends: willowy Helen Vanderbilt, who'd recently published three chapbooks of unpublishable poetry, zaftig Margery Kaplan, who'd gone to high school with Natalie and now raised basset hounds, and a lantern-jawed Henry James scholar named Abner Cassidy, Natalie's former lover and present adviser, to whom I took an instant liking despite his carnal knowledge of my bride.

"I am grateful to thee, Archimago," she told me on our wedding night, Archimago being our favorite *Faerie Queene* character, a protean magician deployed by Spenser to symbolize, variously, hypocrisy, Satan, and the pope. "Not every man would put up with a melancholic Emily Brontë freak who can't finish her dissertation."

"If 'twould please thee, Malecasta, I shall fly to the moon and paint it the color of thine eyes," I replied, Malecasta being the mistress of Castle Joyous, the sensualist's paradise, a magnet for every letch and satyr in Faerie Land.

To consolidate her rising spirits, Natalie began following a regimen that, while it sounded like something out of a particularly vapid self-help book, actually seemed to work. I couldn't say whether her deliverance from Despair—"his raw-bone cheeks, through penury and pine, were shrunk into his jaws, as he did never dine"—traced to her nightly doses of St. John's wort, her twenty daily laps in the

YMCA pool, the Tuesday-night fiction-reading group she'd organized at the Caffeine Fiend, my jovial willingness to be the butt of
her jokes, or a combination of all four remedies. In any event the
ogre loosened his grip and slunk back to his lair, a place "dark, doleful, dreary like a greedy grave that still for carrion carcasses doth
crave."

It was not long after Natalie's recovery that, courtesy of our
subscription to the *Boston Globe,* Londa's name and photograph
began appearing routinely in our lives. During that era, of course,
hardly a week went by without a Dame Quixote story seeing print,
but this was front-page stuff—the revelation by the Reverend
Enoch Anthem, founder and chairman of a postrationalist think
tank called the Center for Stable Families, of an outrageous scheme
hatching in that bastion of degenerate feminism, Themisopolis.
Somehow Anthem had obtained an audio recording of a meeting
between Londa's staff and the vice president of the Baudrillard
Simulacrum Corporation, a Toulouse-based manufacturer of Dis-
neyesque audio-animatronic robots. When the FBI decided that
Reverend Anthem's case against Londa was fundamentally preposterous, he took his complaint to the *Washington Post,* whereupon the
tale proliferated like a bacterial culture, flourishing coast-to-coast
in a thousand cybernetic petri dishes.

If Anthem's account of Baudrillard recording could be believed,
many ideas were entertained on that sweltering August afternoon, from the clever to the harebrained. In one particularly wild
scenario, an enormous robotic replica of Abraham Lincoln, scaled
to the ponderous proportions of the famous D.C. sculpture, would
appear on the Capitol steps, screaming a challenge to the assembled representatives. "Does any man amongst you cleave to an ideal
higher than his own reelection? Who will tell me of the time he favored the demands of his conscience whilst resisting the tyranny of
his constituents?" An equally outlandish project had the Sisters Sabacthani smuggling some simian androids into the Primate House

of the Washington Zoological Gardens. The next day's visitors would witness the New World monkeys lamenting the destruction of their relatives' jungle habitats, a crime readily traceable to American fast-food corporations bent on creating new grazing lands for beef cattle. But it was Operation Redneck, the most demented of the afternoon's brainstorms, that caught Enoch Anthem's attention. The plan called for the Baudrillard people to construct a score of android joggers indistinguishable from their flesh-and-blood prototypes, each decked out in a T-shirt endorsing reproductive rights, gay marriage, evolutionary biology, or some other institution of which Jesus Christ disapproved. Sooner or later a reactionary motorist, intoxicated by beer or piety or both, would run down one of these benighted athletes, a gesture that the motorist would not live to regret, for the robots were in fact ambulatory bombs, wired to explode on impact.

A lardish man whose small head, bulbous frame, and anxious demeanor put me in mind of a bowling pin about to topple, Enoch Anthem spent the next three weeks attacking Operation Redneck through mass mailings, saturation blogging, and dozens of appearances on what Natalie called the "revengelical" networks. He accused Londa of concocting "a terrorist plot worthy of those who crucified our Lord," and, by the pollsters' reckoning, a majority of Americans agreed. The image of even the sleaziest yahoo being blown sky-high by a leftist French C-3PO did not sit well with Mr. and Mrs. John Q. Public.

Ever since Natalie had gotten me to admit that appreciable levels of sexual tension had characterized the classroom climate back on Isla de Sangre, she'd been vaguely jealous of Londa. But, like almost every feminist in the Western world, Natalie also admired Dame Quixote, and she urged me to proclaim publicly that my former pupil would never implement anything so rash as Operation Redneck. I was within hours of phoning the *New York Times* when Pauline Chilton, that canny spinmistress, announced that Dr. Sabacthani would be holding a press conference "for the purpose of answering Reverend Anthem's absurd accusations." Once again, it seemed, Isis and Horus and Thoth had come to my rescue. For the immediate future, at least, I would be permitted to remain outside Londa's sphere.

Over a hundred journalists attended the event, which Natalie and I watched on television while consuming gourmet microwave pizza. Londa acquitted herself brilliantly, using the occasion not only to assail Enoch Anthem as "a man who wouldn't recognize a joke if it walked into his house with a duck on its head" but also to remind her fellow Americans that "the Themisopolis community has an impeccable record of eschewing violence in all its forms, which puts us one up on the Center for Stable Families." Before the week was out, the polls disclosed that Mr. and Mrs. John Q. Public had forgiven Dame Quixote her offensive fantasies.

"Londa was wrong about one thing," I told Natalie. "Operation Redneck was pure whimsy, but there really *is* an ambulatory bomb inside the walls of Themisopolis."

Natalie had heard me question Londa's sanity before, but she'd never found my arguments persuasive. "How long till she detonates?"

"I'll give her three years at the most."

"Hey, Archimago, want to hear something you don't want to hear? Okay, sure, you're the Dame Quixote expert around here, and I'll admit it's possible she's riding for a fall. But I can't help wondering whether, deep down, you believe that fighting the good fight against clowns like Anthem is a *man's* job."

"She snuffed a candle with her palm. She stuck a thorn under her thumbnail."

"An interesting person, no doubt about it. If you ever see her again, I want her autograph."

ON THE EVENING OF OUR FIRST wedding anniversary, I came home bearing a dozen roses, presenting them to a startled Natalie with a theatrical flourish and a facetious remark about the care and feeding of the Japanese beetles inhabiting the bouquet. Our eyes met. Natalie was ravishing even when pained and embarrassed.

"Dear Abby," I said, "my wife forgot our wedding anniversary. Should I feel hurt by this role reversal, or should I laugh it off?"

Seeking to break the grip of the Spenserian monster Error, Natalie forced a smile, squeezed my hand, and invited me to dine with her at the Tasty Triffid, our favorite vegetarian restaurant. I accepted graciously. We made pagan love on the couch, then went out to eat. I spent the soup course joking about a hypothetical restaurant for total carnivores, the Bleeding Carrot, its menu featuring zucchini-flavored sausage, chicken wings prepared to taste like broccoli, and ersatz cauliflower made from pork. My wife pretended to be amused. She owed me that.

Later, standing on the front stoop while Natalie rummaged through her handbag searching for her keys, I realized I might have forgotten to lock the store safe: hardly a crisis—the chances of a break-in were low. Still, I felt compelled to check. I told Natalie I'd be back in time for another roll in the bower, then dashed off.

My habitual pedestrian commute took me along an asphalt path girding the south bank of the Charles, a pleasant twenty-minute stroll past willow trees and park benches. By day this promenade teemed with joggers, bicyclers, mothers pushing strollers, and those good-hearted folk whom the ducks had conditioned to toss bread into the water, but by night it was normally deserted, despite secondhand illumination from the Storrow Drive streetlamps. Alone, I moved through the soft summer air, listening to the river lap the shore with the soft, rhythmic gurgling of Error suckling her progeny.

My solitude did not last. Within minutes I became aware, subliminally at first, then with a disquieting certainty, of a stooped and sinister presence dogging my steps, flitting in and out of the shadows like an immense luna moth paying court to the moon. An asthma victim, evidently, every breath an effort. Doubtless Boston had its share of compulsive stalkers and after-dark psychos, but why had this wheezing Jack the Ripper picked *me*?

Keep moving, Mason. Left foot, right foot, left, right. I patted my jacket pockets, hoping I'd brought the cell phone. No such luck. The nearest police station occupied a location known to several thousand Bostonians, and God, but not to me. In my spinning brain, a tactic materialized. If I sprinted to the store, I could probably put a locked door between Jack and myself in a matter of minutes.

The stalker drew nearer, hyperventilating like an expectant mother practicing her Lamaze exercises. I broke into a run. Parked cars flew past, lighted windows, dark trees, malevolent Dumpsters. At last the store loomed up. The key vibrated in my hand. Somehow I jiggered it into the lock. Securing the door behind me, I fingered every switch within reach. The secular radiance of sodium vapor flowed forth. I drew a thick breath, my heart thumping in my rib cage as I wondered what to do next: call the cops, call Natalie, or arm myself with the clawhammer from the toolbox Dexter kept under the counter.

The hammer seemed the best option, and I was about to grab it when Jack hobbled into view, his silhouette filling the doorframe, his voice effortlessly penetrating the bulletproof pane. "Keep the door shut," he insisted, four clipped and staccato syllables. "When you let me in, it must be a free choice, no coercion, no threats."

"What do you want?"

He ignored my question. "I'm completely serious," he said. "A free choice."

"Who are you?"

"Like that *other* free choice you made about me."

"I've never met you."

"This is true, Father. Acknowledge me when you're ready. I'm a patient fetus."

My intestines tightened. Father? Fetus? What?

"Where are you from?" I asked the man who thought he was my

son. "Which institution? I can't help you. Really. Only the doctors can help you."

"Perhaps you and Mother would've named me Peter. Or Nigel. Biff. Oliver. Marcus. Kelton. Call me John Snow. Things would go better between us if you unlocked the door. John Snow and Mason Ambrose, talking face-to-face."

Without knowing why, I did as the intruder requested. As he struggled across the threshold, I thought of the Kohlbergian dilemma with which I'd presented Londa: Helga Eschbach breaking into the pharmacy to steal the radium extract.

Not until he'd reeled into the light did I realize that, far from being a conventional urban menace, this vagabond was fundamentally pathetic, not Jack the Ripper but John the Broken. He moved with the gait of an arthritic locust. His defective spine had imprisoned him in a permanent cringe. His right arm hung limp as a bell rope, while his left eye, unyoked from his nervous system, turned upward in perpetual contemplation of clouds and geese.

"You called me Father," I said.

"Would you prefer Papa? *Mon vieux père?*"

A spasm of sorrow contorted John Snow's face, which was pocked and stippled like a golf ball. He wore torn Levi's, a soiled beige windbreaker, and a scuffed baseball cap sporting the Red Sox logo. Shuffling forward, he fixed me with an expression mingling disdain with curiosity, and I saw to my horror that his bushy eyebrows and Roman nose corresponded to my own, even as Natalie's genes accounted for his ample lips and dimpled cheeks.

"I am an immaculoid," he continued. "Pure as milk, clean as soap, spotless as the lamb. Maturational age, thirty years. Chronological age, twenty days."

"Did Charnock send you after me? Dr. Vincent Charnock?"

"Pure, clean, spotless, and yet you scraped me out of the world."

I staggered toward a newly arrived shipment of Harvard Classics and slumped onto the carton, all the bones and fibers and fancies of my *Dasein* trembling with perplexity. By what means had the degenerate behind this scheme obtained the residue of Natalie's D and C? Did he pay for the material or simply steal it? No need for the whole fetus, of course. The tiniest scrap of tissue would have sufficed. A single healthy cell.

"All satisfaction is denied my kind," John Snow said. "We can smell the rose but never savor it. Taste the cherry but never relish it."

A single cell. Next stop, the petri dish, followed by the high-tech beaker, and then the ontogenerator.

"Never to enjoy the sun's warmth on my face—that's what you did to me."

And finally the DUNCE cap. John Snow's creator, I decided, was surely Charnock, using the RXL-313 to salve his guilt over sluicing away seven viable embryos.

"Never the sweetness of an ice-cream cone."

Or, if not Charnock, then . . . Londa? Unthinkable, but not unimaginable.

My visitor sprawled on a carton of high-school biology texts and stared in fascination at his good hand, as if just now realizing that his arm terminated in this marvelous device. He leaned toward me. Strangely enough, my anxiety faded, supplanted by an unexpected affection. When John Snow moved to kiss me, I did not recoil but submitted my cheek to the gesture.

"Does the name Londa Sabacthani mean anything to you?" I asked.

"Stainless as a saint." He rose from the biology texts, fixing me with his mother's blue eyes.

"Was Londa your creator?"

"Innocent as rain." He approached the entryway and, in a surprisingly vigorous move for one so enfeebled, yanked open the door. "Natalie Novak made me. Mason Ambrose made me."

"Must you leave already?" I asked.

"Never the fragrance of a pine forest."

"Are you going to visit Natalie?"

"Every child deserves a maternal caress, whether it gives him pleasure or not."

"Will you see her *tonight*?"

"Not tonight, but soon. I intend to call her Mother. She won't like it. Never the song of a lark. Sleep well, Father. Happy wedding anniversary. You shouldn't have murdered me."

John Snow slipped soundlessly into the night, closing the door behind him, and for a full ten minutes I simply sat on the Harvard Classics, my mind as blank as a newborn vatling's soul.

Chapter 9

MOVED BY THE FRUSTRATION her lustful son endures when the chaste and lovely Florimell declines his offer of rape, a malevolent woodland witch hatches a plan. She will present her jilted offspring with a simulated maiden, easily overwhelmed and eminently ravishable. Thus does the byzantine plot of *The Faerie Queene* give birth to yet another strange creature, the False Florimell, an alchemical concoction on whom the witch has bestowed burning lamps for eyes, golden wire for hair, and an indwelling sprite "to rule the carcass dead," the carcass in question being a fusion of painted wax and, of all things, snow, a material the witch presumably selected in sly mockery of the actual Florimell's virginity.

Sly mockery was probably the last thing on the mind of whatever unbalanced biologist had fashioned my nocturnal visitor and named him John Snow. Most probably he wanted to convey his belief that this fetus, like all fetuses, was innocence incarnate, snow become flesh, far closer to God's original intentions for the human race than those depraved *Homo sapiens sapiens* who'd actually inherited the Earth. Smart money said the immaculoid's creator had never read a single word of *The Faerie Queene*.

Against all odds, I remembered to check the safe—it was indeed locked—whereupon I left the store and sprinted pell-mell down Comm Ave. By jostling pedestrians and ignoring a half-dozen bright orange DON'T WALK signs, I reached our front stoop in under ten minutes. Natalie stood silhouetted in the parlor window: the Sisyphus of Sherborn Street, jogging on her treadmill. I lurched through the front door, rushed across the marble foyer, the cracks running every which way like John Snow's disordered dendrites, and ascended the staircase two steps at a time. In my imagination a horrid tableau appeared, the immaculoid hovering over Natalie as she ran frantically in place, faster and faster. John Snow remained at her side, spewing out accusations.

I burst into the parlor. Natalie threw the switch. The treadmill jerked to a halt.

"Welcome back," she said, panting.

"Something happened tonight."

"You look like you've seen a ghost."

There was ultimately no way to talk about John Snow without upsetting Natalie, but I still decided to broach the subject obliquely. "Do you remember the False Florimell? Sometimes called the Snowy Florimell?"

"What about her?"

"The first doppelgänger in literature, cooked up by an evil witch. Here's the truth of it, darling. Somebody has made a living facsimile of our son."

"What son?"

"You know what son. He calls himself John Snow."

"You're not making much sense."

"Our fetus has come back."

"That's preposterous."

"No. Technology."

We spent the rest of the night in our claustrophobic kitchen, talking and drinking coffee, and by dawn Natalie had become convinced that someone—Vincent Charnock or Londa Sabacthani or perhaps a third party—had used the ontogenerator and its collateral DUNCE cap for a stupefyingly sick purpose. Caffeinated but exhausted, we shuffled into the bedroom. A leprous, smirking moon glowed through the window. Heavy traffic growled and squealed its way along Comm Ave.

"He intends to track you down," I said. "Be prepared to have him call you Mother."

"Mother, and also murderer?"

"Yes, but that's just the DUNCE cap talking. Believe it or not, I felt a certain tenderness toward him. Especially when he kissed my cheek."

The last time Natalie and I had gone to bed sobbing in each other's arms, John Snow had been the cause. Tonight, déjà vu—the same desperate embrace, the same passage into sleep on a stream of tears, only now the occasion was not our fetus's death but his equally distressing resurrection. I vowed that if Londa was behind this business, I would accept that long-standing invitation to appear on *Cordelia Drake Live,* telling the viewing public that my former pupil, though ostensibly a humanitarian, was not above dabbling in biological diabolism. If you want my opinion, Cordelia, Dr. Sabacthani is out of her skull.

I awoke at noon and composed an e-mail to Londa, a message that would come as either a bolt from the blue or proof that her plot against me was proceeding apace. In a few terse sentences, I told her about my bookstore, my marriage, my success in publishing *Ethics from the Earth,* and finally my fetus, calling his advent—for I wanted to think the best of her—"a bit of news that will shock you." I stressed the ambiguity of the situation, the strange combination of pathos and banality that characterized John Snow's speech, his unsettling aura of sadness leavened with menace. "Might we get together soon and discuss this misbegotten beaker freak?" I clicked on Send and hoped for the best.

Later I went trolling for the Mad Doctor of Blood Island, feeding "Vincent Charnock" into my search engine and, when that failed, "ontogenerator." Zero. Growing desperate, I hunted for Web pages containing "immaculoid" or "John Snow" or "Smell the rose but never savor it." Zilch.

On Saturday night Natalie suffered her first visitation. She and Helen Vanderbilt, the self-appointed poet, were leaving a revival of *My Dinner with Andre* at the Coolidge Corner Cinema when a gaunt man shuffled out of the darkness, laid a hand on her shoulder, and introduced himself. Their conversation was brief but pointed. The immaculoid called her "a ruthless exterminator of defenseless babies." Natalie countered that carrying him to term might have killed her.

"Then there would have been no net loss of life," he replied.

"Evidently there was an absolute gain," Natalie said.

"I am not alive," John Snow asserted.

As he slipped back into the shadows, Helen turned to Natalie and said, "What the fuck?"

The creature kept his distance on Sunday, but then the haunting began in full, continuing unabated for the rest of the week. He attended our every waking minute, sometimes by his physical presence, more often through our troubled thoughts and acid spasms of dread. Each ticking instant lay heavy with this parody of our son—John Snow and his malign purity, his cosmic complaint, his unending devotion to our disquiet.

That summer, owing to the Caligulan protocols by which the Hawthorne English department operated, Natalie was obliged to shoulder a four-course load: Freshman Composition, British Renaissance Poetry, Greek Drama, and Arthurian Romance. Almost every time she entered the classroom, John Snow would be waiting in the far corner, slumped in a chair, clicking his fingernails on the retractable Formica writing board. He never participated in the discussions, though sometimes a non sequitur would escape his lips like a shout from a Tourette's victim. "Booted into the abyss!" "She praises humanists and murders humans!" "Never to feel my heart soar when Perry Como sings 'I Believe'!" Natalie told her undergraduates that John Snow was her highly medicated brother, recently delivered into her charge by a state mental institution. Her explanation went unquestioned. Anyone who'd taken a course in the College of Continuing Education had encountered adult students far weirder than this demented auditor.

When not harassing Natalie, the immaculoid would appear at the bookstore, gimping past the shelves, then flopping into an empty chair in the coffee bar. I allowed him to run up a tab. Most of the time he simply sat there, bathing his insensate tongue in a latte and reading a random selection from our science-fiction and fantasy shelves, though occasionally I had to endure his outbursts. "Tossed away like an orange peel!" "Deny the devil his curette!" "Impaled alive by my own parents!" Despite the discomfort he caused our customers, no one asked me to eject him. In those days many a homeless schizophrenic roamed the Boston streets, and by an unspoken ethic we shopkeepers were expected to supply these wretches with free coffee, shelter from the rain, and as much patience as we could muster.

On Tuesday and Thursday mornings, relatively tranquil periods at the store, I usually found time to speak with John Snow. Our encounters were unenlightening. He refused to tell me who had supervised his birth, how he supported himself, or where he spent his time when not hectoring his supposed parents. Only once did a question of mine catch him off guard, and he answered it with a frankness that I suspected would have displeased his maker.

"I can't help noticing you aren't a well man," I told him. "Does an immaculoid have a normal life span?"

He shook his misshapen head and coughed. "My days are numbered."

"Do you anticipate living for five more years? One more year?"

"Soon my purpose will be complete."

"What purpose? To drive me crazy? To make Natalie miserable?"

But the fetus had exhausted his reserves of candor. With the apparent aim of ending our conversation, he leaped from his chair and screamed, "Masturbate I must, but each orgasm is duller than the last!"

The customers variously gasped, moaned, giggled, and pretended to be somewhere else.

"Ejaculation without elation! Can you imagine?"

On Sunday morning Londa finally answered my e-mail. No greeting, no "Dear Mason," just a single sarcastic sentence. "When the gumbo girl was anxious to communicate with her old morality teacher, he hit Delete, and now she's supposed to roll out the fucking red carpet?"

My answer was simple. "You owe me a civil reply, and you know it."

She was back at her keyboard within the hour. "I have many enemies, but Mason Ambrose isn't one of them." She went on to say that my success as a bookseller delighted her, that she'd made *Ethics from the Earth* required reading among her staff, and that Natalie must be "a very smart lady if she decided to marry you." Concerning the John Snow crisis, Londa claimed to be as much in the dark as I. "How strange to think there's a fourth beaker freak in the world. Find your way to my door, Socrates, sooner rather than later, and we'll talk of life and its mysteries. Yolly will be thrilled to see you—Quetzie, too—and once you're actually standing in my presence, I might deign to give you a hug."

I JOURNEYED TO THEMISOPOLIS at a leisurely pace, sleeping in funky motels and prospecting for bibliographic gold in every thrift store and antique shop between Boston and Philadelphia. By the time I'd crossed the Maryland border, the trunk of my Subaru wagon held some rare Willa Cathers, a couple of Theodore Dreiser first editions, and the obscure Thomas Bergin translation of *The Divine Comedy*. I checked into a Chadds Ford bed-and-breakfast called Harriet's Hideaway, then switched on my cell phone and contacted Londa's reedy-voiced appointments secretary, who told me that tomorrow's password would be "Godzilla." I slept in Harriet's guest room, snatched a couple of warm bagels from the breakfast spread, and continued down Route 1.

No artist's brush, no photographer's lens, no digital Da Vinci's pixels could have captured the grandeur of Themisopolis in its glory days, though I could imagine Edmund Spenser's quill rising to the occasion. Book One of *The Faerie Queene* is not long under way when the Red Cross Knight is obliged to enter "a stately palace built of squared brick, which cunningly was without mortar laid." Our hero takes particular delight in the gleaming walls, "golden foil all over them displayed, that purest sky with brightness they dismayed." Approaching the City of Justice for the first time, I gasped in astonishment at the flowering cherry trees flanking Avalon Lane, the billowing fountains of Hypatia Circle, and, in the distance, the luminous marble walls of Themisopolis proper. Only when I reached the main entrance, its bronze gates flashing in the sun like the doors to God's private bank vault, did my awe turn to bewilderment. Here on the periphery of Quehannock State Park had arisen an institution consecrated to benevolence and the Beatitudes, yet it presented to the world a face as formidable as any maximum-security prison.

I deposited the Subaru in Visitor Parking and proceeded on foot, inhaling the candied scent of the cherry blossoms. Observing my approach, a wiry woman with a buzz cut sauntered out of the sentry box holding an acrylic clipboard, her sturdy frame clothed in a black leather jacket studded with surly nodes of metal. From her shoulder holster poked the snoutish grip of an automatic pistol.

"Godzilla," I said.

"Name?"

"Mason Ambrose."

The guard consulted her clipboard, handed me a map, and thumbed a button on her remote control. Gradually the mammoth gates parted, clanking and creaking as they disclosed a lavish panorama of spires, gables, clock towers, and groves of sycamores and maples.

It wasn't really a city, of course. As I strolled down Shambhala Avenue, surveying the sunny piazzas, commodious bike paths, neo-Bauhaus buildings, pleasant manicured quadrangles, and knots of passersby—scientists in lab coats, engineers in button-down denim shirts, graduate students in turtleneck sweaters—Themisopolis struck me more as a genteel community college, or perhaps a meditation retreat for Westernized Buddhists who saw no incompatibility between higher consciousness and creature comforts. Reaching the Boudicca Street intersection, I started across Alethia Square, a flagstone courtyard featuring a bronze statue of Themis herself, blindfolded as always, sword held high, her famous balance scales connected to an electric motor, so that the two pans moved in a seesaw cycle, up, down, up, down, beneath the weight of invisible deliberations.

A woman came zooming toward me on a Vespa. She jammed on the brakes, dismounted, and pulled off her helmet, unfurling a banner of auburn hair.

"Londa!" I shouted.

She looked almost the same as on that long-ago night when she'd kissed me following Proserpine's immolation—older, of course, but not significantly older: barely a day over twenty-five.

"Try again."

I immediately guessed my mistake. "Yolly!"

"Bull's-eye, Mason."

We shook hands, a ritual to which Yolly brought an improbable sensuality. "Nifty scooter," I said.

"I still prefer horses."

"Dear old Oyster."

"Believe it or not, he's among the living, collecting his pension on a farm outside Leesburg. A touch of arthritis, but the cortisone keeps him on his feet."

I told Yolly that of all my Blood Island reveries, none enchanted me more than a girl mounted on a Chincoteague pony, galloping across the scrub.

"Those were the days," she said in a neutral tone, as if those days were neither good nor bad and what mattered were the days ahead.

We proceeded to swap memories like two third-grade Sabacthanites exchanging Dame Quixote trading cards on a school playground. Donya's little planetarium, Brock's weird paintings, Charnock's uncanny chimeras, the red coral, emerald moss, psychedelic blossoms, dour alligators, manic monkeys. Much to my surprise, I learned that Yolly had always thought of me not as some aloof intellectual but as "that cool young philosopher guy who understood Londa better than Londa did."

"Sometimes I thought I understood her, yes."

"She's still the pick of the litter," Yolly said. "It's funny, we're supposed to be carbon copies of each other, but Londa got all the best traits—the brains, the drive, the looks."

"Nonsense," I said. "If I weren't married, I'd ask you to the senior prom."

"Hey, Mason, remember where you are," she said breezily. "In Themisopolis we know nothing of senior proms, double-dating, June weddings, or any of that normalcy stuff."

At which juncture, as if to corroborate Yolly's claim, two women strolled by hand in hand wearing silver-studded black leather, one partner hulking, the other merely zaftig, automatic pistols rolling on their considerable hips. Each looked as if she could ride, repair, and quite possibly dribble a motorcycle.

"Our security force is second to none," Yolly said, gesturing toward the passing daughters of Sappho. "When Jordan first got a load of them, she said they should be wearing metal brassieres and winged helmets, so we started calling them the Valkyries, which is better than what Enoch Anthem's cyberflunkies call them—the Dyke Brigade. A misnomer, by the way. Anybody can sign up as long as she's a woman and can shoot straight. About a third of our Valkyries are suburban housewives who couldn't take it anymore."

I told Yolly I was gratified to learn that Jordan hadn't dropped out of her life. She replied that in fact her legal guardian was on the payroll, coordinating the lobbying efforts of the Elizabeth Cady Stanton Foundation out of an office in D.C.

"The boss said to give you two choices," Yolly informed me. "You can grab yourself some breakfast in the Vision Institute food court, or you can have coffee with her and Quetzie right now."

"For thirteen light-years I traveled across the vast emptiness of space, searching for the lost cult of the feathered iguana. Take me to your leader."

IN A GESTURE SO BLATANTLY ALLEGORICAL it would have embarrassed even Edmund Spenser, Londa had sited her headquarters atop the tallest building in Themisopolis, a graceful fieldstone tower known as Caedmon Hall. Hera in her heavenly palace. Ishtar in her Sumerian aerie. Yolly and I ascended via a glass elevator, the glimmering car shooting skyward like the Eighth Avenue Express roaring through a vertical subway tunnel. We disembarked into a stylish reception area appointed with live ferns and dead postimpressionists, presided over by Londa's appointments secretary, Gertrude Lingard of the reedy voice and, I now learned, the equally reedy physique. Beyond lay a labyrinth of offices, the largest of which belonged to the sloe-eyed Dagmar Röhrig, who had famously turned down a Hollywood contract to become Londa's manager. The beauteous Sabacthanite was too busy yelling at somebody over the phone to engage us in conversation, but she flashed us an efficient smile and waved toward the holy of holies. Yolly rolled back a frosted-glass door, and we proceeded across a semicircular space so thickly carpeted it was like walking on an immense sponge, the curved picture windows offering epic views of the surrounding farmlands, until we reached a terrace crowded with flowering plants, their fronds and vines fountaining from earthenware pots.

The first time I ever saw Londa, she was emerging from the floral embrace of a tropical rain forest, and now once again she appeared before me wreathed in blossoms—tulips, lilacs, orchids, plus several hybrids I couldn't identify—Quetzie perched on one shoulder, the opposite hand gripping a transparent watering can shaped like an alchemist's alembic. Instead of a crown she wore a telephone headset, and before acknowledging my presence she spoke into the spindly microphone, telling her listener—an annoying person, to judge from her tone, a politician or lawyer or Phyllistine—that there was nothing more to discuss, then removed the headset and extended her hand. Our fingers connected, and the gesture instantly transmuted into a protracted hug.

"It's been an eternity," she said.

"Much too long, at any rate," I said.

"An eternity and then some," she said, breaking our embrace. She was dressed all in white, as if intending to portray the False Florimell at a costume party. White cotton slacks, white silk blouse, white linen jacket, white silk scarf. Time had largely exempted her from its passage: a few creases around her mouth, some crow's-feet stamped by a fledgling crow—that was all. To my bookseller's sensibility, she suggested a leather-bound volume so skillfully crafted that years of affectionate thumbing had left only the faintest traces.

"Believe me, dear," I said, "the last thing you needed this past decade was a Darwinist Jiminy Cricket lodged in your ear, singing his advice."

"As a matter of fact, it was the *first* thing I needed."

Sensing that a quarrel might be brewing, Yolly stepped between us. She kissed my cheek, urged me to drop by more often, patted the iguana on the head, and reminded her sister to call Senator Kitto by three o'clock. Londa relaxed, as did her auxiliary conscience.

"Quetzie is a handsome devil," the iguana squawked.

Diplomatic mission accomplished, Yolly excused herself and trotted off, explaining that she had a meeting with the Wollstone-craft Fund.

"She sleeps with women," Londa informed me. "Men, too. If there were a third sex, she'd sample it as well."

"I had a feeling."

"I sailed to Lesbos once, along with a ravenous save-the-whales lady named Loretta—pretty thrilling while it lasted, but I'm not really wired that way. Have you ever wanted to screw a man?"

"Only Oscar Wilde, and he's seeing somebody else."

"Quetzie is a handsome devil," the iguana said.

"I wish I could be more like Yolly," Londa said. "She finds time for—I believe it's called *fun*. Goes skiing in Vermont. Plays poker with the Valkyries. Follows her libido where it leads her. It's strange, my little sister is really my *big* sister, somebody I can look up to. For two years now, she's been working on a fantasy novel about a mystical book nobody can understand."

"If she needs a model, let me suggest anything by Heidegger."

"I've read the first chapter. Wonderful stuff, very erotic." She stroked her iguana's plumage. "Guess what, Quetzie? On his way over here, Mason started wondering if I'll try coaxing him down to my secret beach."

"The last thing on my mind," I said, though it was actually the second thing on my mind, the first being John Snow.

She took my hand, massaging the palm, then guided me toward a coffee bar as elaborate as the one that kept Pieces of Mind afloat. "Don't worry, we goody-goody altar girls aren't into adultery, though it happens that my bedroom"—she gestured vaguely toward a dark alcove—"is twenty feet away."

"You sleep in your office?"

"I sleep, eat, drink, scheme, and wrestle private demons here."

"You should get out more."

"Jordan tells me the same thing. You moralists all think alike."

"Cogito ergo sum," Quetzie noted.

"Until two weeks ago, I was dating a computer geek," Londa said. "A sweet guy, very sincere, but he never understood the difference between a relationship and a flow chart. Before that I fell for a film professor at Georgetown. We broke up because I didn't cry at the end of *La Strada*. Somewhere along the line I had a wild affair with a tennis instructor from Owings Mills. Opposites attract. They attract, and they stick together, and then nothing else happens. The verdict is in, Mason. I'm not cut out for romance."

Computer geek, Fellini scholar, tennis instructor: I loved every one of Londa's suitors, for without their attentions she would probably have tracked me down in person and thrown my life into disarray. I also hated them. How dare they presume to know my vatling's heart?

I lifted a glass carafe from the burner and filled a mug bearing the Themisopolis logo, Lady Justice on a galloping horse, balance scales held high. When the brew touched my tongue, I shuddered to experience the familiar flavor of rococonut milk.

"I detect a trace of Proserpine," I said.

"Not enough to cause an opium dream, just your basic euphoria-inducing dosage." Londa filled her own mug, a real collector's item decorated with Weill and Brecht's Pirate Jenny waving a cutlass and saying, THAT'LL LEARN YA. She sipped. "The crop we harvested is still in the Faustino freezer. Henry sends us a shipment every now and then. The Hallucinogen-of-the-Month Club."

I swallowed some tranquillity and said, "Londa, I'm going to ask this only once. Are you the cause of my immaculoid?"

She fluted her lips, siphoning up a measure of well-being. "We must approach this mystery rationally. Do I have a motive to torment you? Let me think. If it weren't for those goddamn ethics tutorials, I might be leading an enviable existence right now. House in the suburbs, white picket fence, golden retriever, a couple of kids. But thanks to you the house burned down, the fence collapsed, the dog ran away, and the kids are in jail."

"I ruined your life, no doubt about it. But I still need to hear you had nothing—"

"I had nothing to do with your immaculoid." She fixed me with her fiercest basilisk stare. "Do you believe that?"

"Yes." I did.

"All you need is love," Quetzie said.

"I imagine this Mr. Snow has put a strain on your marriage," Londa said.

"We'll survive."

"I must meet your fortunate bride."

"She's one of your biggest admirers."

"As you may have noticed, I've got a regular goddamn fan club," Londa said, sucking coffee through the crack in her smirk. "I used to be a member, but then I outgrew the whole thing. There comes a time in every girl's life when she throws away her *League of Londa* comic books."

Spontaneously we drifted toward a conference table holding an architect's model as intricate as Donya's toy amusement park. It was all there, Londa's riposte to the Phyllistines—the Vision Syndicate, the Artemis Clinic, Arcadia House, the Institute for Advanced Biological Investigations. The longer I contemplated this solar-powered El Dorado, the more it received my begrudging esteem. How far my pupil had come since her Faustino days of chain-smoking Dunhills

and wondering how she might insert "fuck" into her next depen-
dent clause. God knows I wasn't about to acquire a Dame Quixote
T-shirt, but perhaps I'd been wrong to turn my back on Themisopolis.

"Edwina would be proud of you," I said.

"And what about my auxiliary conscience? Is he proud of me?"

"Your auxiliary conscience thinks he must've done something
right."

"There's a good chance Yolly and I will leave the world a better
place than we found it," she said in a corroborating tone. "Don't tell
anybody, but the Susan B. Anthony Trust is about to supply the U.N.
with enough information to nail more than a hundred traffickers in
female sexual slavery. Operation Velvet Fist. And we've got another
miracle in the pipeline. You've never heard of a drug called Xelcepin, but after the institute runs some clinical trials, we hope to announce a breakthrough in the treatment of ovarian cancer."

For the first time in years, a snippet from *The Egyptian* flashed
through my brain—the courtesan disrobing before Sinuhe, showing him the malignancy that had deformed her beauty. No wonder
drugs for Nefer. Only suffering and blood and futile prayers to
Isis.

"In certain contexts, my difficulties with John Snow seem triv-
ial," I said.

Londa's next remark caught me by surprise. "You know what's
appalling about you, Socrates?" she said, passing a hand over the
miniature city.

"Pray tell. What's appalling about me?"

"You think I had a choice about all this. You think Themisopolis
was an act of free will."

"Of *course* you had a choice."

"I'm trapped, dearest Mason. I'm locked inside my own lousy
comic book, Dame Quixote versus the whole goddamn Phyllistine
world." She grasped my shoulders, rotating me until our eyes met.

"Don't you have *any* idea what you did to me? Are you *completely* clueless?"

"Not *completely*."

"You carved a thousand facets in my face, so I'd never run out of cheeks to turn. You took the stone that never hit the adulteress and hung it around my neck." She issued an indecipherable laugh, then released her grip. "All signs point to Charnock."

"I had the same thought," I said, pleased to realize she'd changed the subject. "Unfortunately, he's dropped off the face of the earth."

"And landed in the armpit. Armpit, North Carolina, to be precise, otherwise known as Jacob's Notch, an insolvent little town on the Pasquotank River. He's become an aquatic hermit, living on a houseboat. Once a month I get a screed from his laptop, no punctuation, all lowercase. Our species has lost its collective mind. Modernity is a swindle. The future belongs to the ants."

"Did he mention making another vatling?"

"Nope. Shall I have a Valkyrie ride down to Jacob's Notch and give the old man a scare? Major Powers would be good for the job. She'd crack him like a walnut."

"Thanks. I'd like to try a simple conversation first."

Not far from the Vision Syndicate replica lay an object resembling a hockey puck. In fact, it was a hockey puck. The label read CIRCUS OF ATONEMENT. "And what goes on here?" I asked, pointing to the thick disk. "Gladiatorial combat?"

"Testosterone has no friends in Themisopolis."

"Then what?"

"Our chief source of recreation."

"What sort of recreation?"

"A *secret* recreation," Londa replied, her tone clarifying that the topic would enjoy no further elaboration just then. Again she waved her hand over the model City of Justice. "You'd be amazed at all the details the architects got into this thing." She pointed toward the building in which our fractious and disjointed encounter was now occurring. "Pop the roof off Caedmon Hall here, and you'll see a tiny clockwork Londa trading barbs with her old morality teacher. Can you stay for lunch? I'll order Chinese, and afterwards we'll drop by the Circus for some postprandial entertainment."

A tempting offer, as I was truly enjoying her company, but my obligation to Natalie came first. "I have an appointment with the Mad Doctor of Blood Island," I said, edging toward the rolling glass door. "I'll let you know if I need you to sic Major Powers on him. Anything to get that damn immaculoid out of Natalie's life."

"Not only is he a great conscience, folks, he's also a loving husband."

I slid back the door and crossed the threshold. "If there's a stone around your neck, it's because you put it there."

"No, Socrates. You did it. I wonder if I'll ever forgive you."

NOON FOUND ME EMBEDDED in a traffic jam on the D.C. Beltway, mired and miserable like the carp Londa had almost drowned on the Faustino patio. I called Natalie and told her I was bound for North Carolina, hot on the trail of Vincent Charnock, the likely source of our difficulties. "Assuming he's the culprit," I asked, "is there any message you want me to give him?"

"John Snow came to my Arthurian Romance class this morning," Natalie said. "He kept quiet the whole hour, and then he started screaming, 'She wouldn't take the risk!' Here's my message to Dr. Charnock. 'I hope you fucking rot in hell.'"

I circumvented D.C., then headed southeast until I reached Norfolk, where I checked into a Wanderer's Lodge, flagship of a burgeoning hotel chain whose self-conscious name, postmodern décor, and pop-cult mystique catered to middle-class bohemian nomads who fancied themselves following in Kerouac's exhaust fumes. My sleep was fitful and dreamless—perhaps I never slept at all—and shortly after 9:00 A.M. I hit the road again, three Wanderer's Lodge cranberry muffins huddled in my stomach like scoops of library paste. Soon I reached the Carolina border, where the essential sign appeared, JACOB'S NOTCH NEXT EXIT. Once I was within the town proper, getting a fix on Charnock proved simple. The scraggly young man who ran the bait shop, the wisecracking belle behind the 7-Eleven cash register, and the skinny kid skateboarding across the First Baptist Church parking lot all eagerly pointed the way. It was as if the locals knew that one of these days the crazy misanthrope living on the river would have a visitor—an estranged brother, an IRS agent, a private detective, a hit man.

When I finally came upon my quarry, he was slumped in a captain's chair on the afterdeck of his houseboat, smoking a cigarette and staring at a stand of cattails, a depleted fifth of Old Kentucky bourbon snugged between his bare feet. He rubbed the bottle with his toes. A tattered straw hat sheltered him from the sun. I couldn't decide which was the greater wreck, Charnock's body or the dilapidated vessel he called home. Moored to a floating dock, the *Ursula* was a conglomeration of warped planks, rusty nails, and a superstructure suggesting a derelict chicken coop. Of the paint job little remained but leprous scabs and burst blisters.

"Hello, Vincent."

Evidently he recognized my voice, for without lifting his head he said, "I figured you'd show up one day, Ambrose. Did you come to question me, kiss me, or kill me?"

I stepped from the wharf to the afterdeck. Strangely, the boards didn't crumble beneath my feet. "Kiss you?"

"For inventing the machine that resurrected your son."

"John Snow is not my son."

"And Brutus is an honorable man," Charnock said, winching himself to his feet. He tossed his cigarette in the water, picked up the Old Kentucky bottle, and poured the few remaining swallows into a plastic tumbler embossed with the Creature from the Black Lagoon. Spiky whiskers speckled his jaw and neck, so that his head suggested an immense seed pod looking to attach itself to a passing sweater.

"The bastards betrayed me, Ambrose. They promised to keep me in the loop. They lied."

"What bastards?"

"The ones who hired me to teach them the art of ontogenesis. Their leader was in the news a couple of months ago, railing against Operation Redneck."

"Enoch Anthem?"

"That's the bastard."

"I've never even *met* Enoch Anthem. Why the hell would he single out Natalie and me?"

"It was the *other* bastard who singled you out. Anthem's consigliere—you know who I mean?"

"No."

"That tough-as-nails postrationalist up in Boston. Felix Pielmeister. I gather you two have a history."

"Pielmeister? Jesus."

"I also gather that the professor and you and a glamorous complit lady used to hang around the same bookstore, and it wasn't long before he figured out you and she were an item, eventually a pregnant item. When he realized you'd gotten an abortion, he decided your fetus should become the first of the mackies."

I moaned and gripped the gunwale. Pielmeister. Horus help me. Isis be my light. During the past week I'd driven nine hundred miles, traveled through eight different states, and slept in five strange beds, and it turned out that the answer to the mystery lay on my doorstep—or as Dorothy told Glinda at the end of Donya's favorite movie, "If I ever go looking for my heart's desire again, I won't look any further than my own backyard, because if it isn't there, I never really lost it to begin with," a sentiment whose breathtaking incoherence I'd never fully appreciated before.

"You have to realize, this project of Pielmeister's was never mostly about him settling an old score with you," Charnock continued. "He and Anthem are out to get *everybody* who did what you did.

I must admit, even though they stabbed me in the back, I'm damn impressed with those two. They have moral fiber. Think about it. Six thousand fetuses stalking their unfeeling quasiparents—the greatest antiabortion protest in history!"

"Six thousand? Thundering Christ."

Charnock pressed the tumbler to his lips and let the bourbon trickle into his throat. "Anthem's organization paid me a fortune for the RXL-313 schematics, and now they've got three ontogenerators, maybe four. Your John Snow is actually John Snow 0001. Next will come John Snow 0002, followed by John Snow 0003, not to mention Jane Snow 0001 and all her sisters. I didn't want the three million dollars. I gave it to the Red Cross. What I wanted was to be in the loop." He pulled off his straw hat and fanned his sweating face with the brim. "There are wheels within wheels here, Ambrose. Everybody's heard of the Center for Stable Families, but nobody knows it's a beard for a subterranean network called CHALICE, the Christian Alliance of Immaculoids, Chiliasts, and Evangelicals. And here's the rub. The CHALICE biologists don't understand the RXLs. They miss the nuances. Did you know that if a newborn baby started listening to a recital of the human genome sequence, that monotonous melody of G's and T's and C's and A's, he'd still be hearing it when he turned fifty, the same damn base notes, guanine, thymine, cytosine, adenine, over and over in countless combinations? As a matter of fact, the song doesn't end until he's ready to die. No wonder CHALICE screwed it up. No wonder your son has an atrophied arm and a crooked spine, not to mention his limp—he's got a limp, right?"

"And a lazy eye. He says his days are numbered."

"When the mackies start dying like flies, Anthem will realize what a blunder he made, taking me out of the loop. Thirsty?"

"Now that you mention it."

In a gesture more affectionate than he might normally have accorded an unfeeling quasiparent, Charnock set his hand against my back and guided me toward the superstructure. We crossed a mildewed parlor, its fitted benches stacked with books, mostly Russian novels—I don't know whether, per his gazebo conversation with Edwina, he'd gotten around to reading *War and Peace,* but at least he owned a copy—and proceeded to the galley. A diverse collection of half-empty wine and liquor bottles crowded the countertop, obscuring the buckled Formica.

"What's your pleasure?"

"How about a rum and Coke? Hold the rum."

Charnock opened his built-in refrigerator and removed a solitary Diet Pepsi. "Don't you want me to hold the Coke instead?"

"I never consume alcohol before noon."

"Neither do I." He handed me the Pepsi, then screwed open a fresh Old Kentucky bottle and splashed several ounces into his Gill Man tumbler.

"It's eleven-thirty."

"Not in Madrid."

I ripped the tab off my Pepsi, then chugged down all twelve ounces in the same short interval that Charnock required to finish his bourbon.

"So tell me, what's the most fascinating thing about your son?" he asked. "His bedrock nihilism? His bottomless contempt for his parents?"

"He's not my son," I said.

"Sorry. Forgot."

"He's not."

"Right."

I realized I was staring at a box of Earl Grey wedged between a quart of brandy and a fifth of vodka. "Might I have some tea?"

"Caffeine is bad for your digestion." Charnock filled a small copper kettle with water, set it to boiling atop his Primus stove. "Let me tell you something. Even after I came to detest Edwina's project, I still admired her style. A decisive woman. She got a craving for total motherhood, and so she made it happen. Adorable Donya, vivacious Yolly, brooding Londa."

Two minutes later my host yanked the screaming kettle off the stove, filled a grimy ceramic mug, and began dipping a tea bag up and down in the hot water as if making a candle. He gave me my tea, then replenished his tumbler with bourbon. We drank in silence, drifting through the superstructure and back onto the afterdeck. The sun beat down on the river, baking the sodden banks into aromatic loaves of mud.

"You obviously came to question me," Charnock said at last. "But what about kiss and kill?"

"Neither."

"You signed off on your own son's murder, yet you balk at shooting a useless old drunk? Philosophers are supposed to be rational."

"The D and C was absolutely necessary," I hissed. "Natalie might've died of a blood clot." A quick, short leap brought me from the *Ursula* to the dock. "Thanks for the tea. The conversation, too. My wife sends you a message. 'I hope you fucking rot in hell.'"

As I started up the hill toward town, I realized I was still holding Charnock's ceramic mug, a situation I immediately remedied by smashing it against a rock.

"They're coming, Ambrose, six thousand strong!" he called after me. "The greatest political demonstration of all time! The whole world will tremble beneath their unborn feet! Ontological terrorism elevated to an art form!"

THE IMMACULOIDS WERE COMING. Ontological terrorism. Lurid as it sounded, I had no reason to doubt Charnock's forecast, and so upon returning to Norfolk I pulled into a Dunkin' Donuts, grabbed my phone, and, after pleading my case to Gertrude Lingard, got Londa on the line. If Charnock could be believed, I told her, he'd sold his soul and his schematics to a shadowy society whose members included not only Enoch Anthem but also the very professor with whom I'd sparred during my dissertation defense.

"They call themselves CHALICE," I said. "The Christian Alliance of Immaculoids, Chiliasts, and Evangelicals."

"Beware of Phyllistines bearing acronyms," Londa said.

"Charnock thinks they have at least three ontogenerators. They're planning to cook up an army of fetuses and set them loose on the world."

"What a totally atrocious idea."

"It was a dark day when Anthem and Pielmeister found each other, and a darker day when they learned about Charnock's damn machine."

"Raiders of the Lost Christian Consensus. Keep me posted, Socrates."

Next I called Natalie. The news of Pielmeister's involvement flabbergasted her, but she was cheerier than the last time we'd talked. Our fetus had not attended the most recent meetings of British Renaissance Poetry, Greek Drama, or Arthurian Romance.

"Listen, darling, this shitty thing we're going through, Charnock says it's about to happen to *lots* of couples."

"How many is lots?"

"Thousands."

"Is that supposed to comfort me?"

"I thought it might. Does it?"

"No. Maybe. I don't know. Hurry home. If I have to deal with that fucker again, I'm going to jump out a window."

I spent the next thirteen hours on the road, stopping only to empty my bladder and fill my gas tank. By 2:00 A.M., Natalie and I were lying in bed together, conjoined like adjacent jigsaw-puzzle pieces, drifting off to sleep.

A storm was raging when I awoke, alone now, the thick gray rain clattering on the windows like scrabbling claws. My stomach seemed filled with electrified acid, as if I were digesting a flashlight battery. I glanced at the alarm clock. It was almost noon. Soon Natalie would be back from British Renaissance Poetry. I staggered to the kitchen and phoned Dexter, telling him about the rarities I'd scored en route to Maryland. He said we'd sold two copies of *Ethics from the Earth* while I was gone and that the schizophrenic I'd taken under my wing had been asking about me.

Natalie and I entered the living room from opposite directions, our gaits identical, a despairing shuffle. Stark red veins encircled her eyes like meridians, their lids swollen with weeping.

"I don't hate him, not exactly," she said. "But I can't take much more of this."

My anger was primal, fury refined to a malignant elixir. I became my own sort of immaculoid, pure in wrath, pristine in spite, and it was this incarnation of Mason Ambrose who now grabbed an umbrella, rushed into the storm, and drove nine blocks to the Silbersack Building, home of the philosophy department. I dashed down the second-floor hallway like a small but implacable cyclone, then blew uninvited into Pielmeister's office, an exquisite little sanctum, all oak wainscoting, teak molding, and cedar beams. No doubt he had appointed it himself. Augustinians knew their wood.

Pielmeister stood hunched over a cardboard carton, filling it with books. He was doing it exactly wrong, jamming the corners of the covers against each other when he should have been laying the volumes spine to spine. The denuded shelves held only a few forlorn paperbacks, plus the half dozen awards he'd won for his theological treatises. One such commendation depicted Hugh of St. Victor, another represented Thomas Aquinas. Spiritual bowling trophies.

"Good afternoon, Ambrose." His supreme tranquillity sent a chill through my bones. "Let me guess. You've been connecting the dots."

"I'd like to connect a gila monster to your scrotum."

He fiddled with the carton flaps and after several attempts managed to interlace them. "Whatever inconvenience John Snow is causing you, it's nothing compared with the anguish you inflicted on *him*."

"Fuck you."

"Fuck me indeed. But why confine ourselves to generalities? If we're going to have one of your nuanced secular discussions, let's fuck me in the ear and fuck me in the eye and fuck me up the ass."

He seized the carton and bustled out of the room. I followed directly behind him like a mackie dogging its quasiparent.

"Changing offices?" I asked. "Or did you get fired for bullying one too many grad students?"

"I'm leaving this place."

"Really? You're breaking my heart. I'll have to keep reminding myself that the Hawthorne community's loss is Enoch Anthem's gain. I'm right, aren't I? Anthem offered you a job?"

"Matter of fact, I'll be heading up his Bureau of Apologetics."

"Congratulations," I said, then added, hoping to unnerve him, "Maybe you'll get to lead the great antiabortion protest Charnock told me about."

Pielmeister remained his usual granite self. "You would do well to ignore half of what Charnock says and discount the other half. The man's delusional."

"Ontological terrorism, he called it."

"I don't know what you're talking about."

For the next several minutes, I became Pielmeister's doppelgänger, matching his steps as he exited the building and made his way across Parking Area C to his Ford SUV. The rain had stopped. Puddles dotted the macadam like shards of a shattered mirror. Pielmeister opened the hatch, which was already stuffed with book boxes, and attempted to insert the last carton. He failed. He rotated the carton about its horizontal axis. Again he failed. He tried the vertical axis. No luck. I'd always known that academics were people who got paid to problematize the putting of square pegs into square holes, but I'd never before seen such a vivid demonstration.

Pielmeister set the carton on the passenger seat, slammed the door, and looked me in the eye. "Wake up, Ambrose. History is happening right in front of your nose, and you're totally blind to it. Even as we speak, Protestantism and Anglicanism are melting back into their parent Catholicism, and soon that great insatiable body will suck up all the rest, Eastern Orthodox Mariolaters, American heartland charismatics, sodbusting Mormon polygamists, speakers-in-tongues, thinkers-in-apocalypses, snake handlers, scorpion swallowers, wasp whisperers, until Christendom has once again been made whole, pole to pole, crust to core, Greenwich to Gisborne and back again!"

"With liberty and justice for all blastocysts."

"Go ahead, scoff. Scoff all you want. The paradigm shift is upon us, sweeping away the things of Caesar and Sabacthani. Nominalist and humanist, queer and condom monger, peacenik and Bolshevik—doomed, damned, every last one of you. Checkmate, sir. Twilight of the iconoclasts. Secularism is dead, Christ has switched off the Enlightenment, and that exotic bird, the ruby-throated Darwinist, will soon go extinct as the dodo."

"Charnock tells me you've got thousands of immaculoids in the works."

"Give up, Ambrose," Pielmeister said, smiling through his beard. "Tip your king. Corporate Christi has arrived. We're putting the crucifixion back where it belongs, dead center, but this time no silly trickles when the spike hits the Savior—now we'll get a geyser, spurt city, oiling the gears of the paradigm shift, jetting clear to heaven."

"My wife is having a nervous breakdown," I said.

"She has a conscience, then?"

"You shit."

"The amoeboid conscience of Natalie Novak."

Deep within some subbasement of my brain, a hideous id-thing cracked out of its egg. My gorge rose like lava fountaining from a volcano, and I lunged at Pielmeister, closing my hands around his throat.

214

He broke my grip. I slapped his cheek. He stomped on my foot. I grabbed his beard and spit in his face. Is there anything quite so ludicrous as two intellectuals grappling in a philosophy-department parking lot? Each of us wanted to pummel the other to a pulp, but neither knew how to go about it. We couldn't even name the blows, much less inflict them deliberately. Quite possibly we were landing uppercuts, roundhouses, sidewinders, haymakers, and bolo punches. There was no way to tell. Eyes turned black, knuckles acquired the look and texture of uncooked bacon, and lips burst open like blood packets on a Sam Peckinpah set. Somehow Pielmeister scrambled behind the wheel of his SUV, started the engine, and pulled away, enveloping me in a stinking aura of greenhouse gases.

I yanked the phone from my jacket and called Natalie.

"I beat him up," I told her.

"Beat who up?"

"Pielmeister. He did the same to me. We drew blood."

"Can you get home by yourself?"

"With more blood to come. Spurt city. The world is changing, Natalie. Corporate Christi has arrived, and soon we'll all be crushed, you and me and the Sisters Sabacthani. Well, maybe not Londa. No, never Londa. I made her out of steel. When this nightmare is finally over, my vatling will still be standing."

Chapter 10

THE MARCH OF THE IMMACULOIDS began early in October, suffusing the normally genial ghoulishness of the Halloween season—the grinning rictus of the jack-o'-lantern, the clownish gyrations of the rubber skeleton, the cartoon malevolence of the cardboard witch—with authentic horror and genuine dread. No group was exempt from the plague. The walking unborn descended upon rich and poor alike, black and white, Jew and Gentile, Catholic and Protestant, atheist and evangelical. Hundreds of semifathers endured humiliation at the hands of their fetuses, but it was the semi-mothers who suffered the most, particularly those who'd kept their pregnancies and subsequent abortions a secret: teenagers who'd never told their parents, wives who'd been thinking of leaving their husbands, mistresses who'd decided things were already complicated enough.

While the immaculoids' coming was theoretically the sort of graphic and sensational event on which the television medium thrives, the networks simply couldn't get an angle on it. Convinced that the phenomenon was essentially an epic human-interest drama, CNN, Fox News, MSNBC, and the rest initially broadcast a panoply of feature stories, all cleaving to the same maudlin plot. Act one, the mackie appears on his quasiparents' doorstep and is rebuffed. Act two, the quasiparents see the light. Act three, the fetus is welcomed into the family. The problem was that the story typically included a fourth act, and the network was now obliged to present a follow-up report that nobody wanted to see. How John Snow 0714 set his quasiparents' house on fire. How Jane Snow 2039 got her semifather arrested on a false charge of sexual abuse. How John Snow 1190 switched his semimother's birth control pills for placebos, with predictable consequences. How Jane Snow 1347 bankrupted her quasiparents by transferring all their savings to the South Dakota Pro-Life Coalition.

In some cases the TV journalists were forced to file dispatches from a realm they normally avoided at all costs, the low-ratings domain of acid irony and mirthless absurdity. One immediately thinks of John Snow 2047, crucifying himself on the lawn of the family's ranch house, a martyrdom made possible by the carpentry skills of his twin brother, John Snow 2048. Then there was Jane Snow 1264, summarily executing her quasiparents with a Colt .45, a case that the antiabortion judge dismissed on grounds of retroactive self-defense. And John Snow 0339, brutally impregnating his sixteen-year-old semisister, who shortly thereafter announced that, having discussed the matter at length with Enoch Anthem, she would bring the baby to term.

Of course, the average immaculoid narrative was neither heartwarming nor horrifying but merely sad. The fetus came knocking, and the beleaguered semimother would subsequently find herself divorced or disowned or both, end of story. "We've never seen such a potent and dramatic pro-life demonstration, and we salute the anonymous activists who organized it," enthused George Collander of BUBBA, Baptists United against Butchery, Bestiality, and Abomination. The therapeutic community was equally keen on the mackies, who'd triggered among the semimothers a bizarre variation on postpartum depression, "reversed-abortion angst," as one psychiatrist termed it. Faced with the unprecedented epidemic, scores of previously underpatronized counselors and analysts were blessed with more cases than they could handle.

Given the degree of public indignation over the immaculoids' excesses, Attorney General Monica Giroux made a perfunctory stab at locating their creators and enjoining these ontological activists against further mischief. When the federal grand jury asked for my deposition, I revealed what Vincent Charnock had told me—that two of America's leading postrationalists, Enoch Anthem and Felix Pielmeister, were planning to unleash legions of aborted fetuses on their unsuspecting quasiparents. Naturally the jury sought to subpoena Charnock so he could corroborate my accusations, but he and his houseboat had vanished without a trace. For reasons best known to himself, the father of the RXL-313 was presumably hiding in an obscure cove along the Intercoastal Waterway.

In defending his client, Anthem's lawyer cleverly cast my testimony as the fantasies of a man "whose previous attempt to win an audience for his atheism took the form of a ludicrous Darwinist tract called *Ethics from the Earth*." He went on to explain how in my former capacity as Londa's tutor, I had "gleefully filled her head with the materialist philosophy that underlies Themisopolis." Pielmeister's lawyer had an even easier time impugning my motives. Bitter over the professor's disinclination to support my Ph.D. candidacy, I now sought revenge by "forging a spurious link between this controversial pro-life demonstration and one of America's most respected theologians." After twenty minutes of deliberation, the grand jury declined to indict either man.

Today it's generally acknowledged that if Alexander Hornbeam, that most pious of FBI directors, had instructed his agents to monitor our nation's abortion clinics, sooner or later they would have caught an Anthem acolyte in the act of pilfering some D and C residue. By subpoenaing the hard drives and filing cabinets of the Center for

Stable Families, this same Hornbeam could have uncovered a trail leading to the penumbral organization called CHALICE. Given the man's attitude toward all things fetal, however, this simply wasn't going to happen. As he told one CNN reporter, "Naturally I'm concerned that so many women are being bothered, annoyed, inconvenienced, and driven to suicide, but isn't it high time that a day of reckoning befell America's pro-death feminists?"

At first Natalie and I didn't understand why we enjoyed a better relationship with John Snow 0001 than most quasiparents had with their fetuses. Eventually we figured out that CHALICE was programming its pawns with ever-increasing levels of vindictiveness. As the primal immaculoid, ours was also the least hostile, endowed with sufficient free will to make Natalie and me not merely the focus of his scorn but also the objects of his curiosity.

That year, we decided to attempt a quiet Christmas at home. Natalie's parents had recently moved to São Paulo so that her father, a retired political-science professor, could research his book about globalization. My own progenitors, meanwhile, were inhabiting their respective vales of self-delusion, Mom living with a Dallas real-estate agent who'd promised to make her rich, Dad writing a spec screenplay while holed up in a Los Angeles efficiency apartment down the street from my sister Delia, who was presently enjoying syndicated celebrity status as Scarlet O'Horror, hostess of *Frisson Theater*. Natalie and I agreed, however, that if the opportunity presented itself, we would ask John Snow 0001 to spend Christmas Eve with us—and the opportunity indeed arose, one blustery December afternoon when we all coincidentally converged on the Pieces of Mind coffee bar. It was Natalie who made the pitch, interlacing her sentences with so much hemming, hawing, and verbal filigree that at first John Snow 0001 didn't realize what she was getting at. When he finally grasped the nature of her invitation, our netherson insisted he had other plans for that particular night. We were simultaneously saddened and relieved—saddened because he was, after all, our fetus, relieved because we had no desire to spend any night, and most especially Christmas Eve, answering accusations of homicide.

On the morning of December 25, shortly after dawn, our barbaric door buzzer, that chain saw in the brain, shattered our sleep and catapulted us from bed. Even before reaching the window, I'd guessed who the intruder must be. I glanced toward the street, and there he was, standing on the front stoop, gripping a large canvas tote bag and stomping the snow off his boots.

"If he tries to intimidate me," Natalie said, "I'll spit in his eye."

"Scramble some eggs," I told her.

"I think not."

Reeling with approach-avoidance syndrome, I descended to the ground floor and greeted our fetus with a tepid "Merry Christmas, Mr. Snow."

"Merry Christmas, Father," he replied in a splintery whisper, stepping into the foyer. He wore a down-filled orange parka and a ragged woolen scarf. "Christmas is the birthday of Jesus Christ, a fact you doubtless knew."

"And of Isaac Newton."

"Jesus Christ is the Savior of mankind," John Snow 0001 said. "Have no fear—this visit won't last more than twenty minutes." He set down the tote bag and rubbed his chest with his functional hand. "I don't really mind the cold. An unpleasant feeling is better than none."

As we mounted the stairs, the immaculoid explained that his nervous system had finally started delivering sensations. Stimuli were getting through. Qualia no longer eluded him. Biting wind, burning matches, stirring marches, soothing lullabies, anchovies, chocolate bars, creosote, thorns.

"Last night I had a bad headache," he said, "which means I had a *good* headache—do you follow my reasoning, Father?"

"I believe I do."

Natalie was waiting for us in her threadbare red terry-cloth bathrobe. Briefly I took satisfaction in my knowledge that a blue velour caftan would soon supplant this pathetic rag. She extended her hand. Our fetus grasped it firmly, then leaned forward and kissed her cheek. She clenched her teeth, the skin along her jaw growing tight as a drumhead.

"I'm not a monster, Mother," he told her.

"Neither am I," she replied.

"Let me take your coat," I offered.

John Snow 0001 popped the line of brass buttons on his parka, but instead of shedding it he shuffled toward our gaudily decorated Christmas tree, a portly Scotch pine rising from an atoll of presents wrapped in recycled Sunday funnies. "I've brought gifts," he announced proudly, lifting his tote bag high.

"How thoughtful," Natalie said evenly. Now a softness entered her voice, plaintive to a degree that probably surprised her. "We didn't get you anything. I'm sorry, Mr. Snow."

With supreme logic our netherson replied, "You didn't know I was coming."

He proceeded to distribute our gifts. Natalie received a pendant he'd made by braiding bits of aluminum foil into a long, crinkled snake, then bending it into a heart shape. She slipped the twine loop around her neck, aligning the pendant between the lapels of her robe. The red terry cloth showed the silver foil to good advantage. I received a necktie made of nylon swatches cut from a discarded umbrella. The third gift was for both of us, a goldfish bowl containing two grasshoppers that John Snow 0001 had caught the previous summer and, against the odds, kept alive for six months. He'd outfitted their habitat with grass and twigs. Amory and Claudius were orphans, he explained. They wanted Natalie and me to adopt them.

I set the bowl on our favorite piece of furniture, a sleek, glass-doored bookcase from IKEA. The top shelf held six copies of *Ethics from the Earth* flanked by *The Phenomenology of Spirit* and *Tractatus-Logico Philosophicus*. In the outside world, Hegel and Wittgenstein kept company only with other geniuses, but here they had to associate with me.

"Would you like to stay for breakfast?" I asked the immaculoid, then immediately thought better of the idea. I turned to Natalie, soliciting forgiveness. Her eyes released daggers and other pointed objects.

"This has been a good visit," John Snow 0001 replied, "but I should get home before my rage boils up again."

"Where is home?" I asked.

Strangely enough, his answer was straightforward. "They've put us up in all sorts of places. Flophouses, church basements, college dorms, abandoned buildings, the YMCA. At the moment I'm living in a tower."

"What tower?" Natalie asked.

With his working hand John Snow 0001 caressed the star atop our Christmas tree. "It's a good place. Plenty of room. I did nothing to deserve that trip to the abortionist."

"The Prudential Tower?" I asked. "The Hancock Building? A clock tower? A bell tower?"

Bending low, our netherson pressed his face into the pine branches. The needles brushed his newly sensate cheeks. He inhaled deeply and declared, "This is surely how a pleasant fragrance smells." He took a step backward. "And the visual appearance—for a person who came from a womb, such a sight would be entirely lovely. I, too, find it agreeable."

"Do you need anything in your tower?" Natalie asked. "A blanket? An air mattress?"

A barking laugh spilled from the immaculoid's lips. He aligned the flaps of his parka, snapping each brass button into its shell, then yanked open the door. "You shouldn't have scraped me away."

Rummaging around in her shoulder bag, Natalie retrieved her

madras wallet. She removed her ATM card and pressed it into our netherson's functional hand. "Withdraw as much cash as you want. The PIN is one-eight-one-eight, Emily Brontë's birth year."

"Eighteen eighteen," he echoed tonelessly. "Thank you. I believe I'll purchase a heating device. I'm told the weather will get colder before it gets warmer." He turned abruptly and bolted down the stairs. "It was not necessary to exterminate me."

"God bless you, Mr. Snow," my wife called from the doorway.

"I've started reading Heidegger," he said, his voice fading like vapor from a fogged mirror. "You robbed me of my *Dasein,* Mother. The hottest places in hell are reserved for women like you."

NATALIE AND I DIDN'T KNOW what to make of our Christmas presents from John Snow 0001. Should I start wearing my umbrella necktie, Natalie her foil pendant, as tributes to the loving son we'd almost brought into the world? Or should we toss these trinkets in the trash as the reproachful tokens he'd almost certainly intended them to be? On Boxing Day, before setting out for lunch at the Tasty Triffid, Natalie dutifully adorned herself with the pendant, while I put on the necktie. The instant our food arrived, we removed our accessories without exchanging a word and stashed them in Natalie's shoulder bag.

The New Year was not long under way when Amory and Claudius died. I glanced at the bookcase and there they lay, two dry and delicate corpses, recumbent in the bottom of the fishbowl. Their passing perplexed me. Hadn't I given them plenty of water to drink? A surfeit of leaves to nibble? Evidently their little orthopterous clocks had simply stopped. I wrapped the grasshoppers in a white handkerchief, bore them to our rooftop garden, and buried them beneath the philodendron.

Shortly after 5:00 P.M., we heard from our fetus again. He'd left a message on Natalie's voice mail, explaining that he'd used the ATM card for several notable purchases, including a cell phone and a kerosene heater. He wanted us to visit him. His home was an abandoned switch tower in the freight yard adjacent to South Station.

"Please come," he said. "It's quite important." A long pause. "I believe I'm very sick."

Possessed by some raw Darwinian instinct, as primal as *Danaus plexippus*'s need to pollinate, we sprinted to the parking garage, scrambled into the Subaru, and set out in quest of our fetus. Reaching South Station at the height of rush hour, we exploited the hurly-burly and the gathering gloom to climb unseen off the platform and make our way across six parallel sets of tracks. My heart pounded frantically, though I couldn't say how much of this internal percussion owed to my fear of our being arrested, how much to my anxiety over our fetus's health. At some undefined point, we crossed from Amtrak's realm into the freight yard. Tank cars, hopper cars, boxcars, reefers, and gondolas loomed out of the darkness like prehistoric beasts straining to escape a tar pit.

Thanks to our heavy-duty flashlight supplemented by a full moon, we had no trouble spotting the deserted switch tower, a warped and weathered structure reminiscent of Charnock's houseboat. I knocked on the door, half expecting to be greeted by a shrouded skeleton in the ectoplasmic employ of the long-defunct Boston & Maine Railroad, but no one answered. A rickety exterior staircase led to the upper level, where a faint light seeped through the sooty windows. Natalie and I exchanged pained glances and ascended to the observation platform, one wobbly step at a time. I merely had to nudge the door and it swung open, its hinges creaking like an *Inner Sanctum* sound effect.

Strewn with scraps of wood, chunks of plaster, and bits of broken glass, the room was dimly illuminated by an electric lantern whose battery was almost dead. The back wall displayed a faded but elaborate chart depicting the freight yard, each switch circled and numbered, below which our netherson lay shivering on a stained, unsheeted mattress. A down comforter enswathed his body. His newly purchased kerosene heater, an upright thrumming cylinder suggesting an incandescent barber pole, released ineffectual gasps of humidity. Discarded wrappers and packages littered the floor. In recent weeks our fetus had treated himself to Ring Dings, Twinkies, Tootsie Rolls, Triscuits, Slim Jims, Wise potato chips, and Keebler Toll House cookies.

"Thank you for coming," he said.

I extended my hand, cupped his brow. His fever warmed my palm. "Where's the nearest emergency room?" I asked Natalie.

"Mass General."

"Listen, Mother," John Snow 0001 said. "Hear me, Father. I can feel the whole world now. Not just a few things. *Everything*. Isn't that remarkable?"

"We're taking you to the hospital," I told him.

"Right now," Natalie added.

The icy air made specters of our breath.

"The twitchings in my stomach, I *know* that's hunger," the immaculoid said. "And the fire inside my body, it must be a fever."

Natalie asked, "Can you walk? Should we carry you?"

John Snow 0001 seized my wrist. "Here's something even stranger. All these words coming out of my mouth—they're the ones I *want* to be speaking." He relaxed his grip. "A week ago I would've said, 'You're taking me to the hospital? Sure you don't want to get out your curette and slaughter me all over again?'"

Acting in unspoken but complete accord, my wife and I crouched over our fetus and unpeeled the comforter. As Natalie slid her arms under his back, I took hold of his legs, and together we lifted him several inches off the mattress.

"No!" he screamed. "It hurts too much!"

We set him back down.

"What hurts?" Natalie asked.

"Everything."

"We would never hurt you on purpose," Natalie said.

"I know, Mother. Before, I would've said, 'You certainly hurt me on purpose when you lanced me like a boil.'"

Natalie shuddered.

"The paramedics have painkillers," I told our fetus, slipping the phone from my jacket pocket. "They'll give you a shot of Demerol, then rush you to the hospital in their ambulance."

With the suddenness of a frog gigging a dragonfly, John Snow 0001 snatched the phone away and hugged it to his chest. "I can picture it all in my mind. Sharp and clear, like a leaf floating on still water."

"Picture what?"

"My entire race. The mackies. Moving against the city."

"What city?" I asked. "Boston?"

Before he could answer, a coughing fit seized him, the gouts of breath bursting from his windpipe along with a sprinkle of saliva. Natalie reached into the rubble and retrieved a half-liter 7-Up bottle. She gave our fetus a foamy gulp of warm soda. He coughed again, bathing us in carbonated spray, then took a second gulp. Sucking in a deep breath, he squeezed my hand and looked me in the eye.

"Themisopolis," he said. "The place where they perform the abortions."

"The immaculoids will attack Themisopolis?" I asked.

"And you know something?" he said, nodding. "I'm not . . . what's the word? I'm not *jealous*." He coughed. "The other mackies will get to join the crusade, but I'll be too sick to go"—cough—"and I don't *care*. What they're planning to do"—cough—"it's *wrong*. Gasoline and firebrands, that's simply *wrong*."

"Gasoline?" I said.

"And firebrands."

"When does the crusade start?" Natalie asked.

"Soon, they told us," our fetus replied.

"*Who* told you?" I asked. "Enoch Anthem? Felix Pielmeister?"

"What I really want to know is how Amory and Claudius are doing."

"They're doing fine," Natalie said.

"We love them very much," I said.

A tremor passed through his body, and then came a series of overlapping vibrations, a seismic dying for our netherson. Natalie and I threw ourselves atop the creature, massaging his muscles with taut, nervous fingers, as if we were making John Snow 0001 all over again, sculpting him from an immense lump of clay.

"Can I"—cough—"ask you a question?"

Natalie's tears glistened in the lantern's sallow glow. "Of course."

"What is it like"—cough—"to be alive?"

I grimaced and winced. Tenured philosophers have a taste for grandiose questions, and failed philosophers relish them even more. What is it like to be a bat? What if our senses disclose only the shadows of reality? What if our language prevents us from thinking the most important thoughts of all? But my skull was empty just then, a grail devoid of wine, water, or any other useful fluid. I could not have said what it was like to boil an egg, much less to be alive.

"City on fire!" our fetus cried. "Jehovah's holy torch!"

Even as Natalie and I tightened our grip on John Snow 0001, we felt his heat leak away in all its forms—first his acute fever, then his normal mammalian warmth, and finally the spark of life, leaving behind only his cold, confected flesh. Natalie pulled her Christmas gift out from beneath her sweatshirt, lifted the twine loop over her head, and placed the foil heart atop our fetus's chest. Evidently she'd grabbed the thing as we were rushing out the door.

"I meant for him to see I had it on," she said.

"He probably knew we were lying about Amory and Claudius," I said.

Natalie set her palm on the pendant. "I should've shown it to him and said, 'I've never stopped wearing it.'"

WE STAYED IN THE TOWER throughout the night, inhaling the fumes of the kerosene heater and talking about John Snow 0001's short, unhappy incarnation. For Natalie his essential tragedy lay in his knowledge that "he was living an unlived life." He could never escape his realization that his memories were contrived, his opinions programmed, his soul an epiphenomenon of his software. What truly impressed me, by contrast, was his brave and seemingly successful fight against his congenital disconnection from pleasure, so that his final days, miserable though they were by most indices, had included the savor of Ring Dings, the splendor of Twinkies, and the bliss of Triscuits.

"If he'd lived, I wonder, would he have remained sentient?" I asked Natalie.

"We'll never know," she said, combing her netherson's hair.

With the coming of dawn, we snuck across the freight yard and started down Atlantic Avenue, Natalie leading the way, John Snow 0001 wrapped in the comforter, his sorry husk slung across our shoulders. Our fellow Bostonians took little interest in this strange procession. We must have looked harmless, certainly not miscreants disposing of an inconvenient corpse: perhaps rug merchants delivering a Persian carpet to a Beacon Street penthouse, or archaeologists bearing an ancient scepter to the Boston Museum of Art. We reached the car, opened the trunk, transferred the clutter to the backseat—jumper cables, carton of cheap red wine, bag of potting soil, four empty motor-oil cans—and, after working John Snow 0001's stiffening flesh into a fetal position, snugged him into the compartment.

For the next half-hour, I fled the rising sun, driving aimlessly west, then eased the Subaru into the drive-through lane at a Brookline Burger King. I requested a couple of Egg Croissanwiches and some coffee, but when the order arrived, neither Natalie nor I could eat a bite. God knows we were hungry. The problem was that the Croissanwiches were so damn tasty, emanating delights that John Snow 0001 had largely been denied.

We slurped down our coffee and resumed our wanderings. Buoyed by the caffeine, we talked about our netherson's vision of a fetal army firebombing Londa's city. An implausible narrative, we decided, but no more implausible than the immaculoids themselves.

"Pielmeister is capable of anything," I said.

"You really think he would burn Themisopolis?" Natalie said.

"If that's what the paradigm shift requires."

We visited a Starbucks, consumed more coffee, and changed drivers. Logic said the mortuaries would be open now, and so while Natalie piloted us down Beacon Street, I pulled out the phone and called the West Newton Funeral Home. No sooner had I said the word "immaculoid" than the smarmy proprietor, an *r*-dropping Boston aborigine named Stephen Hammond, assured me that he understood our situation. We were the fourth couple this month to approach him concerning the disposition of such a creature.

"Your predecessors opted for cremation," he said.

"I see."

"Simply place the remains in your trunk."

"We did that already."

"There's no shame in this, Mr. Ambrose," Hammond said. "Nobody invited the mackies here."

The instant we pulled into the mortuary driveway, two pale but sprightly young men came bustling onto the veranda, wearing black serge suits and exuding soft gray sympathy. I hoisted myself out of the wagon and unlocked the trunk. The undertakers acted with exemplary speed. The last I saw of John Snow 0001 was a glimpse of his moldering sneakers as the somber men bore him across a vacant lot toward a squat brick building. A round, tapered chimney rose from the roof like a candle on a one-year-old's birthday cake.

With a mournful tread Natalie and I mounted the veranda steps and entered the parlor. The place was a reified lie, its fraudulence so stark as to render any postmodern deconstruction superfluous, all ferns and perfumes and uplifting synthesized harp music, when in fact its business was carrion and lamentation. The funeral director materialized from behind a red velvet curtain, introducing himself in the unctuous tones his profession had perfected down through the generations. He conformed surprisingly well to the mental image I'd assembled over the phone: a balding, roly-poly man with a small white mustache like the bristles on a toothbrush.

"Most of our immaculoid families prefer to leave the ashes here," Stephen Hammond said.

Without consulting me, Natalie said, "We'll take them home."

"No we won't," I said.

For a full minute, my wife and I exchanged annoyed glances and indignant throat clearings. Hammond looked away and took a discreet step backward: apparently a customary move for him—doubtless he'd witnessed many such communication breakdowns between quasiparents. It was Natalie who ended the stalemate, taking my hand, drawing it toward her, and pressing my fingers against her sternum.

"I don't ask for many favors, Archimago."

Fixing my gaze on Hammond, I said, "The ashes will come with us."

The funeral director returned to our sphere, flashing a major smile. His teeth were enormous. I thought of an egg carton with its lid flipped back. Humming in counterpoint to the ecclesiastical Muzak, he guided us to a display case featuring ceramic urns. Natalie selected one bearing an enameled image of wildflowers, explaining that they reminded her of the habitat our netherson had created for Amory and Claudius.

"The procedure takes ninety minutes," Hammond said.

About as long as a D and C, I mused. Later I learned that the same thought had occurred to Natalie.

Under Hammond's guidance we staggered into a small room lined with leather-bound books, reminiscent of the children's alcove back in Pieces of Mind. Rummaging among the news magazines on the coffee table, Natalie extracted a recent issue of *Time* featuring the annual circulation-boosting "So What's the Big Deal About This Jesus Person?" cover story. I selected the complete works of W. H. Auden, then joined my wife on the Naugahyde sofa. I attempted to read, but the poems kept dissolving into typographic jetsam adrift on a white sea. Eventually we put our printed matter aside and held hands. It was like waiting for a muffler installation, only with harps instead of Johnny Cash.

Hammond appeared right on time, bearing the wildflower urn. While Natalie cradled our fetus's remains, I took care of the bill, $530.75 including tax, charging it on our Visa card.

We immediately agreed that John Snow 0001 must not be consigned to the trunk again. This time he would ride up front on Natalie's lap. By noon we were back in our apartment, setting the ceramic vessel atop the same bookcase where our grasshoppers had resided.

"You were right all along," I told Natalie. "I'm glad we brought him home."

"It's the least we owe him."

I stroked the vessel. "I wonder if he's the only child we'll ever have."

"He was not our child."

"He was not our child," I agreed.

GASOLINE AND FIREBRANDS, John Snow 0001 had said. City on fire. Jehovah's holy torch. As I entered the kitchen to call Londa's office, my imagination showed me Cinemascope images of siege towers grinding toward Themisopolis, their turrets crammed with vengeful immaculoids wielding implements of sanctified arson. Gertrude Lingard answered. Her boss, she said, was in Miami evaluating the effectiveness of the Wollstonecraft Fund in helping Cuban and Haitian immigrants find jobs. I tried Londa's cell phone, getting her on the first ring.

Yes, ladies and gentlemen, you may be sure I was profoundly reluctant to tell my vatling that John Snow 0001 had died. Her annoyance with her ponderous conscience, that philosopher who'd inflicted so many facets on her face and hung the uncast stone around her neck, would surely preclude any genuine expression of sympathy. Imagine my surprise when, learning that the creature was no more, Londa choked up—I don't think she was faking it—then went on to assure me that Natalie and I had lost not a son but a cruelly exploited antiabortion icon who was probably better off dead.

It was only after I changed the subject, describing John Snow 0001's forecast of an imminent attack on the city, that the conversation began to unnerve me, Londa's voice becoming incongruously calm, as if I'd said the immaculoids would be spray-painting the walls with graffiti, not burning them down. Dispassionately she proposed that on Monday we make our separate ways to Harford County Airport and thence to Themisopolis, there to share a leisurely dinner while analyzing my netherson's last words.

Like many an obsessive activist, Londa never stopped working, and neither did Dame Quixote or Weltanschauung Woman, and so predictably enough our meal occurred in her executive suite atop Caedmon Hall. We ate at the conference table, adjacent to the model City of Justice, Quetzie roosting on the Vision Institute. When not discussing the possibility of fetal violence, Londa and I shared vegetarian delicacies—"my homage to little Donya," she explained, "everybody's favorite animal-rights advocate"—prepared by the Artemis Clinic's live-in cooking staff, each tureen covered by a silver dome suggesting a DUNCE cap. Since our phone conversation, she had if anything become more cavalier toward the presumed menace. With each new course, I grew increasingly emphatic, averring that a dying immaculoid would not cry "City on fire!" or "Jehovah's holy torch!" without good reason, but only after we'd broached the desserts did Londa deign to explain her nonchalance. She crowned her pecan pie with a globe of vanilla ice cream, ambled toward a filing cabinet, and slid out the upper drawer like a morgue attendant displaying a corpse to a coroner.

"The cornerstone of Themisopolis was barely laid when the threats began," she said. "Each morning's e-mail includes a dozen hate letters, most of them promising to gun down Yolly and me on sight. When it comes to sending us anthrax and explosives, of course, the Internet doesn't work very well, so the Phyllistines have to use FedEx and UPS. At first I was freaked, but then I became—you'd be proud of me, Socrates—I became philosophical about it. We've got a damn smart bomb squad in the mail room, and their dog is even smarter." She brushed her fingers across the files, grabbed a random document, and yanked it before her eyes. "'Your days are numbered, you sick, twisted weirdos,'" she read. She made a second arbitrary choice. "'You know you're the Antichrist, and I know it, and soon the whole world will know it.'" She slid the drawer home. "Junk mail from Jeremiah. Cassandra learns to spam. Forgive me if I don't take your immaculoid's warning more seriously than the ten thousand that came before it."

"Pielmeister," I said.

"What?"

"Felix Pielmeister."

She asked me to elaborate, and I attempted to paraphrase the Augustinian's rant in the Hawthorne parking lot. I told how he'd screamed about geysers of blood, and how before long Corporate Christi would engulf the globe with godly profiteering and eschatological lava.

"He absolutely fucking terrified me," I said.

"Quetzie is a handsome devil," the iguana said.

"And how do you suggest we react to this crisis?" Londa asked dryly.

I couldn't tell whether she wanted my opinion or merely sought to befuddle me into silence. "You're the only superheroine in the room. I'm just another bookseller who never got his Ph.D. I suppose you should post some Valkyries along Avalon Lane and double the watch on the ramparts."

"Here's my idea," Londa said brightly. "Let's spend the rest of the week making merry in the Circus of Atonement. That way we'll be in a good mood when the mackies come and put us out of business."

"Blessed are the facetious."

"But before we hit the Circus, we have to drop by the cemetery."

"Cemetery?"

"White Marsh Cemetery."

"I spent Wednesday morning in a funeral parlor. I have no wish to visit a cemetery."

"When a gumbo girl goes bad, sweetie, she goes very, very bad. It's possible my case is hopeless. You'll have to judge for yourself."

LONDA WAS THE MOST RECKLESS person into whose hands I had ever commended my flesh, a driver for whom the Baltimore Beltway was a latter-day Hippodrome where any sufficiently foolhardy charioteer might garner some laurels and a sack of sesterces. While her palpitating passenger scrunched down in the adjacent seat, staring at the recessed letters spelling out AIR BAG, she intimidated sedans, bullied SUVs, and antagonized tractor-trailers, all the while treating the 65 mph speed limit merely as a baseline against which to measure the caliber of her nerve. By the time we reached the cemetery, the sun had set, the moon had risen, my heart had entered my mouth, and my stomach had migrated into the newly made cavity.

We stopped outside the main entrance, an austere post-and-lintel affair surmounted by a puffy-cheeked angel blowing a trumpet. A heavy black chain presented itself, slung between the wrought-iron gates like an immense watch fob. Someone, a Valkyrie presumably, had hacksawed open the padlock. In a matter of seconds, we broke into the graveyard, a procedure rather easier than peeling the cellophane off a CD, then got back in the Volvo. As the moon brightened and Jupiter bejeweled its portion of the night, we cruised at a respectful velocity past the brooding tombstones, looming vaults, and naked winter trees.

"Cemeteries are the most philosophical of places," I told Londa.

"Whatever you say."

"More philosophical than cafés or beer halls or even the banks of the Nile."

"Undoubtedly."

"As Heidegger would have it, by fully facing the fact of death and deliberately engaging the Nothing, a person can learn to live authentically."

"I'm afraid I don't need a Heideggerian right now, not even one who can deconstruct cemeteries." She reached past me and unlatched the glove compartment. "What I need is a navigator." Two folding maps and a tube of lip balm tumbled into my lap. "Get us to the corner of Hyperion Avenue and Chancery Way."

I spread the map across my knees, edging it into the pool of light cast by the glove compartment's reading lamp, but before I could find the intersection on paper, Londa found it in actuality, thanks to a parked panel truck emblazoned with Lady Justice at full gallop. A half-dozen shadowy figures stood around the adjacent grave like mourners, though their picks and shovels suggested a more controversial agenda. We abandoned the Volvo and joined the leather-clad gang. Upon learning that I was the ethicist who'd supervised their leader's legendary insular youth, the Valkyries presented me with an array of complex facial expressions conveying both their admiration of my success in giving her a moral compass and their wish that I'd made that instrument a bit less baroque.

Londa now introduced me to Major Carmen Powers, a short, perky woman with chipmunk cheeks and a pageboy haircut parted laterally by the metal strap connecting her earmuffs, "the second-highest-ranking member of the Themisopolis security force." The Valkyries' highest-ranking member evidently had better things to do that night than creeping around a freezing graveyard.

I fixed on the tombstone, which shimmered in the full moon like a radioactive menhir. Two bas-relief cherubs protruded from the granite, their pudgy bodies framing an inscription: IN LOVING MEMORY OF ETHAN AND AMELIA PEPPERHILL.

"Ethan Pepperhill," I said. "*The* Ethan Pepperhill?"

Londa grunted in the affirmative.

Of all the congressmen who'd labored to shield the American tobacco industry from the unpatriotic lawsuits of lung-cancer victims, none had been more successful than Ethan Pepperhill of North Carolina. "What's he doing *here*?"

"Naturally he wanted to be buried in his home state," Londa explained, "but he wanted to share the sod with Mrs. Pepperhill even more, and she'd already joined her parents in this neck of the netherworld."

A few errant snowflakes sifted down from the sparkling sky, the swirling crystals meeting the moonlight and turning bright as fireflies. I zipped up my bomber jacket. The Valkyries set to work, breaking the hard January earth with their steel tools. It took them only twenty minutes to penetrate the frost line and begin shoveling away the pliant dirt below. They excavated the glossy oblong box, lifted it free of the hole, and, like newlyweds installing their first refrigerator, set it upright on the mound of freshly turned soil. Major Carmen Powers smashed the clasps with her shovel, and the lid fell away, tumbling into the open grave. Like a gust from a blast furnace, the stench swept over us, and we all went for our scarves and handkerchiefs, pressing them against our faces like poultices. My eyes teared up. I wiped away the salt water and there it was, limned by the lunar glow, the erect remains of the Winston-Salem Corporation's greatest benefactor, dressed in a crumbling tuxedo. Being dead, he looked understandably peaked, though still prepared to wage one more battle against the enemies of free enterprise and spiked tobacco.

A fleeting but bizarre episode followed, grisly even by the norms of this night. Carmen Powers took out her Swiss Army knife, waded through the ghastly fumes, and sawed off Senator Pepperhill's little finger. An unexpected gesture, yet I intuitively apprehended its significance.

I turned to Londa and said, "You've got your own ontogenerator."

"The next big consumer item," she replied, accepting the detached finger from the major.

"This carnival of yours—the performers are all beaker freaks?"

Londa offered me a corroborative smirk, then slid a Baggie from her coat pocket and sealed the finger in plastic. "We'll have Pepperhill on the playbill in a month or two. I picture him walking into a cancer ward with an ice chest containing his recently extracted lungs, offering them free of charge to whoever speaks up first."

I gestured toward the corpse and scowled. "A reverent person—not myself, certainly, but a reverent person would call this desecration."

"No, Socrates, *this* is desecration," Londa said, drawing out a pack of her customary Dunhills. She approached the senator and inserted a cigarette between his lips.

"I thought you'd given up smoking."

"I use these for political purposes only," she explained, then turned to Carmen and said, "It would be fun to read about this in tomorrow's paper. Send an anonymous tip to the night desk at the *Sun*."

"Christ, Londa, aren't you going to rebury him?" I gasped.

"Thanks to Jordan's lobbying efforts, the American Brotherhood of Gravediggers has secured a fair wage for its members. Whoever puts him in the ground tomorrow will be whistling while he works."

"Fuck."

"Lighten up, sweetie." Londa provided the senator with a second cigarette, so that he suddenly seemed to possess the elongated canine teeth of a vampire. "And now we're off to watch the Circus troupers play their parts, the most popular way to pass a Saturday night in Themisopolis. You're only young once, Socrates. Carpe diem."

DEPRESSED BY RECENT EVENTS in White Marsh Cemetery and certain that I would derive no delight from the Circus of Atonement, I spent most of our return trip telling Londa, truthfully, that I was bone tired and felt a cold coming on, if not the flu, so could she please take me to the Themisopolis guesthouse or, better still, a motel, sending along my overnight bag at her earliest convenience? My vatling would hear none of it. What I needed, she insisted, was a rococonut julep followed by a Circus act or two, and within the space of an hour I found myself in her lofty office.

The canopic jar in which she kept her mumquats—authentic Eighth Dynasty, she insisted—evoked for me the most vivid shot in *The Egyptian*: Sinuhe performing his penance in the House of the Dead, a lowly embalmer's apprentice, stirring a stinking vat of natron. Londa made me the promised julep, serving it in a crystal goblet. The nectar did not so much relieve my symptoms as decontextualize them. Once you've been abstracted from your body, the discomfort of an upper respiratory infection loses all claim on your attention.

Bathed in Proserpine's manufactured serenity, I allowed Londa to guide me out of Caedmon Hall and across the flagstone plaza. Soon the Circus of Atonement rose before us, a squat rotunda: black, smooth, featureless—hence the ease with which the architects had represented it using a hockey puck. We passed through an unmarked entryway as inconspicuous as a stage door and entered a dimly lit foyer appointed only with a coatrack, a water fountain, and a vending machine dispensing fruit juice and granola bars. Londa flashed me a cryptic Sabacthanite smile, a sure sign of heavy weather and sizable ironies ahead, then led me past a fan-folded Chinese screen into the darkness beyond.

As we moved along the central corridor, following the curve of the hockey puck, compact prosceniums emerged on both sides, each featuring a live actor earnestly performing a minimalist drama. Nearly every play seemed well attended, only one or two empty seats per theater, but according to Londa the vatling thespians took no pleasure in their popularity, as their DUNCE cap programs precluded any such sensation. They were zombies to the core, beyond delight, outside despair.

Intrigued by the lurid poster, I suggested that we sample *Motherhood Comes to the Holy Father*. We slipped into the theater, taking care not to annoy the actor or disturb the other audience members, and assumed our seats. I quickly became absorbed in a situation of transcendent tastelessness. Through the machinations of a Wiccan sisterhood, Pope John Paul II had awoken one morning to find himself burdened with an unsolicited uterus and a concomitant unplanned pregnancy. Happily for the supreme pontiff, his silk robe billowed so broadly that his condition, like the fifteen Rosary mysteries, remained obscure. I could not imagine how Londa had obtained the tissue sample, and I did not want to know. The present scene was set in a Vatican clinic. Having dropped beseechingly to his knees, the pontiff was begging an audio-animatronic doctor to give him an abortion. A queasiness spread through me—political theater was one thing, feminist Grand Guignol starring reincarnated ecclesiastics quite another—and I politely told Londa that I wished to see no more. As we exited the theater, the Vatican physician presented the pope with a brochure touting the virtues of adoption.

"Do not begrudge us our diversions," Londa said defensively. "The Circus is essential to our mental health."

We continued along the corridor, patronizing each play long enough for the plot to manifest itself. Even as I recoiled at the sheer charnel pornography of it all, Londa's deranged museum brought out the critic in me, and I began evaluating the scripts, performances, and directorial flourishes. Perhaps the mumquat nectar had lowered my standards, but I was deeply moved by *The Martyrs of Modernity,* CEO Warren Anderson's abject apology for the 1984 methyl iso-cyanate leak at the Union Carbide factory in Bhopal, India—eight thousand dead in a week, fifteen thousand by the end of the decade, countless mothers yielding toxic breast milk well into the next cen-tury—a disaster for which neither he nor his corporation had taken any responsibility at the time, instead sending each victim five hun-dred dollars. By contrast, I found little to admire in *The Art of Atroc-ity,* Henry Kissinger's lachrymose lament over the lagniappes he'd added to America's catastrophic involvement in the Vietnam War, including the secret invasion of Cambodia and the Christmas bomb-ings of Hanoi and Haiphong. Far more satisfying was *Searching for My Soul,* in which Ronald Reagan denounced himself not only for supporting Central American death squads but also for curtailing heating-fuel assistance to the elderly, declining to speak out against apartheid, refusing to acknowledge the AIDS epidemic until he had no choice, and appointing a secretary of the interior who believed that the imminent Second Coming rendered environmentalism ir-relevant.

"Could you give us a publicity quote?" Londa asked as we slipped away. "We're always looking for endorsements from celebrity ethi-cists."

I assumed she was joking, but I replied with a blurb reflect-ing my genuine enthusiasm for the piece in question. "In real life Ronald Reagan neither received nor deserved an Oscar, but having seen *Searching for My Soul,* I'm ready to give him one."

We moved on. Davy Crockett's confession, a tour de force called *Moon Over Bexar,* took as its theme the dubious ideals of the Alamo defenders: how they were ultimately seeking to found a republic in which they could own West African slaves, the Mexican government in its wisdom having outlawed that controversial institution. While the beaker freak's bucolic locutions seemed completely natural, he inevitably evoked those scores of post-Crockett scoundrels who'd attained elected office by affecting such folksiness, their talent for faking the common touch matched only by their aptitude for screwing the common man. After sampling the Crockett soliloquy, we dropped by *Jesus Winced,* in which Mary Baker Eddy sought forgiveness from the onstage ghosts of a dozen deceased children whose parents had sacrificed them on the altar of Christian Science. Londa assured me that the youthful specters were audio-animatronic simulacra: no children had been disinterred for this production. Next we joined the audience for what proved to be the evening's most disturbing presentation, *Mega Culpa,* in which the brilliant physicist Edward Teller bemoaned the ebullience with which he'd fathered the hydrogen bomb. At first his anguish captivated me, but then the fusionfamilias tore off his shirt and started chewing into his mortified flesh with a flagellant's whip, and I left in a huff, repulsed by the gratuitous violence.

"Major Powers wrote that script," Londa muttered as we returned to the corridor. "You're right—it's over the top."

Before I could elaborate on my dismay with *Mega Culpa,* my hostess hustled me into the vicinity of two recently deceased and copiously mourned clerics. Prior to his death in an auto accident, Percival Sarnac had been Enoch Anthem's right-hand man, tirelessly transmitting God's views on homosexuality via WXPF-AM in Chicago, "your station for salvation." Before succumbing to leukemia, Leopold Ransom had hosted the talk show *Countdown to Jesus* on the Rapture Channel. And now here they were in the Circus, acting out a love story titled *The Semen on the Mount.* I had to admit

I'd never witnessed a more moving courtship. The fleeting caresses, the furtive kisses, the tender embraces, the candlelit dinner, the passionate grapplings on Ransom's waterbed—it was all impeccably programmed and poignantly performed, and by the time the men had exchanged their wedding vows, most of the attending Valkyries were weeping.

"I have a treat for you," Londa said, ushering me toward a velvet curtain, red and heavy as a coronation robe, "the dress rehearsal of an epic set in the fifteenth century." The adjacent poster identified the show as *Clone of Arc.* "Tonight our youngest malefactor runs through my latest script. We bribed about thirty functionaries and broke a dozen international laws, but at long last Saint Joan's charred femur came into our possession."

"A malefactor? Joan of Arc?"

"I must concede, your admiration for the Maid of Orléans is practically universal. Even the most tough-minded thinker will melt before our dear Joan. Mark Twain devoted his worst novel to her. Bernard Shaw put her at the center of an extraordinarily tedious play—a feat later duplicated by both Jean Anouilh and Maxwell Anderson. She's waiting, Socrates. A private performance. If you liked *Searching for My Soul,* you'll love *Clone of Arc.*"

I stepped behind the red curtain and entered a theater far smaller than the others, barely a dozen seats, all empty. Assuming the best possible vantage, front row center, I fixed on the proscenium, expecting to see the resurrected Joan wearing a prison smock and chained to the notorious stake, her brow speckled with sweat, her eyes glazed with devotion—or perhaps she would be in full armor, mounted on a charger, holding the French standard high as she urged her troops into battle. But instead she stood beside a fir tree rooted in a mound of earth carpeted in lush grass and golden buttercups. She was blindingly beautiful, her raven hair secured in a bun, her voluptuous form wrapped in a muslin shift, her hazel, feline eyes darting in all directions. A gleaming broadsword—Joan's, no doubt—protruded from the hillock like Excalibur rising from its anvil.

"Yes, my achievement was astonishing, *pas de question,*" she began. "I saved a nation. *Vive la France!* But there is still a difficulty, *un grand problème.*"

In an unbroken and balletic gesture, she untied her sash and laid it along her outstretched forearm. The accessory slithered across her skin and floated to the grass, and suddenly I knew how this untried and untested commander had rallied an entire army to her side. In some lubricious sector of his soul, every French infantryman had imagined himself embracing this divine peasant.

"It's an old story, perhaps the oldest on earth," Joan said. "The sky rumbles, the clouds congeal, the sun spasms. Is that a saint I see on high? An angel? The Lord God Jehovah himself? Now a holy voice booms down, instructing the poor prophet to grab a sword and thrust it into a fellow human, or perhaps a hundred fellow humans, or even a million if the cause is sufficiently sacred. The prophet never talks back. The tradition existed before me. It flourishes to this day. The sword, the blood, the freshly created corpses littering the battlefield, exuding the stink of epiphany."

She issued a merry programmed laugh, then hiked up her shift and cast it aside. Her navel contemplated me. Her flesh elicited appreciation from all my senses. Even at this distance, I could smell her lovely pheromones, hear the whisper of her ligaments, feel the softness of her hands, taste her salty thighs.

"I wish I had it to do over again," Joan said. "I would have tried bargaining with my voices." She unfastened her hair. Her tresses spilled onto her bare shoulders and cascaded downward, swirling around her eminent breasts like an incoming tide. "I wish I'd said, 'Why must so many lose their lives, dear God? Why not turn the English swords to glass and their pikes to aspic, so our enemies will capitulate without a fight? Whence cometh thine appetite for carnage, O my Father? Why this thirst for blood? *Pourquoi le sang?*'" She looked me in the eye. "Come hither, knave."

I obeyed, joining the maid onstage. She made a circuit of the fir tree, then approached me in all her mind-boggling nubility. I had consumed too much rococonut milk. Deftly she removed my clothes, then guided me to the hillock and bade me lie with her. Her lovely fingers sculpted me into the rigid amoretto her appetite required. The mumquat juice saturated my neurons. She climbed on top, and soon her moist quoit found its object—no resistance from Mason the morality teacher: all that nectar. Synesthesia overcame me, everything melting together, the warmth of her skin, its fine rural fragrance, the hazel of her eyes, the eddies of her hair, the surrounding meadow.

"On the day we broke the siege," she said, "I disemboweled twenty men, only two of whom were even remotely vile."

In the dream that now suffused my sleeping mind, John Snow 0001 was still alive. The two of us were standing beside an Isla de Sangre swamp, tossing gobbets of raw meat to the alligators like a couple of Boston Common benchsitters feeding the pigeons.

I awoke in time to catch the end of Joan's soliloquy. "There are no just wars," she said. "There are no greater goods."

Evidently I'd wept during my ethereal reunion with John Snow 0001—my cheeks were wet: the dew of my mourning. The maid sprawled beside me, tickling my nose with the stem of a buttercup.

"Four days ago I lost a fetus," I told her. "A miserable and misbegotten creature, but I'm still very sad."

"I wish I had it to do over again," Joan said, echoing herself. "I would have asked God a question or two."

Chapter 11

MANY ARE THE CONSOLATIONS of literature, and not the least such solace occurs when an annoyingly virtuous hero succumbs to carnal temptation. Case in point: the Red Cross Knight who dominates Book One of *The Faerie Queene*, as pious a protagonist as might be imagined, a man whose life's ambition is to enter orthodoxy's dictionary—"see also *holiness, probity,* and *St. George*"—single-minded even by the norms of allegory. So how does this chain-mail messiah behave when the degenerate witch Duessa throws herself at him in the guise of the fair maiden Fidessa? We might expect Sir Red Cross to resist. But no. The enchantress has only to wiggle her wiles, and soon our randy chevalier has "poured out in looseness on the grassy ground," which means exactly what you think it does.

I was staring up at the starry winter sky, drained and sated and vaguely enjoying the sensation of being carried away from the Circus of Atonement on a stretcher borne by Major Powers and another Valkyrie, when it occurred to me that just as Spenser had exonerated his knight, so might Natalie eventually pardon my dalliance with Joan of Arc. Or if my wife failed to forgive me, then perhaps I would in time gain absolution from the readers of the self-serving memoir I was certain to write one day. Or maybe Joan herself would let me off the hook, coming to me and saying, "Your lack of chivalry appalls me, monsieur, but I must allow for certain extenuating circumstances and tumescent conditions."

In keeping with Londa's egalitarian principles, all visiting dignitaries to Themisopolis stayed at Arcadia House, the same neo-Tudor building that sheltered the outcasts and indigents who routinely sought refuge within the city's walls. As she tucked me into bed that night, Major Powers reported that the present population of this heartbreak hotel included seventeen orphans, eleven pregnant adolescents, ten battered wives, five abused girlfriends, and fourteen general pariahs who until recently had been eating out of restaurant garbage pails. Lolling on the mattress, I imagined that I could hear my fellow residents' sobs, whimpers, and moans seeping through the walls: a distressing cacophony, and yet I was glad now to be among these wretches, whose phantom lamentations were serving to deepen my admiration for Londa. Yes, the woman was out of whack, unbalanced by her profligate conscience—how else to interpret the Circus of Atonement?—and yet the harvest of that disharmony, this refuge for the dispossessed, was surely among the world's great marvels.

The following morning, surfacing into consciousness, I immediately wished that I was still asleep. My skull had become a winepress, squeezing forth the latest vintage from the Château de Spinal Fluid. My throat and stomach were joined by an esophagus once owned by a sword swallower. By punching a bedside button labeled NURSE, I prompted a lovely young paramedic to flutter into the room, and presently she confirmed my self-diagnosis: I had the flu, complete with a 102-degree fever. My angel prescribed water, electrolytes, aspirin, and bed rest. I decided to start with the last regimen, wrapping the pillow around my head and snuggling beneath the patchwork quilt.

Several hours later the telephone wrenched me from my dream— Donya and I were wandering the beaches of Isla de Sangre, rescuing stranded sea urchins—and dumped me back into my febrile body. The caller was Londa, inquiring after my health.

"I expect to be on my feet in a day or so," I told her. I wondered if she'd written the *Clone of Arc* script solely with her old tutor in mind: a kinky recapitulation of her seduction attempt back on the island, though with a different climax. "Tell me honestly, dear, did you get a vicarious thrill from my misbehavior last night?"

"What misbehavior might that be?"

I grunted indignantly.

"I'm not a voyeur," Londa said. "I have no idea what happened between you and Joan."

"You wrote the damn script."

"And you chose to *follow* it?" she said with fake dismay. "Am I to infer that you ravished that poor dead gamine? I'm shocked."

"Oh, come off it."

"You ran the bases, Socrates. Fornication, adultery, pedophilia, and necrophilia, all in one fell shtup."

"I didn't ravish anybody. The Circus troupers are zombies. You said so yourself."

"Hey, Mason, I would *love* to spend the afternoon discussing the inner lives of beaker freaks, but I've got a million things on my plate right now. It seems you were right about Pielmeister and CHALICE having grand ideas. Get well, sir. And don't worry about our Joan. She's one tough gumbo girl."

"Grand ideas? What's going on?"

"Gotta run. Drink lots of fluids. Ciao."

I didn't want to stick Themisopolis for a long-distance call, so I hauled myself out of bed and retrieved the cell phone from my bomber jacket, which Major Powers had thoughtfully draped across the solitary chair. My efforts were rewarded not with Natalie's dulcet tones but with a computerized voice urging me to leave a message. What to say? "Reached Maryland safely, caught the flu, had wild, illicit sex with a reincarnated Joan of Arc, miss you, will call again tomorrow, bye"? When the beep sounded, I told Natalie I was sick in bed and hoped to be home in two days.

Briefly I surveyed my quarters. Somebody had retrieved my overnight bag from Caedmon Hall and set it on the dresser, a sturdy antique with a pristine mirror, adjacent to which hung a paint-by-numbers canvas depicting a Gospel narrative that had figured prominently in the emergence of Londa's Purple Pietest self, the episode of the woman taken in adultery. At the center of the tableau stood a seraphic Jesus who looked about as Semitic as Peter O'Toole. "Let him among you who is without sin cast the first stone," ran the superfluous caption, rendered in an Old English font. As I climbed back into bed, it occurred to me that, from CHALICE's viewpoint, Londa and her colleagues had already cast many first stones, rocks of relativism, clods of infanticide, not to mention the megaliths of Lesbos, and it was high time they got their geologic comeuppance.

A TRIBAL CHANT—BASSO, growling, ominous. A frenzied drumming, as if rival marching bands had assembled outside my window, rehearsing halftime routines for the Bedlam-Charenton all-lunatic gridiron match. I blinked myself awake. Morning, or so I guessed. Day four of my Arcadia House sojourn. Throat healed, sinuses drained, fever broken.

"Feeling better?"

A grain of sand had nestled in my eye, bringing a tear, so that Londa seemed encapsulated, a bouillababy in a bubble. "Much," I said, wiping the grit away. The adamant song and the awful pounding continued, threatening to revive my headache. "What's that damn racket?"

Instead of answering, she made a circuit of the room, gathering up my socks, underwear, and street clothes like a suburban mom on laundry day. She tossed the pile on the bed.

"The barbarians are at the gates," she said, and it was then that I noticed her face, as pale and stiff as Senator Pepperhill's. "Get dressed."

I did as instructed, then grabbed my phone, intending to contact Natalie. Before I could key in the number, Londa told me not to bother. The immaculoids were jamming all transmissions from Themisopolis.

"I don't get it," I said.

"You will," she said.

We left the building and hurried down Shambhala Avenue, the raucous voices and the unruly percussion growing louder by the minute. Reaching the main entrance, we stepped into Londa's private elevator—all plush Victorian velvet, like a dumbwaiter on Captain Nemo's submarine—and ascended to the top of the rampart. Apprehension throbbing in my chest, I crossed the windy causeway and, accepting Londa's offer of binoculars, set about absorbing the coming of Corporate Christi in all its lurid spectacle.

An army was bivouacked outside the city, a seething fetal sea, roiling, churning, three thousand pock-faced, silver-haired immaculoids deployed amid rows of canvas tents and nylon pavilions, plus another three thousand arrayed in protest along Avalon Lane, their legions spilling into the snow-covered cherry orchard beyond. Dozens of bazookas, assault rifles, and grenade launchers glistened beneath the gelid eye of the January sun. Scores of placards trembled in the wind, rank upon rank of epigrammatic anger: EVERY CONDOM IS A NOOSE. SPOTLESS AS THE LAMB. NEVER TO SAVOR THE ROSE. D & C = DESTRUCTION & CRUELTY. Dressed in identical orange jumpsuits, the fetuses banged lug wrenches against trash receptacles and beat on fifty-five-gallon drums with clawhammers, simultaneously chanting like institutionalized monks convinced that their madhouse was a monastery.

"They've had us sealed in since Monday afternoon," Londa said, "commuters and residents alike." Elaborating, she explained that upon their arrival the fetuses had employed an electromagnetic pulse to disable the city's cell phones, satellite dishes, and wireless modems, and shortly thereafter they'd severed all phone lines and coaxial cables. "Yolly and I were watching the TV coverage of the siege when—kablooey—the screen turned to static."

"TV coverage?" I said. "Good, great, *that* should put a crimp in Pielmeister's paradigm shift."

"Don't count on it. Two days ago the news helicopters were thick as mosquitoes, but the pilots got jittery when the bazookas came out. Whatever the mackies pull next, the viewing public won't see it."

The sun glinted off the snow, lancing through my irises, skating across my retinas. I yanked the Ray-Bans from my bomber jacket and slid them into place. "Is Pielmeister down there? Anthem?"

"Our favorite Phyllistines are keeping their distance. When CNN interviewed Anthem, he said he couldn't imagine who'd encouraged the immaculoids to bring their complaint to our door."

Although nearly half of Londa's staff commuted to work, the parking lot was barren of all private sedans, station wagons, and SUVs. Instead the macadam held more than a hundred Greyhound buses, plus ten Mayflower moving vans and seven semi-rigs sporting the Mountain Dew logo: not a surprising sight, really—how else could CHALICE have gotten so many mackies and their camping gear onto the scene? Far more disturbing than the mobilization vehicles was the battery of howitzers, ideal for pulverizing our gates, not to mention the thirty-odd Caterpillar hydraulic lifts, perfect for sending waves of fetuses over our walls, and the forty or so diesel tractors pulling trailers filled with gasoline. Texaco was the principal donor, but Exxon, Sunoco, Getty, and Amoco had also made their contributions to the paradigm shift.

"City on fire," I muttered. "Jehovah's holy torch."

"That appears to be their intention," Londa said, each syllable dipped in venom.

"The Maryland governor, what's his name—Winthrop—he'll have to call in the National Guard, right?"

"Tucker Winthrop? Are you kidding? A major Phyllistine."

Londa slipped on her mirror shades. "The last thing Yolly and I saw on CNN was Winthrop's press conference. Quote: 'These poor innocent fetuses are exercising their right of peaceable assembly, and my office has no reason to thwart them.'"

I heaved a sigh and said, "Not to mention their right of peaceable arson."

Londa strode back and forth across the causeway, an image that evoked various Hollywood depictions of Davy Crockett—repentant protagonist of *Moon Over Bexar*—sizing up Santa Anna's army as it paraded past the Alamo. "I'm supposed to join Yolly and our security chief for a noon meeting with the mackie general. I'd like my conscience to come along."

"Your conscience has nothing better to do."

"I appreciate that."

Again I heaved a sigh. "Suppose they gave a paradigm shift and nobody came?"

WE ENTERED THE VICTORIAN elevator and returned to the ground. Yolly was pacing around by the main entrance, accompanied by Dagmar Röhrig and a leather-jacketed Valkyrie who introduced herself as Colonel Vetruvia Fox: an astonishingly intense woman, small but fearsome, a lark of prey. An instant later the gates pivoted away with the ponderous force of a hippopotamus shifting in its wallow of mud. Remote control in hand, our escort stepped forward, Captain John Snow 0851 according to the embroidery on his jumpsuit, a cadaverous mackie with hair the texture of a Brillo pad. He asked Colonel Fox for her sidearm. She surrendered her Glock 19 with a resentful snort. The fetal army had stopped chanting and drumming, but we still endured a barrage of bitter grunts and toxic glances as, burdened by his immaculoid limp, Captain Snow led us through the encampment. Angry words appeared wherever we turned. BURN, BABY KILLER, BURN. OUR PORTION WAS ABORTION. NEVER TO FEEL A PUPPY'S TONGUE. ABLATED LIKE A TUMOR.

Our destination proved to be a prefabricated tin shanty reminiscent of Charnock's Quonset-hut complex back on the island, cold as an igloo, drafty as a crypt, without a single kerosene heater in sight. Apparently these immaculoids were all still strangers to sensation. Captain Snow seated us at a collapsible aluminum picnic table, directly across from a short, scowling fetus labeled Major John Snow 3227 and his commanding officer, the squint-eyed, simian-shouldered General John Snow 4099. Wrapped in shadows, a dozen mackies of indeterminate rank stirred in the background.

"The evacuation begins at dawn," General Snow announced, his exhalations turning visible in the frigid air.

"We expect you all to show up promptly," Major Snow said. More palpable breaths. Everyone seemed to be speaking in *League of Londa* dialogue balloons.

"Evacuation?" snarled Colonel Fox.

"What?" gasped Dagmar.

For some reason Captain Snow preferred to remain erect, strutting back and forth on the dirt floor. "We'll march the lot of you to Quehannock State Park, where your commuters will find their missing cars and vans," he said. "Next we'll issue cell phones to your residents, so they can commission private transportation and thereby continue the exodus."

Colonel Fox stared at the vaulted ceiling and muttered, "Fuck this." The tin walls replayed her words, turning her throwaway epithet into a malediction.

General Snow glowered at the Valkyrie and said, "In other words, your people will be at a safe distance when the conflagration starts."

"Conflagration?" said Yolly, who'd evidently not spent much time mulling over the implications of the gasoline trucks parked outside the city.

"Conflagration," General Snow repeated, rolling the word around on his tongue like a cherry stone.

A hush descended. The stillness held dominion for two full minutes. Wordless dialogue balloons hovered here and there throughout the hut.

"What makes you think we won't stand our ground?" Londa asked, digging into her thumb with the nail of her index finger.

Major Snow issued a toothy immaculoid smirk. His diseased mouth suggested an encounter between a piano keyboard and a sledgehammer. "If it's a fight you want, Dr. Sabacthani, we'll gladly give you one. But remember that every mackie will be dead of his infirmities within the week. You'd be battling the very legions of despair."

"We have guns," Colonel Fox noted.

"We have more guns," countered General Snow.

"We have the high ground," Colonel Fox asserted.

"We have the howitzers," General Snow said.

"We have the wisdom of experience."

"We have the lethality of innocence."

"We have esprit de corps."

"We have nothing to lose."

A second silence came, during which I contemplated General John Snow 4099. Beyond his programmed frown, lazy eye, and immaculoid pocks, I caught glimpses of the handsome face he might have owned had his godfather been Charnock and not some incompetent CHALICE technician. His heritage, I decided, was heterogeneous. Several months earlier, a comely Asian soul had connected with an attractive human of Caucasian descent. I imagined that the two of them truly loved each other and might eventually bring forth several splendid children who would all make a sincere effort to forgive their late pyromaniacal semibrother.

"We suggest that between now and sunrise you gather together any possessions of sentimental value," said Captain Snow.

"Unlike our curette-happy parents, we are not heartless," said Major Snow. "We shall permit you to retain whatever photographs, tchotchkes, and liberal-intellectual spider plants you keep on your desks."

"No weapons, of course"—General Snow threw Colonel Fox a gloating glance—"no pistols, no rifles, those all stay behind, likewise your laptops, cell phones, PDAs, iPods, hard drives, and storage media. You'll be strip-searched and X-rayed, so there's no point trying to smuggle any computer chips past our guard."

Londa went after her hangnail with a vengeance, peeling away a quarter-inch scroll of skin. She was trembling now, and not from the cold.

"If you won't allow us any CD-Rs," Colonel Fox said, training her laser gaze on General Snow, "then shut off your electromagnetic pulse for a couple of hours so we can send our files over the Web."

"You don't seem to understand," the immaculoid commander replied. "When the city burns down, all of your unscriptural initiatives must burn down with it."

"Unscriptural initiatives?" Dagmar gestured wildly in the direction of Themisopolis. "Do you have any idea what sort of data we've got back there?"

For the next several minutes, she expounded upon two enterprises Londa had mentioned during my first visit to the city, Project Xelcepin, aimed at producing an ovarian-cancer treatment of unprecedented efficacy, and Operation Velvet Fist, a full-bore assault on the international sexual-slavery trade. Both of these breakthroughs were girded by digital information. Apropos of Xelcepin: the complex protocols for administering the drug and the recent results of a double-blind trial. Concerning the prostitution rings: the secret identities and hidden lairs of more than one hundred slave traffickers, plus the locations of several dozen churches and private homes where the exploited women could seek sanctuary right before the U.N. made its move. Precious data, priceless facts, all of them still awaiting exportation beyond the walls of Themisopolis.

"We're okay with wiping out ovarian cancer, and on the whole your antiprostitution campaign sounds like a good thing," General Snow said. "What worries us is the *other* data you'd like to carry out of here."

"What other data?" Dagmar demanded.

"Don't be coy," General Snow said. "We know that Project Xelcepin is a front for the scheme that *really* matters to you, the development of . . . what's it called?"

"Nildeum," Major Snow said.

"Nildeum," echoed General Snow. "The breakfast cereal additive that makes children stop believing in God."

"This meeting has outrun its usefulness," Yolly observed.

"It's time we took leave of these clowns," Colonel Fox concurred, squeezing Londa's arm.

My vatling made no response. She simply ripped away her hangnail and regarded the far wall with the sort of glassy stare Henry Cushing's young audiences had doubtless accorded *Professor Oolong's Oompah-pah Zoo.*

"And we also know what you're *really* designing at the Vision Syndicate," Captain Snow said.

"The automotive fuel whose secret ingredients are corn oil and menstrual blood," Major Snow said.

"We've worked out the implications," General Snow said.

"We're no dummies," Captain Snow said.

"Once women realize they can sell their menstrual blood for thousands of dollars, they'll try to produce as much of the stuff as possible," Major Snow said.

"We're talking about de facto infertility," Captain Snow said. "Diaphragms, IUDs, condoms—whatever it takes."

"We're out of here," Yolly said.

"You people won't rest until every oil company in America has gone bankrupt," General Snow said, "and pregnancy has become a thing of the past."

* * *

A HEAVY SNOW was falling when we left the mackie headquarters and started back toward the city, though I doubted that the flakes would be sufficiently large, wet, or plentiful to insulate Themisopolis from the coming inferno. Midway through our return journey, Londa stopped walking, as if she'd acquired the plaster flesh and steel bones of Alonso the Conquistador, but she managed to communicate her immediate wishes through clipped phrases and spasmodic gestures. We carried her, literally carried her, to my room in Arcadia House. At first she simply sat on the mattress, grinding her molars and wringing her hands, but finally she spoke, telling her manager to have the city's administrators and division heads assemble in an hour at the Institute for Advanced Biological Investigations.

Not long after Dagmar's departure, the immaculoids' chanting and drumming started up again. Londa cast her livid gaze first on Colonel Fox, then on Yolly, and finally on me.

"The strategy session that matters isn't the one I just arranged," she said. "It's the one that's going to happen right now."

By scouring the paramedics' station, Yolly managed to scare up everything we needed for a tea party—Earl Grey, chai, lemon, sugar, biscotti—not a merry Donya sort of tea party, but the grimmest such gathering imaginable. As the tea bags steeped, Colonel Fox took out her PDA and began working the keyboard with her ballpoint pen, the point striking the membrane with the precise pistoning action of a sewing-machine needle as she summoned crucial statistics to the miniature screen.

"Monday afternoon, as soon as I saw those swarms of mackies, I started running the numbers," she said. "Our present civilian population is three thousand seventeen. I immediately subtracted the orphans and pregnant teens, also the zombie troupers—there's no time to reprogram them for defilade—which gave me a hypothetical fighting force of two thousand and fifty-eight, including professional staff and maintenance workers. Next I conducted an informal survey and learned that about a third of those potential defenders, six hundred and eighty-five, are prepared to take up arms and hold the fort. Naturally we can count on total commitment from my Valkyries."

"That's maybe nine hundred against six thousand," Yolly concluded, aghast.

Colonel Fox lifted a biscotto and set it between her teeth like a cigar stub. "Not great odds, I grant you. But we can still win. The minute the fetuses draw blood, they'll lose public support. Even Governor Winthrop won't dare say it's just another antiabortion demonstration. He'll have to send the National Guard to our rescue."

"Unless the immaculoids have already massacred us," Yolly observed.

"And here's another factor in our favor." Colonel Fox flipped an insouciant hand in the general direction of the mackie encampment. "Those are pretty unhealthy creatures out there. I doubt that they can shoot straight."

"You heard General Snow," Yolly protested. "Their despair makes them abnormally dangerous."

"With all due respect, Yolly," Colonel Fox said, "never employ the enemy's propaganda in assessing the enemy's strength."

Londa arced her thumb and middle finger into the shape of calipers, using the instrument to massage her temples. She lifted her head and fixed on the Valkyrie commander. "You make a compelling case for manning the walls." She climbed off the mattress and presented me with a meandering grin. "Nevertheless, I've decided to follow the advice of my morality teacher. Go ahead, Mason. Tell me what to do."

"You're dumping the decision in *my* lap?" I said.

"I'm confident you can rise to the occasion."

"This isn't fair."

"Sorry, Socrates," Londa said. "I'm responsible for Themisopolis, and you're responsible for me. You knew it might one day come to this. Take a posh job tutoring a gumbo girl for a hundred dollars an hour, and eventually there'll be hell to pay."

My body, it seemed, had become fused with some sinister machine, its gyroscopes spinning in my aorta, its meshed gears nibbling at my stomach. I swallowed some tea and studied the paint-by-numbers tableau over my dresser: Jesus holding up a potential and soon-to-be-proverbial projectile, the famous unthrown first stone, inviting the vigilantes to contemplate its fearsome solidity, even as they took stock of their soggy souls.

"I've always liked that story." I gestured toward the painting. "It cuts through a lot of nonsense."

"Mason used to have us act it out," Londa told Colonel Fox. "He played the mob leader. My friend Brittany was the adulteress, and I was—"

"Let me guess," Colonel Fox said scornfully. "You were the rock."

"It's not generally known that Jesus had encountered a similar situation the week before—same adulteress, different mob," I said, improvising wildly. "Only he didn't intervene. He just stood and watched as a passing Pharisee told the vigilantes, 'Let all the sinners gathered here start stoning the woman, while the flawless among you undertake to defend her.' So the mob broke into two groups, pelters and protectors, and soon the stones were flying every which way. When the dust settled, all the pelters lay dead, but no protector had received so much as a lump on the head. And the Pharisee said, 'What a glorious outcome—the defeat of the vengeful.' And Jesus asked him, 'What if the protectors had been slaughtered instead?' And the Pharisee replied, 'That, too, would have been glorious—the martyrdom of the righteous.' And Jesus said, 'We can do better than that.'"

"Listen to your conscience," Yolly implored her sister. "We have to make a strategic retreat."

"If we don't fight, we'll lose the data," Colonel Fox said with equal urgency.

"Remember how you programmed Joan of Arc?" I asked Londa. "'There are no just wars. There are no greater goods.'"

"No just wars," Yolly echoed.

"A miracle drug for ovarian cancer," Colonel Fox said. "The end of sexual slavery."

Londa approached the dresser and stared into the mirror. Whether by serendipity or intention, her reflected eyes lay along the same horizon as the lush blue Protestant orbs of the Jewish rabbi.

"It's really no contest, is it?" she said.

"None at all," I replied.

"Mason, you earned every penny of that hundred dollars an hour," Yolly said.

"You've got a coward for a conscience," Colonel Fox told her boss.

"By this time tomorrow," Londa said, "we'll all be out of here, no massacre, no martyrs, not one life squandered, and I'll be wishing I was dead."

I LAY AWAKE for many hours, perhaps the entire night—certainly no dream came: no alligator feedings with John Snow 0001, no sea urchin rescues with Donya. Dawn found me thrashing around amid my blankets like the reanimated Lazarus struggling against his winding-sheet. I summoned my remaining strength and staggered to the dresser, where I studied the play of the morning sunbeams on the Gospel canvas. In this light, the adulteress and her Nazarene advocate seemed positively beatific, painted not by numbers but by numinosity.

I scrambled into my clothes and packed my overnight bag, whereupon the Sisters Sabacthani appeared, Yolly looking haggard and jumpy, Londa maintaining an uneasy détente among her warring selves. Each woman had brought along a small valise, and Londa also carried a birdcage. Its outraged occupant, Quetzie, repeatedly poked an indignant snout through the bars.

"Tell me this isn't happening," Yolly said. "Tell me it's all a mumquat dream."

"It's happening," I said.

The instant the mackies issued us a cell phone, Londa explained, we would call Jordan and have her retrieve us from the state park. Apparently Londa's decision to surrender Themisopolis, which she'd represented as "my former morality teacher's decision to surrender Themisopolis," had been well received by the medical and research personnel, who'd hastened to point out that they'd signed on to practice healing and pursue knowledge, not to cross swords with fetuses. Several Valkyries, custodians, and groundskeepers had volunteered to stay behind and wage guerrilla war against the arsonists, but Londa had told them, "I don't want your blood on my conscience, and I don't want it on my conscience's conscience either." Of all the creatures in our care, only the zombie troupers would not be joining the retreat. They were mere enfleshed machines, after all, insensate as sock puppets, and by Londa's account they had opted to remain in the city and allow the mackie flames to end their meaningless programmed lives.

I grabbed my overnight bag, and then the three of us left Arcadia House, marched across the quadrangle, and headed down Boudicca Street past the leafless, brainless ranks of trees, each elm and sycamore oblivious to its imminent incineration.

The mood at the main entrance was dour, somber, almost funereal. Knapsacks on their backs, suitcases at their sides, the city's entire population had collected in silent clusters of twenty and thirty. I spotted several terrariums and pet carriers—gecko, ferret, parakeet, Chihuahua, tortoiseshell cat: Londa wasn't the only person who'd be saving an animal from the conflagration. Everyone spoke in whispers. To judge from their empty holsters and disgruntled deportments, the Valkyries had complied with the directive to leave their guns behind. I was pleased to note a team of paramedics administering to our orphans and pregnant teens, making sure they all had their mittens, scarves, and medicines.

For twenty minutes we huddled in the raw morning air, stomping our feet and rubbing our hands, and then the gates opened to admit a company of three hundred heavily armed immaculoids, Lieutenant Colonel Jane Snow 3221 in command. With rude shoves, loutish punches, and the occasional coercive boot, the fetuses herded us through the portal and into a kind of open-air rat maze improvised from sawhorses and quivering streamers of yellow barricade tape. An additional immaculoid regiment appeared, breaking us into groups of ten and forcing us to negotiate the labyrinth, until eventually we stood before a line of nylon pavilions, eight labeled WOMEN, four MEN. Lieutenant Colonel Snow explained that we were about to be "processed"—checked for smuggled goods—and anyone who resisted would be "treated as callously as our parents treated us."

More waiting, a full hour this time, an interval during which I beheld the immaculoids climb into the forty gasoline trucks and drive them, engines gasping with diesel flatulence, through the gates toward the city's combustible heart. Goaded by the butt of an assault rifle, I followed my nine fellow evacuees into pavilion number 12, where Sergeant John Snow 0875 required us to strip down to our goose pimples. Our teeth chattered furiously. We sounded like a castanet band. A squad of enlisted immaculoids X-rayed our innards with portable radiology gear, searching for ingested computer chips and swallowed microfilm capsules. A second squad commandeered our wristwatches, credit cards, and loose change, any of which might have been storage media in disguise. Squad number three examined our clothing, probing pockets, turning gloves inside out, inspecting every seam and cuff. A fourth cadre took out utility knives and peeled away the linings of our valises and suitcases like fur trappers skinning beavers. My overnight bag came back to me in tatters, but at least I'd passed the test, as had the rest of my group—not a single piece of contraband among us.

At long last the sergeant issued the blessed command. "Get dressed, and no stalling!"

As the next band of ten entered the pavilion, the mackies' gun muzzles nudged us through the rear flaps. An instant later the Sisters Sabacthani emerged from pavilion 3. Londa still held Quetzie's cage. Stupefied by the cold and grateful for the restoration of our clothes, we became putty in the hands of Lieutenant Colonel Snow and her regiment, and nobody raised the feeblest protest during our subsequent ordeal, which had us first standing around Hypatia Circle for two hours while the remaining Themisopolians were processed, then tromping four miles across frozen fields covered with thorny vines as treacherous as barbed wire, until at last we spied a line of snow-dusted evergreens marking the eastern edge of Quehannock State Park.

The fetuses and their rifle butts continued to treat us harshly, pressing us toward our destination at a rapid clip. Upon reaching the parking lot, the Themisopolis commuters rebonded with their cars and vans, then took off, even as Lieutenant Colonel Snow and her subordinates moved among the rest of us, passing out the promised technology. When Londa received a cell phone, she sidled discreetly away from the mackies and, after ringing up Jordan, spoke to her in a whisper. At the end of the conversation, she offered Yolly a freighted nod whose significance eluded me. I took the phone and called Natalie, but she didn't answer, so I left a message assuring her I was out of harm's way and would probably spend the night in Jordan Frazier's Georgetown apartment.

Within a half-hour the evacuation vehicles started arriving—sedans, station wagons, hatchbacks, SUVs, pickup trucks, limousines, hired taxis. Particularly conspicuous were the shuttles bearing the logos of various Maryland hotels and motor inns, Londa's medical staff having arranged for our orphans and outcasts to enjoy commercial lodgings until more permanent accommodations could be secured. I took comfort in the thought of our paramedics tucking in these wretches for the night, assuring them that a second City of Justice would one day rise from the ashes.

Jordan was among the last chauffeurs to appear, vaulting athletically from the cab of her Plymouth Carmilla minivan. I wanted to tell her she looked fabulous—her buoyant brown eyes and lavish smile had ceded little to the years—and how much I admired her lobbying efforts on behalf of Sabacthanite ideals. But I was so frazzled I could only give her a doleful hug and thank her for being the one bright spot in an otherwise wretched morning.

Under the immaculoids' watchful gaze, we climbed into the minivan, Yolly settling beside Jordan while Londa, Quetzie, and I assumed the backseat.

"On track with Plan Omega?" Londa asked Jordan as we cruised out of the park. "Matériel in hand?"

"Lady Justice is looking out for us," Jordan replied cheerfully.

Plan Omega? Matériel? The terminology of the moment made me nervous.

"I'm confused," I said.

"Have patience," Londa said.

Yolly inserted *Linda Ronstadt: Greatest Hits* into the dashboard music center. As the Carmilla resounded with "You're No Good" followed by "Silver Threads and Golden Needles," Jordan piloted us to I-95, hit the accelerator, and zoomed into the fast lane, everybody except me singing along with the recording. By the time we reached the Havre de Grace turnoff, Ronstadt and her backup trio were belting out "That'll Be the Day."

Jordan followed the exit ramp to a Burrito Junction, where she parked and killed the engine.

"Can't we do better than this?" I pleaded. God knows I was hungry, but I wasn't in the mood for fatty ground beef enshrouded in a soggy tortilla.

"We aren't here to eat," Londa explained. "We're here to use the restrooms. Let's say we get into our disguises in ten minutes max—okay, gang?"

"Disguises?" I said.

Londa squeezed my knee. "On her way to pick us up, Jordan bought everything we'll need to turn ourselves into immaculoids. Orange jumpsuits, silver wigs, grease pencils."

"I could find only three suits," Jordan said, "but as your getaway driver I don't really need one."

"Getaway driver?" I said.

"Last night we burned three hundred gigabytes onto sixty CD-Rs and hid them inside our statue of Themis," Londa explained. "Not the first place the mackies will think to look, but not the last either, so the sooner we go fetch the data—you and me and Yolly—the sooner, the better."

"All three of us?" I said.

"The plan turns on us having as many Sabacthanites inside the city as possible," Jordan said.

"Sounds dangerous," I noted.

"Only if we do something amazingly stupid," Londa said.

"*Really* dangerous," I said.

"We can count on you, right, Mason?" Yolly asked.

Of course they couldn't count on me. Who did they think I was, goddamn Anthony Quinn in *The Guns of Navarone*? "I would say we need *two* getaway drivers."

"Sheesh!" Jordan exclaimed.

"Mason," said Yolly through clenched teeth.

"I'm a philosopher," I said, "not a fucking commando."

Londa unsnapped her seat belt, curling one arm around Quetzie's cage, the other around my shoulder. "Hey, Socrates, don't you recognize a second chance when you see one? Help us get those CD-Rs, and the world will forgive you for cooking me up."

It wasn't merely the carrot of redemption that sent me to the Burrito Junction men's room that afternoon. The ovarian cancer drug also figured in my reasoning, as did the slave traffickers. Initially I bobbled the job, applying the greasepaint so liberally I gave myself a leper's decaying cheeks, but by rubbing the stuff away with paper towels I eventually acquired the pocked complexion Plan Omega required. Before returning to the minivan, I donned my silver wig and studied my face in the mirror. An aging mackie stared back at me—not a generic aging mackie but the one whose features I knew best, the former inhabitant of an abandoned Boston switch tower. If I could believe his dying words, John Snow 0001 would have refused to join the imminent burning of Themisopolis. He was a highly principled fetus, a fact of which his semifather would always be proud.

Chapter 12

TO SNEAK INTO THE OCCUPIED CITY on a mission whose unmasking would surely occasion our deaths—to lay hold of the treasure without drawing the attention of six thousand watchful fetuses—to spirit the data away the instant the immaculoids turned their backs: a foolhardy plan indeed, bound to spark tension and discord within our ad hoc commando unit, and so I was hardly surprised when a heated argument erupted between the Sisters Sabacthani. Londa, our reckless rationalist, wanted Jordan to drive right up to the city gates, on the theory that the mackies would be too distracted to note the incursion. Yolly, our sensible sybarite, insisted that we park at least a mile from the ramparts. Better safe than sorry. Just when it seemed the women might come to blows, Jordan resolved the controversy by stopping the van on a spot she insisted was the precise Pythagorean midpoint between Londa's impetuosity and Yolly's prudence.

At three o'clock, eight hours after our captors had marched us through the police-tape labyrinth, Jordan presented Londa with a Phillips screwdriver, Yolly with a cell phone, and me with a knapsack full of Gatorade and cereal bars. Itching beneath our fetal patinas, we dashed down Avalon Lane past the dormant cherry trees until we reached the encampment. Now Londa increased the pace, leading us through the grid of tents and pavilions to the parking lot. Running faster still, we swerved among the moving vans, buses, and semi-rigs, the air growing ever thicker with the aggressive aroma of gasoline. At last the great portal loomed up, its bronze gates hanging open, doubtless so the mackies could make a quick retreat if the conflagration got out of hand. The noxious fumes became sharper yet, reaming our nostrils, scoring our tonsils, scouring our lungs.

A final sprint, and we were inside the city, where I beheld a scene so appalling that for a moment I simply stood and stared, frozen in begrudging awe of CHALICE and its fetal minions. Having attached auxiliary pumps, hoses, and nozzles to the forty gasoline trucks, the immaculoids were busily siphoning this liquid munificence and releasing it in wild ejaculatory spurts. Whatever one thought of Enoch Anthem and Felix Pielmeister, they were consummate apocalypticians, men who could envision a Judgment Day of surpassing surrealism and render it in fossil fuel.

Normally the city's sewer system would have channeled the deluge underground, but the mackies had stoppered all the gratings with swatches cut from their canvas tents. Slowly, inexorably, the gasoline collected in the streets, the puddles fringed by iridescent rainbows. My brain seemed to float free of my body, a neural balloon, borne by the Texaco zephyrs. Despite the urgency of our situation, or perhaps because of it, the women started squabbling again, Yolly insisting that we proceed at the immaculoids' characteristically crippled gait, Londa arguing that we run like mad. The right tactic soon became apparent: we needn't limp at all, the mackies being far too busy constructing their holocaust to notice the impostors in their midst.

We charged down Shambhala Avenue, weaving among the ever-expanding petroleum pools, and a few minutes later arrived in Alethia Square. Resolute as ever, bronze heart throbbing with her undying devotion to fairness, Themis held her motorized balance scales aloft. The fumes pursued us like vengeful ghosts. Londa dropped to her knees before the statue, so that she briefly appeared to be a pagan supplicant worshipping an idol—or, more likely in this case, Sinuhe's iconoclast sister faking adoration—then took out the screwdriver and fitted it into a screw holding the access plate to the pedestal. She rotated her wrist. The screw resisted. She cursed and increased the torque. The screw surrendered. My headache spread through its bony enclosure, colonizing every sinus. Londa loosened all four screws. The access plate hit the flagstones. She thrust the screwdriver into the hollow, triggering the emergency shut-off mechanism. The balance scales ceased oscillating, as if after all these years Lady Justice had finally reached a quintessentially equitable decision. From the depths of the pedestal, Londa retrieved a crumpled Kevlar satchel—it looked like an enormous green change purse—and hugged it to her breast.

The sewers were backing up rapidly, turning the city into a nightmare Venice, its canals swollen with dark, seething torrents of Regular, Plus, and Supreme. From these ghastly waterways there now arose a shimmering gallery of hydrocarbon mirages. I pulled out the Gatorade bottle and took a big gulp, seeking to wash the Cretaceous taste from my mouth. My eyes swam with tears. My dizziness increased. A blackout seemed imminent, but I fought to forestall it, chewing the insides of my cheeks and slapping my brow with the flat of my hand.

Yolly yanked the cell phone from her jumpsuit. Obviously the immaculoids had shut off the EMP, for she reached Jordan without difficulty, telling her to expect us shortly. "The data's in hand," she informed her guardian, at which instant the fetuses, having set their torches ablaze, thrust them into the gasoline.

In a blinding flash, Lake Sunoco caught fire, and then the rest ignited, Amoco Run, Getty Lagoon, Texaco Tarn, the river Exxon, and soon all five bodies were flowing together, a confluence of infernos, so that a roaring wall of flame now stood between the city gates and ourselves. A great swell of scalding air rolled toward us like a boiling tsunami. We dropped to the flagstones. For a full minute, we lay prone in the courtyard, gasping and coughing, while Londa explained that we had only one option. We must make our way to the Circus of Atonement, descend to the basement, and hide in the ontogenerator until the firestorm passed.

"The vat's lined with silica ceramic," she noted. "Heat-resistant as hell's hinges."

Clutching the satchel more fiercely yet, Londa lurched to her feet and led us on a frantic dash down Boudicca Street. Billows of smoke filled the sky, vast and black as the clouds whose cache had scrubbed Noah's contemporaries from the earth. Cinders flew everywhere like squalls of demonic snow. Insectile sparks stung our cheeks and brows, fiery hornets, incandescent wasps.

As we drew within sight of the Circus, Yolly called Jordan again, informing her of the obvious fact that Themisopolis was burning and the less obvious fact that so far we'd all avoided incineration—a circumstance we intended to prolong by taking refuge in the ontogenerator. Next Londa got on the phone, telling Jordan to move into the nearest hotel and stand ready to retrieve us at a moment's notice.

The plaza outside the rotunda was unexpectedly crowded. Galvanized by whatever survival instinct had leaked into their algorithms, the Circus troupers had armed themselves and fled the building—a sensible step but insufficient, for their path was blocked by a fetal battalion, one hundred strong. Clearly a massacre was in the offing, the immaculoids' assault rifles being considerably more powerful than the troupers' theatrical props. Joan of Arc wielded her sword, Pope John Paul II his crozier, Davy Crockett his Kentucky rifle, Edward Teller his flagellant's whip. Mary Baker Eddy had emerged into daylight accompanied by her band of audio-animatronic victims, all of whom had evidently forgiven her, for they gathered protectively around her like a bodyguard of midgets. Fresh from their church wedding, Percival Sarnac and Leopold Ransom brandished gold altar crosses, which they evidently intended to use as cudgels. The most poorly equipped performers were Warren Anderson, Henry Kissinger, and Ronald Reagan, their only weapons being spindly aluminum stands stolen from the Circus's lighting system.

Sensing her authority and perhaps also remembering her victories, the troupers rallied to Joan of Arc's side. For a fleeting instant, the maid and I exchanged glances of mutual recognition, acknowledging our moment of choreographed passion.

"There are no just wars!" she exclaimed in obedience to her DUNCE cap programming. "There are no greater goods!"

So intense was the immaculoids' delight in having an entire theater company to annihilate, they simply ignored Londa, Yolly, and myself as we slipped behind the Maid of Orléans's ragtag army. Reaching the rotunda entrance, we paused to survey the pitched battle. It was predictably quick and entirely brutal. Anderson, Kissinger, and Reagan were the first to fall, blasted to pieces as, floodlight stands raised high, they attempted to poke out their assailants' eyes. The fetuses fired again, killing Sarnac and Ransom before they could bludgeon anyone with their crosses, and then came the third volley, raining down on my poor Joan and leaving her as perforated as St. Sebastian after the archers had martyred him. More bullets flew. Before succumbing to their wounds, the pope coshed a fetus with his crozier, Crockett shot one between the eyes, and Mrs. Eddy issued a piercing battle cry, ordering her entourage into the fray. The audio-animatronic children fought bravely, collectively dragging a mackie to the ground before salvos of lead separated them from their electric intestines.

Throughout the slaughter I occasionally glanced at Londa, who seemed proud that her troupers were displaying such fortitude in the face of the mackie host. Even before the butchery ended, I realized that while she still detested the primal Ronald Reagan, the original Warren Anderson, and all their Phyllistine kind, their repentant reincarnations had emerged in her eyes as brave and even noble beings. As we slipped into the Circus, Londa looked over her shoulder, anxious to glimpse her slain creations before their bodies turned to ash.

MANY ARE THE CONDITIONS under which a man might relish intimate confinement with a comely heterosexual woman and her polymorphous-perverse sister, but I soon realized that my interval in the subterranean ontogenerator would not be one of them. Londa and Yolly hated our situation no less than I. True, they were accustomed to these sweltering diving bells, not so much from their prenatal immersions as from the deliberate descent they'd made with Donya in Torre de la Carne several months after their mother's funeral, an episode they now proceeded to relate in detail, describing how it had reinforced their sisterly bonds even as it enabled them to absolve Edwina of her sins. Nothing in their previous experience, however, had prepared them for this premature burial with its benumbing boredom, unrelieved claustrophobia, and relentless requirement that we twist ourselves into poses suggesting some sadistic school of yoga.

But for our battery-operated fan—its feeble plastic vanes plying the glutinous atmosphere like spatulas stirring mud, replenishing the vat's stale air via the vent in the hatch—we might very well have suffocated. Hour after hour we sat on our haunches, simmering like meatballs in a Crock-Pot as the bellowing flames consumed the city. Yolly tried contacting Jordan again, hoping her guardian might use cell-phone technology to send some soothing music our way. The connection failed. Even as it saved our skins, the titanium chamber blocked all communication with the outside world.

We slaked our thirst courtesy of the Gatorade, assuaged our hunger with the cereal bars, and preserved our sanity by telling

stories. For my own contribution to this oral anthology, I drew upon
Edmund Spenser's epic, recounting the Red Cross Knight's three-day
battle with the great dragon, scourge of Faerie Land. When Londa's
turn came, she enumerated the misdeeds of those Phyllistines she'd
been intending to put in the Circus: Ethan Pepperhill, of course, as
well as Pol Pot, Idi Amin, Slobodan Milošević, and Joseph Stalin, assuming the necessary grave-robbing arrangements could be made.
Our stellar performer, predictably, was Yolly, who told us the plot of
her evolving fantasy novel. Set in Ondoluria, a feudal world where
books were living creatures, *The Citadel of Paradox* concerned a band
of adventurers—three men and four women, ever eager to enter into
carnal configurations with one another—who'd undertaken a long,
perilous, continent-spanning quest to heal the sole and sickly copy of
the *Epistemologia,* a protoplasmic encyclopedia containing the whole
of human and divine knowledge.

"So what do you think?" Yolly said upon finishing her presentation. "Am I on the right track?"

"A very Yolly sort of epic," Londa said approvingly, and indeed it
was, full of horses and eros and the juices of life.

"Maybe the quest should be part of a larger narrative," I suggested.
"Once your adventurers restore the book to health, they attempt to
decipher it, and just when they're about to give up, a cosmic Rosetta
stone falls into their laps."

"I like that," Yolly said.

"What sort of knowledge does the book contain?" Londa asked.
"The periodic table of the elements? Maxwell's equations? The Beatitudes?"

"All of the above, I should imagine," Yolly said, stroking the
green satchel. "Not to mention a cure for ovarian cancer and a map
disclosing the whereabouts of every sexual slaver in the galaxy."

ON THE MORNING OF THE THIRD DAY, we decided to take
the risk and test the air beyond the ontogenerator. The instant we

popped the hatch, an agile breeze wafted into the vat, cooling our cheeks and brows. A gust from the gods, I decided—a breath from noble Horus, a laugh from wise Thoth. The inferno, it seemed, had burned itself out.

We ascended to street level, reveling in our newly acquired femurs and knees, and exited the rotunda. Yolly called Jordan on the cell phone, telling her to jump into the van and drive like a maniac. Before us lay a lunar plain, bleak, shattered, sterile. Emerging from our titanium womb, we had entered a void. We had been born into death. The fire had gutted the buildings, blasted the trees, and turned the gasoline trucks into amorphous lumps of metal. Galaxies of particulate matter swarmed and swirled everywhere, their motes dancing like cathode-ray static. An unnamable sensation screwed through my nasal passages, a stench compounded of evil resins, depraved plastics, and satanic polymers.

Like survivors shambling away from a crashed jetliner, we stepped uncertainly across the Circus plaza, moving past the charred bodies of the zombie troupers. Poor Joan of Orléans—twice born, twice burned. We headed down Boudicca Street, Londa hunched protectively over the Kevlar satchel like a mother shielding her infant from a rainstorm. Caedmon Hall, Arcadia House, the Vision Syndicate, the Artemis Clinic, the Institute for Advanced Biological Investigations: all had been reduced to naked matrices of blackened beams and melted girders. Combers of ash rolled across the scorched terrain in a vast, unnavigable sea. Parts of the city were still cooking, wisps of smoke rising from the carbonized timbers as the crackling embers issued a disquieting cadence.

Gradually we became aware of the immaculoids, most of them now corpses, having variously succumbed to asphyxiation, dehydration, and the defects bequeathed them by incompetent CHALICE technicians. Of the remaining mackies, barely fifty were yet standing, wandering amid the cinders like extras in a cinematic collaboration between George Romero and Martin Heidegger, *Dasein of the*

Dead. The other survivors floated upon the ocean of ash, gagging and thrashing as the gray waves sucked them down.

In time our fitful journey brought us to Alethia Square. Themis had fallen, her bronze knees turned to butter by the heat. The blind-folded goddess lay supine in the courtyard, scales at her side, staring at the winter sky. Curious, I touched her sword, still warm, where-upon a series of short, sharp reports reached my ears—*pop, pop, pop, pop.*

At first I thought it was an automobile backfiring—could Jordan be here already?—or perhaps a metallic echo caused by the cooling of Themis's hollow innards. Then I glanced at Yolly. For an instant she simply stood there, jerking like a gaffed fish. A sound of primal dismay, more animal than human, broke from Londa's throat. Yolly pitched forward and collapsed on the flagstones beside the statue's massive head.

I spun, glancing in all directions. No sniper caught my eye. I saw only the granular air. Londa tossed the satchel aside, sprinted to the statue, and, falling to her knees, cradled her spasming sister.

"Get it out!" Yolly cried.

Lurching forward, I melded with the pietà. Just below Yolly's left shoulder, a ragged wound blossomed like a carnation, petals of blood spreading outward from the axis. Her complexion grew white as alabaster. She pressed her spine against Themis's cheek and shiv-ered.

"Jordan's coming!" I insisted, squeezing Yolly's hand. "We're taking you to the hospital!"—the very words I'd spoken to my neth-erson five days earlier.

"It burns!" Blood dribbled from Yolly's mouth like the effluence of a punctured scream. "Get it out!"

"We'll get it out!" Londa shouted.

"It burns!"

Yolly's fingers turned to ice. Her eyes rolled upward as if to scan the inside of her skull.

Fetal snorts filled the air. Pivoting away from Yolly's dead and grimacing face, I glanced once again across the square. Smoke pouring from the muzzle of his assault rifle, General John Snow 4099 came gimping down Shambhala Avenue, the last of the immaculoids, manifestly pleased that he'd recognized us beneath our disintegrating disguises. I estimated I had fifteen seconds to live. No philosophical truths flitted through my brain. I did not learn the veracity or falsity of Platonic idealism. I did not see God. I merely let out a yelp of despair and vomited onto the flagstones.

Were it not for Londa's next action—grabbing the satchel and hurling it toward the approaching fetus—we would surely have died then and there, joining Yolly and the Circus troupers on Corporate Christi's roster of victims. Instantly General Snow fell upon the green bag, tearing it to pieces. Soon sixty shining CD-Rs lay strewn around the courtyard like wafers baked for a postindustrial Eucharist. Next the mackie went to work with his rifle butt, an assiduous alchemist grinding pestle against mortar, so that the discs became a thousand glittering shards, but this was not enough, for now he splintered the splinters, transmuting the data into spoonfuls of chaos and pinches of mockery and glittering smidgeons of nothingness.

Acting on raw instinct, Londa and I pulled Yolly's body to a standing position and laid it athwart our shoulders. We began our retreat, hurrying along Shambhala Avenue as the satisfied snarls of the dying fetus grew ever fainter. Passing through the city gates, we staggered across the parking lot and entered the encampment, except there was no parking lot, no encampment, only my Heideggerian hallucination, a bottomless abyss swallowing the tents, pavilions, howitzers, hydraulic lifts, moving vans, buses, semi-rigs, cherry trees, and fountains. One instant Jordan was there, standing beside her minivan, staring at Londa and me and Yolly's corpse, and the next she was gone, consumed along with Avalon Lane and Hypatia Circle and Quehannock State Park, and before the illusory vortex ingested me, I briefly wondered what precise portion of the universe might satisfy its appetite. The answer, of course, lay somewhere in the *Epistemologia,* that omniscient anthology with its recipes for ambrosia, spells for raising the dead, and compendium of methods by which a philosopher might commit suicide without effort or pain. I merely had to crack the spine and read.

THESE DAYS MANY HISTORIANS and social commentators perceive a tragic grandeur in the fall of Themisopolis. According to this theory, Londa and Yolly Sabacthani were too spiritually advanced to prosper in the mundane world, their vision too noble to survive the slings and arrows of Corporate Christi. The destruction of the city, the loss of the data, the murder of Yolly—these disasters were inevitable given the rarefied plane on which the sisters' souls resided.

While I would award this interpretation high marks for romanticism, I personally favor a more prosaic argument. In my view, Londa and Yolly made the banal and common mistake of underestimating the opposition. The vatlings' tragedy lay not in their presumed surfeit of purity but merely in their failure to appreciate the enemy's surplus ruthlessness.

Unlike her superstar twin, Yolly had never been accorded her own action figure, trading cards, board game, or comic-book series, and yet she was a celebrity in her own right, and I was not surprised when her death made the front page of the *Harford County Aegis,* the *Baltimore Sun,* and the *Washington Post*—plus several hundred other papers, I later learned, commanding more ink in some cases than the collateral incineration of Themisopolis. Predictably, Maryland's Governor Winthrop told the reporters that Yolly had "died accidentally when a legitimate antiabortion protest went awry," and at the time Londa, Jordan, and I were too dazed and depleted to offer a rebuttal. Instead we simply huddled in Jordan's Georgetown apartment, trying to reweave the unraveled threads of our lives.

Throughout this wretched period, the emotional atmosphere

among us was, to say the least, tempestuous. Jordan blamed Londa for talking her into Plan Omega and me for not talking Londa out of it. Londa reviled her former tutor for giving her such a malignantly idealistic psyche, even as she faulted Jordan for making Yolly only slightly less obsessed. As for me, I alternately heaped scorn on Londa for thinking up the whole crazy Omega scheme and abuse on Jordan for facilitating it.

When not trading accusations with my roommates, I instinctively sought solace from Natalie, telephoning her every morning and afternoon, but I never caught her at home. The one time she called back, leaving a message expressing her sorrow over Yolly's death and her frustration that we weren't connecting, I was down the street buying whole wheat bread and red wine, the staples of our unhappy community.

In deference to Yolly, we all agreed to suspend our mutual antipathy long enough to select a burial site—an easy task, as it happened. Two years earlier, on a pellucid October afternoon, Yolly and Jordan had gone hiking around Parnassus Acres, the Virginia horse farm where Oyster was spending his dotage. When they reached the cherry grove, Yolly had casually mentioned that in the world of her novel an Ondolurian normally arranged to be buried in an orchard, so that his remains might nourish the trees and his descendants continue to know him in the succulent person of apples, pears, peaches, figs, or plums.

Parnassus Acres belonged to a divorcée named Sally Quattrone, a middle-aged neo-hippie who practiced shamanic trance, Tibetan channeling, and other disciplines that in her neighbors' eyes verged on sexual perversion. When we approached Sally with the idea of interring Yolly among the cherry trees, she was understandably nonplussed, but then we gave her the extant pages of *The Citadel of Paradox*—Jordan had been keeping a printout in her apartment, reading it with an eye to one day offering Yolly a critique—and a single perusal was sufficient to win Sally over. She would happily facilitate our scheme, providing we didn't harm any roots, a point she underscored with a quotation from the novel celebrating "those fleshy, fibrous anchors binding Tolvaganum the Oak to Goncelia the Earth, and Goncelia the Earth to Tolvaganum the Oak."

Two burly Valkyries helped us dig the grave, a familiar enough task for them: six days earlier they'd driven their shovels into the frozen ground of White Marsh Cemetery in prelude to disinterring Ethan Pepperhill. After wrapping Yolly's remains in a shroud, Jordan, Londa, and I lowered the corpse into the cavity, threading it through the tangle of roots. The task proved emotionally draining for both women, and they immediately fled the scene, leaving the Valkyries and myself to restore the dirt.

Twenty-four hours before the scheduled memorial service, Henry, Brock, and Donya flew from Key West to D.C. and checked into the Mayflower Hotel. I could hardly imagine a sadder set of circumstances under which the Hubris Academy faculty might hold a reunion, and yet the arrival of the Isla de Sangre contingent had an immediate and salutary effect. Simply knowing that the youngest Sister Sabacthani was in town—Donya, the better angel of all our natures—inspired Londa, Jordan, and me to stop quarreling and cultivate a more seemly grief.

On the morning of the funeral, we all met for breakfast at an Art Deco café near Jordan's apartment. My male colleagues had come through the decade unspoiled. Far from diminishing his good looks, Brock's wrinkles actually augmented his aura of bohemian rascality, and it occurred to me that he might have applied the lines himself: the Mad Artist of Blood Island, embossing his face with an exquisite chisel. Henry's billowing paunch struck me less as a sign of laxity than as a deliberately acquired enhancement. He arrived bearing good news. After years of being strung along by various Nickelodeon executives, he'd just learned that the current regime had loved, absolutely loved, his concept for *Uncle Rumpus's Magic Island,* and they were equally enamored of his sample scripts. As soon as Donya was safely installed in the freshman class at Yale, her guardians would head to New York City, Henry to attend a series of preproduction meetings, Brock to start designing Plessey the Plesiosaur, Siegfried the Snapping Turtle, Basso Profundo the Bullfrog, and the rest of Uncle Rumpus's friends.

The instant I laid eyes on Donya, I realized I'd been wrong to stay away from Isla de Sangre all these years. In maturing from a freckled preschooler to a feline eighteen-year-old, she'd become the spitting image of the adolescent Londa—lithe, graceful, tall as a sunflower—but the resemblance, thank heaven, was confined to the physical. She had none of Londa's scary intensity, none of the fervor that had raised and then razed Themisopolis. It was hard to believe that the self-possessed young woman now sitting before me eating a vegetarian omelet had once almost severed her little finger to protest the outcome of a croquet game.

We finished our breakfast, climbed into Jordan's van, and drove to Parnassus Acres, where Dagmar Röhrig and Vetruvia Fox joined our mournful company. Somehow Londa's disciples had gotten wind of the imminent ritual, and about three hundred were waiting for us, wearing Weltanschauung Woman sweatshirts and Dame Quixote baseball caps. Patiently but firmly, Colonel Fox explained to the acolytes that gate-crashing the funeral would be a poor way to honor either sister, and so the Sabacthanites retreated to the adjacent dairy farm, where they milled around smoking dope, strumming guitars, and singing songs from Pischel and Ploog's Tony Award–winning rock opera about Londa, *Doctor Madonna*.

For several minutes the six of us stood in the orchard and said nothing, the communal aphasia of the bereaved, and then the ceremony officially began with Jordan reading a passage from *The Citadel of Paradox* in which a vain prince suddenly grasps the inner beauty of the hideous toads of Nobdagob Bog, "who asked nothing of the world save mud and methane, swamp and solitude." Henry came forward next, setting a bouquet of amaranth on the grave, after which Londa recited Emily Dickinson's "Because I Could Not Stop for Death," and then I offered up my favorite stanza of all time, Lord Byron's "She walks in beauty like the night / Of cloudless climes and starry skies; / And all that's best of dark and bright / Meet in her aspect and her eyes. . . ." The instant he'd heard the news, Brock had sculpted a piece of Blood Island driftwood into a little horse, and now he used Sally Quattrone's trowel to plant this elegant eohippus several inches down, beneath a rock that marked the spot—I could guide his hand with great confidence—where Yolly's heart lay.

Shivering in her windbreaker, tears trickling down her face like meltwater from an icicle, Donya delivered an oration she'd composed the night before, a verbal collage assembled from her e-mail exchanges with her elder sister. Repeatedly, with great patience, Yolly had explained to Donya why there was no shame in being a gumbo girl, and she'd also helped her little sister undertake an Internet search for Edwina's mother and father—that is to say, Donya's mother and father, and Yolly's, too, and Londa's. Before they died, Francine Sabacthani, née Miller, and her husband, Arthur Sabacthani, had been high school biology teachers, dedicated to their profession, beloved by their students, and bewildered that their only child had turned out to be a genius.

Not long after Donya's tribute ended, Londa slipped away without explanation, sidling into the swamp like an Ondolurian setting out to save the *Epistemologia.* Although Dagmar insisted that Londa simply needed to be alone for a while, Donya soon grew fretful. Perhaps her remaining sister was going to shoot herself, she speculated, or maybe she intended to jump into a pool of quicksand.

My search took nearly an hour, and by the time it ended, the sun was setting, gilding the trees and thickening the shadows. I found Londa sitting by a brook whose sparkling course marked the border between Parnassus Acres and the neighboring dairy farm. Having constructed a cairn on the bank, she was now systematically disassembling the pile and throwing the stones into the water.

"I love Donya," she said without looking up. "And I love Jordan, too, and Henry and Brock, and when you're not being a jerk, I even love you. But I loved Yolly most of all."

"Of course."

"Tell me I didn't kill her."

"You didn't kill her."

"I killed her." She hurled a stone. It bounced off a drifting log and plopped into the brook.

"No. It was the mackie." I glanced toward the far shore. A scarecrow stood guard over a barren field—not a gaunt Ray Bolger off to see the Wizard, but a joyless sentry stuffed with corncobs. "You probably feel like murdering Pielmeister right now."

"If I'm an honest woman, then I must look my morality teacher in the eye and say, 'You're right, sir. I want to see Pielmeister dead and buried and eaten by maggots, likewise Anthem, Winthrop—that whole ugly crowd.'" Our gazes met. "You'll be happy to hear I'm planning a different destiny for the Phyllistines. It's fine to love your enemies, but it's even better to *cure* them, wouldn't you say?"

"Not necessarily."

"Curing is better than loving."

"Maybe. I don't know. Let's go back to the funeral."

Seizing the handiest rock, she wound up her arm like a gaucho preparing to unleash a bola. "Watch me, Socrates. Watch me take a lump of enlightenment and plant it in that scarecrow's brain."

"Donya's worried sick about you."

She released the rock, and it flew across the brook, coming to rest exactly where she'd predicted, north of the scarecrow's nose, south of his dome, like David's missile lodging in Goliath's brow.

"Bull's-eye, Socrates. I knocked out his pineal gland and replaced it with a vastly superior transplant. The pineal gland is a divine organ. It's the locus of the human soul. Your friend Descartes revealed that to the world."

"Not his finest hour. The man was no neurologist."

"I just did to that scarecrow what you did to me. I gave him a soul. Now he's cured."

I made no reply but took Londa's hand and led her away from the brook. The closer we drew to the orchard, the more certain I became that no seer or sibyl would ever step forward to bless Londa's plan to rehabilitate the Phyllistines. Unfavorable stars hung over the enterprise, ominous entrails, disapproving runes. And yet when Donya ran across the field and threw her arms around both of us, I grew suddenly convinced that, for her surviving sister's sake, my vatling would reject this nascent scheme and all such demented projects to come. Before the year was out, I told myself, any visitor to Londa's abode would hear a biblical verse that through constant casual repetition she'd inadvertently added to Quetzie's repertoire.

"Let us reason together," the feathered reptile would say. "*Cogito ergo sum,* and all you need is love, and Mason is a genius, and let us reason together."

Part III
Prometheus Wept

Chapter 13

I KNOW WHAT YOU'RE THINKING, ladies and gentlemen. The instant I heard Londa speak of transplanting superior pineal glands into the Phyllistines' brains, I should have realized that the loss of Yolly, Themisopolis, and the omnibenevolent data had warped her in ways that went well beyond mere bereavement or simple rage. Were I not myself close to madness in those days, I would have contacted some avatar of the law and explained that the most benign of Londa's selves, the rational and circumspect Scarlet Darwinist, had evidently perished along with her younger sister. Keep an eye on Dr. Sabacthani, I would have implored this hypothetical Javert. Observe her night and day. She has ceded her psyche to the sinister Crimson Kantian and the capricious Purple Pietist. But instead of alerting the agents of justice, I simply limped back home to Boston and attempted to get on with my life.

Perceptive readers that you are, you may have already deduced why Natalie made only a perfunctory effort to contact me during my sojourn in Jordan's Georgetown apartment. But I myself remained clueless. It never occurred to me that my wife had better—that is to say, worse—things to do with her time.

His name was Castorp Muller, his parents having suffered from an unfortunate preoccupation with *The Magic Mountain,* and he was both a Hawthorne M.F.A. candidate in fiction, endlessly noodling with his half-written, half-assed, wholly autobiographical novel, and a member of the Tuesday-night reading group Natalie had organized, for its therapeutic benefits, several months after the abortion. The sea change in their relationship traced to the club's decision to read *Ship of Fools*: an incendiary choice, as it happened, splitting the membership into a feminist contingent obsessed with Katherine Anne Porter's gender, and a humanist faction who believed that refracting the novel through a political lens trivialized the author's larger artistic accomplishment. Eventually these exchanges became so heated that, following each formal meeting at the Caffeine Fiend, everyone would head for the Shepherd's Pie to cool down with lager and stout. At first this drinking society comprised all nine *Ship of Fools* enthusiasts, but in time the demands of academic life reduced their number to five, then three, until finally the party comprised a volatile total of two.

Already a hero in Natalie's eyes for having taken the feminist side in the Porter controversy, Castorp Muller boasted the additional virtue of seeming to enjoy her conversation unreservedly. On only one occasion was I privileged to observe the man in action, but the memory remains vivid. Natalie and I had run into him, looking spiffily world-weary in his goatee, red bandanna, and black fisherman's sweater, at the Coolidge Cinema's weekly midnight revival of *The Adventures of Buckaroo Banzai,* and after the show the three of us retired to a nearby bistro. I soon apprehended the fellow's talent for ostensibly hanging on to Natalie's every word, his uncanny ability to interrupt her so subtly that she never even noticed. I should have thrown in the towel immediately. Here was a man who could bring a woman to orgasm simply by listening to her.

As their Tuesday-night ritual progressed from a pleasant diversion to the week's most passionately anticipated event, the conversation between Castorp and Natalie inevitably focused on John Snow's presence in her life. Apparently Castorp's self-centered empathy enabled Natalie to get through each new phase of the crisis—our netherson's sudden advent, his increasingly abusive behavior, his unexpected Christmas visit, his final disposition in a ceramic urn atop our bookcase. But Castorp the fiction writer began to conceive a broader narrative. By way of helping Natalie discover her heart's own truth, he encouraged her to free-associate like a neurotic on Freud's couch, and before long they had collaboratively constructed a story in which I was the villain and she the victim.

According to the Muller-Novak version of her tribulations, she had wanted to bring the baby to term, but she knew I would never forgive myself if anything bad happened to her during the pregnancy. In other words, her decision to abort was in essence a submission to my will. But for my paranoid attitude toward her blood clots, she would now be enjoying unequivocal motherhood, when instead she'd become the object of her unborn child's infinite scorn.

At some point during the siege of Themisopolis, this cute couple began enjoying illicit afternoons in Castorp's apartment, a situation that Natalie successfully—and, I'm chagrined to report, effortlessly—kept under wraps for two whole months following my return from D.C. Ever on the lookout for a way to break the bad news, she finally got an opportunity courtesy of the same reading group that had blessed her with Castorp. Arriving home one evening after drumming Victorian poetry into several dozen pairs of indifferent undergraduate ears, she noticed that idle curiosity had prompted me to remove the seminar's current selection, Harry Mulisch's *The Procedure,* from the coffee table. Years ago at Villanova, I'd been assigned this neglected but beguiling moral fable, in which Mulisch takes a twelfth-century kabbalist's ambition to create a clay golem and cleverly counterpoints it with a contemporary Dutch biologist's success in wringing organic molecules from the same substance. Natalie immediately plucked the book from my hands and recited a passage concerning Rabbi Löw's attempt to enlist his son-in-law, Isaac, in the momentous project.

"'Isaac's hair and beard are red as a blazing fire,'" she read, "'which seems to point to an ecstatic character, but the opposite is the case. Esther, Löw's daughter, also found that out too late; but that's nothing out of the ordinary, since virtually everyone marries the wrong person.'"

She closed *The Procedure* and said, "Is Mulisch right? Does virtually everyone marry the wrong person?"

"I recently saw a statistic suggesting that mutually satisfying marriages are not the norm," I said.

"There's something I've been meaning to tell you. I believe I married the wrong person."

I chuckled in amusement. She laughed in distress.

"In fact, I *know* I married the wrong person," Natalie continued, whereupon I began to feel sick, and then it all spilled out, the trysts with Castorp, the joys of having a friend who would rather talk to her than read Kierkegaard, my determination to maneuver her into the abortion clinic, my failure to comfort her adequately back when John Snow 0001 was calling her a murderer, my initial resistance to bringing the immaculoid's ashes home.

I freely admitted that these accusations were not without merit, which of course did me no good, since this wasn't about my shortcomings—it was about Natalie being in love with Castorp. We wandered into the living room and took up positions on opposite sides of the couch, goalies in that most ancient of indoor sports, domestic discord. For the next four hours, we vilified one another as our marriage burned down all around us. At the dismal hour of 2:00 A.M., my desperation peaked, and I declared that I would seek out Dr. Charnock and convince him to fashion an infant from John Snow 0001's bottled ashes, so that we would have our son again. Natalie reminded me that we'd never regarded the immaculoid as even the remotest simulacrum of a son, ours or anybody else's, and this was not the time to start pretending otherwise.

"You're taking this much harder than I'd imagined," she said. "Look at it this way. Now you're free to go chasing after Londa. You've always been half in love with her."

"Londa is a deeply disturbed person. You're the woman I love."

"Hey, Mason, I'm willing to sit here and talk till dawn, but we'll just keep covering the same damn ground."

"You want to be with Castorp right now, don't you?" I said.

"More than you can imagine."

"I'm sure you're being truthful. Philosophers appreciate the truth. Now please lie to me. Tell me I have a chance."

"It's over, Mason. Sorry. I'm so crazy about Castorp, I can hardly stop singing."

At the methodical pace of a pallbearer, I rose from the couch, walked to the bookcase, and with both hands took hold of our fetus's brittle sarcophagus.

"Don't do something you'll regret later," she said.

"Fuck you."

I raised the urn high above my head and sent it on a collision course with the hardwood floor. The moment of impact was gratifyingly spectacular, ten thousand glittery splinters radiating outward from the impact point. I thought of bombs exploding, universes expanding, paradigms shifting. With a demented cackle I dropped to my knees and, reaching into the rubble, closed my fist around a scraggly carbon glob.

"I hope you and Castorp have lots of children." Rising, I assumed the posture of a catapult. "I hope you have so goddamn many children the *Catholic Worker* names you Baby Factory of the Year."

"Mason, don't," she said between gritted teeth.

"Heads up, Natalie! John is coming to get you! This snowball has your name on it!"

I laughed and launched the projectile. The lumpish remains

found their target, splattering across Natalie's chest. She screamed and called me a piece of shit, a not inaccurate evaluation under the circumstances, then stormed out of the apartment. There could be no doubt concerning her destination.

My heated brain became home to a lurid psychodrama. In this dark reverie, I removed my clothes and rolled around naked on the floor, grinding the urn fragments into my back, after which I sought out Natalie and showed her my mortified flesh. But martyrdom has never been my métier, and in this case it wouldn't have accomplished anything, so I simply located the dustpan and returned to my knees and got to work.

IT TOOK US a mere five weeks to legalize our enmity. The Commonwealth of Massachusetts had long ago recognized the pragmatic concept of no-fault divorce, which during the course of our negotiations I started calling recursive-blame divorce, and because our mutual assets were few and our children nonexistent, the whole process set us each back only three hundred dollars. When it was over, we shook hands on the steps of the Massachusetts State House, wished one another well, returned to our separate domiciles—Natalie and Castorp had just bought a condo on Beacon Hill—and set about the business of never seeing each other again.

The rest of my winter passed in three unrelated activities: feeling sorry for myself, presiding perfunctorily over Pieces of Mind, and appearing before Virgil Harkness's Congressional Commission on Fetal Activism. Although his heart wasn't in it, Senator Harkness had hastily convened his panel upon realizing that for most Americans the immaculoid phenomenon had proved impossibly distressing, and these shaken citizens wanted the government to protect them from any future such invasions. The initial sessions were televised, but C-Span viewers soon found them unpalatable (too much talk about mackies driving their quasiparents to suicide), and so the network began broadcasting the far livelier Chaffey Hearings into allegations that certain gratuitously compassionate physicians in Pennsylvania were systematically violating the Mother Teresa Anti-Euthanasia Laws. Somewhere in my disorganized cache of DVDs is the C-Span coverage of a bitter Londa, a shattered Jordan, and a depressed Mason presenting their testimony to Harkness and his colleagues. Among the highlights of this *digital vérité* collector's item is a sound bite of Londa admitting that her now-defunct Institute for Advanced Biological Investigations had "acquired an RXL-313 ontogenerator with an eye to conducting human duplication experiments" and forthwith urging the committee to "excavate this treacherous device from the ashes of Themisopolis and oversee its destruction." The C-Span video also includes a brief segment of Jordan imploring Harkness to hunt down the "self-righteous criminals" who, through their fetal proxy General John Snow 4099, had "murdered Yolly Sabacthani in cold blood." But my favorite clip shows me assuming a gesture of *j'accuse* while explaining that, if I knew their exact location just then, I would point my indignant digit directly at Enoch Anthem and Felix Pielmeister, "who almost certainly convinced General John Snow 4099 that it was open season on the Sisters Sabacthani."

As unimaginative sycophants go, Harkness was a fairly decent chap, and he took my indictment of Anthem and Pielmeister seriously enough to dispatch a team of FBI agents to the Center for Stable Families. In giving their depositions to the G-men, Anthem and Pielmeister vociferously denied any connection to the mackies beyond, as Pielmeister put it, "an unashamed sympathy for their pro-life agenda," but eventually it became obvious that the two suspects and the Harkness Commission had struck a deal, for a week later the FBI invaded an abandoned limestone processing plant near Bellefonte, Pennsylvania, and found therein a clandestine bioengineering laboratory. The prize of the haul was three ontogenerators, and the following day Harkness, in keeping with Londa's recommendation, convinced Governor Winthrop to send a Maryland National Guard unit to Themisopolis and recover the device through which she'd populated the Circus. Before the month was out, the Harkness Commission had arranged for the effective extinction of this technology, contracting with the U.S. Coast Guard to load all four ontogenerators onto a container ship, bear them twenty leagues due east of Cape Hatteras, and there consign the machines to a watery grave.

Even though the chances of another grand-scale immaculoid protest were essentially zero, there being no more RXL-313s in the world save the moldering remains of the prototype back on Isla de Sangre, I suspect that for the likes of Felix Pielmeister, Enoch Anthem, and Tucker Winthrop this was a golden age. Recent biblical exegesis by Anthem's newest organization, Hermeneutics Unlimited, had established beyond doubt that Jesus Christ was adamantly opposed to universal health-care insurance, class-action lawsuits, and corporate whistleblowers. Several prominent postrationalist theologians had successfully exposed public education for the misguided Marxist boondoggle it was, while a majority in Congress now advocated replacing the secular school system with private academies committed to sparing children the bad news that Charles Darwin had brought back from the Galápagos Islands. As for the dubious projects nurtured by the so-called City of Justice, it would be years, perhaps a decade, before the data pulverized in Alethia Square could be replicated by the scattered staff of the Susan B. Anthony Trust and the tattered remains of the Institute for Advanced Biological Investigations.

One particularly telling sign of the times was the consummation of Ralph Gittikac's campaign to rebuild the RMS *Titanic*. Much to my amazement, our primal Phyllistine had gotten the luxury liner's doppelgänger off the drawing board and into the water. Gittikac's Getaway Adventures was now taking reservations for the "Great Cathartic Voyage of the *Titanic Redux*," scheduled to sail from Southampton, England, on the first of July and arrive in New York City on Independence Day.

From the Phyllistine perspective, of course, one felicitous development eclipsed all the others. According to a confluence of rumor, gossip, and paparazzi espionage, Londa Sabacthani was no longer a force to be reckoned with. Evidently she'd been checking herself into one Manhattan mental institution after another, even as her press secretary, the faithful Pauline Chilton, proceeded to frost her client's fruitcake condition with obfuscation and euphemism.

With my marriage a void, my vatling an inmate, and Corporate Christi poised to conquer the world, I found it increasingly difficult to get up in the morning. Day by day I retreated ever farther into the deepest reaches of myself: Mason Ambrose, shipwreck victim, washed up on the deserted shores of his own *Dasein,* a condition that he perversely compounded by disconnecting his phone, selling his computer, and instructing the post office to hold his mail. No man is an island, John Donne had famously insisted—very well, true enough, but I had certainly become whatever landmass entailed an equal measure of estrangement: a tidal peninsula, perhaps, joined to my fellow beings by the narrowest of shoals. Wandering my barren beaches, I encountered no auspicious footprints in the sand, and the corked bottles I retrieved from the surf contained only blank scraps of parchment, their messages long since bleached away by the sun.

My condition worsened, from isolation to desolation. Acting on impulse—if a man gripped by stupefying malaise may be said to act on impulse—I appointed Dexter Padula the sole manager of Pieces of Mind and sold him the bulk of my shares, using the ready cash to pay the rent three months in advance, send anticipatory checks to the gas company, and provision my rooms with certain essentials: a case of canned salmon, the Erlanger House *Collected Works of Friedrich Nietzsche,* twenty bottles of red wine, a stack of Vaughan Williams CDs. I closed the door, turned off the lights, and waited for Godot. The days elapsed at the velocity of molasses. Camus, I decided, had gotten it right—there is only one important philosophical question: why not suicide? My apartment was an embarrassment of possibilities. A set of stainless-steel steak knifes. A heavy-duty extension cord, easily fashioned into a noose. A fire-escape platform offering a thirty-foot fall to a concrete alley.

To this day I'm not certain how I survived my long, dark fortnights of the soul. Through some felicitous synergy of Nietzschean fortitude, cabernet sauvignon, and "The Lark Ascending," I continued to elude the abyss. And then came my deliverance. I was sitting beside my bedroom window, staring across the alley into the parlor of my closest neighbor, Thomas Cochran, a Medieval Studies professor so ancient of days that his colleagues joked how he'd joined the department back when it was called Contemporary Theology. At some point during my twelve-week immurement, Dr. Cochran had acquired an enormous plasma television set, and to my astonishment the screen now shimmered with a familiar Cinemascope long-shot. There he was, my old mentor Sinuhe, walking the banks of the Nile. Half in jest and half in desperation, I told myself that this sign had arrived from a supernatural realm, and the meaning was unequivocal: my philosophy career had not yet run its course. Rather than become a corpse, I must follow up *Ethics from the Earth* with additional impertinent Darwinist tomes that nobody wanted to read. Isis expected it, Horus would settle for nothing less, and who was I to defy the gods?

TWENTY-FOUR HOURS AFTER the Egyptian deities made their wishes known, I received an equally welcome visitation when young Donya came knocking at my door. I was ill-prepared to receive her. Unsightly stubble covered my chin, uncivilized aromas wafted off my skin, and my apartment looked like a rutting ground favored by caribou. She didn't seem to notice—a spontaneous Platonist, that girl, ever on the scent of the eternal, unconcerned with the immediate world's superficial splotches and transient smudges.

After revealing that she now lived a mere two hours from

Boston, her e-mail correspondence with several renowned marine biologists having netted her a summer internship at the Woods Hole Oceanographic Institute, Donya explained herself. Everybody was concerned about dear old Mason—Donya, Henry, Brock, Jordan, especially Londa—so Henry had persuaded the younger Sister Sabacthani, the only Massachusetts member of our fellowship, to track me down. I related how the collapse of my marriage had landed me in Spenser's Cave of Despair, but I had more or less recovered, having found a provisional answer to Camus's notorious question. Any day now, I told Donya, I would start writing a new treatise on evolutionary ethics.

"To be honest, I wasn't terribly anxious about you," she said. "Those who can kill themselves do, and those who can't, teach philosophy. It's weird big sister who's got me worried. Did you know her iguana died?"

I shook my head. "You're worried about Londa because her iguana died?"

"I'm worried about Londa because she's Londa."

"Poor old Quetzie. What happened?"

"Nothing. A bad case of mortality. At least she has a clear conscience on that score."

Forty minutes later, having disinfected myself, put on a clean shirt, and located a viable credit card, I accompanied Donya to the Tao of Sprouts in Copley Square. The best local vegetarian restaurant was still the Tasty Triffid, but returning there without Natalie on my arm would have been excruciating. While the chef heated our ratatouille, Donya reminisced about her childhood, breezily recounting a Yolly story I'd never heard before—how she'd once made a hilarious home video by taking her documentary footage of Blood Island fiddler crabs and altering the soundtrack, so that the creatures appeared to be playing a Beethoven string quartet. Throughout Donya's anecdote my eyes rarely left her face. How strange to be sitting across from this willowy adult version of the

diminutive six-year-old who'd once served me peanut-butter sandwiches and chocolate-chip cookies in a tree house. Strange, and also
a little sad, because the preschool Donya was gone forever now—
wasn't she?—as irretrievable as Edwina or Yolly or John Snow 0001.

Our ratatouille arrived. We consumed several ambrosial morsels, then broached the evening's unhappy topic.

"Apparently she's plotting something—a weird big sister sort of
something, ingenious and dangerous and very likely to end badly,"
Donya said.

"The last I heard, she was on a grand tour of New York's loony
bins."

"A subterfuge."

From her shoulder bag Donya produced a sheaf of computer print-
outs, crumpled like the treasure maps Brock used to create for her cartography lessons. E-mails from Londa, she explained, then read me a
series of snippets, and I soon concluded that Donya was correct concerning her sister's sanity. These weren't the ravings of a madwoman
but something even more disturbing: the effusions of a frighteningly
rational person systematically setting a trap for her enemies.

> Call me an egotist, dear Donya, but I believe I've devised a
> way to cure the Phyllistines.

> I won't deny it: certain aspects of Operation PG are morally
> ambiguous. I'd better secure Mason's services the instant
> he resurfaces.

> The pieces are falling into place. At first the Phyllistines will
> denounce me, but in time they'll realize I've delivered them
> from their own evil.

> Matthew logically locates the Sermon on the Mount on a hill,
> but Luke places the same speech on a plain. I have sched-

uled Operation PG for the middle of the Atlantic Ocean. Future historians will probably stick it in the Gobi Desert.

"What do you suppose the PG stands for?" Donya asked. "Parental guidance? Pride goeth? Phyllistine Götterdämmerung?"

"Pineal gland," I groaned. "Londa's into Cartesian physiology."

"I've got her last message memorized. 'Zero hour is barely a week away, so please make every effort to locate Mason. The plan requires his input.'"

"Zero hour. Christ."

Donya pulled a phone from her jacket, plunking it down on the table with the weary air of a jaded Russian-roulette referee preparing to adjudicate a game. "Every time I call, she chatters merrily until the subject turns to Operation PG, and then she clams up. You'll probably have better luck."

Londa answered with a chipper "All you need is love." After insisting how wonderful it was to hear my voice, she turned suddenly somber and proceeded, characteristically, to take charge of my life. I was to catch the 6:45 A.M. Amtrak out of South Station and get off four hours later in Manhattan. She would meet me in Pennsylvania Station near the Seventh Avenue exit, right by Hudson News.

"I hope your wife can spare you for a while," Londa said. "I'm in dire need of an ethics tutorial."

"Three months ago Natalie ran off with a failed novelist who found fucking easier than plotting. I'm free as a bird."

"Oh, my poor Socrates, you didn't deserve that. Was Joan of Arc part of the problem?"

"Not as much as Katherine Anne Porter."

"Are you on the mend?"

"Healthy as a horse. Speaking of health, Donya tells me you've found a way to rehabilitate the Phyllistines. Operation PG. Let me guess: pineal gland."

"Details at eleven."

Throughout the rest of our meal, Donya brought me up to date on the Hubris Academy faculty. Traumatized by the Themisopolis catastrophe and despondent over the loss of Yolly, Jordan had disavowed political activism and was now pursuing her Ph.D. at the University of Toronto. Henry had begun portraying the host of *Uncle Rumpus's Magic Island* on Nickelodeon, and the initial ratings suggested that America's four-year-olds had found a new idol. The Rumpus franchise had also proved a boon to Brock, whose agent had arranged for him to receive a portion of the licensing fees generated by the characters he'd created for the show. Thanks to Plessey the Plesiosaur and friends, Brock was in danger of becoming embarrassingly rich.

Later, as Donya and I strolled down Beacon Street, she rhapsodized about the Oceanographic Institute—by her account a truly utopian community, its scientists ever eager to pour their molten obsessions into the crucible of her curiosity. Her immediate guru was a cephalopod expert, whose explorations of the giant squid's singularly accessible nervous system bade fair to revolutionize the field of neurophysiology. The resident arthropod aficionado had likewise taken an interest in Donya, initiating her into the cult of the preternaturally primitive horseshoe crab. Somehow we managed to get all the way to her car without mentioning Londa again, a fact on which Donya remarked as she slid behind the wheel.

"To tell you the truth," she said, "even while I was talking about squids, I was thinking about you-know-who."

"Me, too."

"Watch over her, will you, Mason?" Donya snapped her seat belt into place, then twisted the ignition key. The engine coughed to life. "Back on the island, she needed a morality teacher, and now she needs a guardian angel, and once again you're the man for the job."

ALTHOUGH THE AMTRAK timetable had promised a noon arrival, my train didn't pull into Pennsylvania Station until 12:13

P.M., which meant that by the corporation's amoeboid clock, ever beholden to the whims of the freight lines, we'd actually hit New York ahead of schedule. We were nevertheless objectively late, and I was not surprised when, approaching the Seventh Avenue exit, suitcase in hand, I came upon Londa pacing in circles and checking her watch. Still very much a celebrity and hence vulnerable to unwanted attention, she had affected a disguise: dark sunglasses, scarf across her mouth, hair stuffed beneath a black beret. Only after we were secluded in a Yellow Cab, moving uptown in fits and starts, did I get a good look at her face. I hadn't seen her since Yolly's funeral, an afternoon on which grief had bloated her features. Today I was sharing a taxi with the most attractive woman in Manhattan, a svelte enchantress with high cheekbones and opalescent eyes.

"Donya told me about Quetzie," I said. "Please accept my condolences."

"It's all right," she said wistfully. "He didn't know he was supposed to live any longer. Maybe he wasn't."

"That lizard had a more complicated relationship with language than Wittgenstein. Hey, Londa, I've never seen you looking better."

"That's hard to believe. I've been working around the clock."

"On curing the Phyllistines?"

"I even worked on my birthday. We beaker freaks have birthdays—you knew that, didn't you?"

"Of course."

"Naked came I from my mother's vat."

Later that afternoon, surveying Londa's claustrophobic living room on the second floor of 56 West Eighty-second Street, I tried to decide whether she was a tidy housekeeper. The place was awash in clutter, but on closer inspection I realized that most of the detritus traced to a single source, her preoccupation with both the maiden voyage of the original *Titanic* and the imminent cruise of Ralph Gittikac's *Titanic Redux*. Her apartment would probably seem quite neat were she to jettison the myriad books, DVDs, news clippings, brochures, handbills, and blueprints concerning the primal Ship of Dreams and its equally decadent descendant.

"Want my advice?" I wedged my denim jacket into a hall closet crammed with jeans, blouses, skirts, and sweatshirts. "Stop brooding about the *Redux*. Rich people get to go on luxury cruises, poor people don't, and there's nothing you or I or Thoth on his throne can do about it."

"I *always* want your advice, Socrates," Londa replied, "and in the case of Operation PG, I *lust* for your advice. I'll happily put you up at the Essex House, but I'm hoping you'll reconcile yourself to my futon. My next deontological crisis could strike at any time, day or night."

"The futon's fine. Shall we begin the tutorial now?"

"First food, then philosophy."

Not only were Londa's housekeeping skills beyond evaluation, I learned nothing that day about her cooking abilities, for the lunch she now fed me consisted of reheated fried rice and sesame scallops from the previous evening's Chinese dinner. Throughout the meal we chatted superficially, Londa systematically deflecting my questions about Operation PG, but then events took a surprise turn when she dropped a manila envelope into my lap and announced that it contained "the single most libidinous object in New York." Instead of explaining herself, she suggested that I investigate her claim while she took a shower.

Londa trotted off to the bathroom, and an instant later came the rubbery percussion of the spray hitting the plastic curtain. I shoveled some *Titanic* memorabilia off the futon, sat down, and separated the envelope from its contents: a charged artifact indeed, the twelve-page manuscript of her old one-act play, *Coral Idolatry*.

"'A sea nymph lives with one purpose in her heart!'" she called from the bathroom, projecting her first line over the water's drumming. And suddenly I was back on Isla de Sangre, watching her portray the undine Sythia climbing onto the shore. "'She seeks a mortal who will love her, betroth her, and lavish his body upon her, for in this manner alone might she acquire a soul!'"

Londa glided into the room wearing nothing but her facial expression. A smile. The residue of her shower spilled from her drenched auburn hair and sluiced along her limbs.

My throat constricted. My blood rolled in all directions. Nothing about the moment failed to astonish me. There she stood, the unhorsed Dame Quixote, the deposed empress of Themisopolis, dripping and glistening as if newly emerged from Charnock's broth—"Her birth was of the womb of morning dew"—and I knew that despite everything, despite her plots and zombies and titanic machinations, I was in love with this person and always would be.

"'Two hundred days have I followed the submarine currents, seeking the legendary Isle of Sérifos, whose pleasure-loving Hedonists never hesitate to avail themselves of succulent sprites and willing sylphs,'" she continued. Her aureoles were the size and hue of gingersnaps. "'Could it be that my search is finally ended? Will the man I see before me grant my wish?'"

I peeled off my turtleneck. The undershirt came with it, accompanied by the crackle of static electricity. "No problem with lavishing my body, Miss Nymph, but the betrothal will have to wait."

"Stick to the script, Mason. Your line is 'Forgive me for gaping, but I'm astonished to find myself a mere stone's throw from a creature of your kind.'"

"'Forgive me for gaping, but I'm astonished to find myself a mere stone's throw from a creature of your kind.'" I subtracted my jeans, jockey shorts, and socks from the situation, then scrambled to my feet, clutching my script in one hand and brushing Londa's cheek with the other. "'Until now I've observed undines only from afar. Whenever I take ship, I stand on the deck and stare out to sea, hoping to glimpse a nymph sporting with the dolphins.'"

"'My name is Sythia. Are you a Hedonist?'"

"'Call me Thales, disciple of Epicurus.'"

She wrapped a damp hand around my wrist and led me down the hall to her boudoir. There was no bed in sight, simply a queen-size mattress strewn with quilts—not a large beach, but sufficient for this performance. "'Epicurus? Then I must surmise that for you the essence of pleasure is the removal of pain.'"

"'True, fair Sythia. Once pain is gone, pleasure admits of variation but not of increase—'"

"If we made love until the sun comes up, you might decide that ecstasy comes in gradations," she said.

"I thought we were sticking to the script."

"Poetic improvisation is encouraged."

"Then I suggest we improvise an elision and jump to page four. Stage direction: 'Sythia kisses Thales squarely on the lips. Thales reciprocates.'"

Sythia did as the text required, according Thales a protracted kiss. Fingers scurried across bodies not their own. Blood vessels swelled. Words were exchanged concerning the sea nymph's fertility, as neither party desired a fetal outcome to their frolic, and they agreed to meet this contingency with a selection from Sythia's collection of exotic condoms from the four corners of the world.

She liquefied, my passionate vatling, and inevitably I thought of those colorful enzymes—crimson, purple, gold, turquoise—in which Charnock had braised her nascent frame. We sat on a floral quilt and connected face-to-face. She told me I made a fine supplementary superego but an even better subsidiary id. I replied that I'd nearly forgotten what a splendid thing was the mammalian mode of descent.

"A miracle, really," I said. "No dreary anthropomorphic deity could have thought it up in a million years."

"True enough," Londa said. "And yet the most erotic sentence I ever heard doesn't come from *Fanny Hill* or *Justine* or *Lady Chatter-*

ly's Lover. It comes from the Anglican Book of Common Prayer."

"The most erotic sentence?"

"With my body I thee worship."

NO PILLOW TALK for my undine, no basking in the afterglow, no lolling about on the shores of Sérifos. This was Londa, after all, the driven Crimson Kantian, the edgy Purple Pietist. She slid free of my embrace, grabbed her cell phone, and slipped away, leaving me to contemplate in private the afternoon's remarkable events. A few minutes later, her urgent mutterings wafted into the room. I heard an occasional "Dagmar." She was talking to her manager, doubtless about their plan to fix the Phyllistines.

My mind raced like a machine shorn of its flywheel. Was it possible that Londa's reasons for staging this off-off-Broadway performance of *Coral Idolatry* were less romantic than I'd imagined? Had she merely sought to win my approval of Operation PG? I placed my palm in the quilted cavity from which she'd emerged. The fabric was still warm. No profit in pessimism, I decided. For the immediate future, I would refrain from thinking the worst of my undine. Gradually my anxiety faded, and I drifted off to sleep, lulled by the comforting rumble of the rush-hour traffic rolling up Amsterdam Avenue.

It was dark when I awoke—8:17 P.M. by the gimlet gaze of the digital alarm. Slowly I slid free of my dream, an expressionist extravaganza that found Charnock and me sailing his houseboat across a nameless sea, pursued by pirates, menaced by sharks, and engulfed by a maelstrom. Londa brought me her restive flesh and a crystalline goblet of mumquat nectar. For the next two hours, we lay together, entwined like strands of DNA, my vatling demonstrating an uncanny talent for combining recitative and fellatio, her morality teacher reciprocating with *a cappella* cunnilingus, neither of us pausing except to use the bathroom or sip more serenity. At length Londa asserted that I would do well to get a good night's sleep, as tomorrow we were leaving on a long journey.

"I just got here," I protested.

"First thing in the morning, we're hitting the road, Thales and Sythia, off on another adventure. We'll be away three months at least, maybe four."

"Four months? You're not making much sense, darling."

"Don't worry if you don't have enough underwear with you. Where we're going, consumer goods grow on trees." She presented me with her cell phone. "Call your landlord. Tell him to sublet your apartment from now till New Year's."

"This is crazy."

"No, it's your gumbo girl. Trust her."

A wave of fatalism washed through me, a not entirely unpleasant sensation. Trust her? Why not? What did I have to lose?

I pestered Verizon for Fred Packer's number, punched in the digits, and caught him in a good mood, the Sox having just vanquished the Yankees on a ninth-inning grand slam. He said he'd try to find a substitute tenant for one semester, though naturally it would be easier to lease the apartment for the whole school year. Either way works, I told him, figuring that once Operation PG had run its course, Londa and I would start playing house here in Manhattan.

Next I called Dexter Padula, telling him he could have my remaining shares in Pieces of Mind if he would hire a van, drop by my apartment, remove all possessions of value, and stick them in a storage shed. He agreed without batting an eye, no doubt delighted that his increasingly unreliable business partner was getting out of the game entirely.

"So what happens after we cure the Phyllistines?" I asked Londa. "Your disciples will expect something even grander from you. They'll want you to become a deity."

She snickered and said, "I'm not ruling out that possibility."

"What sort of deity? A hamadryad? Plato's demiurge? The Creator God of Judeo-Christian revelation?"

"That job's already taken," she said.

"But you could do it better," I said.

"When it comes to the physics, no, but in other areas—you're right."

Londa's voice fell, her eyelids drooped, and her mouth opened in a cavernous yawn revealing all thirty-two of her mother's straight, white teeth.

THE DIGITAL ALARM roused us at eight o'clock. Londa served me coffee and a toasted poppy-seed bagel. Naturally I'd imagined that our departure from Manhattan would occur by car, taxi, bus, train, or some other horizontal means, so I was taken aback when she announced that we'd be traveling by helicopter.

"Traveling where?" I asked, harboring not the remotest expectation of a straight answer.

"To the radiant crux of justice."

As a mellifluous July morning flowed over the city, Londa and I stepped into the hallway gripping our respective suitcases. We lowered the fire ladder from the ceiling and climbed to the roof, where a helicopter stood ready to receive us, rotor blades churning, cockpit enclosed by a dirty Plexiglas blister—a hydrocephalic dragonfly. Dagmar Röhrig sat behind the controls. We fought our way through the prop wash, climbed into the cab, and secured our luggage. Londa seated herself in the copilot's chair, and so I joined my suitcase in the storage compartment, involuntarily assuming a painful and unnatural posture. I wondered if all trips to the radiant crux of justice required such contortions of their pilgrims.

"Did we make the *Times*?" Londa asked.

"The front page," Dagmar replied. "Also the last three minutes of *Coffee Klatch* and the news banner on the Flatiron Building."

We flew south along the Hudson River docks, soared across

Upper New York Bay, and swung so close to the Statue of Liberty I could see the startled faces of the tourists clustered in her crown. After skirting the western lobe of Brooklyn, we veered away from the rising sun and entered upon the vast foaming tracts of the North Atlantic. Each time I posed a question to Londa or Dagmar, she declined to answer, insisting that the present mission was too complicated to be summarized in a few sentences shouted over the roar of our engine—a feeble excuse, since the women were perfectly happy to compete with that same racket when speaking to one another. From the snatches I caught of their conversation, I gathered that our destination was the *Titanic Redux,* currently somewhere on the high seas, steaming toward New York.

As we zoomed across the whitecapped ocean, mile after nautical mile, I resolved to inhabit the moment as fully as I could. Here I was rambling around with a goddess whose soul I'd once assembled and whose body I'd recently worshipped in the best High Church style, beginning an exploit that, whatever its hazards, would most likely include intervals of bliss aboard a luxury liner. Apart from certain disconcerting mysteries, my situation had much to recommend it.

After a flight of perhaps an hour, I once again attempted to make Londa stop ignoring me.

"Let me guess," I said. "You've bought the *Titanic Redux,* and you and Dagmar plan to spend the summer cruising from port to port, living like royalty."

"We haven't bought her," Londa explained. "We've hijacked her."

"*Hijacked* her? No, Londa, no! Bad idea!"

"Even as we speak," Dagmar said, "Colonel Fox's commandos are parading around the decks, keeping everybody in line."

"This is madness!"

"True, but it's a very *efficient* madness," Londa said. "In a single

toss of the net, we caught three hundred of America's top Phyllistines, all ripe for enlightenment. Enoch Anthem is part of the haul,
and your old nemesis Felix Pielmeister."

"I can't believe I'm hearing this!"

"God knows I wanted to discuss the project with you ahead of
time, but you'd disappeared down your spider-hole," Londa said.
"Try withholding your judgment till you've grasped the broader
picture."

"Screw the broader picture! We're going to have that ethics tutorial, and we're going to have it *right now*!"

"Shut up, Mason!" Dagmar screamed. "You're making me nervous! Can't you see I'm trying to fly a goddamn helicopter?"

At noon we sighted the *Titanic Redux,* her stem cutting a great
billowing furrow in the endless blue field. With the sun almost directly overhead, I couldn't be certain of her bearing, but a glance
at the chopper's compass confirmed my intuition that, although we
were still flying east, the ship was now on an aberrant course, south
by southwest. I decided to forgo the ethics tutorial, demanding instead that Londa answer two questions. Why wasn't the sea swarming with Coast Guard cutters, and why wasn't the sky dark with
CNN helicopters?

By way of a reply, she produced from her shoulder bag an object
suggesting a DVD remote control, its numbered keys encircling
a small red button, ominous as a smallpox pustule. Thanks to the
Valkyries' derring-do, she explained, the *Titanic*'s largest forward
hold was filled with plastic explosives of her own design.

"A momentous instrument, wouldn't you agree?" she said. "A
Godgadget if ever there was one. Colonel Fox and her Valkyries
have eight more just like it. The outside world is appropriately impressed. The instant the Coast Guard or a SWAT team or a news organization appears on the scene—*ka-boom,* the Ship of Dreams gets
blown to kingdom come."

"Fuck this!" I shouted, a hundred times more furious than when I learned she'd burned her palm in homage to Stoicism. "You'd kill all those Phyllistines, not to mention the other passengers, the officers, the crew, the Valkyries, Dagmar, yourself, and *me*?"

"Of course not," Londa replied. "First we'll evacuate the innocent, and *then* we'll blow up the ship. That's the whole *point* of a radio-controlled detonator." She stroked the metallic casing of her Godgadget. "Now, there's always a possibility, and I mean a *distinct* possibility, that this thing is a fake, no more lethal than a water pistol."

Her cryptic disavowal soothed me. Not much, but a little. "I want the truth," I told her. "Is that thing wired to the detonator or not?"

"Sorry, Mason, my lips are sealed—the only way I can keep *your* lips sealed, too."

"Until I have more data," I said, "I'll assume the best of you."

"You're a peach, Socrates. Believe me, we'll do that ethics tutorial at my earliest convenience."

Now the mighty vessel loomed up, her magnificence multiplying with each passing instant, she of the noble prow, majestic decks, soaring masts, and raked funnels exhaling cottony puffs of smoke. A seagoing skyscraper, tilted ninety degrees, plying the waves under full steam. Londa grabbed the radio mike and contacted the bridge, instructing the skipper to hold steady. The man's reply reverberated through the Plexiglas blister. In a tone wavering between defiance and bewilderment, Captain Drew Pittinger said that, while he would do as instructed, he was still master of *Titanic Redux*.

"You are indeed her master," Londa replied. "And I am her queen."

For a full minute, we followed the frothy wake, and then Dagmar increased our speed and circled the stern mast. Anticipating our descent, the assembled voyagers—sunbathers, fishermen, noonday strollers—dispersed in all directions. We dropped from the sky like a slain duck. The poop deck made a perfect helipad.

As Dagmar shut off the engine, Londa explained that the people we'd just sent scurrying inhabited the plebeian confines of F and G decks. On the *Titanic Redux,* as on her ill-starred predecessor, social stratification was the norm. At the moment, these third-class passengers were more likely to receive engraved invitations to the White House than admittance to the boat-deck promenade.

"But all that's about to change," Londa insisted. "By the time the sun rises tomorrow, the last shall be first, and the first shall be last, just like in heaven."

Chapter 14

GO AHEAD, ADOPT AN APE, it sounds like fun, a chimpanzee or maybe even an orangutan, but be prepared to justify your decision when he eats your neighbor's begonias. By all means, have a baby, you deserve a descendant, but stand ready to defend your parenting skills when he grows up to become a serial killer. *Mais oui,* acquire a belief in God, theism is a popular and comforting lifestyle, but first do your homework, learning how the world's great minds have explained the Creator's seeming indifference to human suffering, lest you waste your time fretting about tsunamis and cystic fibrosis.

How might I rationalize my initial acquiescence to Operation Pineal Gland? Why did I make no immediate effort to thwart this frankly criminal escapade? In retrospect, I realize that my infatuation with Londa kept me from seeing that her scheme was irredeemable. Then, too, I must confess that my contempt for Ralph Gittikac and his fellow Phyllistines made me believe that at some level they deserved whatever they got. Eventually I started thinking like a moral philosopher again, but throughout my first day aboard the *Titanic Redux,* I was in thrall to a mixture of love and disgust, that poisonous compound with which the devil's apothecary is always so well stocked.

No sooner had I retrieved my suitcase and stepped free of the helicopter than Colonel Fox came striding across the poop deck. She acknowledged her leader with a crisp salute, her leader's manager with a respectful nod, and her leader's conscience with a bruising scowl. Obviously she'd not forgiven me for convincing her boss to abandon Themisopolis to the mackies. Londa returned the salute, then hustled me through the nearest hatchway, explaining that I could best serve the cause of justice by lying low for the next twenty-four hours. I replied that the cause of justice and Operation Pineal Gland were evidently two different things, but before I could elaborate, a sprightly, apple-cheeked lieutenant appeared, outfitted in the standard Valkyrie black leather jacket, an AK-47 slung over her shoulder, and introduced herself as Marnie Kristowski, "your faithful aide-de-camp," though my instincts told me she was expected to function more as my custodian. Londa promptly fobbed me off on this vivacious daughter of Odin, asserting that "the *Redux* hijacking will in time make complete sense to the entire world, you included, Socrates," then turned abruptly and headed back to the poop deck.

"Been a security officer long?" I asked Lieutenant Kristowski as she grabbed my suitcase and directed me toward the companionway.

"Barely a month, sir. I was one of those kids who grew up reading *League of Londa* comics. Did you know you're in number forty-six?"

What a ghastly thought. "No kidding."

"It's not *literally* you, but you were clearly the inspiration. Dr. Sabacthani goes back to her birthplace, somewhere in Indonesia, and meets Masai Ambooloy, the kung fu alchemist-philosopher who taught her the way of the Splanx."

"The Splanx?"

"An occult mental discipline. The Splanxist can send out psychic waves that scramble her enemies' brains. Masai Ambooloy, Mason Ambrose—get it?"

"Number forty-six? I'll have to track it down."

"My all-time favorite is the lead story in issue thirty-two. A gang of South American drug lords has imprisoned Dr. Sabacthani in a concentration camp, so the Valkyries engineer a flock of giant condors and ride them to the rescue. Those condors are probably the main reason I'm wearing this uniform."

We descended to D deck and entered a commodious second-class cabin that, though lacking a porthole, was chockablock with other amenities: a private bath, a writing desk, a refrigerator, a room-service intercom, and—in a break with the period purism that characterized the *Redux*—a home entertainment center crammed with classical CDs, including, appropriately enough, Wagner's *Ring of the Nibelung* with its stirring "Ride of the Valkyries." The kitchen staff knew of my special status, Lieutenant Kristowski explained, so whenever I felt hungry, I should simply get on the horn and order any menu items that tickled my fancy.

She saluted and slipped away, leaving me to spend the next four-teen hours under idyllic circumstances. In the refrigerator lay two dozen cans of Guinness, moist black cylinders of civilization. The bookshelves held a fiction collection ranging from J. R. R. Tolkien's melancholy optimism to Ernest Hemingway's bracing fatalism, the reading chair was a foam rubber throne, and the D-deck stewards delivered broiled lobster tails to my door as casually as a mailman bringing the day's credit-card offers. Even the bed was luxurious—down blankets, silk sheets, satin pillows—though not quite luxuri-ous enough, I soon learned, to quiet my mind and calm my nerves. Londa has not gone insane, I told myself as I thrashed around on the mattress. In time her capsized soul will right itself, and she will be restored to me. But still I could not sleep.

* * *

CONTEMPLATING OPERATION Pineal Gland through the pellucid lens of hindsight, I realize that it comprised a dozen distinct though interconnected strategies, one of which continues to elicit my awe. I speak of Londa's decision to have Colonel Fox and her thirty bravest soldiers purchase second-class tickets on the maiden voyage of the *Titanic Redux*. Shortly after coming aboard in Cherbourg, these stalwart commandos had pooled the contents of their steamer trunks, each jammed with ostensibly innocuous materials that, cleverly combined, became a panopoly of automatic weapons and explosive devices. The Uzis and the AK-47s proved every bit as philosophically persuasive as Londa and Colonel Fox had hoped—the famous argument from imminent oblivion—and the Valkyries had little difficulty filling forehold number 3 with plastique, winning the crew's allegiance, convincing the service personnel to join the insurrection, and coercing Captain Pittinger into informing the outside world that any attempt to foil the hijacking would trigger a horrendous but not unprecedented maritime catastrophe. The coup de grâce had occurred twelve hours before our helicopter landed on the poop deck. With wry smiles on their lips and taut fingers on their triggers, Colonel Fox's commandos had rounded up all the first-class passengers and ordered them to hunker down in their staterooms until further notice.

Indulging in her affection for the theatrical, Londa waited until exactly 12:18 A.M. before addressing our captive Phyllistines, for that was when the first-class passengers aboard the original *Titanic* had been roused from their quarters on April 15, 1912. She even insisted that the hostages dress exactly as had their twentieth-century counterparts, in pajamas and life jackets. Although the majority of her audience—an elite group of two hundred and twenty-five corporation presidents, congressmen, lawyers, judges, arms merchants, government advisers, and political operatives—was predictably male, our catch also included three female CEOs and a woman lobbyist for the petroleum industry. Using their rifle butts like cattle prods, the Valkyries herded their prisoners down the C-deck passageways and into the reception room outside the Grand Dining Saloon, leaving the Phyllistines' ancillary spouses and children to brood and fidget in their cabins. Dressed in a glossy black microfiber suit, Londa strode past the murmuring crowd with a stateliness appropriate to her status as queen of the ship. Her decision to include her conscience was evidently an afterthought—my invitation had arrived at the stroke of midnight, delivered in person by Lieutenant Kristowski—yet she seemed pleased to have me by her side, and as we ascended the great marble staircase, she squeezed my hand and whispered, "'She seeks a mortal who will love her, betroth her, and lavish his body upon her. . . .'"

Colonel Fox and Major Powers awaited us on the first landing. The Valkyries exchanged conspiratorial nods with Londa, who then faced the highborn mob like Marc Antony preparing to turn Rome's citizens against Caesar's assassins.

"Masters of the universe!" she shouted over the hubbub. "Mistresses of creation! Your attention, please! I have astonishing news!"

The multimillionaires ceased their disgruntled muttering and grew provisionally quiet.

"My name is Londa Sabacthani, and I'm here to inform you that, like her legendary ancestor, the *Titanic Redux* has struck an iceberg."

Instantly the muttering resumed, though now in a register of outrage. Ralph Gittikac stood up straight, dropped his Hapsburg jaw, and shouted, "I know who *you* are, but do you know who *I* am? You're talking to Ralph Winston Gittikac, CEO of Gittikac's Getaway Adventures and director of Project *Titanic* Ascendant, and when this ridiculous caper is over, I'm going to jam your sorry ass in jail!"

Apparently Gittikac didn't recall meeting the adolescent Londa twelve years earlier in the Bahía de Flores, and I figured she had no particular reason to remind him of the encounter.

"Where's Captain Pittinger?" demanded a lithe Phyllistine whose matinee-idol features were probably not unrelated to his personal fortune. "What've you done with him?"

"Are you aware that I'm a United States senator?" snarled a ruddy man wearing a silk bathrobe over his pajamas. "Have you any idea how much trouble you're in?"

"Let's get something straight!" Colonel Fox snapped, lifting her Uzi high above her head in a pose suggesting the Statue of Liberty's glamorous young anarchist sister. Her fellow Valkyries likewise brandished their weapons. "There are worse things than listening respectfully to Dr. Sabacthani, like getting blown into such tiny pieces the sharks will use you for spare change, which is exactly what's going to happen if you don't shut the fuck up!"

Silence enshrouded the reception room like snow blanketing a meadow. Surveying the chastened plutocrats, I traded stares of reciprocal contempt with Felix Pielmeister, who appeared dignified despite his pajamas and life jacket, and glances of mutual recognition with Ralph Gittikac, who would have looked like a humorless boor even in a Brooks Brothers suit.

"As I was saying, the *Redux* has struck an iceberg," Londa continued. "Not an ordinary iceberg, but a malignant mass composed of your own frigid vanity and frozen gall."

The crowd indulged in snorts and huffs but stayed on the circumspect side of articulation.

"That's the bad news," Londa continued. "The good news is that the ship will not founder. As your damaged souls begin to mend, the gash in our hull will heal as well. In short, masters of the universe, think of us not as your captors but as your teachers."

Jowls flapping, nostrils flaring, Enoch Anthem stepped free of the mob and, folding his arms across his barrel chest, addressed Londa in a bravely stentorian voice. "Teachers?! *Teachers?!* What you are is a bunch of sicko lesbian pirates, and I hope I'm there to see the fireworks when Jesus gets his hands on you!"

Colonel Fox responded to Anthem's outburst by aiming her rifle vertically and squeezing off a round. Squalls of plaster sifted down from the shattered ceiling. A dozen arms reached out and pulled Anthem back into the collective Phyllistine body.

"Allow me to introduce your other benefactors." Londa leaned toward me and, in a gesture more condescending than affectionate, tweaked my cheek. "This is Mr. Ambrose, my ethical adviser. The woman who fired at the ceiling is Colonel Fox, our chief of security. Beside her stands Major Powers, second in command." Beaming a smile that would have looked equally at home on Anthem's sanctimonious face, she abruptly pulled the Godgadget from her jacket. "Yes, masters of the universe, the rumors are true. Our hold is packed with explosives, a fact that has so far kept your would-be liberators at bay. Make no mistake. The instant we get word that a Coast Guard cutter or a SWAT team helicopter is chasing us, we'll lock you up, flee in the lifeboats, and detonate the plastique." She extended her index finger and allowed it to hover menacingly near the red button. The plutocrats engaged in a synchronous cringe. "Even as I speak, many of you are imagining you might pave the way for a rescue operation by wresting the transmitter from me. Such a gesture would be futile—am I right, Colonel Fox? Major Powers?"

The officers flashed their Godgadgets, holding them up like scalpers hawking Super Bowl tickets. "Three of our subordinates have transmitters as well," Colonel Fox said, "and there are three more hidden around the ship."

"But for now let's drop this depressing talk of bombs and address a happier topic, your imminent ethical growth," Londa said, repocketing her transmitter. "At dawn we reach our first port of call, Brigantine, New Jersey, where we shall unburden ourselves of your spouses, your children, and our second-class passengers. After the evacuation, you and the third-class passengers will trade places, the latter taking over your staterooms while you all move into the spartan cabins on G deck. It occurs to me that the mere experience of living so close to the waterline might effect your cure. What do you think, Colonel?"

"I've never seen a smarter gaggle of capitalists," Vetruvia Fox said. "Unless I miss my guess, they're about to become the most progressive plutocrats in Christendom."

"And you, Major?" Londa asked.

"We've caught ourselves some real sharp cookies, and that's the truth," Carmen Powers said. "When I think of how deeply they comprehend the stock market, I know they'll have no trouble with the Beatitudes."

"Tell me, Mr. Ambrose, do you share the prevailing optimism?" Londa asked me.

"Oh, yes," I hissed between clenched teeth. What else was I supposed to say?

Londa scanned the mob with a piercing eye, fixing first on Ralph Gittikac, then on Enoch Anthem, and finally on Felix Pielmeister. "Could it be that your teachers are right?" she said, each syllable dripping with derision. "A few days of tender loving privation, and you'll all acquire a moral compass? I like to think so. In any event it's time we returned you to your quarters. Enjoy your staterooms whilst ye may, masters of the universe, for there are no Persian rugs on G deck, nor damask curtains, nor flutes of champagne—as a matter of fact, it's rather like a darkling plain down there, where ignorant armies clash by night."

SOCIALIST IN WORLDVIEW and cynical in sensibility, Colonel Fox predicted that the third-class passengers would leap at the opportunity to trade stations with the Phyllistines. What she didn't understand was that the cheapest *Titanic Redux* tickets had been purchased not by oppressed Old World wage slaves eager to inaugurate a dictatorship of the proletariat, but by unionized European factory workers and civil servants who had no particular problem with the prevailing economic order and whose presence on the ship reflected a simple desire to cross the Atlantic at a bargain rate. When the Valkyries explained to these thrifty British, Irish, Scottish, French, Swiss, Belgian, Dutch, Italian, and German voyagers that rather than spending the rest of their vacations in the United States, they could remain on the *Redux* and be treated like royalty, only three dozen out of five hundred and fourteen accepted the offer—a number sufficient for Londa to claim that she'd turned the status quo on its head, though hardly the Marxist revolution forecast by Colonel Fox. I could not fault the vacationers' wariness. Given a choice between putting to shore right now and spending three weeks in the company of thirty-one Uzi-armed harpies on a floating munitions dump, I likewise would have erred on the side of caution.

At first light I staggered from my cabin and ascended the companionways, arriving on the boat deck right before we dropped anchor off the Jersey coast. A dozen seamen and all four junior officers hovered near the lifeboats, removing the canvas tarps, plugging the drainage holes, unlocking the davits. Soon the second-class passengers appeared, most wearing expressions of blasé resignation, as if throughout their second-class lives they'd endured many such instances of monumental inconvenience. Next came the plutocrats' families—two hundred and eight angry wives, three befuddled husbands, several dozen confused children—followed by those scores of third-class passengers who'd been rational enough to turn down Londa's offer of an all-expenses-paid cruise to the heart of her darkness. Last to arrive was the *Redux*'s twenty-one-piece orchestra, along with forty or so stewards, waiters, and scullerymen who'd decided to jump ship while they could.

Perched on the wheelhouse roof, amplifying her authority through a battery-powered megaphone, Londa directed the evacuation with the zeal of a creationist impresario barking outside a carnival tent where a vatling Charles Darwin was tearfully recanting the theory of natural selection. She assured everyone that the bay was only slightly choppy this morning, "which means you'll have no trouble rowing to Brigantine," then added that there were still plenty of unreserved first-class staterooms for any third-class passengers who wanted to "stick around and be waited on hand and foot by CEOs who earn upwards of two million dollars a year."

As Londa made her pitch, I retreated to the bridge and continued observing the spectacle from the starboard wing, where I was soon joined by my aide-de-camp, gripping a pair of binoculars. It happened that Lieutenant Kristowski was a native of these shores, having grown up in the Atlantic City suburb of Absecon. "The state flower of New Jersey is the common violet," she explained, smirking, "the state bird is the eastern goldfinch, and the state fragrance is unrefined petroleum."

I scanned the lifeboats, each hovering two feet above the deck on its davits. Londa, shouting, announced that before taking a seat each departing voyager must present his passport to a junior officer and demonstrate that he'd not exceeded the luggage quota: a single valise or sack jammed with cash, jewelry, medicines, laptop—whatever items he'd deemed indispensable. Many evacuees refused to climb aboard until they'd received an officer's personal assurance that their remaining worldly goods would be stowed away and ultimately returned. In lieu of conventional baggage, three plutocrat wives had brought along their dogs—pug, basset hound, cairn terrier—and because each pet was secured in a plastic carrier, nobody raised any objections.

Once Londa felt satisfied that the loading operation was proceeding apace, she permitted the captive Phyllistines to leave the staterooms and come on deck. Per Colonel Fox's orders, they arrived still dressed in their pajamas. Searching for their families, our hostages surveyed the crowded lifeboats with eyes that betrayed, variously, rage, bewilderment, shock, and longing. A succession of farewells followed, some quite poignant, though probably none as wrenching as the partings that had occurred a thousand leagues to the northeast on the morning of April 15, 1912. Reaching over the gunwale of her lifeboat, Enoch Anthem accorded his chubby, whey-faced bride a protracted embrace. Ralph Gittikac was obliged to perform an especially elaborate adieu, as he'd embarked with an entourage that included his wife, their four daughters, and his divorced sister's grumpy adolescent son. Felix Pielmeister did not appear on the boat deck that morning, so I assumed he'd left Southampton unaccompanied.

On Londa's orders, the junior officers swung the lifeboats out over the water—a frightening experience for the evacuees, judging from their howls and shrieks—then further employed the davits to send these same voyagers on a brief but bumpy downward ride. Throughout the lowering process, the Brigantine harbor police, tooling around in their patrol boats, worked diligently to keep the local fishing dories and pleasure craft out of the *Redux*'s vicinity. For the moment, at least, our plastique was having the effect Londa desired.

Within a half-hour, all the evacuees were bobbing about on the pounding, foam-flecked bay. Their attempts to work the lifeboat oars proved unintentionally comical, but their incompetence hardly mattered, as the tide was rolling landward. Assuming no boat sprang a leak, our superfluous passengers would reach Brigantine in time for lunch.

Borrowing the binoculars from Lieutenant Kristowski, I studied the crowded shore. It seemed that half the population of New Jersey was milling around on the beach, and I wondered what had inspired them to get up so early on a Saturday morning. While some onlookers had probably come to glimpse the fabled ship, others doubtless hoped to witness a rescue attempt by the Coast Guard or a SWAT team, still others to express their solidarity with the abducted plutocrats. And surely our audience included scores of Sabacthanites: youthful idealists who owned complete runs of *The League of Londa,* boasted full sets of Dame Quixote trading cards, and spent their free time mastering the way of the Splanx.

Even as the evacuees headed for Brigantine, a flotilla came cruising toward us: two tugs hauling a barge bearing the additional coal required by this unforeseen amendment to the maiden voyage—so ran Lieutenant Kristowski's explanation—plus three bumboats loaded with food, sundries, and prescription-drug refills, Major Powers having researched the hostages' medical histories as part of the general strategizing for Operation PG.

"So what's our next port of call?" I asked my aide-de-camp.

"There isn't one, sir. We're going to steam in circles until our hostages get cured or the Coast Guard shows up."

"And what happens if the Coast Guard shows up?"

"We can count on Dr. Sabacthani to exercise restraint," Lieutenant Kristowski said, pulling out her Godgadget. The metallic casing glinted in the morning sun. "Samson didn't slay those four thousand Philistines until he was up against the wall, and Dr. Sabacthani won't start whacking away at our own Phyllistines until it's absolutely necessary."

SHORTLY BEFORE NINE O'CLOCK, the *Titanic Redux* weighed anchor, the bumboat supplies having been stowed away, the coal barge lashed to our stern, and the demoted plutocrats exiled—sans clothing, laptops, cell phones, radios, money, and other such earthly possessions—to their draconian digs in the bowels of the ship. As the great voyage to nowhere began, I bade Lieutenant Kristowski adieu and retired to the Café Parisien, a swank first-class eatery on B deck, featuring bilingual menus and international cuisine. The cooks were happy to whip me up an extravagant breakfast: cheese omelet, Belgian waffles, croissants, fruit salad. I carried the feast to the table myself, as the former first-class passengers hadn't been assigned their duties yet. No sooner had I taken my first bite than the stirring "Gonna Fly Now" theme Bill Conti had composed for *Rocky* filled the air, borne throughout the café—and the rest of the ship, too, I assumed—by the public-address system.

"Good morning, masters of the universe and mistresses of creation!" boomed Londa's disembodied voice over the brass-heavy melody. The music diminished in volume, and she proceeded to lecture the hostages in the tone of a Devil's Island commandant intimidating new arrivals. "This is Dame Quixote, welcoming you to the premiere of *The Last Shall Be First,* the one and only radio program originating aboard the *Titanic Redux*—local in its coverage, planetary in its reach, universal in its message!" The music swelled, then dropped away as Londa resumed talking. "Before long, dozens of stations will be broadcasting *The Last Shall Be First* to every corner of the globe. Doubtless your friends and relatives will tune in each episode, eager to know about life aboard the Ship of Dreams."

A tremulous anticipation seized the recently promoted first-class passengers in the Café Parisien. They set down their utensils and cocked their ears toward the loudspeaker, a fluted cone mounted on an Art Nouveau pillar.

"Many of you are familiar with the Revelation to Saint John— hardly the noblest book in the Bible, though certainly the most garish, bursting with action and special effects, the summer blockbuster of the New Testament. I'm sure you remember the spectacular onslaught in chapter six, the thrilling cavalry charge of War, Famine, Pestilence, and Death. Look inward, masters of the universe, and you will realize that the horseman called War has already arrived. I speak now of the conflict raging within each of you, that grand battle between your inflated self and your atrophied soul. As for Famine, Pestilence, and Death, they are not far behind."

After this pompous prelude, Londa shifted to pragmatic matters. A new monetary system had been instituted aboard the *Redux,* she explained, predicated on a medium of exchange called the lucre. Thanks to the bumboats, seven thousand freshly printed lucres in several denominations now filled the bank vault. For the duration of the voyage, the former first-class passengers would toil at "monotonous but spiritually rewarding jobs," receiving a wage of five lucres per day.

"Would you like my advice? Practice frugality and you'll be able to make all sorts of impulse purchases, such as, for example, food."

She went on to assure the Phyllistines that although their private health-insurance policies were invalid under the new regime, their physical well-being would not suffer. The ship's pharmacy was brimming with the drugs they took for their assorted ailments—diabetes, kidney disease, congestive heart failure, depression—and every pill would be distributed free of charge.

"In other words, simply by booking passage on the *Redux,* you became beneficiaries of our socialized health-care system. I can't help pointing out that two of your fellow voyagers, Senator Frank Endicott of Iowa and Senator Rupert Marbury of Alabama, have worked unstintingly to keep America's citizens from enjoying affordable medical insurance. You can thank whatever gods may be that Endicott and Marbury are not in charge of political arrangements aboard this ship."

For the next twenty minutes, the plutocrats learned of the scrubbing, scouring, waxing, polishing, scraping, painting, swabbing, lifting, loading, toting, fetching, ferrying, and fawning jobs they would be performing in the days to come, and then the audio engineer snuck in the *Rocky* theme.

"And so, masters of the universe, until the next exciting episode of *The Last Shall Be First,* this is Dame Quixote wishing you a memorable and enlightening voyage!"

The music swelled to a crescendo. I took a final sip of coffee, sopped up a dribble of egg with a waffle, and considered what to do next. My great urge was to seek out Londa and tell her that in my opinion this crude approach to curing the Phyllistines was certain to fail, but I figured she hadn't slept in the last twenty-four hours, so it would be prudent to postpone my visit. With a confused heart and an ambivalent gait, I returned to my D-deck cabin, where I spent the rest of the day revisiting Middle Earth while glutting myself on room-service lobster tails, delivered in person by Senator Endicott. I thanked him for his trouble. He told me to go crack a walnut in my ass.

At nine the next morning, episode two of *The Last Shall Be First* came pouring from the ceiling speaker and gushed uninvited into my brain. As the *Rocky* theme faded, Londa started gleefully enumerating the menial tasks the plutocrats had completed during their first day under the new regime. I looked around for ways to silence the broadcast. Eventually I resorted to repositioning my writing desk under the speaker, stacking books on top, and capping the pile with a pillow pressed tightly between Londa's sardonic recitation and *A Farewell to Arms.*

I passed the afternoon putting Hemingway's novel to a different use, immersing myself in Frederic Henry's problems by way of escaping my own, most especially my anxiety over being in love with a person whose aptitude for malice seemed to increase every day. Shortly after six o'clock, Lieutenant Kristowski appeared at my door with an invitation from on high. If it would not be inconvenient, might I come to OPG headquarters for "mumquats and moral discourse"?

"Lead the way," I told my aide-de-camp.

"Did you hear this morning's broadcast, sir? Sounds like those folks on G deck are going to get their improved pineal glands sooner rather than later."

ALTHOUGH THE B-DECK corridor presided over by Dagmar Röhrig had been designated the reception area, anyone seeking an audience with Dr. Sabacthani was in fact received by two Valkyries who regarded most supplicants with the same caliber of suspicion Omar the Doberman had accorded all visitors to Casa de los Huesos. They were a redoubtable pair, the imposing corporal evoking the bronze Themis who'd once graced the fallen city, the lithe sergeant suggesting Alonso the Conquistador following a sex-change operation. A simple nod from Lieutenant Kristowski was sufficient to make the guards step aside—she outranked them both—whereupon Dagmar abandoned her desk, guided us along a glass-walled promenade offering spectacular views of a calm North Atlantic sea, and ushered us into the Louis XIV parlor suite that now functioned as Londa's command-and-control center.

True to her solidarity with the downtrodden, she'd peeled away the suite's opulent trappings, so it was up to my imagination to supply the brocade draperies, Persian carpets, gilt-framed mirrors, and Fragonard reproductions that had doubtless once appointed the place. Although her surroundings were spare, Londa herself had opted for elegance that evening, her lips daubed with magenta, her exquisite skin wrapped in a strapless green taffeta evening gown. After gesturing Dagmar and Lieutenant Kristowski away, she gave me the sort of deep, aqueous kiss at which undines are adept, then sidled toward a serving table where a samovar stood heating over an open flame.

"Ever drunk your nectar warm, darling?" she asked, indicating the great silver urn. "Dagmar recommends the experience, so I thought we'd try it." She worked the stopcock, filling a black ceramic mug with a steaming measure of Proserpine. "Naturally I hoped we'd get together before now, but it's been pure madness around here, with more chaos to come."

"I heard your first two broadcasts. I guess you think you're being unbelievably brilliant inflicting poetic justice on the Phyllistines—"

"Not brilliant necessarily. Clever, I suppose. Droll."

"But paying them starvation wages, that's *cruel*."

She presented me with eight savory ounces of equanimity. "At the risk of sounding rather too forward, I'll get right to the point. I would like to formalize our bond."

My heart seemed to rotate on its axis. Formalize our bond? What was she suggesting? That we march straight into Captain Pittinger's cabin and demand that he marry us? A bizarre nuptial tableau flashed through my mind, at once beguiling and repulsive, Londa and myself standing before the master of the *Redux,* the vatling in her evening gown, her groom wearing a three-piece Italian suit that had previously belonged to a plutocrat, Dagmar and Lieutenant Kristowski getting ready to pelt us with rice. Did such a union make sense at any level? Would marrying Londa give me some sort of psychological leverage, a kind of Splanx-like power by which I might convince her to shut down Operation PG?

"My most precious and impossible undine," I sighed. "My infinitely exasperating sylph."

Londa stared at me as if I'd started speaking Chinese. "I'm wild about you, too, Mason, but that's another day's conversation. Right now we have to fix the Phyllistines."

"You said this was about our *bond*."

"Correct. Ambrose and Sabacthani, united against the misogynists and theocrats." She turned the stopcock and filled a second mug. "Ah, *now* I get it—you're referring to *another* sort of bond: Sythia and Thales, rolling around on their secret beach." Her tone was wistful, as if our lovemaking had occurred in some mythic realm beyond time and space. "Believe me, Mason, I get goose bumps just thinking about that day, and if it gave you further proof of my good intentions, so much the better."

My overwhelming impulse just then was to bounce the ceramic mug off her skull. "Are you saying that because you fucked me, I'm now supposed to go along with this hijacking crap?"

"I suggest we not dwell on those aspects of Operation PG you find objectionable. Let's focus on the greater good."

"May I once again quote you to yourself? 'There are no greater goods.'"

"That's Joan of Arc's line."

"Written by Londa Sabacthani."

"Your nectar's cooled off by now. Try some. You'll feel much better."

I took a protracted swallow. "Shall I tell you the truth? For a minute there, I imagined you wanted Captain Pittinger to marry us."

The perplexity that came to Londa's face was even deeper than before, as if the issue of my lips had changed from Chinese to bumblebees. She sipped some nectar, then marched to the writing desk: a typical piece of *Redux* furniture, so graceful it seemed intended solely for penning sestinas and would turn to sawdust the instant anybody used it for paying a bill. Sliding open the top drawer, she removed her fanciful account of her nonexistent preadolescence. "I saved only two mementos from Faustino—*Coral Idolatry* and this quaint and curious volume." She deposited *The Book of Londa* in my hands, its brown leather binding scuffed like an old shoe. "I've been using it to scribble down anecdotes from my life. At some point in the story, fiction turns to fact. Note the most recent entry."

As the mumquat molecules navigated my bloodstream, I did as Londa instructed. The specified page contained a mere sixty words, rendered in a script so ragged I wondered if she'd composed it under Proserpine's influence.

Today my auxiliary conscience and I shared mugs of nectar in my office. We weren't far into our conversation when he told me he fully supports the grand experiment in social justice now unfolding aboard the Redux. He even offered to sign this entry as a testament to his blessing, hence the "Mason Ambrose" at the bottom of the page.

She reached into the drawer again and retrieved a fountain pen: a genuine Montblanc, quite possibly the only aristocratic gewgaw she'd allowed herself after stripping the suite of its elitism. "I need your blessing," she said, pressing the pen into my palm. "It would make all the difference."

The nectar bathed my brain, bestowing a simulated serenity, but I was too distressed to enjoy it. "I can't."

"Of course you can."

"No," I said, regarding the fancy pen as I would a rattlesnake.

"Always the philosopher. Always the contrarian. Very well, Socrates—think it over. Think it over a whole fucking bunch. The evening's young."

"I've already thought it over."

"All I want is your goddamn signature."

I threw the pen across the room.

"I'm supposed to *beg* you—is that it?" she said.

"No, you're supposed to bring the ship about, steam back to Brigantine, and set the hostages free. If Donya were here, she'd tell you the same thing. Yolly, too. Even Edwina."

Londa's eyes grew shadowed and narrow, like visor slots in a knight's helmet. She gulped some nectar, snatched her journal away, and unleashed a diatribe of vast scope and epic sweep. Left to their own devices, she insisted, Ralph Gittikac and his compatriots would turn the planet into a toxic waste dump. If Enoch Anthem and his brethren retained their stranglehold on the zeitgeist, life would become even more wretched for those Americans who'd made the mistake of being born poor, unhealthy, gay, pigmented, or female. Once Pielmeister and his kind finished bringing Corporate Christi into being, a dark age would descend upon the human spirit, unredeemable by any imaginable renaissance.

"I forget, Londa, what sorts of weapons did the disciples bring to the Sermon on the Mount? As I recall, Mark says Browning machine guns, but Matthew reports AK-47s."

"Don't become my enemy, Mason. I have enemies enough."

In a quick, unbroken gesture, I tore the last page from *The Book of Londa* and jammed it into the flame beneath the samovar. Londa shuddered but did not move. I pulled my hand away and released the burning page. Buoyed by a draft, it turned into a lamina of ash, then floated to the floor and consumed itself.

I said, "John writes that the Good Samaritan acquired his legendary benevolence only after Jesus handcuffed him to a fig tree under the scorching sun."

"Have it your own way. We won't be lovers. We won't be friends. We won't be fellow warriors in the great crusade."

"In Luke's version, however, the conversion takes a bit longer."

"Kindly leave my office before I count to ten. One . . . two . . ."

I strode toward the door. "First Jesus locks the Samaritan in a dungeon for six months, then lays into him with a horsewhip."

"Three . . . four . . ."

"Until finally the Samaritan becomes a man of compassion."

"Five . . . six . . ."

I was gone before she got to seven.

NOW THAT THE GREAT SCHISM had occurred, a rift as wrenching for me as it was doubtless inevitable from the plenary perspective enjoyed by Isis, Horus, Thoth, and the rest of my antique pantheon, I assumed that Londa would exact a swift revenge. I imagined her canceling my room-service privileges and requiring me to join the Phyllistines in waiting on our first-class passengers. And yet I retained my pampered status—though apparently Londa did tell the security force I was no longer to be trusted.

"It's none of my business, sir, but I gather that you and Dr. Sabacthani had quite a falling-out," Lieutenant Kristowski said.

"True," I said.

"What did you do to offend her?"

"I quoted her to herself."

"I used to do that to my boyfriend," Lieutenant Kristowski said. "It's why we broke up. I'm sure Dr. Sabacthani doesn't hate you. Do you hate her?"

"No."

"If I had to take a guess, sir, I'd say you're in love with her."

"That may be the case."

"You philosophers like to make things complicated, don't you? If you ever need a break from your brain, drop by our shooting range on C deck. I'll teach you how to fire a Galil."

Throughout the second week of the voyage, as the ship oscillated aimlessly between the thirty-third and thirty-fifth parallels, I undertook a kind of anthropological study, systematically analyzing the behaviors of victims and oppressors alike as they played out their parts within the privileged precincts of A and B decks. Besides the three dozen former third-class passengers, our local elite included nineteen stewards, twenty-one scullerymen, and—when they weren't on duty shoveling coal in the boiler rooms—fifteen stokers. As far as I could tell, our entire population of parvenus had already gotten the hang of arrogance. Before making a particular demand, the first-class passenger usually invoked the captive plutocrat's name: an easily obtained datum since, pursuant to a directive from Major Powers, the Phyllistines had all signed their pajama pockets with indelible Sharpie pens.

"Albert, old sport, at four o'clock I shall require a repast of oysters and beer on the first-class promenade."

"Enoch, this martini glass appears to be empty, a situation I expect you to remedy without delay."

"Quentin, would you kindly visit the library and scare me up a Tom Clancy novel?"

"Donald, be a dear and retrieve your wife's cardigan from my stateroom."

"Felix, my man, it has come to our attention that fresh croissants are now available in the Café Parisien. Bring me a dozen in five minutes flat, and I'll reward you with a lucre."

I wondered what a devout Fabian like George Bernard Shaw would have made of Londa's deranged experiment in social engineering. He probably would not have approved. It was one thing to argue, per *Pygmalion,* that the class system was arbitrary and unnatural, quite another to demonstrate that, given the opportunity, the working poor of America, the United Kingdom, and Europe would happily turn themselves into callous egomaniacs every bit as tyrannical as Henry Higgins.

Owing to both my personal investigations and my daily conversations with Marnie Kristowski, I had a pretty good idea what was happening in the Phyllistines' heads. As in their previous lives, the subject of money rarely left their thoughts, but the focus of the obsession had changed, from piling up mountains of wealth to figuring out whether they had enough ready cash to buy toothpaste from the pharmacy and toilet paper from the commissary. For the brute truth was that five lucres a day—thirty-five lucres a week—did not go very far aboard the *Redux*. In accordance with Londa's latest fiat, a loaf of bread now cost thirty lucres, a quart of milk forty, and a box of raisins eighty. I shuddered to imagine the consequences if she ever repealed universal health insurance. No doubt she would start charging the same outrageous prices as the druggist in a certain famous moral dilemma.

It was alternately painful and amusing to watch our hostages laboring in the Grand Saloon and its adjacent kitchen, where their duties included arranging the place settings, taking the orders, serving the food, busing the tables, and doing the dishes. Our first-class passengers showed their inferiors no mercy. They addressed the plutocrats as "garçon" and "Jeeves," required them to memorize long wine lists, sent back half the entrées, and left worthless tips in the form of dollars, pounds, and euros. At the end of each meal, the more spiteful parvenus heated their plates over the dinner candles, thus guaranteeing that the Phyllistines would have to spend hours scraping away baked-in bits of poached salmon and encrusted morsels of kidney pie.

When it came to maintaining their staterooms, our first-class passengers held their servants to the highest standards. Every day, whether the task needed doing or not, the plutocrat responsible for a given suite was expected to vacuum the carpet, dust the furniture, disinfect the toilet, launder the linen, wash the portholes, clean the curtains, make the beds, and, after stripping the wardrobe of its jackets and pants—most of which had once belonged to the plutocrats themselves—brush each garment with a lint remover. Our parvenus soon became sticklers for detail, and God help the G-deck passenger who neglected to turn down the sheets or leave a chocolate on the pillow.

Londa took particular delight in publicizing the astonishing monetary harvest the Phyllistines had been reaping prior to their departure from Southampton. Third-class passenger Gary Pons, the whiz kid behind the Macro-Mart phenomenon, pulled down a cool five million a year, more than three hundred times the take-home pay of his average employee. Sheila Portman, CEO of several fast-food empires, enjoyed an annual salary equal to two hundred times the income of anyone who scrubbed the floors of her Grab-a-Crab restaurants. Morris Hampton, owner of the supernaturally profitable Prester Pharmaceutical Laboratory, had in recent years accumulated sufficient wealth to purchase private yachts for all four of his ne'er-do-well brothers.

"You wouldn't know it to look at him, since he's a physically diminutive chap," Londa said, wrapping up an especially caustic installment of *The Last Shall Be First,* "but it turns out that Frank Diffring, the guiding light behind Blue Château hotels, is nine hundred times worthier than the women he hires to change the bedding in those exemplary inns."

Thirty-five lucres a week—and if that wasn't pathetic enough, Londa soon arranged for inflation to plague our unhappy community, so that the plutocrats' newfound ability to budget judiciously for toothpaste and toilet paper suddenly stopped mattering. Now the big challenge was to get through the day on your meager allotment of plain tofu and rice, supplementing these rations with string beans gleaned from the Grand Saloon floor, bread crumbs scavenged from the parvenus' plates, and apple cores retrieved from the garbage pails. In short, a low-grade famine had come to the *Redux,* the second horseman of Londa's aquatic apocalypse, though whether that wasted rider would trample the Phyllistines or reunite them with their souls, I could not begin to say.

LIKE MANY BRILLIANT PHILOSOPHERS—and, closer to home, like many middling philosophers who never managed to get their Ph.D.s—I've always been susceptible to insomnia. Throughout the voyage of the *Redux*, this condition visited me with alarming frequency. Typically I would awaken at 5:00 A.M. and, knowing that my restlessness was certain to persist, make my way to the weather deck. For the next ninety minutes, I would pace in circles around the foremast, head tilted back, meditating on Orion, Ursa Major, Cassiopeia, that whole glowing host. I shall never cease to marvel at the clarity of stars when viewed from midocean, each as sharp and bright as the laser pointer God uses when lecturing the angels on evolution. At length the constellations would fade, and I would greet the rising sun with an awe verging on adoration—I was no longer Sinuhe just then but another character from *The Egyptian*, the monotheistic pharaoh Amenhotep IV, prostrating himself before a graven image of his divine and shining Aton—after which a delicious drowsiness overcame me, and I would return to my cabin for a long nap before Londa's usual nine o'clock broadcast roused me from my dreams.

On the morning of my thirtieth day aboard the *Redux*, my post-devotional sleep was terminated by an especially distressing episode of *The Last Shall Be First*. Londa began by expressing her "profound disappointment" in the hostages' performance to date. Her office had received myriad complaints: spots on the crystal, stains on the tablecloths, socks inadequately mended, shoes not sufficiently shined, toilets neither spick nor span. But incompetence was not the primary reason that fifty percent of our G-deck passengers were about to lose their jobs. Sheer economic necessity had proved the deciding factor. The fewer superfluous workers we employed in servicing the staterooms and the Grand Saloon, the more likely the voyage was to turn a profit.

"Downsizing is an imperative with which certain of my listeners are well acquainted—especially you, Corbin Thorndike, president of Aries Athletic Wear, and you, Barry Nelligan, founder of Beyond Style, and you, Wilbur Conant, CEO of Ultra Office, and you, Alexander Lerner, board chairman of General Heuristics. In your former careers as corporate heads, you collectively outsourced two hundred and thirty-four thousand manufacturing jobs to atrociously run factories in Asia and Latin America. But hear me now, masters of the universe. The *Redux* is a generous ship. Of the one hundred G-deck residents we're about to drop from the payroll, none will become destitute, for in our compassion we've decided to retire all our stokers and offer you their jobs at four lucres a day. True, the boiler rooms are an austere environment—quite similar, in fact, to the sweatshops that figure so crucially in your corporations' prosperity: long hours, foul air, hazardous working conditions, infrequent bathroom breaks. The temperature is one hundred and ten degrees Fahrenheit in the shade. But at least you'll be gainfully employed."

She went on to assure our former third-class passengers that those plutocrats not assigned to the boiler rooms would start working double shifts. To wit, the parvenus needn't fear a decline in the stateroom service, and the Grand Saloon would remain a place where one might enjoy a gracious dining experience along with the collateral satisfactions of treating the staff like dirt.

"For many of you, I imagine, the thought of your imminent demotion is distressing," Londa said. "But here's a late-breaking story to cheer you. Despite frenzied efforts by well-funded lobbyists, we shall continue to bless all G-deck residents with free health insurance. In other words, your pill bottles will remain full, and should you perchance fall sick, the *Redux* will cover your medical bills."

The new economic order was in place barely a week when a

combination of curiosity and boredom persuaded me to venture into the bowels of the ship and observe the situation in the boiler rooms. My Virgil for this Dantean descent was Lieutenant Kristowski, who gladly accepted my offer to assist in her daily task of bringing tepid water to the patrician stokers, along with cold beer for their guardian Valkyries. Prior to our departure, we loaded our backpacks with plastic pints of Poland Spring and crammed twelve thermoses of Tadcaster ale into a canvas duffel bag. We shouldered the water and set off, the bag swinging between us like a hammock as we clambered down a series of aft companionways reminiscent of a fire escape, though in this case we were seeking, not fleeing, an inferno. Throughout our journey we discussed that most fascinating and confounding of topics, Londa Sabacthani. In a tone more equivocal than she probably intended, Lieutenant Kristowski announced that she'd decided to give her employer the benefit of the doubt concerning the boiler-room scheme, and I replied that thus far I could discern no doubt on which to predicate a benefit.

As we reached the lowest deck, a stifling gust of heat blew toward us, and our conversation tapered into silence, as if the blistering air had melted our words away. A huge iron slab, embroidered with rivets, blocked our progress. The presiding sentry, a statuesque Valkyrie sergeant whose name patch read SKEGGS, thanked us so extravagantly for her gift thermos that if a video camera had caught her reaction, the result would've been a singularly persuasive commercial for Tadcaster ale.

"It's a real honor having you visit us, Mr. Ambrose," said Sergeant Skeggs, draining the thermos. "May I ask you a question? My boyfriend could use some ethical fine-tuning himself, so I'm wondering—how did you make Dr. Sabacthani the way she is?"

"Londa was a blank slate when she became my student," I said. "I doubt that her story is relevant to your problem."

"You don't know Douglas."

"He's not a tabula rasa—I can tell you that."

"Maybe," said Sergeant Skeggs. "In any case, what did you *do*?"

"We started with role-playing exercises," I said. "Get your search engine to track down 'Lawrence Kohlberg' and 'moral dilemmas.' K-o-h-l-b-e-r-g."

"I'll give it a try."

"Eventually we did Jesus. Be careful with the Sermon on the Mount. It's not for amateurs."

"I hear you. Thanks. It all sounds a lot easier than hijacking a fucking ocean liner."

The guard threw a switch on the wall, whereupon the watertight door screeched and squealed its way upward like a portcullis. Lieutenant Kristowski and I crossed the threshold. Swathed in swirling tendrils of sallow steam, eight enormous horizontal cylinders dominated boiler room 1, each demanding ceaseless attention from a team of Phyllistines, the first member responsible for opening the furnace door and feeding the fire with shovelfuls of coal, the second for stirring the burning fuel with an iron lance inserted through the stokehole, the third for keeping the adjacent bin filled with wheelbarrow loads of anthracite drawn from a communal heap. The spectacle transfixed me. For a full minute, I simply stood and stared, my eyes dazzled by the glare, my ears throbbing with the roar of the furnaces, the billows of horrific scarlet heat casting my mind back to Themisopolis's fiery demise. Now the lieutenant and I started working the room, moving among the stokers like a couple of minor-league angels ministering to Ben-Hur and his fellow galley slaves. My first customer was chubby Wilbur Conant—so read the name on his sweat-soaked pajama top—his soft features and stern expression suggesting a teddy bear who'd gotten in touch with his dark side. Upon receiving his pint, the CEO of Ultra Office set down his shovel, removed the cap with a single twist of the wrist, and consumed the entire portion in a prolonged gulp.

"I remember you from that first night, when those dyke bitches gathered everybody together outside the Grand Saloon." Conant ran his tongue across his lips in search of stray drops. Medallions of soot and splotches of coal dust speckled his chest. "Tell me, Mr. Ethical Adviser, where's the goddamn *ethics* in condemning us to this stinking place?"

"Dr. Sabacthani wants you to start thinking about your life in new ways," I replied.

"Yeah? Well, I'll tell you something. Most of the time, I'm exhausted, and hungry, too, and until you showed up, I was dying of thirst. Under conditions like that, how am I supposed to get any goddamn *thinking* done?"

"I can see your point."

"I'm not a monster, Mr. Ambrose. I've sponsored orphans in India. I give to the United Way. You don't know me, and neither does Dr. Sabacthani."

I assured Wilbur Conant that Dr. Sabacthani did not think him a monster, merely an avaricious miscreant who trafficked in the form of legal slavery called sweatshop labor. While this characterization obviously displeased him, he offered no rejoinder beyond ratcheting up his scowl and asserting that "sweatshop labor" was an exaggeration.

My next thirsty plutocrat was Beyond Style's dynamic manager, Barry Nelligan, whose face had on three occasions graced the cover of *Fortune.* A trim, athletic man who bore a startling resemblance to the young Robert Redford, he seemed to take a certain pride in artfully jabbing his lance through the stokehole. After thanking me for the water, Nelligan wiped the sweat from his forehead and said, "I've got a message for Londa Sabacthani. Tell your client I forgive her, for she knows not what she does. You understand what I'm getting at?"

"I believe I grasp your allusion."

"The crucifixion, right?"

"I'm afraid Dr. Sabacthani wants nothing to do with me these days."

"Oh, really? Well, if you ever bury the hatchet, let her know she can torture me all she wants, and I'll still forgive her."

For the next half-hour, Lieutenant Kristowski and I moistened dry mouths and cooled blistered brows, until at last we'd serviced all twenty-four amateur stokers. In most cases the Phyllistine's understandable bitterness was leavened by a less predictable reaction: a show of stoicism, a declaration of innocence, an outburst of contrition, a recitation of philanthropic acts, and in a few instances—the sentiment I'd first encountered in Barry Nelligan—a short speech absolving Londa of her sins. For better or worse, it appeared that Operation PG was an experiment of greater psychological complexity than I'd allowed.

Upon reaching the far end of the compartment, Lieutenant Kristowski approached a tall Valkyrie whose gray blouse matched the oiled metal of her rifle, making the weapon seem less a gun than a fashion accessory, and presented her with a thermos of ale. The guard swilled down half the contents, then opened the watertight door.

We crossed over and began bringing our charity to boiler room 2. Halfway through my toils, the formidable figure of Felix Pielmeister emerged from the steam, naked to the waist, huffing and grunting as he filled his wheelbarrow with coal. Sensing my presence, he leaned his shovel against the barrow and fixed me with a brutish stare, as if auditioning for the part of Yank, the gorilla-faced stoker in Eugene O'Neill's *The Hairy Ape*.

"I knew we'd meet again one day," I told him, "though I didn't think the location would be hell itself."

"Your antics before the Harkness Commission were despicable," Pielmeister rasped. Sweat sparkled on his chest. Burns and blisters peppered his skin: evidently he was slow to dodge the errant embers forever spewing from the furnaces. "How irresponsible of you to blame me and Reverend Anthem for that Sabacthani woman's death."

"Irresponsible. Yes. Also reckless and rash. So tell me, what did you and Anthem say to the mackies when you gave them their marching orders? 'Remember, my precious vigilantes, Themisopolis is the abortion capital of the world. The Sisters Sabacthani deserve to die.'"

Pielmeister glowered, grabbed his shovel, and added another measure of coal to the barrow. His thirst, I figured, must be intolerable, and I was not surprised when he gestured toward my backpack and said, "Got any more water in there?"

"Lots of water. Too proud to ask me for a drink?"

"Hardly. Pride is a sin. So is withholding water from a thirsty man."

"What's your preference?" I set my backpack on the floor, unzipping it to reveal my seven remaining pints of Poland Spring. "Today's choices are perfect for a man of your persuasion. This one holds the joyful tears Mary shed after the Annunciation. This one comes from the basin in which Pilate washed his hands. And here we have the wine that Satan turned back into water following the wedding at Cana."

"You're loving this, aren't you, Ambrose?" Pielmeister laid his shovel athwart the barrow. "You're having the time of your life."

"Please satisfy my curiosity," I said, tearing a bottle from its plastic tether. "Am I the first person you ever screwed out of a degree?"

"Are you going to give me that water or aren't you?"

"I like to think I was the first. That would be quite a distinction."

"You've cast your lot with a lunatic—I hope you realize that. Your protégée is out of her mind, and one way or another she's going to wreck this ship and destroy us all."

I tossed the bottle to Pielmeister, who caught it in one hand. He wrenched off the cap and began guzzling. I did not stay to watch him finish but returned to my Kantian duty, irrigating the arid throat of Senator Rupert Marbury, soothing the desiccated tongue of Macro-Mart wizard Gary Pons, salving the parched tonsils of Aries Athletic Wear CEO Corbin Thorndike, while all around me the furnaces seethed and bellowed, spewing sparks like those burning braziers in which the priestesses of Isis—not the least of the deities to whom Sinuhe had bent his body while withholding his devotion—would glimpse the future.

How good a prophet was Pielmeister? What was the caliber of his brazier? I hated to admit it, but I feared he'd seen our collective fate. Sooner or later, Londa would bring the *Titanic Redux* to the edge of the world, and then with both eyes open and both hands on the helm she would contact the engine room, order them to crank up the turbines, and sail us into the void, all ahead full.

Chapter 15

ON THE FIRST SUNDAY IN AUGUST, while the equatorial sea raged with Charybdian fury and the *Titanic Redux* entered her fourth week of functioning as Londa's empire and toy, the most disturbing installment yet of *The Last Shall Be First* resounded through the ship. I was sitting in my cabin, sipping room-service coffee, oblivious to the screaming storm, when the broadcast started spilling down from the ceiling like acid rain sterilizing a lake. Once again I resolved to muffle the program with my pillow, but then I became transfixed by Londa's message of the day, a mordant account of what the Phyllistines could expect from the next phase of their treatment.

"Yes, masters of the universe, we finally see the light. We now accept the arguments by which certain clear thinkers among you convinced the U.S. Congress to gut and geld so many pieces of environmental legislation. I'm speaking of you, Clarence Garmond, enterprising chairperson of the White House Council on Air and Water Quality, and you, Robert Arnold, tireless lobbyist on behalf of the Greater Pacific Electric Company, and you, Senator Chad Wintergreen, assiduous pimp for the petroleum industry."

A tawdry wailing trumpet melody underscored the word "pimp," though the Phyllistines were probably too hungry and tired to appreciate the audio engineer's wit.

"And so we've decided to banish environmental extremism from the *Redux*," Londa continued as the trumpet faded, "systematically rescinding those regulations that until now have forbidden us to collect the fumes from our smokestacks and vent them onto G deck."

A wave of nausea rolled through me. I leaned back in my reading chair, grasping the armrests for support.

"We're confident that Messrs. Garmond, Arnold, and Wintergreen will not balk at the introduction of lead, mercury, sulfur dioxide, carbon dioxide, and carbon monoxide into their living spaces," Londa continued. "After all, in their various campaigns against ecofetishism, they managed to assemble mounds of solid right-wing scientific evidence proving that heavy metals and hydrocarbons pose no long-lasting threats to human health. Of course, those of you already suffering from lung ailments may find your symptoms aggravated, but I'm sure you're prepared to endure such discomforts in the name of a profitable voyage."

I jerked free of my chair and stood staring at the speaker, as flabbergasted as Joan of Arc hearing from her celestial sponsors.

"Of one thing we may be certain. As news of the venting initiative spreads around the globe, scores of self-righteous physicians will raise their voices in alarm, glibly predicting that the third horseman, Pestilence, is about to go galloping through the *Redux*."

Thanks to the dexterity of her audio engineer, the sound of thundering hooves counterpointed Londa's image of equestrian contagion.

"But even if those smug doctors are right, you needn't fret, as you can still avail yourselves of our free medical services. True, we *have* started reviewing the position papers that G-deck citizens Endicott and Marbury once wrote by way of persuading their fellow senators to torpedo universal health insurance. But if I were you, I wouldn't worry. God will provide."

The engineer eased in the *Rocky* theme.

"Will an epidemic of lung ailments be visited upon the Ship of Dreams? Will the *Redux* administration continue to coddle its third-class passengers with socialized medicine? To learn the answers, or at least to hear a repetition of the questions, tune in tomorrow!"

Blood boiling, dudgeon rising, I bolted from my cabin and charged through the maze of D-deck corridors like a maiden in flight from the Minotaur. I scrambled up the companionways and, arriving on the boat deck, dashed across the wheelhouse, much to the sputtering dismay of the officer on duty. A Valkyrie with the proportions and demeanor of a New Jersey nightclub bouncer interposed her body between myself and the communications shack, its door shut tightly against potential intrusions by livid Phyllistines and outraged superegos.

"Dr. Sabacthani thought you might show up," she said, waving her Uzi in my face.

"Listen to me, Londa!" I yelled toward the shack. "Cease and desist! No toxic fumes on G deck!"

The Jersey bouncer wrapped her thick, intractable fingers around my upper arm.

"No fumes, Londa!" I persisted. "The whole world will turn against you!"

Chuckling at the low comedy of the situation—a gangly neo-Darwinist philosopher struggling to break a musclebound Valkyrie's iron grip—the bouncer rudely escorted me back to my cabin. She forced me into the reading chair, fixed me with the burning gaze of the believing Sabacthanite, and wafted out one of those reverential banalities so characteristic of Londa's security force.

"What you have to understand," she said, "is that there's a good reason for everything Dame Quixote does."

The bouncer stalked out of the room, leaving me to spend an ethically indefensible afternoon getting drunk on Guinness while consuming plate after plate of broiled lobster tails.

No less chilling than its predecessor was the next installment of Londa's radio show, a roll call of those G-deck residents who'd experienced asthma attacks during the first day of the venting initiative. Once again I sprinted to the communications shack and screamed my outrage in Londa's direction until the bouncer whisked me away. Twenty-four hours later, I endured another broadcast, Dame Quixote's report on how the emphysema rate was climbing under the deregulation regime, and so for the third time that week I ascended to the wheelhouse and shouted my impotent objections.

Shortly after the bouncer deposited me in my quarters yet again, I realized that a day might dawn when I would be called upon to testify against Londa in a court of law. Would I leap at this opportunity? Greet it with fear and trembling? Whatever the case, my Kantian duty was clear. I must obtain an oxygen rig and inspect the venting initiative firsthand.

As usual, Lieutenant Kristowski proved willing to help—I didn't tell her the real reason I wanted to visit the hostages' quarters, claiming instead a morbid interest in their latest ordeal—and the following morning she appeared at my door bearing a face mask, regulator, and scuba tank. I thanked my aide-de-camp, strapped on the gear, and descended to G deck. Entering the plutocrats' domain, I immediately found myself negotiating a web of heating ducts, PVC pipes, vacuum-cleaner tubes, and fire hoses, all carefully configured to foul the corridors with the ship's effluvium. A half-dozen Valkyries, likewise equipped with oxygen rigs, presided over this jerry-built torture device. The air was visibly gritty, sallow as an October moon, a jaundiced miasma suggesting the collective exhaust from a thousand tractor-trailers barreling down Interstate 80. There was no need to take notes—for how could I ever forget the misery of the Phyllistines now wandering the corridors, their eyes streaming tears, bronchial tubes wheezing, diaphragms racked by coughing fits?

I deposited the oxygen rig in my cabin, then found my way to the C-deck infirmary and marched uninvited through a door marked HOWARD FLETCHER, M.D. A gangly man with skin as pallid as goat cheese, Dr. Fletcher stood before a vertically mounted light table to which was secured a chest X-ray, its subject's lungs and ribs rendered in electromagnetic chiaroscuro. I introduced myself as "a former member of Dr. Sabacthani's inner circle, now a defector."

"I believe you about the inner circle part," Dr. Fletcher said, then explained that he recognized me from the television coverage of the Harkness hearings. "As I recall, you once tutored her in moral philosophy."

"That was ages ago. Believe me, when they put her on trial, I'll gladly denounce her from the witness stand."

"Christ, Ambrose, you should be denouncing her *right now*. You should be denouncing her right now to her *fucking face*."

I told him that Londa had exiled me from her sphere—not exactly a momentous event, I hastened to add, as these days she took the advice of no one but herself, and there were doubtless times when she ignored that counsel as well. Muttering under his breath, Dr. Fletcher went back to studying the chest X-ray, but an instant later he looked me in the eye and said he would grant me a five-minute interview.

In the ensuing conversation, the doctor revealed that, owing to the venting initiative, his staff was now obligated to obtain daily blood samples from the hostages. If any third-class aristocrats exhibited signs of lead contamination or mercury poisoning, he was prepared to offer them chelation therapy, but so far they all seemed free of heavy metals.

"Which is not to say I'm remotely happy about what's happening down on G deck," Dr. Fletcher said. "Almost everybody who came aboard with a preexisting lung condition is doing badly. Yesterday I treated five asthma patients. This morning it was four emphysema cases, plus something that looks suspiciously like pneumonoconiosis."

I thanked the man for his time. He said he hoped my testimony would "land that bitch in prison for the rest of her life," then added, lest I imagine that he thought me heroic, "So tell me, who were your other morality students? Richard Nixon? Osama bin Laden?"

I clenched my jaw, hard enough to induce tinnitus, then returned to D deck, where the day's second great humiliation awaited. Major Powers stood in the corridor, her waist girded by a utility belt suggesting the holstered arsenal of a Dodge City marshal, and I soon apprehended that she'd just finished converting my cabin to a jail cell. Steel rods and two-by-four studs reinforced the door, and instead of a knob there was now an outside latch equipped with a padlock.

"Fuck this," I said.

The major opened the door and, gesturing with her screwdriver, directed me across the threshold. "Perhaps you'd prefer one of those smoggy hovels on G deck?"

"Tell Londa she's making a big mistake."

"What a coincidence—that's her message to you. 'Tell Mason he's making a big mistake, condemning the deregulation regime before it's had a chance to prove itself.'" The major followed me into the cabin, then pointed to the six-inch slot she'd jigsawed into the bottom of the door. "That's right, Mr. Ambrose, you'll still get your beer and lobster, and your cat, if you have one, can come and go at his leisure."

"I was just talking with Dr. Fletcher. He thinks you're all a bunch of thugs."

Major Powers made no reply but instead reached into her jacket pocket and produced a cardboard sleeve holding a compact disc. "Londa had me troll the Internet and download a bunch of low-end Frankenstein movies for your amusement and edification," she explained, setting the disc atop my DVD player. "*I Was a Teenage Frankenstein,* that sort of thing."

"It's nice to know she still loves me."

"She said you'd find them, quote, 'relevant to solving the riddle of Edwina Sabacthani.'"

The major made a snappy about-face and returned to the corridor.

"One final message from headquarters," she said before locking me in. "'Tell Mason that at some point in their relationship an undine and an Epicurean will set out to change one another, and the results are always disastrous.'"

THUS DID I FIND MYSELF living under house arrest aboard the *Titanic Redux*. In retrospect I realize I was enduring the sort of cushy incarceration our Phyllistine captives would have enjoyed had they been convicted of their various crimes against the planet and its life-forms. But at the time I found no irony in my imprisonment, only infinite frustration, for I was evidently missing the most significant events of the voyage.

The first thunderbolt struck during Londa's regular nine o'clock broadcast. "Good news, masters of the universe! My staff reports a virtual orgy of self-reflection on G deck, and Colonel Fox believes that many of you are now on the road to recovery—and so we've decided to put your rehabilitation on hold. Even as I speak, we're shutting down the venting initiative, and in a matter of hours the ship's regular staff and stokers will come out of retirement to take over those character-building jobs that have absorbed you of late."

She spent the rest of the program telling her captives what to expect in the days to come. One by one they would be brought up to OPG headquarters for an interview "not unlike those that routinely occur between felons and parole officers." As the evaluation progressed, Londa would assay the hostage's soul, and if she deemed him cured, he would be put ashore when the *Redux* reached the Florida Keys on September 17. Anyone who failed the examination would remain on the ship "under the regrettable but necessary plastique regime," until he, too, became fluent in the Beatitudes.

"How many G-deck residents have thus far acquired a moral compass?" Londa wondered aloud. "Some? Most? All? None? Be sure to tune in our next exciting episode!"

Prompted by a combination of inquisitiveness and fear, I indeed tuned in the next exciting episode—that is, I decided not to censor it with my pillow—and a half-dozen subsequent episodes. What I heard astonished me even more than Edwina's long-ago disclosure that she'd quadruplicated herself. For if Londa could be believed, Operation PG was a resounding success, with nearly every Phyllistine lamenting his former indifference to the downtrodden and his past offenses against Lady Justice.

"Tomorrow we drop anchor off Key Largo," she said over the swelling *Rocky* theme, "whereupon two hundred and eighty-eight of you will be ferried to Miami. Those dozen voyagers who still require treatment will remain on board until they are likewise ready to join the fellowship of the gentle."

As the music reached its crescendo, I muttered an acid paraphrase of Londa's final sentence—"Those dozen voyagers who refused to tell me what I wanted to hear will remain on board until I brokered a deal with the FBI"—for such was the depth of my hostility toward Operation PG, my skepticism regarding the Phyllistines' redemption, and my disgust with Dame Quixote and all her poisonous dreams.

Hostility, skepticism, disgust: and yet—wonder of wonders, joy of joys—these sentiments were evidently misplaced. Although Londa did not permit me a shortwave radio or an Internet connection, she did allow Lieutenant Kristowski to drop by D deck once a day and shout the latest news through my barricaded door, and each such bulletin proved more heartening than the last. Against all odds, defying every rational expectation, our recently released Phyllistine legislators were sponsoring Beatitudinous measures around the clock, aimed variously at sparing the planet the ravages of industrialization, curbing the theocratic agenda of the Center for Stable Families, undermining Corporate Christi, and raising the republic's foreign-aid budget to levels commensurate with Jesus of Nazareth's reported enthusiasm for generosity. Our liberated CEOs, meanwhile, ashamed of their former complicity in sweatshops and global poverty, were arranging for the planet's toys, running shoes, designer clothing, household appliances, and cybernetic consumer goods to be assembled in convivial environments by reasonably contented workers who received fair wages. As for our rehabilitated lobbyists, they were switching allegiances with an alacrity to tax the vocabulary of even the most articulate neo-Nazi radio host—for after you've labeled them traitors, quislings, and agents of Lucifer, what *else* can you call them?—and in nearly every case the reformed influence peddler announced that his new cause, whether it was educating preschoolers, protecting rain forests, or securing affordable day care for single mothers, had blessed him with an unaccustomed quantity of self-respect.

Concerning our immediate circumstances, Lieutenant Kristowski reported that after leaving Key Largo the *Redux* had steamed to Isla de Sangre, and she presently lay at anchor in the Bahía de Colón. Captain Pittinger and his officers, as well as the deckhands, stokers, stewards, galley staff, and medical personnel, had all been sent home, and in a goodwill gesture Londa had transferred the twelve unrepentant Phyllistines—a group that, predictably enough, included Enoch Anthem, Felix Pielmeister, and Ralph Gittikac—to second-class cabins on E deck. Throughout the luxury liner, the lieutenant told me, an eerie quietude reigned: not surprising, really, since the guards now outnumbered the prisoners. Plenty of food remained in the pantries, and the Valkyries were amusing themselves by preparing gourmet meals for one another. Owing to our explosive cargo, the outside world was still disinclined to harass us, though it wasn't clear how much longer the standoff would prevail before somebody blinked, balked, or blew up the ship.

Hour by hour the glad tidings poured in. The civilized world watched in awe as drug companies voluntarily lowered their prices, cigarette manufacturers launched class-action lawsuits against themselves, and automakers burned the midnight oil seeking ways for future generations to burn innocuous fuels instead. But you know more about these halcyon days than I, ladies and gentlemen. After all, you were sitting in front of your television screens every night, watching heaven come to earth, while I languished in my boring windowless cabin, watching grade-Z Frankenstein movies.

When not contemplating Mary Shelley's cinematic descendants, clearing away the resultant cranial cobwebs with the aid of J. R. R. Tolkien and Guinness stout, or sending impotent messages to Londa imploring her to let me out of the clink, I talked through the door with Lieutenant Kristowski. Despite her inveterate faith in Dame Quixote, my aide-de-camp was having as much trouble as I believing that the miracle had occurred. "To be truthful, I wasn't always sure she'd bring it off," the lieutenant said. "There's a moment in *The League of Londa* number twenty-four when her followers lose faith. Dame Quixote has resolved to talk the world's leaders into destroying their nuclear weapons, and of course her disciples think she's gone off the deep end, but she actually makes it happen, universal disarmament. You must be pretty proud of yourself, giving her such an ironclad conscience."

"Proud? Right, Lieutenant. You bet. I taught her everything she knows. Love your enemies, and if that doesn't work, grind them into the dirt. Turn the other cheek, and if the bastard slaps you again, imprison him on a polluted luxury liner. Next time you meet a rich man, try dragging him through the eye of a needle, and if the experience leaves him a bloody pulp . . . well, you certainly shattered his complacency, didn't you?"

"Really, sir, I don't think this is a time for negativism," Lieutenant Kristowski said.

"Londa would agree with you. That's why she keeps me in jail."

"You never told her to grind her enemies into the dirt."

"Back when we were mentor and mentee, I told her that at least once a day. Obviously she learned her lesson. I'm a better teacher than I know."

IN THESE SNEERING, jeering, jaded times, we tend to forget how close my vatling came to redeeming Western civilization through Operation Pineal Gland. For a full seven weeks following the release of the cured plutocrats, an epidemic of decency raged through the corridors of power and the citadels of privilege. Sometimes the blessing in question traced directly to the activism of a former *Redux* hostage, sometimes to a mover and shaker who'd been moved and shaken by a rehabilitated Phyllistine's example. It seemed not only that the meek stood a plausible chance of inheriting the earth, but that the concomitant taxes would be paid by, of all people, the rich. Within the walls of corporations once shamelessly engaged in gangbanging the biosphere, moderation was now the watchword, even as a previously unthinkable distinction—that between an honest profit and a profit beyond cupidity's wettest dream—was openly discussed in boardrooms everywhere, with the latter judged inimical to the common good. Behind the ramparts of America's gated communities, a discourse had arisen whereby the promiscuous accumulation of wealth was regarded less as a mark of genius than an index of sin.

The bubble, I am told, did not so much burst as implode. Apparently one could practically hear the sluggish suck of unearned income returning to plutocrat pockets, the plaintive peal of progressive legislation falling into procedural purgatory, and the agonized cries of Lady Justice squirming and writhing in the jaws of alleged necessity. It was as if the rehabilitated Phyllistines and their acolytes had awoken one morning and said to themselves, "Wait a minute. What's going on here? This is the United States of America, not fucking Camelot. What were we *thinking*?"

Believe me, ladies and gentlemen, I understand why many of you recall the golden age of Operation PG with fondness. If the Beatitudes broke the bank once, the argument goes, the same thing could happen again, so let us celebrate the dream, short-lived though it was. For what it's worth, however, I have come to regard Londa's transient success as an unequivocal tragedy. Far better for the merciful, the gentle, and the spit-upon if they'd remained permanently in the shadows and never endured the fate that actually befell them, a day in the sun followed by the cruelest imaginable eclipse.

Though filtered through several layers of pine and oak, Lieutenant Kristowski's sobs clawed at my soul, the most wrenching such sounds I'd heard since the choral grieving at Yolly's funeral. Numb with sorrow, paralyzed with despair, my aide-de-camp could barely bring herself to relate the dispatches now arriving from all directions. Sweatshops once again running at a pace to wreck their employees' health and rack their spirits. Developers devouring ecosystems as if—the very outcome this violence seemed intended to secure—there was no tomorrow. Legislators cutting nutritional programs for the urban poor even as these same elected representatives rigged the tax code to guarantee that no CEO need ever suffer empty-yacht-berth syndrome again.

"Back to square one," I moaned.

"Dr. Sabacthani will think of something," my aide-de-camp asserted in the bravest voice she could muster. "She always does."

Lieutenant Kristowski's instinct was doubtless correct. Dr. Sabacthani would think of something. And at that particular moment, sitting in my prison as *Lady Frankenstein* played across my plasma television monitor, I could not imagine a more disturbing prediction.

* * *

WHILE THE UNRAVELING of Operation Pineal Gland broke my heart, it also hardened my resolve, convincing me to do all within my power to prevent the circumstances through which Londa Sabacthani had come into the world—her vatling birth, DUNCE cap infancy, scattershot moral education at the hands of a dubious philosopher—from ever converging again. How I longed to break free of my prison and appear on Londa's doorstep: not in my persona as her ethical adviser, of course, a sympathetic Jiminy Cricket nudging her back onto the straight and narrow. Her caller, rather, would be an insect of Gregor Samsa pedigree, bent and grotesque, graphically mirroring her own misshapen soul. Or perhaps I would become an arthropod more monstrous yet, a chittering, chitinous mutation out of some 1950s science-fiction movie, *It Came From Beneath the Family Hearth.* You may fancy yourself a semidivine genius, I would tell her, but in truth you're just another autocratic narcissist whose followers have guns. You're not a demigod, Londa Sabacthani, merely a demagogue.

As the days slogged by, I came to wish that my DVD library actually included some of those 1950s giant-insect thrillers. In my experience such spectacles were marginally diverting, which is more than I could say for my digitalized Frankenstein omnibus. Despite their promising titles, none of these films could be rehabilitated through hermeneutics. There was no compelling discourse on gender occurring between the frames of *Lady Frankenstein,* no postmodern insouciance afoot in *Jesse James Meets Frankenstein's Daughter,* no tacit political subtext crying out for deconstruction in *Frankenstein Conquers the World,* no allegory on adolescence to be gleaned from *I Was a Teenage Frankenstein.* There was only tedium, and turgidity, and my gradual realization that Londa was severely mistaken to imagine that these cinematic catastrophes could provide any insight into her mother's mind.

Month three of my imprisonment was not long under way when,

early one morning, Major Powers popped the padlock, marched into my cabin, and, after hauling my semiconscious self out of bed, explained that Londa wanted to see me. I dressed frantically—linen slacks and a silk shirt that in fact belonged to one of our twelve onboard Phyllistines, Clarence Garmond of the White House Council on Air and Water Quality—and soon we were on B deck, marching toward Londa's headquarters. Although I'd never doubted Lieutenant Kristowski's report that the *Redux* lay moored in the Bahía de Colón, I was startled to look beyond the glassed-in promenade and see not the usual expanse of ocean but a range of forested hills wreathed in clouds. It was a typical Isla de Sangre dawn, pure travel brochure, the rising sun fruiting the trees with emeralds and filling the bay with a million buoyant diamonds.

Major Powers and I arrived in time to observe the changing of the guard, two steely-eyed Valkyries stepping away as their day-shift counterparts—the avatar of Themis and the transsexual conquistador—came on deck. A shroud of melancholy enswathed all four sentries. Dagmar Röhrig sat slumped behind her desk, staring despondently into space as if practicing to play herself in a Hollywood adaptation of a forthcoming *League of Londa* comic in which Dame Quixote's staff lapses into suicidal depression following the demise of Operation PG. Saying nothing, she waved us into the parlor suite.

Londa lay sprawled across a green velvet divan, wrapped in shadows, a raven cloaked by its own wings. Major Powers made a discreet exit. A calculated cough escaped my throat. My vatling struggled to her feet and stepped into a shaft of sunlight streaming through the porthole. Her auburn hair was a snarled skein. Her eyes suggested corroded pinballs. Her flesh looked battered and swollen, as if she'd been swallowed by Spenser's allegorical Error, judged indigestible, and vomited out.

"Guess what, Socrates?" she muttered. "You've been replaced.

Like a worn-out fan belt, or a TV show with low ratings. I've got a new conscience now."

Although rococonut milk was Londa's anesthetic of choice, today she'd opted for rum. She approached her antique desk and, taking hold of a half-empty Captain Morgan bottle, slopped a measure into a cracked white coffee mug.

"Is this development supposed to make me jealous?" I asked.

"Yes."

"It doesn't." Actually it did.

She swallowed some rum, then moved her hands with the staccato awkwardness of a stymied charades player, eventually directing my gaze toward the porthole and the island it disclosed. "The Wild Woman of the Jungle."

"What?"

"My new ethical adviser. The Wild Woman of the Jungle. The feisty lady has blessed every aspect of Operation PG—past, present, and future. She even signed *The Book of Londa*. Our relationship is not ideal, but she understands me better than you do."

"That rum bottle understands you better than I do."

She took another gulp of Captain Morgan. "Be honest, Mason. You think I've lost. Lousy position, down a rook, and my opponent's about to queen a pawn. But as we all know, sweetie, the winner's not the player with great position, an extra rook, and a pawn storming the back row—it's the player who can flash her opponent a smirk and say, 'Checkmate.' The whole world will be listening to tomorrow's broadcast, but my message will hold particular interest for our recently released Phyllistines. They have one last chance to get it right."

"And what if they *don't* get it right?"

"You always ask such penetrating questions, Mason. I swear, the day you die, Aristotle and Plato will petition God to have you transferred south. If you can't liven up limbo, nobody can."

"Limbo doesn't exist anymore."

"Neither does God. Been enjoying your Frankenstein films?"

"They're garbage. What if the released Phyllistines ignore you?"

Londa sipped rum and removed a Jerusalem Bible from her desk drawer. "Major Powers tells me there's a great speech in *I Was a Teenage Frankenstein*. 'Come, come, my boy, say good morning to your creator. Speak! You've got a civil tongue in your head—I know you have, because I sewed it back myself.'" She flipped open the book and made a beeline for the Gospels. "This Jew you think is such a splendid moral philosopher—you know what he *really* is? He's Victor Frankenstein's monster. Go digging through the New Testament, and eventually you'll unearth enough material to stitch together any sort of Jesus you want. When you neo-Darwinist sentimentalists go about it, you naturally assemble the brother-loving, mother-loving, other-loving, love-loving rabbi of your cuddliest fantasies. But suppose we want to build ourselves a different kind of Christ—say, the lock-and-load Messiah of the Rapture-mongers? No problem. Take the Gospel According to Matthew. Chapter eleven, verse twenty-three, Jesus blithely condemning an entire city to hell—men, women, children, and fetuses. Chapter thirteen, verse forty-two, the Messiah merrily throwing sinners into a blazing furnace. Chapter eighteen, verse thirty-five, the Prince of Peace threatening his followers with torture if they fail to accord their estranged relatives sufficient forgiveness." She snapped the book closed. "What if the Phyllistines ignore me? Simple, Socrates. Colonel Fox brings Enoch Anthem onto the weather deck, and the first thing he notices is the dozen nooses dangling from the foremast shrouds."

"Nooses?"

"The apocalypse, Anthem now realizes, is about to become complete. War, Famine, and Pestilence have already visited the ship, which leaves only the pale rider on his pale horse."

"No, Londa! Forget it! Absolutely not!"

"I see your point of view. I really do."

In a gesture so cartoonish it was doubtless prefigured in some *League of Londa* splash panel, I strode toward her with arms raised, my fingers curled into talons. To this day I'm not sure what I had in mind. Did I intend to close my hands around her throat and threaten to strangle her if she didn't surrender to the FBI?

She foiled the attack with her Godgadget, pulling it from her hip pocket and pointing it in my face. I froze, arrested by my vision of a rather different sort of splash panel: the *Redux* exploding, bright orange billows of flame and ash roiling outward from ground zero, a stark black KA-BOOM superimposed on the blast wave in ono-matopoeic capitals.

"Back off, Socrates."

I retreated two steps.

"Have you any idea how empowering this device is?" Her index finger danced above the transmitter, directly over the red plastic node. "At the press of a button, I can change the channel of reality itself, from Quotidian Central to the Armageddon Network." She brought the remote to her lips and kissed it. "By my calculation, the threat of Enoch Anthem's execution will inspire thousands of his followers to find their inner Samaritans. But perhaps my predic-tion will fail, in which case I'll have to lynch Anthem and play the game all over again with a second hostage—Corbin Thorndike, say, or Ralph Gittikac, or your friend Pielmeister." Circling back to her desk, she threw a switch on the intercom and delivered an order to Dagmar. "My lame-duck conscience has become impossibly annoy-ing. Kindly instruct Major Powers to remove him from my vicin-ity."

"Imagine you've borrowed my ax," I said. "When I come to claim it, I'm obviously in a lather, and so you—"

"And so I defend myself by splitting your head open," Londa said.

"And so you refuse to give it back."

"Ah, yes, I forgot that step. The Wild Woman would be ashamed of me. I refuse to give it back, and *then* I split your head open."

I cursed Londa to her face, specifying the precise ratio between her corporeal contents and shit, whereupon Major Powers appeared and casually imprisoned me in a half nelson.

"Your husband is dying of cancer, but a radium extract might save him," I told Londa as the Valkyrie dragged me away. "You can't afford the druggist's outrageous price, so here's the question. Should you break into the pharmacy and steal an ampoule?"

"Of course I should steal it," Londa said. "And the next morning I'll return to the store with my borrowed ax, and I'll hack the pharmacist to pieces for the greedy Phyllistine he is."

SHORTLY AFTER MAJOR POWERS brought me back down to D deck and locked me in my cabin, I arranged to prevent *The Last Shall Be First* from ever intruding on my awareness again. The procedure proved surprisingly simple, a mere matter of transforming a coat hanger into a metal rod and thrusting it repeatedly through the perforated ceiling plate. Each time my rapier pierced the paper speaker, I experienced a small thrill. To cleanse my cabin of Londa's voice wasn't the same as thwarting the vatling herself, but it was a start.

At the end of the week, I suffered two minor misfortunes when my wristwatch and my travel alarm both ceased to function. My immediate impulse was to ask Lieutenant Kristowski for replacement batteries, but she no longer came down to D deck—evidently Londa had decided to deprive me of all human contact. And so it happened that, with no clock at my disposal, no sun within view, and my food appearing at random intervals, I lost track of time. My dawns, mornings, afternoons, dusks, evenings, naps, dreams, and reveries forsook their normal boundaries, melting into one another even as my Wagner recordings and cheapjack monster movies coalesced into a surrealist German opera whose cast had been exhumed and reanimated by Victor Frankenstein. When at last a fellow being darkened my door, I could not say for certain if a week had passed, or a fortnight, or an entire month.

My visitor was Major Powers, crashing unannounced into my cabin and brandishing a pair of steel handcuffs whose intended destination was brutally apparent.

"You're going ashore," she told me. "Londa has arranged for you to meet with her new ethical adviser."

"I'd rather see whether *I Was a Teenage Frankenstein* gets better the tenth time around."

"The Wild Woman is expecting you," Major Powers insisted, yoking my wrists together. "Sorry about the bracelets, but Londa says you've been acting strange lately."

"Could I ask you a stupid question? It is morning, noon, or night?"

"Morning in New Delhi, night in London, noon aboard the *Redux*."

Now Lieutenant Kristowski appeared, according the handcuffs a quick scowl and an unhappy sigh. It pained her to see Masai Ambooloy's prototype treated so harshly, but then her face softened, as if she'd just told herself, for the thousandth time, that Dr. Sabacthani worked in mysterious ways.

My reluctant wardens guided me out of my cabin and down the D-deck corridor toward the companionway. Although neither woman was in a talkative mood, I managed to elicit a few provocative facts concerning Londa. By Major Powers's account, she'd recently vacated the ship and moved back into Faustino, relaying her commands to Colonel Fox via cell phone. Despite the "ostensible failure of Operation PG," Londa had triumphed over her despair and was now brimming with "new ideas for curing the Phyllistines," which was exactly what I didn't want to hear.

The natural music of Isla de Sangre greeted our arrival on the boat deck, a polyphony of breaking waves, squawking toucans, screeching parrots, and gibbering monkeys. Colonel Fox was waiting for us near one of the *Redux*'s three remaining lifeboats, hanging from its davits like a baby's cradle. As Major Powers and Lieutenant Kristowski prepared the vessel for launch, Colonel Fox made an ominous announcement—"Before you go ashore, Londa wants you to see something"—then propelled me through the deserted wheelhouse to the lookout booth on the starboard wing, a vantage that gave me an unobstructed view of the weather deck.

The rigging now featured a dozen nooses, each dangling from its own ratline. Was I surprised that Londa had gone ahead with her plan to turn the foremast into a gallows? Not really. What shocked me was the bodies, one suspended from the starboard shroud, the other from the port, both twisting in the noonday sun like exhibits in a butcher's window. Vultures and seagulls made languid circles around the dead men, periodically swooping down and partaking of the feast their carrion god had spread before them. Judging from the pitted condition of his flesh, Enoch Anthem had probably been lynched several days before Corbin Thorndike—unless it happened that for a bird of prey a cleric is tastier than a CEO.

Seconds after my mind absorbed the grisly scene, my stomach registered it as well, and, leaning out the landward window, I vomited my breakfast into the Bahía de Colón.

"We're not yet sure how many such executions the future holds," Vetruvia Fox said, noting my distress, "but Londa is confident that the meek will inherit the earth long before we run out of hostages."

The colonel took my hand and propelled me toward Major Powers and Lieutenant Kristowski, who in our absence had managed to ready the lifeboat for lowering, its elliptical form casting a sharklike shadow on the water. I must confess, ladies and gentlemen, that my first rational remark concerning the fate of Anthem and Thorndike was informed less by moral outrage, humanist sympathy, or even simple sorrow than by mere flippancy. Am I more of a cynic—and less of a Cynic—than I would like to believe?

"Those decaying corpses will look terrific on the cover of *The League of Londa*," I told Lieutenant Kristowski. "Even at the height of its glory, *Tales from the Crypt* never had a grabber like that."

✳

Chapter 16

✳

IN RECENT YEARS I HAVE MANAGED to acquire, against the odds and despite my bank account, a complete set of *The League of Londa*. Number 46, which I purchased on eBay, arrived in the mail only yesterday, and it indeed features a story about Londa's inscrutable mentor, the philosopher-alchemist Dr. Masai Ambooloy. I even appear on the lurid full-color cover: superheroine and mentor standing shoulder to shoulder amid a fretwork of film noir shadows, cooking up a homunculus in a subterranean laboratory. The resemblance between Dr. Ambooloy and myself is so precise that, were I a litigious man, I might sue the artist for appropriating my face.

But if I am to enjoy an exalted status in your eyes, ladies and gentlemen, let it not be as Dr. Ambooloy. Rather, let my mythic alter ego be that eternal friend of the human race, Prometheus. Does this mean I fancy myself a Titan, a son of Gaea, a ruler of the universe? Hardly. My point is simply that I was among those who gifted Edwina's vatlings with the ambiguous boon of scruples. Like Prometheus, we acted out of compassion for our charges. You must believe that. We loved those children. If I had it to do over, I would surely have spared Londa the Beatitudes and shielded her from the Good Samaritan. But I would still have brought her the fire.

As Major Powers, Lieutenant Kristowski, and I took leave of that hubristic ship to which the Titan race had lent its name, the late Enoch Anthem continued to haunt me, and Corbin Thorndike proved equally pitiless. Their suspended remains broached my skull, split my brain, seared my visual cortex. Throughout our trip to Isla de Sangre, I sat in the bow of the lifeboat and moaned. The two Valkyries ignored their wretched passenger, concentrating instead on rowing us safely past the reef. It occurred to me that during our earliest lessons I might have fruitfully presented Londa with a role-playing exercise spun from the sinking of the original *Titanic.* "Imagine this scenario, young woman. You made it into lifeboat number five, which like most of the others was not filled to capacity. The great ship has gone down, and you can hear the screams of the less fortunate passengers, bobbing about in their life jackets as they freeze to death. The quartermaster commanding boat number five calls for everyone's attention. 'Raise your hand,' he tells his forty-one charges, 'if you believe we should go back and pull some of those screaming souls from the water.' Now, here's the question, Londa. Do you endorse the quartermaster's plan? Or are you swayed by the argument that scores of panicky survivors will try scrambling into the lifeboat, capsizing it in the process?"

We came to rest in a palm-sheltered cove that, despite various overland explorations during my Blood Island sojourn, I'd never seen before. While Lieutenant Kristowski remained behind on the beach, guarding the boat, Major Powers led me along a labyrinthine path winding past mammoth plants from whose floral fecundity streamed turbulent swirls of red and yellow blossoms. On all sides fat vines formed graceful parabolas, macaws swooped from tree to tree, and dragonflies darted about like remote-control syringes inoculating the air against Phyllistine pollution. All during the journey, I repeatedly explained to Carmen Powers that while

I was quite willing to speak with the Wild Woman of the Jungle, I would not listen to any glib rationalizations of the dead men on the foremast. The major had no reaction to this high-minded sentiment, but at one point she looked me in the eye and said, in a surprising spasm of candor, "As long as *you* were her conscience, there was hope."

Our hike ended before a vast expanse of inland water, not the pristine Laguna Zafira on which I'd once lived but rather its aquatic opposite, dark, bleak, silent, and tide-fed, its shores fringed with mottled masses of algae. A decrepit and perforated wooden dock, free lunch for myriad marine invertebrates, extended six feet from shore. My immediate obligation, the major explained, was to stay here and wait for the Wild Woman. If the meeting between her ethical advisers went well, Londa would see fit to remove my handcuffs.

Carmen Powers slipped away, leaving me to sit on the dock and brood. The afternoon stretched into an orchid-scented dusk that soon became a shimmering tropical night bathed in amber lunar hues, even as the air resounded with the music of countless insects, a cicada for every star. A dozen jellyfish rode the tidal currents, their umbrella bodies glowing an iridescent blue. At length a female figure appeared on the water, wrapped in mist and limned by moonbeams, standing erect in the stern of a skiff as she poled her way toward the ruined pier. She was blessed with Londa's commanding height, athletic build, and imperial poise. As this lithesome Charon drew nearer, my vatling's lovely features emerged from the gloom, her green eyes piercing the fog like beacons.

"I've seen the bodies on the foremast, Londa," I said in the most venomous voice I could summon. "The vultures have done their worst."

Charon stood up straighter still, exuding a pale presence: white shirt, white slacks, white face—a vision that suggested alternately a

June bride and a shrouded cadaver. "I'm not Londa," she rasped.

"Okay, fine, and I'm not Mason, and those two corpses are Gilbert and Sullivan."

"Step aboard, Mr. Ambrose. Have a seat. My shack is on the far side of the lagoon. I'm not Londa."

"Take these damn handcuffs off me."

"Only Londa can do that. The key is with her at Faustino. Step aboard. My name is Edwina 0004. Londa made me. The child is the mother of the woman. We're having steamed crabs for dinner. I caught and cooked them myself."

AH, THE BRILLIANCE, the audacity, the recklessness of my vatling. The wanton genius. The transcendent cheek. So your original conscience isn't willing to rubber-stamp your sins? Have no fear. *Pas de problème.* Simply drop by Torre de la Carne, reactivate the ontogenerator, reprogram the DUNCE cap, and bring your faux mother back to life. After all, the Übermom was always your greatest friend and supporter, and so Übermom II is certain to prove the perfect superego.

Slowly she poled us away from the dock, guiding the skiff through the alien jellyfish nation. I hunched in the prow and fixed on Edwina 0004, studying the moonlit elegance of her cheekbones, the graceful sweep of her jaw. The resemblance to Londa was at once disturbing and inevitable: the primal Edwina had been Londa's present age when she died, so it followed that the Wild Woman and my vatling would mirror one another—indeed, Edwina 0004 lacked only her creator's faint wrinkles and incipient eye pouches. A thirty-eight-year-old who'd yet to celebrate her first birthday, the present beaker freak axiomatically displayed no marks of the life she'd never lived.

Much to my surprise, she was prepared to discourse upon her *Dasein,* and by the time we reached the far shore, all my most burning questions had been answered. Unlike the species from which she'd arisen, an animal that in accounting for itself faced an unhappy choice between a groundless theism and a groundling Darwinism, Edwina 0004 knew how she'd come into the world. She fully grasped her ontological status—doppelgänger of a deceased biologist, puppet of the DUNCE cap's algorithms, mother and mentor to the notorious Dame Quixote—and she radiated a sense of mission. The original Edwina had devoted herself to her triune daughter's welfare, and Edwina 0004, if I could believe her, was equally determined to secure Londa's happiness.

"At one time her happiness mattered to *you,* too," the Wild Woman admonished me. "A golden age, Londa calls it. She hopes it will return."

"Golden ages rarely return," I said, "especially if they never existed."

A coughing fit seized the Wild Woman, the guttural convulsions ringing across the open water, and I wondered whether this particular Edwina, like her predecessor, might be cursed with poor health. "Technically I'm as sociopathic as any newborn vatling, but so far I've committed no crimes," she said. "I haven't burned down Faustino, or pulled the wings off a butterfly, or sneaked onto the ship and slit Felix Pielmeister's throat. This morning I came up with a theory. Want to hear it? My psyche or soul or whatever you call it— my program—it's bursting with love for Londa, and this fount of affection keeps my depravity at bay."

"Entirely plausible," I said, though I doubted that a DUNCE cap program could provide its recipient with anything but the most schematic beneficence. Her depravity, I suspected, was merely biding its time, waiting to sponsor some atrocity or other.

Although the Wild Woman had called her dwelling a shack, it had obviously once been the most picturesque of lakeside cottages, a virtue it might still boast had the jungle not laid claim to the exterior. Flowering vines enswathed the walls like veins coursing through aged skin, dark roots emerged between the porch planks like ebony piano keys, and the roof had become a feral Swinburnian garden of bougainvillea and Spanish moss.

"Back when I was the primal Edwina, this place was my secret world," said the Wild Woman, leading me through a tidy kitchenette into a cozy living space dominated by a table overspread with the promised feast of freshly caught crabs, their cooked shells as red as my childhood wagon. "Here and only here could I escape the commotion of myself."

"Speaking of escape . . ." I cast an indignant eye on my shackles.

"Even if I had the key, Londa wouldn't want me to use it. She loves you, but she doesn't trust you."

I sat down and, through a series of gestures made oafish by the handcuffs, dismantled a crab. We ate in silence. Evidently Londa had stenciled some first-rate recipes onto Edwina 0004's tabula rasa, because the meal left nothing to be desired. The wine, too, was admirable, a Chablis drawn from a rack in the kitchenette, though we had to consume it at room temperature, there being no refrigerator on the premises.

"Last night, while you and I were sleeping, thirty thousand children died of malnutrition," Edwina 0004 suddenly declared, using a grapefruit spoon to extract a final tidbit from her crab shell. "We're all guilty bystanders to that tragedy, but certain bystanders are more guilty than others. Some, in fact, are accessories to the crime."

"I quite agree," I said. "But that hardly gives Londa the right to *murder* those accessories."

"Believe it or not," said the Wild Woman, swallowing a morsel, "just hearing another person say my daughter's name gives me a thrill. 'But that hardly gives Londa the right to *murder* those accessories.' Please, Mr. Ambrose, let me hear you say 'Londa' again. Any sort of sentence will do, just so it includes her name."

"Sure. How's this? It would be my guess that Londa has gone completely insane."

Edwina 0004 sipped her Chablis. "It's such a *privilege* being a mother. I'm relishing every minute. 'It would be my guess that Londa has gone completely insane.' Marvelous. As you doubtless know, if Western Europe and the United States committed seven billion dollars annually to the cause of clean drinking water worldwide, that investment would save four thousand lives a day. Might I convince you to say it again? 'It would be my guess that Londa has gone completely insane.' I pity any woman who isn't a mother."

I daubed the corners of my mouth with a tattered but spotless napkin. "How about we change the subject, okay?"

"Seven billion dollars. That's less than what Europeans spend each year for perfume and Americans for cosmetic surgery. Before he went to the gallows, Enoch Anthem spoke often about Christ turning water into wine, but he never once implored Christendom to turn perfume into water. God, I do love it—I love being a mother. Annual global expenditures to fight AIDS, a disease that kills millions each year, amount to three days of military appropriations. Londa, Yolly, Donya. I love them all. Three children in one. One child in three. My dearest, sweetest Yolonda."

Our encounter continued in this vein for another hour, Edwina indicting the geopolitical status quo by piling gruesome fact upon gruesome fact, until at last she fixed me with Londa's most piercing gaze and said, "My daughter was right. She predicted you would join our side once I made my presentation."

"All mimsy were the borogoves," I said, "and the mome raths outgrabe."

"That, too." She smiled seraphically. "Remember our first meeting? Mason and the primal Edwina, sitting on wicker chairs in the geodesic dome? I gave you a mumquat from Proserpine. The mattress in the sleeping loft is a bit lumpy, but the one in my bedroom is soft as a cloud. Shall we draw straws?"

"The loft is fine," I said, moving my fettered hands in a circumscribed gesture of nonchalance. "But I must ask you something. After Londa decided to create you, did she take the trouble to—?"

"To dig up the primal Edwina? Or did she simply use a specimen of her own DNA?"

"That's my question, yes."

"What do you think?" she asked.

"I have no idea."

"Yes you do," the Wild Woman said.

"Knowing Londa, I would imagine she did it the hard way."

My hostess nodded, then pressed both hands against her brow, as if to assuage a headache. "According to my program, she exhumed and reburied her mother with the greatest care. A wayfarer happening upon the grave would never know it had been disturbed. That's the sort of person my daughter is—respectful of the dead. She does us both proud, wouldn't you say?"

I COULDN'T SLEEP THAT NIGHT, though the problem was neither the lumpy mattress, the despicable handcuffs, nor the Wild Woman's ghoulish origins, but the far more vexing issue of Londa's madness. The problem was the corpses on the foremast. To quiet my mind, I meditated on Zeno's paradox, recited Aristotle's taxonomy of causes, and tabulated leaping sheep. Nothing worked—not even the additional glass of Chablis I obtained through a furtive visit to the kitchenette.

Shortly after dawn, I descended from the loft. The Wild Woman was up and about, dressed now in khaki pants and a safari shirt. Insomnia had lately plagued her as well—such was the testimony of her face, so haggard she looked more like Londa than ever. Silently we breakfasted on raw oysters washed down with freeze-dried coffee. The caffeine proved sufficient to open our eyes and get us talking past each other again, with my hostess attempting to convince me that her daughter was a libeled saint, certain to be vindicated by the verdict of history, while I countered her arguments with unassailable mountains of unequivocal evidence, not one particle of which successfully completed the arduous trek from Edwina 0004's ears to the rational portions of her brain. Throughout this vaporous exchange—this nonversation, if you will—she filled her knapsack with bananas and cashews: snacks for our hike to Faustino, she explained.

"Londa is eager to see you again. Now that I've entered her life, she's prepared to forgive you your trespasses, a majority of them at least, maybe even your refusal to bless Operation PG."

"And who's going to forgive Londa *her* trespasses?"

The Wild Woman scowled impatiently. "Who do you *think*?"

NO DIRT ROAD, no jungle trail, no thoroughfare of any sort lay between the lagoon and Faustino, and so we spent the better part of the morning hacking our way through the undergrowth. The heat was relentless, the mosquitoes gave us no quarter, and Edwina 0004's incessant chatter—another depressing and pointless catalog of Phyllistine transgressions—drove me crazy. At long last we reached the valley of acacia groves and, passing beneath the dysfunctional crossing gate, its arm raised in an eternal *Sieg heil,* headed down the dirt road toward the mansion.

Against my expectations, my first glimpse of Londa that afternoon aroused in me neither rage, revulsion, nor righteous indignation. There she was, dressed absurdly in a saffron silk muumuu and a Florida Marlins baseball cap, humming off-key as she stood on the veranda casually whipping up a jug of sangria, and this utterly banal tableau filled me with longing for the virtuous vatling I'd once known and also—I make my confession with great reluctance—for the fanatical vatling she'd become.

Whooping with joy, trilling with delight, the women raced

toward each other, Londa traveling from the veranda to the ground in a single balletic leap. Their embrace was spontaneous and passionate, and for a brief instant I fancied that the primal Edwina was actually walking the earth again, reveling in motherhood. Threaded onto a gold chain, the Godgadget hung from Londa's neck like a crucifix, and I cringed at the thought that in hugging so tightly, these two beaker freaks might inadvertently detonate the explosives in forehold 3. At last Londa pulled free of her—her what?—her mother? daughter? sister? student? conscience? doppelgänger?—then returned to the veranda, where she poured a round of sangria for all.

"Cheers," she said, clinking glasses with Edwina 0004. "Tell me, *Maman,* what sort of philosopher have you brought me today?"

"The former master has become the humble disciple. He bows to your wisdom, and he loves you more than ever."

I needed the whole of my cerebrum to process these words, my analytical left hemisphere rejecting Edwina 0004's ridiculous assertion that I was now a Sabacthanite, even as my irrational right hemisphere contemplated the strange truth that yes, I still adored my vatling. I gulped some sangria and locked eyes with Londa. Our expressions, I imagined, were nearly identical: two fleshy Necker cubes, their aspects alternately reflecting our requited adoration and—flip—our bitterness over various mutual betrayals and—flip—the adoration and—flip—the bitterness.

"As I was leaving the *Redux,* I thought of an ethical dilemma," I told her.

"The good old days," said Londa, with only a modicum of sarcasm.

"Imagine you're in lifeboat number five, rowing away from the wreck. Screams fill the air—the abandoned passengers, afloat in their life jackets, freezing to death. There are twenty-four extra spaces left. Do you vote to go back, or do you—?"

"Or do I decide that a mob of survivors will arrive en masse and sink the boat? Difficult question, Socrates. Give me till sundown."

"In the meantime, kindly unshackle me."

"Sorry. Can't. As Mother says, you love me, but there's something you love even more. You love the idea of hogtying your homicidal gumbo girl and bringing her to justice."

A protest formed on my lips—*No, Londa, I just want to be rid of the damn handcuffs*—even as I admitted to myself that Mason unbound might try to do exactly what she imagined. But before I could make my complaint, Londa took Edwina 0004 by the arm and escorted her into the mansion.

Throughout the rest of the day, the women focused their physical and emotional energies on each other, gleefully pursuing those mother-daughter activities that had so gratified the primal Edwina during her final months. They erected a badminton net on the lawn and played a series of three games, all of which Londa won. They took tea and biscuits on the veranda, simultaneously pursuing a conversation whose levels of rapport and intimacy were doubtless off the charts. As the sun descended, arraying the tropical sky with sashes of gold and turquoise, they slipped into identical yellow spandex bathing suits and went down to the beach, intent on frolicking in the surf.

Having nothing better to do, I prowled through the library where Londa and I had first enacted the Riddle of the Borrowed Ax and the Fable of the Stolen Radium. In time I gravitated to the philosophy section, spontaneously unshelving a key influence on *Ethics from the Earth*: John Caputo's *Against Ethics,* with its wry argument that lofty theories of virtue have done the world a grand total of no good. Briefly I traded stares with Alonso the Conquistador and, intuiting that he approved my choice, ferried it to the reading table, where I set about revisiting the various passages spun from Heidegger's *Es gibt*—"There is"—which for the author meant "There is obligation," savoring them as I might a rococonut julep.

"Obligations happen, bonds are formed, tables are set, and the earth is covered in cold white snow, while the surf roars, while the stars dance their nightly dance, while worms inch their way toward forgotten graves."

At seven o'clock my stomach began to rumble. As if cued by this gastric clamor, Londa suddenly appeared, dressed once again in her saffron silk muumuu and holding a silver salver heaped with lobster canapés, caviar-smeared crackers, salmon croquettes, and oysters Rockefeller, all of which she'd pilfered from the *Redux* shortly before taking up residence at Faustino. She'd also brought a local delicacy, a blue ceramic flagon filled with mumquat nectar. I set the book on the reading table, splayed and spine up, so that it suggested a capital A. A is for *Against Ethics*. Adam's fall, Augustine's confessions, Anthem's broken neck. Londa pulled up a chair. The Godgadget was no longer slung about her neck—hardly a cause for celebration: with eight duplicates on board, she could permanently mislay her own, or deliberately destroy it, or wrap it up in ribbons and give it to me for my birthday, and the deterrent would remain in place.

We fed ourselves uncouthly, wolfing down one dainty after another, sluicing them into our stomachs with large swallows of serenity, and then Londa gestured toward *Against Ethics* and asked, "What's that one about?"

"Obligation," I said. "The Loch Necessity Monster."

"Caputo's a Kantian, then?"

"More of a Kierkegaardian."

"Are we still friends?"

"No."

"Enemies?"

"That's quite likely the case."

"Lovers?" she asked tentatively.

"Perhaps that's how history will remember us."

She ate the last of the lobster canapés. "I would vote to go back."

"What?"

"I'm in boat number five, remember? I would vote to go back and rescue as many passengers as possible. They're exhausted and weak and half frozen. It's preposterous to imagine they would swamp us."

"Good answer," I said, consuming the last oyster Rockefeller.

From her pocket Londa produced a toothed steel rod, pressing it into my palm. The key, she explained. I immediately attempted to free myself, but thanks to the handcuffs this ambition proved paradoxical, like trying to write on a pen using the pen with which you're writing. Londa came to my aid, popping both shackles in a matter of seconds.

I swung my arms in joyous circles. "What did I do to deserve this?"

"You haven't done it yet, but you will. Listen, darling. I just got off the phone with Colonel Fox. Our liberated hostages are still behaving badly. It would appear that their new and improved pineal glands have atrophied."

"You expected otherwise?"

She pointedly ignored my question. "In keeping with Dame Quixote's ultimatum, I should call Colonel Fox back and arrange for Pielmeister to join his fellow incorrigibles on the foremast—unless you think Gittikac, Wintergreen, or North would be a better choice."

"The hell with Dame Quixote. The hell with her ultimatum."

"A worthy sentiment, Mason. I quite agree. The hell with them. Hear my proposition. I'm assigning you to Mother's old bedchamber, second floor, the suite with the grandfather clock outside the door. The Wild Woman will sleep in my room. I'll come to you at midnight. We'll drink nectar together and kiss our pain away, and for a few glorious hours we'll become the same person. At dawn we'll start talking again, a full-blown philosophical conversation, Socrates and his gumbo girl, all morning and maybe all afternoon, however long it takes us to figure out what my next move should be."

"I already know what your next move should be. Surrender to the FBI, then convince the Valkyries to do the same."

"Such high expectations you have for your student," she said.

"The mark of a caring teacher."

She brought a hand to her mouth, her thin fingers set across her lips like sutures, then used the opposite hand to silence me. "No words," she whispered. "From now until the sun comes up, no words."

I nodded. She dropped her hands, brushed my cheek, and, shifting softly within her muumuu and her equally enveloping inscrutability, slipped out of the room.

WITH ITS DRIVING RAIN, explosive thunder, and brilliant bursts of lightning, each discharge flashing through the black sky like an aneurysm bursting in God's brain, the tempest now raging up and down Isla de Sangre inevitably evoked the stormy night Henry and I crept into Torre de la Carne and observed Yolly's advent. In a matter of hours, the island would, Isis assenting, Thoth willing, witness the birth and maturation of a rather different creature. If I played my part well, wielding my philosopher's scalpel with consummate skill, by noon tomorrow I would give the world a rehabilitated Londa Sabacthani, moral agent extraordinaire, committed to shutting down Operation PG before it spilled more blood.

True to my expectations, the primal Edwina's former boudoir was a paragon of opulence, shaming even the most extravagant stateroom aboard the *Titanic Redux*. The canopy bed was especially splendid, a hushed bower girded by green velvet curtains fastened to the posts by silken cords. As the wind rattled the casements, hurling barrages of droplets against the panes, I set about increasing the ambient eroticism—lighting the ensconced candles, igniting a stick of patchouli incense, equipping the CD player with Castelnuovo-Tedesco's Guitar Concerto No. 1 in D Major, arraying the nightstand with the mumquat flagon flanked by crystal goblets—then took a quick shower and, returning to the bedchamber, put on a black satin caftan, the sole garment hanging in the closet.

Midnight arrived, heralded by the grandfather clock in the hall, and as the twelfth chime died within its depths, Londa appeared before me, wearing only a white silk dressing gown. We embraced. No words. I untied her sash and parted the halves of her gown, portals to her beauteous estate. Grasping my caftan by the shoulders, she slipped it smoothly over my head. No words. We climbed onto the mattress and, like Tristan and Isolde hoisting the sails of their love barge, pulled the silk cords loose from the bedposts, so that the curtains glided noiselessly into place.

In a matter of minutes, the wind and the tide carried us far from shore. And still no words, though of course we didn't need them, being absorbed in the discourse of our skin, Londa's carnal morphemes, lickerish sestinas, and wet lexica, her conscience's lubricious phonemes, tactile stanzas, and spasmodic sonnets. How abundantly I loved my creature that night. I loved her confabulated flesh and ontogenerated smile, her synthetic psyche and labyrinthine mind. I loved each cell in her marrow, every synapse in her brain, all the mites in her lashes. Occasionally we procured the flagon and filled our goblets, and at one point we broke our vow of silence and recited Shakespeare to one another—"So long as men can breathe or eyes can see, so long lives this, and this gives life to thee"—the nectar all the while heating our blood, until at last our private orgy ended, and our love barge came to rest, and we descended into a delicious and unfathomable sleep.

THE CONCERT BEGAN with warbling finches, and soon the squawks of the parrots arose, followed by the cries of herons and flamingos. Golden shafts of sunlight slanted through the gaps in the bed curtains, and I knew that the storm had blown out to sea. I yawned, stretched, and with a slow downward stroke propelled myself into wakefulness. Time to beguile Londa with all my powers of reason. Time to make the Scarlet Darwinist once again sovereign over her soul.

But she was gone, my errant undine, absconded from our love barge. I drew a slow breath. No need to fret, I told myself. She was merely taking a shower, or once again sharing tea with her mother on the veranda, or enjoying a morning swim in the bay. Or perhaps Londa had acquired the primal Edwina's habit of spending Saturday morning in the conservatory, though I imagined that the place must be more Swinburnian than ever, all canker and rot and wilt.

I slipped into my street clothes and began the search, repeatedly calling Londa's name as I checked the bathrooms on all three floors, then descended to the foyer and headed for the veranda. Suddenly Edwina 0004 stood in my path, dressed in her safari jacket and demanding that I join her for coffee in the geodesic dome. She claimed to know Londa's whereabouts. Our forthcoming conversation would be of epochal significance, she said, keyed to matters of life and death.

"Londa's life, to be specific," she insisted as we arrived among the languishing orchids and expiring ferns. "Londa's death."

The coffee urn held a potent mocha java. I filled my mug to the brim and, settling opposite Edwina 0004 at a small wrought-iron table, ventured small electric sips.

"Let me summarize the situation as baldly as I can. My daughter is now my prisoner." With unnerving sangfroid the Wild Woman poured a fragrant cup of hazelnut from a glass carafe. "Earlier this morning I put your handcuffs on her, then locked her in Dr. Charnock's old laboratory."

It took me a moment to absorb this unlikely but not unwelcome piece of news. I reached across the table and squeezed the Wild

Woman's wrist. "Believe me, Edwina, you did the right thing."

"My action knew nothing of virtue. Four hours ago an especially aggressive component of my program kicked in."

"The next step, I assume, is to contact the authorities."

For a brief dreamy interval, Edwina 0004 ignored me, casting a weary gaze all around the dome. "I think this is where I died," she rasped. "Yes, I'm sure of it. How strange. I passed away in this very room, under a mutant mangrove." She looked me in the eye. "The authorities? If you had the total picture, you would never say that. So here it is, Mr. Ambrose. Full disclosure. Bless me, Father, for I have trafficked in moral ambiguity."

A ball of lead congealed in my stomach like a failed alchemy experiment. How foolish of me to have forgotten that we were living on Isla de Sangre, illogic's own atoll, locus of the Fountain of Terrible Ideas. "I'm listening," I said apprehensively.

Edwina 0004 seized a bread knife and sliced a raisin bagel. "I'll start with a question. Why do you suppose Londa created me?"

As would any self-respecting philosopher at this juncture, I frowned pensively and drank more coffee. "She wanted to get her mother back, simultaneously replacing me with a more permissive adviser."

"Correct. Go on."

"And apparently she thought your advent would somehow allow the primal Edwina to keep on enjoying the pleasures of motherhood."

"True, every bit of it, but you've barely scratched the surface."

"The story of my life."

"The *real* reason I was brought into the world . . . I have difficulty saying this."

"Yes?" I took a measure of coffee into my mouth, allowing it to trickle slowly down my throat.

"Londa created me for the purpose of murdering her."

I aborted the swallow, spraying coffee into the air. "What?"

"I'm a homicide machine," the Wild Woman continued. "Or, if you prefer, a suicide implement. I detest this situation, but there's nothing I can do about it. Londa is far more complex than you realize. You can't begin to imagine the intensity of her distress over Enoch Anthem's death. The instant the man stopped kicking, she suffered excruciating pangs of remorse."

My hands trembled, setting the coffee to swirling in its mug. Was I in fact sitting three feet away from Londa's designated assassin? I wished I had an auxiliary conscience of my own just then, somebody who would tell me exactly what to do—such as dragging Edwina 0004 into the jungle and roping her to a tree.

"Excruciating pangs," I echoed. "Though not quite excruciating enough"—an unbidden sarcasm entered my voice—"to stop her from killing Corbin Thorndike, too."

"That second hanging tortured her even more than the first. Her pineal gland began to bleed." The Wild Woman mortared the halves of her bagel together with cream cheese. "The Londa who stood on the weather deck watching those two Phyllistines twist in the wind, was she a creature out of control? Of course. But here's the thing, Mr. Ambrose. She *knew* she was out of control, and in time she saw the answer, or thought she did, and so she cooked me up, Edwina 0004, Anthem and Thorndike's personal avenger, and that's why she's locked away in Charnock's lab right now, listening for my footsteps, and why we're here in the dome, having this discussion."

"But you *love* Londa. You're her *mother*."

"I'm her mother, yes. But I'm also my algorithms."

"No, Edwina. This is *crazy*."

"Are you appealing to my conscience, Mr. Ambrose? I don't have one. There was no convenient ethicist around when I was growing up."

My coffee kept swirling. I slammed the mug onto the table. "Listen, Edwina, there's no need to *murder* her. Here's the plan.

We'll go to Charnock's lab, take her into custody, turn her over to the G-men—and then we'll try our damnedest to make sure she gets a fair trial."

"Perhaps some hypothetical Edwina could do that," the Wild Woman said, voraciously consuming her bagel. "Edwina 0005 maybe, or Edwina 0006, or conceivably even the primal Edwina. Not I. My program won't permit it. I shall execute Londa, or I shall set her free. Either, or—that's me. Utterly binary. Totally digital. But there's *another* reason we won't be turning her over to the G-men. The symptoms should arrive any second now."

"Symptoms?"

"First a tingling in your hands and feet, then a throbbing behind your eyes, and finally a loss of gross motor functions."

My heart began racing, not only in reaction to the Wild Woman's revelation but also, no doubt, from the chemical contents of her treachery. "You *drugged* me? You goddamn fucking *drugged* me?"

"More of Londa's ingenuity, a mixture of nectar and curare. It attacks the midbrain and spinal cord only. You needn't worry about blindness, aphasia, or respiratory complications."

My best course, I decided, would be to find an emetic and cleanse myself of the contaminated coffee. I bolted from my chair, started toward the dome entrance—and then it happened: not the predicted tingling, not a throbbing behind my eyes, but something considerably more frightening, a sharp blow, whack, as if Socrates's borrowed ax had contacted my cranium. My knees went rubbery, my spine became jelly, and I collapsed on the dirt floor.

"If Londa has calculated correctly, you won't black out." The Wild Woman stood over me, devouring the last of her bagel. "The paralysis, however, should last at least two hours, and by then she'll be beyond all medical and philosophical intervention."

I languished on my back and stared at the glass ceiling, wheeling my limbs like a beetle pinned to an entomologist's corkboard. The curare colonized still more of my nervous system, so that the same tragedy that had befallen Proserpine now visited me. I was a basket case, stranded in my cortex. "Edwina—please—you don't have to *kill* her."

"That statement is more accurate than you might imagine." She crouched beside me like a mother helping her toddler build a tower from alphabet blocks. "Permit me to describe my program's most provocative feature. If you were to look me in the eye right now and forbid me to destroy Londa—you and only you, Mr. Ambrose— my need to murder her would vanish, replaced by a compulsion to go unlock Charnock's lab and remove her handcuffs. Isn't that re- markable? Six words from you, 'Thou shalt not murder thy daugh- ter,' and the death sentence is lifted. But then, of course, Londa will start doing those things we've come to expect of the world's most famous vatling. Calling up the Valkyries, for example, and instruct- ing them to lynch Felix Pielmeister."

"Shit."

"I'm not sure *why* she placed her fate in your hands. My guess is that she's never forgiven you for declining to sign *The Book of Londa*. Go ahead, Mr. Ambrose. Say, 'Thou shalt not murder thy daughter,' and I'll set her free."

"Set her free to murder Pielmeister."

"Most likely. But maybe not. We all know how unpredictable she is. She'll probably hang a second hostage in the bargain. Gittikac, Wintergreen, North—there are nine Phyllistines in the queue. Give me your answer."

"I *can't*."

"I know, but give it to me anyway. Come on, Mr. Ambrose. You're fond of ethical dilemmas. What's the lesser evil here? What's the greater good? Make your choice—*now*. Pick the door that leads to the lady, because the tiger is ravenous this morning."

My decision to walk out on my dissertation defense—that had been a choice. My resolve to continue tutoring Londa after learning her true heritage—that, too, had been a choice. My insistence that she abandon Themisopolis and allow the immaculoids to burn it—once again, a choice. But this wasn't a choice. This was something else. This was the death of a thousand cuts.

I boxed the compass with my eyes—north, north-northeast, northeast, east-northeast, east, east-southeast, southeast, all the way to north-northwest—until at last my gaze came to rest on the Wild Woman. "I'm going insane."

"You'd be well within your rights to do that, but first you must flip the coin. On the count of ten. One . . . two . . . three . . ."

"I need more time."

"Four . . . five . . . six . . ."

"*You're* the one who should die," I protested.

"I don't disagree. Seven . . . eight . . . nine . . . do I hear it? Do I hear 'Thou shalt not murder thy daughter'?"

Like my tongue, lips, larynx, and ocular muscles, my salivary glands remained in working order. I did my best to spit in Edwina 0004's face, but the projectile fell short and landed on her safari jacket.

"Know something, Mr. Ambrose? In your shoes I would've answered that way, too." She stood up, straight and tall as when she'd first come toward me in the skiff. "But I'm not in your shoes. I'm in my own shoes, a mother's shoes, so naturally I've decided to use those shoes to kick you in the teeth."

It was not a shoe, however, but the pointed tip of a hard leather boot that collided with my mouth. Thanks to the curare, I didn't feel a thing. Apparently she struck me pretty hard. There was much blood.

"If you wish to bury the body, come down to the beach," said the Wild Woman, striding away. "She hopes to draw her last breath in sight of the Red Witch."

The blood continued pouring from my mouth and streaming onto the floor. Had my nervous system been more functional, I could have shifted to a prone position and, extending my index finger, used the spilled blood to draw a stick figure on the flagstone path, or scrawl an Egyptian hieroglyph, or write my name. But instead I simply lay there, glued in place and transfixed by an astonishing thought. I had just saved the life of my worst enemy, even while arranging the annihilation of the person I loved best.

Chapter 17

TO HOBBLE THE BODY, a good Cartesian dualist would say, is not necessarily to impede its complementary opposite, the mind. A Hegelian idealist might take the argument even further, asserting that a physical handicap may under certain circumstances increase a person's mental prowess. By this theory, Charles Darwin's chronic exhaustion became a lens focusing his intellectual energies on the origin of species, Friedrich Nietzsche's racking ailments sponsored the composition of his wrenching aphorisms, and Stephen Hawking's amyotrophic lateral sclerosis underwrote his exploration of those astronomical abysses he called black holes.

The longer I lay paralyzed in the geodesic dome, however, the more skeptical I grew regarding any attempts to correlate suffering with wisdom. Stuck on my back like an inverted turtle, staring at the play of morning sunlight on the glass triangles, I reviewed the shocks of the past forty-eight hours—the corpses on the foremast, the Wild Woman's lineage, Londa's suicide scheme, the curare in my coffee—searching for insights. In declining to shut down Edwina 0004's assassination program, had I committed a terrible sin? Prevented the executions of ten innocent Phyllistines? Become a party to a murder? A hero to the angels? I contemplated the triangles, and pondered my questions, and arrived at the nexus of nowhere.

My material self, it seemed, had fallen prey to a kind of neuromuscular relativism. We recognize no universal requirement to serve you, my brain cells declared. We have no absolute duties, my tissues insisted. But after two hours of such discourse, the very interval predicted by the Wild Woman, my body transcended its chemically induced indifference and regained its traditional sense of mission. Joint by joint, ligament by ligament, I struggled to my feet, then spent a minute reacquainting my flesh with my spirit. I wriggled my toes, splayed my fingers, clapped my hands, massaged my neck. As my pain receptors came back on line, my gums started smarting from the damage inflicted by the Wild Woman's boot.

"She hopes to draw her last breath in sight of the Red Witch," Edwina 0004 had said. "Draw her last breath," a locution that suggested a gradual passage, not the abrupt obliteration of "drop dead" or "keel over."

I raced to the primal Edwina's bedchamber and retrieved the mumquat flagon. Chimes filled the hall, the ominous bongs of the grandfather clock, tolling the noon hour. Each brassy reverberation energized me, and before the twelfth chime sounded I had dashed across the veranda, raced down the steps, and hurled myself into the forest.

IN THE TWENTY YEARS that had elapsed since Londa attempted to stage *Coral Idolatry* on her secret beach, the crimson invertebrates had kept adding their exoskeletons to the Red Witch, so that her once-conical hat now resembled a jester's cap and bells. Otherwise the place hadn't changed much. Conch shells, glistery pebbles, tufts of seaweed, a few dead starfish. Even the piece of Cretan bull driftwood remained intact. The tide advanced in thick staccato whispers, like syllables of an incantation sprung from the witch's brittle lips.

Londa sat on the sand beside a tide pool, head bobbing, legs splayed, back pressed against a boulder. Firming my grip on the flagon, I vaulted the bull and ran toward her. My vatling's eyes were closed, her cheeks pale, lips pulled back in a fierce grimace. A low, liquid moan soughed through her clenched teeth.

The Wild Woman had pursued her program with a vengeance. She had played her part in full. A rivulet of dark, frothy blood streamed from the midriff of Londa's white cotton blouse. It rolled down her white denim shorts, spilled across her thighs, bubbled onto the sand, and flowed along the beach like a freshet bound for the sea.

She pressed her manacled hands against the wound, but the blood kept coming, coating her fingers like potter's slip. She shivered as if packed in ice. For an indeterminate interval, my thoughts stopped dead—perhaps some residual curare had penetrated my brain—and then the questions came, flooding my cranium like the petroleum that had inundated Londa's city. Should I tear off my shirt and bind her wound on the spot? Carry her back to the mansion? Would the act of moving her reverse whatever clotting process had already begun?

I planted a foot in the tide pool, got down on one knee. The scent of iron filled my nostrils. Londa's eyes flickered open. Her tongue thrust forward, accompanied by two dribbles of blood that scored her jaw with crisp red lines, giving her the appearance of a ventriloquist's mute puppet. I expected a scream of pain to follow, but instead she winced and said, with typical Weltanschauung Woman bravado, "Present evidence suggests that the curare did not kill you."

"Christ. What happened?"

"She stabbed me."

"With a knife?"

"Sword. My idea. It came from our conquistador."

"Alonso?"

"Yes. Don Quixote's first name—did you know that? Alonso."

"I brought you some nectar."

"Good. Great. Lay it on me, Socrates. Turns out I'm not much of a Stoic after all."

She tried to speak again, but the words lodged in her throat. Her molars came together, clicking out a meaningless message in an unknowable code. I brought the flagon to her lips. She drank greedily, sputtering and gagging like my netherson perishing in his tumbledown tower.

"Get out your notebook," she said at last. "It's not every day a philosopher is privileged to watch somebody die. I might say something profound."

"I'm taking you to Faustino," I told her. "We'll call in a medevac chopper."

"I was expecting a razor-sharp pain. Instead it's more like somebody's punching me in the stomach, again and again and again."

I gave her a second swallow, then slid one arm beneath her legs, another around her shoulders. Her face relaxed, and her teeth stopped chattering. She smiled, awash in the nectar's counterfeit contentment.

"Brace yourself," I said. "On the count of three, I'm going to pick you up."

"No, Socrates. Sorry. I've lost too much blood. The sand soaked it up. Imagine the castle we could build. Take your arms away."

"Faustino, that's the plan. Faustino, then a chopper."

The nectar continued to bless her. "What's eating you, Socrates? Ashamed of your complicity in all this? Cheer up. You made the best of a bad situation: kill one beaker freak, save ten Phyllistines. Very Utilitarian. Let me go. I mean it."

I relaxed my muscles but kept my arms in place. "They won't convict you, I promise. We'll hire the best lawyers money can buy."

"Praise the humble mumquat. Glory be to all rococonuts everywhere. Other than the raw existential terror, I don't feel a thing." And still she bled, growing paler with each passing instant. "Your arms are really bothering me."

"And once your trial is over, you can go back to work. Londa Sabacthani, bane of Phyllistines, bulwark against Corporate Christi."

"Sorry. No. This doesn't end happily. Get that through your thick philosopher's skull. I won't be dragged in chains to Rome. Cleopatra had the right idea. She opted for the asp."

Isis forgive me, Thoth absolve me, I did as Londa wished, withdrawing my arms and jamming my hands into my pockets.

"'When I am dead, my dearest'—do you know Christina Rossetti's poem?" she said. "Henry taught it to Donya, and Donya taught it to the rest of us. 'When I am dead, my dearest, sing no sad songs for me. Plant thou no roses at my head, nor shady cypress-tree.'" A sudden spasm contorted her features. "I wrote you a letter. A confession, actually. Like it or not, your gumbo girl gets the last word. You can't contradict a corpse."

"What sort of confession?"

"Go to the library. Everything's getting dark. Look inside the obligation book."

"*Against Ethics*?"

"Obligation. I think I'm going blind. Kiss me."

I pressed my lips to hers. "This is all my fault." I kissed her mouth, brow, cheeks, and eyes. I kissed her bloody jaw.

"'Be the green grass above me with showers and dewdrops wet. And if thou wilt, remember. And if thou wilt, forget.'"

"Of course I'll remember," I said.

"Hold me," she said.

Obligation. Mine was entirely clear, and now I proceeded to enact it, bestowing what comforts I could as the *Dasein* leaked out of her. I wrapped my arms around her torso, easing her face against my chest.

"Are you holding me? I can't tell. I'm numb as a brick."

"I'm holding you."

"I love you, Mason Ambrose. Make sure Donya finds out about this place. I can picture her standing on the shore, befriending the

Red Witch, telling her what to do. 'The next time any Phyllistines come sailing by here, counting their gold and spilling their garbage, how about casting a spell on them?'"

She twitched and trembled in my embrace. "I'm holding you," I said again.

"'Borrow a trick from your sister Circe. Turn the Phyllistines to swine.'"

"I love you."

"Killed by a Spanish sword. That almost happened to Don Quixote. Lots of times. But he always walked away. He got to die in bed."

"I love you, Londa Sabacthani."

He got to die in bed. Her last words. A few seconds of soft gurgling, and then she grew utterly silent, and her quivering ceased. But of course this was still Mr. Darwin's planet. In the midst of death, we were in life. Macaws screeched. Howler monkeys cried. A pelican flapped across the sky and landed atop the witch. And now came a fiddler crab, pressing against my heel as if it were the portal to some crustacean heaven, an empyrean to which he might gain admittance by rattling the gates with all his invertebrate resolve.

FOR AN INDETERMINATE INTERVAL I hugged her vacant frame, the tears falling from my cheeks and giving their substance to the tide pool. Water to water, salt to salt. Human tears, that unique precipitation, their salinity looming large among those facts suggesting that we terrestrials once belonged to the sea.

When at last my weeping ran its course, I took hold of her body—she was horribly cold but still supple—and carried her beyond the reach of the tide. I set her prone on the white sand, carefully arranging her head and limbs in the posture of one asleep, then entered the forest and harvested a dozen fronds. They covered her completely, head to toe, a green shroud for my beloved.

I returned to the jungle, soon picking up the trail to the Bahía de

Flores, in thrall now to a different obligation, political and perhaps even apocalyptic. Throughout my hike I kept an eye peeled for the Wild Woman, but I didn't expect to see her. Most likely she'd gone into hiding—perhaps in the mansion, perhaps in her cottage—or else she'd left the island entirely and was now headed to Key West in Captain López's cabin cruiser.

Reaching the water, I broke into a jog, following the horseshoe curve of the beach. My obligation assailed me, falling from the sky, bursting from the jungle. I quickened my pace, soon arriving at the dock that Nick, the most ambitious of the primal Edwina's imported adolescents, had built during Londa's first summer on earth. Lashed to the piles were four decrepit vessels, a fleet that various Blood Island squatters and intruders had evidently collected over the years and then abandoned, including an ancient rowboat with two oars, a battered kayak and paddle, a swamped catamaran, and a dilapidated outrigger canoe. After studying each option and imagining the particular way it might fail me, I settled on the rowboat. I scrambled aboard, cast off, and pulled free of the dock, all the while keeping a wary eye on the keelson. The boat was leaking, but not disastrously. Unless I hit an iceberg, I would reach the *Titanic Redux* before dusk.

Stroke by stroke, breath by breath, I made my way along the shoreline, carefully avoiding the surf on one side and the crimson reef on the other as I navigated the southern hump of Isla de Sangre. And, yes, ladies and gentlemen, you may be sure I felt a strong impulse to reverse course, make my way back to Faustino, enter the kitchen, and obtain the required implement. A paring knife would do, likewise a pizza cutter, corkscrew, or French peeler—and once I'd returned to her secret beach and snipped away some portion of Londa, a fleck of her splendid neck, perhaps, or a bit of perfect thumb, I would bear the specimen to Vincent Charnock in his hidden cove on the Intercoastal Waterway, and together we would visit the island and enter Torre de la Carne with blasphemous intent.

But instead I stuck to my plan, rowing into the Bahía de Colón just as the setting sun was coronating the mangrove trees with a blazing scarlet aura. By the time I sighted the *Redux,* my whole body felt pummeled. From muscles I hadn't even realized I owned came every variety of pain and protest. Glancing upward, I beheld a bizarre drama unfolding on the weather deck. Galil pressed against her shoulder, Lieutenant Kristowski was firing round after round at the gulls and vultures circling the corpses on the foremast. I couldn't tell if she meant to kill the birds or merely scare them off, but in either case she evoked Coleridge's Ancient Mariner carrying out his ill-conceived design against the albatross.

"Ahoy, Lieutenant Kristowski! Ahoy! Ahoy!"

She fired again, and this time her bullet found a gull. The feathery white corpse plummeted to the weather deck. Its fellow scavengers took note of the event and flapped away.

"Lieutenant Kristowski!"

She leaned over the rail and, assessing my predicament, began outfitting a davit with a breeches buoy. I lashed the rowboat to the anchor chain, climbed into the harness, and placed my fate in the lieutenant's hands. Methodically she turned the crank, reeling me free of the rowboat and drawing me skyward like a ripe bouillababy rising from its enzyme bath.

"Are you hurt?" she asked after I was safely on deck. "You're covered with blood."

"It's not mine. I must see Colonel Fox. Major Powers, too, and Dagmar Röhrig. There's no gentle way to say this. Dr. Sabacthani is dead."

"Dead, sir? Jesus. *Dead?*"

"Dead."

"How?"

"Suicide. She stabbed herself."

"With a knife?"

"A conquistador's sword."

"Dead. That's awful."

"Not entirely."

"I know what you mean," Lieutenant Kristowski said.

TWO HOURS LATER, having taken a shower and changed my clothes, I entered Londa's denuded suite, slouched against the antique desk, and, gesticulating wildly, stammering like Demosthenes, repeated for Vetruvia Fox, Carmen Powers, and Dagmar Röhrig my various conversations with Edwina 0004. Her ontogenerated origins were not news to my listeners, as both Colonel Fox and Major Powers had attended her birth, firing up the machine on Londa's instructions, then lowering the fetus into the maturation chamber. My narrative of their leader's ultimate purpose in bringing forth the Wild Woman, by contrast, took all three hijackers by surprise. As the women fixed me with ever widening gazes, I revealed that Edwina 0004 was in essence the child of her creator's death wish, that the murderous component of her DUNCE cap program had started functioning about ten hours earlier, and that Londa's body now lay on an obscure Blood Island beach. I confessed that I could have saved her with a single glance and a six-word sentence but had instead allowed the Wild Woman to carry out the assassination.

"What a horrible choice," Colonel Fox said in a voice as flat as glass. I could not tell whether she meant to express sympathy for my plight or disgust with my decision.

"Londa insisted that this new Edwina was merely her second conscience," Major Powers said, "but we suspected there was more to the story."

"Something crazy and pathological and perverse," Dagmar said. "Something quintessentially Londa."

I studied the weary hijackers, their moist eyes, trembling jaws, quivering lips, each face conveying its own distinctive mixture of anguish and relief. Not for an instant did they imagine that lynching Felix Pielmeister or Corbin Thorndike or Ralph Gittikac would bequeath the earth to the meek—and now, suddenly, here I was among them, revealing that Londa would never again demand such ferocity of her apostles. Even as they grieved, their gratitude washed over me like a wave of warm rococonut milk.

Slowly, piece by piece, the women constructed a plan. Its essence was capitulation. Its particulars included removing the corpses from the foremast, putting them on ice, convincing the enlisted Valkyries that surrender made sense, and telling the world that Operation PG had been terminated. But the first order of business, Colonel Fox insisted, was for Major Powers and Lieutenant Kristowski to retrieve Londa's body, without which the FBI might never regard the case as closed. When the G-men arrived, Colonel Fox would explain that, tortured by guilt and unable to abide captivity, Londa had stabbed herself to death, a story that in its own way was absolutely true.

"I've been honest with you," I told the hijackers, "and now I'd like some candor in return."

I didn't have to say another word. Moving synchronously, the women took out their Godgadgets and pushed the red buttons in tandem. I steeled myself. No detonation reached my ears. No blast wave shook the hull. The *Redux* remained at anchor in the tranquil bay.

Major Powers pushed her button a second time. She merely wanted to emphasize the point, but I still flinched. "You see, Mason?" she said. "You were a better conscience than you knew. Londa wasn't really putting us at risk—not through our Godgadgets anyway."

"Are the explosives themselves also a lie," I asked, "or just the part about their being wired to the transmitters?"

"Take a trip to forehold three," Colonel Fox said. "You'll find a long serpent of plastique weaving through the champagne cases and the sardine crates."

"I believe you," I said.

"Londa liked to bluff, no doubt about it," Dagmar said. "But she liked holding aces even more."

I SHALL NOT DWELL on the denouement of the *Titanic Redux*'s maiden voyage, a succession of episodes that found the Fifth Horseman of the Apocalypse, Expediency, galloping along her corridors and promenades. The television coverage was both exhaustive and exhausting, and most of the key events were later hashed over ad nauseam by Sabacthani obsessives everywhere. Read their books, visit their Web sites, and you'll discover that when it comes to recounting the raw historical data, there's a surprising harmony between the faction that holds Londa a latter-day Joan of Arc and those who believe that she and Judas Iscariot were separated at birth. The dissolution of Operation PG is open to myriad interpretations, but the facts themselves are not in dispute. How Vetruvia Fox broadcast a special edition of *The Last Shall Be First* disclosing that Dr. Sabacthani was dead and the Valkyries were hoisting the white flag. How the U.S. Coast Guard decided to believe Colonel Fox and forthwith dispatched a cutter to the Ship of Dreams, whereupon the cutter's officers and crew purged forehold 3 of the plastique, collected the Valkyries' weapons, and ferried the surviving Phyllistines to Miami along with Londa's remains and the frozen bodies of Anthem and Thorndike. How the FBI, after accepting the Coast Guard's assurances that the liner was no longer booby-trapped, landed a succession of helicopters on the poop deck, evacuating the entire Valkyrie brigade within an hour and flying them to a government detention facility in Fort Lauderdale. How the American system of jurisprudence placed the captured women on trial for hijacking, kidnapping, piracy, torture, and premeditated murder. How the Valkyries' canny and, thanks to Donya's donations, well-funded attorneys succeeded in casting Londa as the one true villain in the narrative, their clients as mere accessories, with the result that every Valkyrie was spared life imprisonment, receiving instead a sentence of ten to twenty years, a penalty that in most cases transmuted into less than five years behind bars followed by a laissez-faire probation. And, finally, how Ralph Gittikac, reviving his impudent project, sailed the *Titanic Redux* from Southampton to New York City without incident, so that his original quarry, "those imps, devils, and angels of catastrophe who haunted the North Atlantic on the fateful night of April fifteenth, 1912," were finally vanquished.

There is one occurrence, however, that you didn't see on TV or read about in any Sabacthanite's blog. I speak of the conversation I had with Felix Pielmeister shortly before he departed the Bahía de Colón for points north. Different ambitions had brought us to the weather deck. The postrationalist merely wanted to get the hell off the ship, the Coast Guard having told him and the other former hostages to gather around the foremast until the evacuation craft was ready to receive them. As for me, I simply needed to survey the rigging and tell myself, over and over, that ten more Phyllistines would have died on these shrouds if I'd terminated the Wild Woman's mission.

"It appears that your protégée didn't sink the ship after all," Pielmeister said. An ellipsis of white scars arced across his brow, a stark testament to his days down among the furnaces. "My powers of prediction failed me on *that* one, didn't they?"

"Don't worry about it," I said. "Jesus was a poor prophet, too. He said his apostles would live to see the Kingdom come to earth. Matthew sixteen, verse twenty-eight. Mark nine, verse one."

A grin broke through Pielmeister's scraggly beard. "You atheists are such fundamentalists, always quoting Scripture. May I ask you a question?"

"As long as it's not about Charles Darwin."

"Is it true what I heard? You played a role in the lunatic's death?"

"I won't deny it."

"Here's what else I heard," he said. "You did it so she wouldn't order my execution."

"I did it so she wouldn't order *anybody's* execution."

"But she told you I was next in line."

"Maybe. Don't take it personally. I just wanted to end her tawdry little reign of terror."

"Nevertheless, you saved my life."

"That's one way of looking at it."

"Thank you," Pielmeister said humbly.

"You're welcome," I replied icily.

"No, I mean it. Thank you. If I can ever do you a favor, simply ask."

"How about canceling the paradigm shift?"

He gave me a look of consummate perplexity. Could it be that Pielmeister no longer believed in Corporate Christi? Was it possible that during his sweltering days in boiler room 2 and his polluted nights on G deck he'd forgotten about the twilight of the iconoclasts? With any luck, I figured, this theological giant would continue thinking small for the rest of his life.

A Coast Guard midshipman approached, a pimply youngster with an Adam's apple as large as his nose, and, tapping Pielmeister's shoulder, requested that he go down to E deck. Pielmeister nodded, then faced me squarely and said, "Good-bye, Ambrose. You're really not such a bad philosopher. Forsake your foolish scientism"—he stretched out his arm, his fingers soliciting contact with mine—"and you might even get your Ph.D."

"Know what you can do with that hand of yours?" I asked.

"What?"

"You can shove it up thy neighbor's ass," I said, an answer that I imagined would have pleased Yolly, almost as much as if I'd thrown Pielmeister into the bay.

Saying nothing, he slid the rejected hand into his pocket. He strode past the foremast and joined the other released hostages, and then the lot of them were swallowed by the sun's noontime glare. Inevitably I thought of Amenhotep IV's lyrical hymn to his shining divinity, the Aton. "Whatever flies and alights, they live when thou hast risen for them," ran the panegyric. "The fish in the river dart before thy face. Thy rays are in the midst of the great green sea." Even Darwin, I decided, could not have said it better.

IN THEORY IT WOULD BE EASY convincing the FBI that I'd played no part in the Valkyries' assault on the *Titanic Redux*. For one thing, I was not a woman. For another, Colonel Fox and Major Powers would vouch for me. Nevertheless, I decided to err on the side of paranoia, and so I secluded myself inside a cold furnace in boiler room 3, crouching amid the carbon detritus and remaining there until the G-men had gotten all their prisoners off the ship.

Smeared with soot and ash, I climbed free of the furnace and with feline stealth ascended the aft companionways. It seemed entirely possible that I now had the *Redux* to myself, though my desire to sit alone in the Café Parisien was nonexistent, likewise my wish to savor a solitary respite in the Turkish bath or enjoy a private screening of *Touched by an Angel: The Complete First Season* in the ship's cozy little movie theater. I had but one ruling passion just then—to return to the island and extinguish the last vestige of a technology that my species would be better off without.

Upon reaching E deck, I entered the maze of corridors and found myself staring at an ax: not the morally charged prop from Plato's famous parable but a fire ax of no symbolic significance whatsoever, sealed behind a pane of glass stenciled with the words EMERGENCY USE ONLY. I detached the ball peen hammer from the wall, broke the glass, and retrieved the ax. *Existential use only,* I mused, hurrying away, *including personal vendettas against infernal machines.* At last I reached the hatch through which the hostages had been evacuated. I turned the lock wheel. The great steel door swung open, revealing a twenty-foot drop to the Bahía de Colón. I inflated my lungs, gritted my teeth, closed my eyes, and jumped. Surfacing, I employed a crude approximation of a sidestroke to bear the ax toward the bow of the ship. Warm and smooth and briny, the tropical waters washed the carbon from my skin. Soon I reached my rowboat, still moored to the anchor chain and miraculously afloat, the keelson covered by several gallons of the Gulf of Mexico.

For the rest of the afternoon the Aton continued to smile upon my mission. Despite a choppy sea, an obstinate breeze, and the weight of my unwanted water, I rowed myself into the Bahía de Matecumba without any serious mishaps—blistered palms, strained muscles, nothing more. I made landfall near the great keep. Ax in hand, I strode across the drawbridge, then climbed the spiral staircase and immediately got to work, wielding my weapon against the RXL-313. I shattered the enzyme tanks, smashed the chamber ports, toppled the gantry, crushed the DUNCE cap, pulverized the plasma monitors, eviscerated the control console. Rampage accomplished, I stood back and surveyed the former laboratory, exhausted, panting, and unconscionably pleased with myself. Even Daedalus, I decided, could sustain no wonders here. Even God would strain to wring from this wreck any creature more substantial than a tick.

The jungle paths leading away from Torre de la Carne were soaked in shadows, but the westering sun shone brightly, guiding me safely past the treacherous roots and perilous bogs, until I arrived, famished, at Faustino, eager to consume whatever *Redux* delicacies I could find. I sat at the kitchen table and worked my way through a wheel of Gouda, a quarter pound of caviar, and half a bottle of cabernet, until I felt both sated and insensate and thus prepared to deal with Londa's letter. Abandoning the feast, I sought the library, my apprehension growing with each step.

Alonso occupied his usual post, discouraging visitors from choosing forbidden texts. Someone, Edwina 0004 presumably, had returned his sword to its scabbard. What thoughts had gone flitting through her head at the moment she'd sheathed that bloody implement? Did she see herself as a child-killer—Medea's doppelgänger—or simply as a machine like the RXL-313 from which she'd come, beyond good and evil? I half expected to find her in the philosophy section, reviling the conquistador for supplying the murder weapon, but the only life-forms around just then were a hairy black spider, a scattering of ants, and a grieving Darwinist from Boston.

Handwritten but legible, the letter was in its promised place: an 8½-by-11-inch sheet marking the Caputo chapter called "Several Lyrical-Philosophical Discourses on Various Jewgreek Parables and Paradigms with Constant Reference to Obligation."

My Dear Mason,

I must write quickly. Any minute now the Wild Woman will be here. Assuming you decline to suspend her destiny, I'll be dead by the time you read this.

Here's what I have to tell you. Two weeks ago my mother's hunger came upon me. I speak now of the primal Edwina, and of her all-consuming desire to have a child. Fashioning Edwina 0004 did not satisfy my craving to procreate—how could it?—so I devised a different scheme.

The person you took to your bed last night was the Wild Woman. The whole arrangement appalled her, but she agreed to play her part out of love for me. There's reason to believe a con-ception occurred. If our child is a boy, I hope you will name him Arthur, after the primal Edwina's father. If a girl, let me suggest Sofia, wisdom.

I can hear my mother's footsteps in the hall. She'll lock me up in Charnock's lab, long enough for you to make your decision, and then she'll unsheath Alonso's sword and bring me down to the beach. My plan is to hide this letter inside Caputo, hoping you'll have cause to visit his pages again.

My sins are many. I failed to cure the Phyllistines. I murdered two men. I forced you to decide between two evils of which neither was the lesser: kill the gumbo girl, kill her not. Forgive me. She is coming. I love you, Mason. You're not a very good philosopher, and you're not really much of a conscience, but you're some sort of great teacher.

Your difficult student,
Londa

Imagine that a team of neuroscientists has just unveiled a technology that lets a person remove all trace of some terrible experience from his brain. Under what conditions, if any, would you use it? What might it be like to go through life knowing you'd once suffered an ordeal so dreadful that it demanded radical excision? How long could you endure this strange affirmative ignorance, this lost access to the unspeakable, without becoming neurotic, or even slightly mad? In the long run, might you not decide that such circumscribed amnesia was worse than whatever memory you'd felt compelled to erase?

The instant I finished Londa's letter, I decided that if an amnesia machine existed, I would avail myself of it immediately. Lacking such a device, I compensated as best I could, returning to the kitchen, lighting a gas burner, and with steely determination edging the message toward the flame. The paper caught fire, transmuting into an airborne carbon curlicue.

My flesh throbbed with the exertion of destroying the ontogenerator. My head reeled from the effort of forgetting Londa's confession. I trod the stairs to the primal Edwina's bedchamber, that bower in which her fourth iteration and I had never made love, then lowered the curtains and surrendered to my dreams.

FOR THE NEXT SIX WEEKS I pursued an Uncle Rumpus sort of existence, combing the shores of my magic isle. I alternated my residency between Faustino and the primal Edwina's cottage, all the while keeping an eye out for the Wild Woman—she with whom I had not slept, that person I did not impregnate—but I saw no trace of her, and eventually I decided she'd gone to the mainland. My scavenging skills were sufficient to keep me nourished, and the lack of distractions boded well for my new project, a sequel to *Ethics from the Earth* that I intended to call *The Serpent Was More Subtle*. The real reason Charles Darwin distresses people, I would argue, is not that he stumbled on an argument against theism. No, the problem was that he *replaced* theism—replaced it with a construct more beautiful and majestic than any account of the Supreme Being outside the Book of Job, a construct that invites us to see every variety of life, from aphids to archbishops, zygotes to zoologists, as vibrant threads in an epic tapestry, its warp and woof stretching across the eons and back to the Precambrian ooze, the seminal sea-vents, the primordial clay-pits, or wherever it all began. An astonishing construct, a mind-boggling construct, a construct of which Jehovah is understandably and insanely jealous.

Despite my tranquil surroundings and my enthusiasm for its theme, *The Serpent Was More Subtle* did not flow easily from my pen. Each sentence was a tribulation, every paragraph an ordeal. The problem, I decided, traced to a combination of writer's block and procrastinator's malaise. And the remedy? I couldn't be sure, but it seemed likely that a return to Boston would do my book more good than harm.

True to his prediction, my landlord had failed to find a one-semester tenant for my Sherborn Street apartment. Instead he'd granted a full-year lease to, of all people, a Hawthorne philosophy Ph.D. candidate who'd loved, absolutely loved, *Ethics from the Earth,* her zeal for the thing eclipsing even Natalie's enthusiasm of five years earlier. A spunky, thirtyish, divorced Spinoza enthusiast with an elfin face and a sensual overbite, Leslie Rosenzweig and I were not long into our first conversation before two noteworthy facts emerged: she found Boston as appealingly exotic as I'd found her native Los Angeles on those occasions when I'd visited my sister—Beantown's buskers and scrod versus La-La Land's surfers and palm trees—and she'd be delighted to let me crash on the living-room futon until I located more convivial digs. Leslie even offered me the master bedroom, citing the satisfaction she would feel in "doing a mitzvah for the inventor of Darwinian deontology." Such a sacrifice, I insisted, was unnecessary: I had no wish to exercise some presumed elitist prerogative over her—as far as I was concerned, all middle-class urban intellectuals were created equal.

Not only did I now have a place to sleep, I soon acquired a social life as well. It turned out that my original vision for Pieces of Mind—here would flower the headiest philosophical discourse to be found west of ancient Athens—was not so silly after all. If an unrepentant neo-Darwinist and a vivacious Jewish Spinozist decided to institute such a dream, then by God it would happen.

Our core group met on Tuesday and Thursday nights, gathering in the science-fiction and fantasy section around a low, circular table barely large enough to accommodate our books, coffee mugs, tea presses, and occasional slammed fists. Leslie and I had peopled the seminar the way the young Orson Welles had mounted his idiosyncratic Shakespeare productions, with an affection for flamboyance. We drew our requisite eccentrics and scenery chewers from the Religious Studies Program, the William James Center, the Lewis Mumford Institute, and the congregation of bookstore barflies who passed their leisure hours at Pieces of Mind. I even allowed certain select members of the Hawthorne philosophy department to join our fellowship. We called ourselves the Whores of Reason, and our conversation was of sufficient general interest to eventually attract a regular audience, as if we were engaged in something rather more sensational than abstract discourse, like cockfighting or an American League pennant race. Week after week our fans would appear, cheering us on as we spelunked in Plato's cave, settled Heidegger's hash, confessed to our guilty admiration for Nietzsche, forged a compromise with pragmatism, relativized relativism, categorically rejected absolutism, and presumed to know Spinoza's unknowable God.

Although I'd never regarded my recent sojourn on Blood Island as an attempt to elude the long arm of the law, the FBI didn't quite see it that way. Pleased to realize that I now had a known and fixed address, a place that a person might approach without fear of quicksand, alligators, venomous snakes, or poisonous jellyfish, two agents from the Boston office began paying me regular visits. I told them more than they wanted to know but nothing they didn't deserve to hear, with the upshot that I was not indicted. When one of my interrogators, a grim and intelligent Russian expatriate named Bolkonsky, said I should thank my "plucky stars" I hadn't ended up in prison along with Fox, Powers, Kristowski, and the rest, I assured him that at dawn I would sing a hymn to the Aton.

Our philosophy group's prestige quickly reached such proportions that the average Boston intellectual crackpot, of which there are many, took pride in being invited to favor us with an informal talk. Although it wasn't my idea to have Vincent Charnock contribute to the Londa Sabacthani Memorial Lecture Series—the suggestion came from Dr. Cochran, the medieval-studies professor whose high-definition television had saved my life by displaying *The Egyptian* at a crucial moment—I did not protest, for the man had clearly turned over a new leaf, several new leaves, in fact. Truth to tell, Charnock had rewritten the entire *Book of Vincent,* not only climbing free of his self-constructed abyss (with a boost from Alcoholics Anonymous) but also funding and administering the Charnock Consortium, a Cambridge-based enterprise that in its devotion to avant-garde cancer research was generally perceived as the stepchild of the incinerated Institute for Advanced Biological Investigations. Having supplied Anthem and Pielmeister with the means for spawning the immaculoids, Charnock would always seem to me an accessory before the fact of Yolly's murder, and yet he'd also evidently become a crusader on behalf of Yolly's hope.

There was one way in which Charnock had not changed. This moralist who'd so adamantly opposed Edwina's removal of Proserpine's brain, and who would doubtless have resisted our uprooting of the sentient mangrove had he been around at the time, remained a steadfast foe of physician-assisted suicide. In his talk that evening, "From Mercy to Mengele," he made a coherent philosophical case against euthanasia. He began by recapitulating Kant's claim that if the practice ever became commonplace, the effect would be to cheapen the intrinsic value of human life, then proceeded to demonstrate that John Stuart Mill's defense of euthanasia suffered from the same fallacy as other Utilitarian positions—namely, an assumption that to mathematize a dilemma was to resolve it. For his coup de grâce, Charnock explained why in his view the institutionalized destruction of individuals facing a life without quality lay on the same continuum as the Third Reich's eradication of those who supposedly had nothing to offer the Fatherland.

Although nobody agreed with Charnock's conclusions—as Leslie later put it, "you could float the *Titanic Redux* through the holes in his argument"—it was an astute and heartfelt performance, drawing applause from the audience, myself included, and our guest was in good spirits when we adjourned to the Shepherd's Pie. We were celebrating two events that evening: Charnock's successful appearance before our group and my recent contract with Prima Facie Press for *The Serpent Was More Subtle,* based on two sample chapters and an outline. Most of us ordered beer. Our speaker opted for a Cherry Coke and nachos. As the conversation heated up, Charnock confessed that he'd begun investigating the problem of physician-assisted suicide because the abortion controversy had proved too much for him, requiring that he search his soul more deeply than was compatible with his sanity.

"I came to feel that if I *really* cared about those seven embryos

I poured into the bay, I should adopt seven unwanted children in their place. Or six at least. Or five."

"Or four unwanted children," Leslie said.

"Or three or two," I said.

"The truth is that I've never felt an urge to nurture," Charnock said.

"Or one unwanted child," Leslie said.

"Edwina certainly felt it," Charnock continued. "She ached for motherhood. She needed it like oxygen."

"So did Londa," I said. "Not at first. But sometime during the hijacking, the impulse kicked in."

"I didn't know that," Charnock said. "I'm not surprised. Like mother, like daughter. This drive to rear the next generation, it's essentially a female instinct, wouldn't you say?"

"Nonsense," Leslie said.

"Nonsense," I agreed, though I had nothing on which to base this assertion, my parenting experiences being limited to John Snow 0001, who hadn't exactly brought out my inner Geppetto.

"To the next generation," Leslie said, raising her pilsner high, and we all followed her lead, clinking our glasses together and giving posterity our permission to come forth.

ON A CHILL, RAINY EVENING in October, three days before Halloween, the Whores of Reason sat down to epistemology as usual. Our reading that autumn had been Hegel's preternaturally dense *Phenomenology of Spirit,* with its audacious account of the individual soul's journey from consciousness to self-consciousness to reason to spirit to religion to perfect knowledge. Although I'd always found this byzantine ascent annoying in its obscurity, I figured that the fault lay with me, and as the evening progressed, Leslie and I began playing good cop–bad cop with Hegel's teleology, your narrator defending the man's attempt to privilege pure thought, Leslie arguing that we shouldn't hesitate to label metaphysical drivel as such. To cinch her case, she related how Hegel had in 1800 written a dissertation proving that, while the definition of a "planet" had varied over the centuries, there could still be, philosophically, only seven planets. "And then, in January of 1801, an eighth planet—the asteroid Ceres—was discovered by a non-Hegelian astronomer named Giuseppe Piazzi," Leslie said. "And so, once again, we see why the real world has always been such an embarrassment to German idealism."

On that epigrammatic note, the clock struck nine, and the meeting broke up—or almost did. What kept everyone in place was the appearance of a stooped figure, wheezing and arthritic, her face obscured by the cowl of a rain-spattered poncho. She was toting, of all things, a wicker bassinet, and before she reached our inner circle, several bystanders remarked that the conveyance held a baby.

Shuffling into my vicinity, our visitor set the bassinet on the table. Thanks to the auxiliary plastic hood and an abundance of blankets, the infant had been spared the wretched weather. Indeed, it was sleeping peacefully, eyes closed, nostrils emitting a pianissimo snore, a tiny sphere of saliva poised atop its delicate lips.

"The hospital insisted that I put something on the birth certificate, so for now her name is Jane," our visitor told me. "That won't do, of course. I'll leave the christening to you."

I surveyed Edwina 0004. Evidently Londa and the Valkyries had assembled her so hastily that they'd introduced a flaw into her genotype. Her skin was as yellow as an ancient newspaper, her eyes had receded into her balding skull, and she had fewer teeth than fingers. The world at large would never recognize this broken crone as the late Dame Quixote's doppelgänger.

"The delivery occurred two months ago at Mass General." From the lining of her poncho Edwina 0004 retrieved a glass baby bottle, pressing it into my hands. "My milk has dried up. I use Similac instead. You make it from powder and water. Her pediatrician is Dr. Ankers in Brighton. The sooner you assume your proper role, the better. If she remains in my care any longer, she'll languish."

I thought of the newborn Sinuhe, cast adrift in a reed boat—
"Thus the city of Thebes was accustomed to dispose of its unwanted
children"—coursing down the Nile before being rescued by the
good-hearted couple who then adopt him. And now this unexpected infant had likewise floated into my life.

"Languish?" I tried returning the Similac to Edwina 0004, but
she refused me with raised palms. "No, you're doing a splendid
job," I told her. "It's raining cats and dogs, but you kept her dry as
a bone."

"I'm a vatling," she replied. "No conscience. Receive your
daughter, Mr. Ambrose, before I harm her."

"Harm her? She's your *child*."

"So was Londa. Name the baby as you will. Good-bye."

With an agility that belied her decrepitude, Edwina 0004 spun
on her heel and hurried out the door. My impulse was to chase her
down and beg her to relieve me of this burden, but just then the
baby woke up and started crying.

"Mason, I don't understand," Leslie said, bending over the bassinet. "Are you the father?"

"That appears to be the case."

An astonishing circumstance, but not without its foreshadow.
Here at Pieces of Mind, my netherson had first made himself known
to me, and now on these same premises another such annunciation
had occurred.

Gently Leslie unwrapped the woolen blanket and, inserting her
hands under the baby's armpits, lifted the squalling bundle free
of the bassinet. The Wild Woman had dressed her in a fluffy pink
jumper. Her eyes, like mine, were a dark shade of brown.

"Give me the bottle," Leslie said, snugging the infant into the
crook of her arm.

"Do you know what you're doing?" I asked.

"I have a black belt in baby-sitting. Give me the goddamn
bottle."

I presented Leslie with the Similac. Edwina 0004's return, her terminal condition, the abandoned infant, my newfound fatherhood: it was all so abrupt, so absurdly sudden, like Ceres appearing before Giuseppe Piazzi. But beyond my confusion, I felt exhilarated, and when my daughter stopped fussing and started feeding, thus prompting the crowd to break into spontaneous applause, my happiness grew greater still. My ignorance was endless—did they sell Similac at the Whole Foods Market? diapers, too? did a baby need shots, like a puppy?—and yet I felt equal to the challenge. She was a regular person after all, of conventional genesis. Ovulation, oocyte, orgasm, obstetrics. We humans had been tackling parenthood, often with impressive results, ever since *Homo erectus* had emerged from *Homo habilis.* When it came to the catastrophe in the bassinet, history was on my side.

THIS BEGAN WITH A BUTTERFLY, and it ends with one, too. We were a party of five that mellow April afternoon, eager patrons of the Hawthorne University Great Insect Carnival, organized annually by the zoology department. Besides myself, our fellowship included Leslie, with whom I'd been exchanging romantic protestations and sharing a Back Bay apartment for the past three months, plus Donya, Donya's charming boyfriend Raúl, and of course little Sofie Ambrose.

Now fifteen months old, my daughter could walk after a fashion. She could also sort her stuffed animals from her alphabet blocks, babble eloquently in a language of her own devising, play level-five peekaboo, and derive considerable amusement from the daily Nickelodeon broadcasts of *Uncle Rumpus's Magic Island,* starring Henry Cushing as every preschooler's favorite bodhisattva. What Sofie didn't do was talk. Not a single word of recognizable English so far. The situation had me worried, but Dr. Ankers was confident that the child would utter a "Da-da" or a "bye-bye" any day now.

Clinging to the southern face of the Environmental Sciences

Building like a piece of avant-garde scaffolding, the Von Humboldt Butterfly Conservatory was a spindly marvel of glass and steel, a kind of secular cathedral dedicated to the adoration of the most exquisite invertebrates Mr. Darwin's algorithms had ever brought forth. Several additions to the permanent collection had arrived in time for the Great Insect Carnival, including a colony of Nabokov's South American Blues, so named because the author of *Lolita,* a first-rate lepidopterist as well as a literary genius, had bestowed on Lycaenidae an innovative and valuable classification system. As our group wandered awestruck among the Nabokov's Blues, Donya and Raúl described their efforts to protect those unique Mexican forests where most of the planet's monarch butterflies passed their winters. It was largely a matter of gauging one's audience. Sometimes Donya and Raúl would attempt to rehabilitate a given land speculator or industrial developer by appealing to his personal moral code, more often by enlarging his private bank account, but regardless of the tactic they usually managed to turn the clueless entrepreneur into a staunch butterfly advocate.

As you might imagine, habitat restoration was just one of the endeavors into which Donya had channeled her trust fund. Beyond her dedication to the welfare of beasts and butterflies, her munificence extended to the human realm; the call of the wild moved her, but so did the cries of the bewildered. I think especially of her invention called the Urban Igloo, an inflatable shelter for homeless people constructed from heavy-duty garbage bags and packing tape. Cheap and portable, every Urban Igloo boasted an ingenious feature—a heating device consisting of a plastic tube terminating in a simple gasket. After installing his igloo on the sidewalk outside an apartment complex, retail store, or corporate headquarters, the occupant would fit the gasket over the exhaust vent of the building's heating system. Thus was an otherwise wasted resource, the liters of warm air expelled by HVAC ducts, put to a sensible use. So far Donya had distributed four hundred Urban Igloos up and down the eastern seaboard, and she hoped to give away a thousand more before the year was out.

There was a mystery here. How did Donya manage to keep subverting the Phyllistines while eschewing the thorny forest of grandiosity into which her elder sisters had wandered? Why would she never even imagine initiating a project like Themisopolis or Operation Pineal Gland or Edwina 0004? Perhaps Henry and Brock had been more circumspect mentors than Jordan and I. Or perhaps Donya's sanity traced simply to her having enjoyed something resembling a childhood. Whatever the answer, one fact seemed clear. The last of the Sabacthanis was also the wisest.

If I am to believe my dear Leslie, your narrator has himself attained a certain sagacity. She claims that Mason Ambrose is "no longer his skull's only tenant" but pays attention to his daughter and even his girlfriend "with touching regularity." And here's something else, ladies and gentlemen. Make of it what you will. In recent months I have shed my reflexive dislike of *The Faerie Queene*. There are passages in Spenser that now move me to tears, and I've come to regard that hidebound dogmatist as some sort of great poet.

Lovely though they were, the Nabokov's Blues did not captivate Leslie and myself for long, and we wandered off in search of gaudier lepidoptera. Our quest took us to the cathedral's core, dense with ferns and blossoms, little Sofie waddling between us like a penguin. Eventually a Central Asian peacock butterfly caught our attention, a magnificent *Nymphalis io* perched on a yellow orchid, each wing stamped with an image suggesting a mask of comedy. I scooped up Sofie and brought her within view of the improbably marked creature.

"See, sweetheart?" I said. "See the beautiful butterfly?"

The child selected that very moment to acquire the gift of language. No baby talk for Sophie. She didn't say, "Bootiful." She said, "Beautiful."

Joy rushed through my veins. My cup overflowed.

"Did you hear that? She said, 'Beautiful.'"

"Mazel tov," Leslie told Sofie. "No doubt about it"—she flashed me a wry smile—"the kid'll grow up to become a philosopher, with a special interest in aesthetics."

Beau-ti-ful. If Sofie's late mother Edwina 0004 could have heard her little girl articulate those syllables, she would have been immensely pleased. Sofie's departed mother the primal Edwina would have been equally delighted. But her deceased mother Londa would have been the proudest of all. And so it was that, conjuring up the face and form of my impossible vatling, I bent low and inhaled the orchid's scent, happy in my knowledge that sometime tomorrow, or perhaps even later today, our daughter would move her tongue and part her lips and say her second word.

About the author

About the book

Read on

Insights,
Interviews
& More . . .

Meet James Morrow

© Didier Leclerc/Atelier N89

JAMES MORROW is the author of nine previous novels, including *The Last Witchfinder*. He lives in State College, Pennsylvania. ᕫ

My First Publisher

THE PHILOSOPHER'S APPRENTICE begins with a butterfly. My career as a novelist began with my mother's willingness to set up her typewriter on the dining table and take dictation from her son as he paced around the room, improvising his first work of fiction. It was 1954. I was seven, an only child, living with my parents in a modest suburban split-level outside of Philadelphia, and the clatter of my mother's battered old Royal imprinting my surrealistic fable was the most thrilling sound I'd ever heard.

After transcribing "The Story of the Dog Family"—six discrete chapters arrayed across three pages—my mother helped me design a cover and then bind the whole thing together with yellow yarn. Over the next two years we produced a dozen more such fantasies, some embarrassingly derivative, others exhibiting flashes of originality, embracing modes that I would ultimately learn to classify as fantasy, science fiction, and boys' adventure. As I often say, "William Morrow is my current publisher, but my first was Emily Morrow."

In the years that followed, I found other outlets for my storytelling drive. I drew comic books, dabbled in playwriting, and, upon reaching adolescence, scripted and produced a half dozen eight-millimeter movies in collaboration with my friend George Shelps. These efforts ranged from a Wellsian sci-fi spectacle titled *The Futurians* to a Hammer Films homage called *Calliostro the Sorcerer* to adaptations of Coleridge's *The Rime of the Ancient* ▶

> " The clatter of my mother's battered old Royal imprinting my surrealistic fable was the most thrilling sound I'd ever heard. "

Mariner and Poe's "The Tell-Tale Heart." Safely ensconced in aluminum cans, this oeuvre still resides in my hall closet.

Emily, meanwhile, was leading a life that, I'm sad to report, knew only intermittent flickers of satisfaction. She had lost her own mother to cancer at an early age, and, in the syndrome William Styron described so vividly in *Darkness Visible*, her grief ultimately played out through that notorious reciprocity between alcoholism and depression. And yet, when it came to my creative endeavors, she was always my fiercest partisan. To keep our movie company afloat, we would screen our productions for the neighborhood kids, and my mother delighted in welcoming these paying customers into our living-room theater and supplying them with free popcorn. And when I needed a presentable manuscript for my first novel, she allowed her life to come full circle, once again typing up her son's fiction, sitting in the same dining room where "The Story of the Dog Family" had emerged twenty-five years earlier.

Act one of *The Philosopher's Apprentice* turns on the machinations of Edwina Sabacthani, a character who, I realize in retrospect, is the inverse of my late mother. Where Emily suffered from abysmal self-esteem, my molecular biologist is a renowned professional who knows exactly what she wants. On first principles, of course, Edwina is the more attractive parent—and yet I am infinitely grateful that I was raised by Emily instead. In a just universe, she would have had herself for a mother. ❦

> ❝ When I needed a presentable manuscript for my first novel, she allowed her life to come full circle, once again typing up her son's fiction. ❞

Women in White

The Author Relates His Journey into the Deepest Reaches of Frankenstein Cinema

AT ONE LEVEL, *The Philosopher's Apprentice* is an homage to Mary Shelley's classic tale of a fatally ambitious scientist and his pathetic humanoid creation, and so I decided that, as part of my calisthenics prior to writing the novel, I would spend several days watching every, or nearly every, feature film bearing the word *Frankenstein* in its title. What better way, I thought, to energize *The Philosopher's Apprentice* with a convivial measure of luridness? Before long, thirty-two DVDs and VHS tapes lay at my fingertips. Now all I had to do was take the dog for a walk, brew a vat of coffee, array myself before our wide-screen television, and begin my trek through the beating heart of celluloid darkness.

Day One: Tales from the Vasarian Woods

After an aperitif of a 1910 short known to film scholars as the Edison *Frankenstein*, I voraciously consume the entire black-and-white Universal series of the thirties and forties, starting with James Whale's stylish 1931 adaptation of Peggy Webling's play and proceeding through the witty *Bride of Frankenstein*, the expressionistic *Son of Frankenstein*, the engaging *Ghost of Frankenstein*, the lively *Frankenstein* ▶

> 66 I decided that . . . I would spend several days watching every, or nearly every, feature film bearing the word *Frankenstein* in its title. 99

Meets the Wolf Man, the byzantine *House of Frankenstein*, and the baroque *House of Dracula*. Set in and around a nebulous, lederhosen-wearing eastern European community occasionally identified as Vasaria, a village that manages to feel simultaneously Gothic and contemporary, these seven classics and quasi classics relate the multigenerational saga of the Continent's most dysfunctional family since the Hapsburgs. Each time I throw a new installment up on the screen, Pooka the border collie fixes me with a gaze that says, "Is this strictly necessary?" My festival is off to a good start.

Day Two: Frankenstein Meets the Übermensch

After experiencing the schizoid time frame of the Universal product, I am eager for the cycle of semi-sumptuous period pieces that Hammer Films produced between 1957 and 1974. After enjoying the sanguine *Curse of Frankenstein*, I savor the atmospheric *Revenge of Frankenstein*, followed by the lavish *Evil of Frankenstein*, the ingenious *Frankenstein Created Woman*, the sardonic *Frankenstein Must Be Destroyed*, and the gruesome *Frankenstein and the Monster from Hell*. Whereas the Universals all pivot on the original creature's aptitude for resurrection, Hammer makes a continuing character of the suavely sinister scientist instead. As I chortle in appreciation of Peter Cushing's Promethean audacity and proto-Nietzschean bravado, Pooka offers me a stare that means, "I perceive that,

> ❝ Pooka [the border collie] offers me a stare that means, 'I perceive that, once again, you have elected to take leave of your senses.' ❞

once again, you have elected to take leave of your senses."

Day Three: From the Nadir to the Pits

Shortly after sunrise I watch *Abbott and Costello Meet Frankenstein*, a 1948 Universal effort bearing no narrative relationship to the classic series. This noisy, crude, and affectionate burlesque makes a perfect transition to the day's main agenda: nine disreputable potboilers that appeared during the same interval as the Hammer renaissance, 1957 through 1974, each shamelessly mining the most exploitable proper name in popular culture. My ordeal lasts past midnight, and when it's over I'm pleased to realize that the grand philosophical questions raised by Mary Shelley—can a person play God without going insane? what does a creator owe his creature?—survive even in the novel's most degraded emanations, including the sublimely ridiculous *I Was a Teenage Frankenstein*, the singularly ludicrous *Frankenstein 1970*, the enthrallingly appalling *Jesse James Meets Frankenstein's Daughter*, the unintentionally surrealistic *Frankenstein Conquers the World*, the infinitely awful *Frankenstein Meets the Space Monster*, the aggressively tasteless *Flesh for Frankenstein*, and the borderline unwatchable *Frankenstein's Castle of Freaks*. As I moan and groan my way through this ziggurat of trash, Pooka goes on the Internet and arranges to be adopted by a shepherd living near Inverness.

Among the sensibilities on display during day three—sybaritism, nihilism, ▶

fin-de-siècle decadence—one proves wholly unexpected: feminism. Beyond the fugitive femme fatale Dr. Sandra Mornay, who contrives to plant Lou Costello's biddable brain in the monster for her own Machiavellian ends, I am also treated to Dr. Maria Frankenstein, heroine of *Jesse James Meets Frankenstein's Daughter* (1966), single-mindedly fashioning a fleshly golem using the last of her beloved grandfather's "artificial brains," as well as Dr. Tania Frankenstein, protagonist of *Lady Frankenstein*, deftly assembling the ideal lover by fusing her intellectual soul-mate's cerebrum to a local hunk's body. While I doubt that any of these films would give a misogynist pause, it's supremely gratifying to watch Lenore Aubert, Narda Onyx, and Rosalba Neri put on their white smocks, pick up their glittering scalpels, and demonstrate that a woman's place is in the lab.

Day Four: Prometheus Redux

Anticipating that day three would catapult me into the pits, I have programmed the rest of the festival with my rehabilitation in mind. The therapy begins at noon with Robert Tinnell's charming and touching tribute to monster-movie fandom, *Frankenstein and Me*. Next comes Mel Brooks's famous parody of the Universal series, *Young Frankenstein*, followed by Roger Corman's earnest adaptation of Brian Aldiss's *Frankenstein Unbound*, after which I savor *Frankenstein: The True Story*, a 1973 made-for-television epic, over three hours long, bolstered by a literate script and A-list actors. With the coming of night

66 It's supremely gratifying to watch Lenore Aubert, Narda Onyx, and Rosalba Neri put on their white smocks, pick up their glittering scalpels, and demonstrate that a woman's place is in the lab. 99

I screen the wry *Frankenstein 90*, which,
being a French perspective on the novel,
dramatizes the scientist's expectation
that his monster will not only refrain
from murdering people but also learn to
appreciate women and exhibit good table
manners. Heartened by this turn of events,
Pooka cancels the Inverness adoption.

By the dawn's early light I insert the
final DVD in the machine. Although *Mary
Shelley's Frankenstein* has many detractors,
I still take immense pleasure in Kenneth
Branagh's operatic interpretation. The
crypto-Freudian creation scene in
particular rewards the suspension
of my better judgment, featuring as
it does a swarm of electric eels bursting
orgasmically from a multi-lobed sac,
wriggling down an immense glass phallus,
spilling into a birth chamber, and vitalizing
the recently stitched-together monster.

The sun rises. The shadows flee.
Slowly Pooka and I mount the stairs,
my mind awhirl with peasants lighting
torches, cerebrums floating in fish tanks,
disembodied arms wriggling their fingers,
and patchwork cadavers shambling forth
from the lab. As I drift to sleep, I hear
my favorite line of the marathon,
a declaration from Colin Clive's
Dr. Frankenstein that was censored
in the original prints but restored for
the DVD release, "Now I know what
it's like to be God!" ∾

James Morrow
A Self-Interview

Your new novel, The Philosopher's Apprentice, *has an intriguing title. Who's the philosopher and who's the apprentice?*

The philosopher is Mason Ambrose, a graduate student at a thinly disguised Boston University who believes he has teased an ethical system out of Darwin's theory of evolution. During his dissertation defense, Mason crashes and burns, but he still makes a favorable impression on one member of the audience: the emissary of reclusive biologist Edwina Sabacthani. The next thing Mason knows, he's been hired to fly to a remote tropical island and teach his "morality curriculum" to Edwina's beautiful adolescent daughter Londa—the apprentice of the title—who is evidently an amnesiac with a severely defective conscience.

Does Mason succeed in giving Londa a moral compass?

He succeeds all too well. It turns out that Londa's psyche is really a tabula rasa, a blank slate, and so she ends up taking Mason's morality curriculum—lessons drawn from Plato, Epicurus, Stoicism, Kant, and the Gospels—rather more seriously than anyone intended. The poor young woman never figures out that she isn't supposed to really *believe* the Sermon on the Mount. And so, when she ventures forth from her tropical utopia, she can't

> 66 The philosopher is Mason Ambrose, a graduate student at a thinly disguised Boston University. 99

help trying to remake our fallen world in her own morally charged image. Naturally, this is a recipe for disaster.

Why is Londa's mind a blank slate?

Shortly after realizing she had a terminal illness, Edwina enacted a scheme that had her making three genetic copies of herself and accelerating their growth to three different stages. Her aim is to experience motherhood in toto before she dies. The plan actually works. Thanks to Londa, Edwina comes to know the pleasures of watching her "daughter" evolve from a teenager to an adult, while her other "children" afford her the joys of interacting with a sprightly eleven-year-old and a delightful preschooler.

So Londa is really a clone? And her sisters are also clones, right?

I suppose so, but let me point out that, from the moment it entered the language, the word "clone" has carried misleading connotations. At the instant of its creation, a clone is merely an embryonic genetic echo of whatever adult organism supplied its chromosomes. It's an identical twin, nothing more. Such a creature will not develop into a zombie, an empathic freak, a doppelgänger, a biddable robot, or any other sort of anomaly. Most so-called cloning stories are really "artificial maturation" or "engineered nurturance" stories, and *The Philosopher's Apprentice* is no exception. The first time I discussed my concept for the novel with my editor, Jennifer Brehl, she told me, "Clones are a tedious subject. I want this novel to be about something else."

So what is The Philosopher's Apprentice *really about?*

The mystery of morality.

Morality is a mystery?

I think it's one of the most baffling phenomena in the whole universe, right up there with consciousness and the fact of being. Why do human beings act nobly under certain circumstances and abominably under others? More mysteriously, why do we identify certain behaviors as noble or abominable? God doesn't seem to have much to do with it. Lately the Darwinists have taken an interest in the problem. They won't solve it, but I wish them luck. ▶

James Morrow *(continued)*

It sounds as if you're a novelist who benefits from interacting with editors.

Well, it certainly helped in this case. Thanks to Jennifer Brehl's prodding, I came to see that, while Edwina Sabacthani's crazy experiment in time-lapse motherhood was interesting as far as it went, the core of the novel was the relationship between Mason and Londa.

Is that why you've described the book as a cross between Shaw's Pygmalion *and Nabokov's* Lolita?

Exactly.

I get the Pygmalion *part. Why* Lolita? *Is Mason a connoisseur of nymphets?*

Good Lord, no. But, you see, the relationship between the philosopher and the apprentice is highly erotic, and, ultimately, romantic—the same arc that Humbert traces in his pursuit of Lolita. And, as with Humbert and Lo, the initial dynamic between Mason and Londa is that of a teacher and his student. I have a teaching degree, and I used to work frequently with schoolchildren, mostly helping them make films and videos, so the education theme in *The Philosopher's Apprentice* is quite autobiographical.

Your previous novel, The Last Witchfinder—*which was quite a good book, by the way . . .*

Thank you.

The Last Witchfinder *also centers on a teacher-student relationship. The heroine, Jennet Stearne, is tutored by her beloved Aunt Isobel in "natural philosophy," that is, science.*

I'd never thought of that connection before.

But whereas The Last Witchfinder *is an unequivocal celebration of the Enlightenment,* The Philosopher's Apprentice *seems more wary of science and its fruits. In fact, one of the central "characters" in the novel is a weird high-tech womb called the ontogenerator. Initially it functions mainly to bring Londa and her sisters into the world, but then people start putting the machine to some pretty sinister uses.*

You're probably thinking of the scenes in which religious zealots pilfer aborted fetuses, turn the discarded tissue into full-grown adults, and then condition these angry "immaculoids" to torment the parents who presumably canceled their prospective lives.

Those scenes, yes. What the heck is going on here? On one level, the immaculoids are sympathetic, but I don't think of you as being in the "pro-life" camp. The Last Witchfinder *was a very feminist novel.*

Once I stumbled upon the concept of the immaculoids—these "adult fetuses" with their programmed grudges—I decided to push it to extremes. Who knows, maybe I imagined that this "thought experiment" would help reframe the abortion controversy. What I love about fiction is the way this form of expression allows an author to wrestle an idea to the ground, as opposed to the bumper-sticker dialectics that pass for political and philosophical discourse in most sectors of our culture. In the age of mass communication, we need the quiet, contemplative, and often ambiguous medium of the novel more than ever.

You're avoiding the question, Morrow. By bringing those wretched immaculoids on stage, don't you end up endorsing the antiabortion position?

While composing *The Philosopher's Apprentice*, I did some public readings of the immaculoid scenes that, halfway through, had some audience members wondering if I might be taking a "pro-life" stance. By the end of the immaculoid episode, though, it's pretty clear that I'm satirizing those ideologues who fetishize fetuses but don't seem to care very much for humankind in general. The immaculoids mean nothing to their creators apart from their utility value as antiabortion icons.

You obviously have a taste for grandiose themes. Where does that come from?

No cleric will tell you this, and most philosophers, educators, and politicians also want to keep the cat in the bag, but it would appear ▶

James Morrow (*continued*)

that human beings haven't the foggiest idea why there's conscious life in our part of the galaxy, nor do we have a glove on why any one of us has been hurtled onto this planet at this moment in cosmic time, in whatever immediate circumstances he or she happens to enjoy. But I figure that, given our "thrownness," as Heidegger called it, we should work hard to become as bewildered as possible by this strange state of affairs, asking the most impertinent and audacious questions we can imagine. To do otherwise—and instead hand over the mystery of it all to dubious cults of expertise—is to waste one's life, I feel.

So, for you, novels are a good way to keep experts from impoverishing our minds?

That's right. In recent years, in interviews very much like this one, I find myself noting what a privilege it is to work within this particular form. Novels give writers and readers unique ways to grapple with the mystery of it all, and thus continue the great post-Enlightenment conversation.

We've talked about Shaw and Nabokov as influences. One of your prepublication critics, covering the book for Kirkus Reviews, *notes that* The Philosopher's Apprentice *also "tips its hat with style to Mary Shelley."*

Frankenstein was definitely a touchstone. In fact, for a while I was calling the novel *Prometheus Wept*, an allusion to Mary Shelley's subtitle, *The Modern Prometheus*. My Londa is indeed a kind of monster: a "moral monster," that is, one cursed with an outsized conscience. And, of course, *Frankenstein* is one of the great novels about the teacher-student relationship. Victor's sin is not so much that he abuses his knowledge but that he breaks faith with his creation. He fails in his prime parental responsibility. To paraphrase Professor Marvel, Victor Frankenstein is a good wizard, but he's not a very good man.

But eventually Londa becomes monstrous in a more conventional sense, doesn't she? By the end of the novel she's almost as brutish as the creature in the Hollywood adaptations of Frankenstein.

As part of the run-up to *The Philosopher's Apprentice*, I watched every *Frankenstein* movie I could lay my hands on. I figured such a festival would help me suffuse the text with a gratifying dose of cinematic sensationalism. I've always liked the truism "All art is entertainment," and its variant "All drama is melodrama." Sure, it doesn't work the other way around—but let's not forget that most serious novelists are out to show the reader a good time. Well, not Henry James, but most serious novelists.

Somebody once remarked, "Henry James chewed more than he bit off."

As opposed to, say, Herman Melville. From page one onward, *Moby-Dick* is almost polymorphously perverse in its commitment to the pleasure principle. I wish more English teachers helped their students engage the classics at the level of raw delight, instead of putting them on the scent of symbols. A novel is not a cryptogram.

Nevertheless, when you named your main character Londa Sabacthani, you were obviously trying for a symbolic effect. Her name evokes Jesus' famous cry from the cross in Matthew 27:46.

What famous cry would that be?

"Eli, eli, lama sabacthani." Translated from the Aramaic, it means, "My God, my God, why have you forsaken me?"

No, that was the last thing on my mind.

You're lying.

Yes, I'm lying. Novelists get paid to lie. We must be constantly vigilant, lest it become a habit. Now let me tell you about my dogs.

I'm afraid we're out of time.

We have an amazing female SPCA border collie named Pooka and a male Doberman mix named Amtrak. He's a wonderful dog, too. We rescued him from a train station in Orlando, and he's never forgotten it. Thank you for a very enjoyable conversation. ∽

Have You Read?
More by James Morrow

THE LAST WITCHFINDER

Jennet Stearne's father hangs witches for a living in Restoration England. But when she witnesses the unjust and horrifying execution of her beloved Aunt Isobel, the precocious child decides to make it her life's mission to bring down the Parliamentary Witchcraft Act. Armed with little save the power of reason, determined to see justice prevail, Jennet hurls herself into a series of picaresque adventures—traveling from King William's Britain to the fledgling American Colonies to an uncharted island in the Caribbean, braving West Indies pirates, Algonquin Indian captors, the machinations of the Salem witch court, and the sensuous love of a young Ben Franklin. For Jennet cannot, and *must* not, rest until she has put the last witchfinder out of business.

"[Morrow] pulls off so many dazzling feats of literary magic that in a different century he'd have been burned at the stake. . . . Watch out for James Morrow: he's magic."
                                —*Washington Post Book World*

The Godhead Trilogy

TOWING JEHOVAH
BLAMELESS IN ABADDON
THE ETERNAL FOOTMAN

James Morrow's Godhead Trilogy was called "one of the wildest series ever written" by the *Denver Post*. Based on the audacious conceit that the Creator of the Universe has not only incarnated himself but subsequently passed away, leaving behind a two-mile-long cadaver, the three books in the cycle— *Towing Jehovah*, *Blameless in Abaddon*, and *The Eternal Footman*—acquired a cult following as they were published in the 1990s. Several critics saw in the Godhead Trilogy a demented updating of Dante's *Divine Comedy*, but whatever their ancestry, these novels stand among the most engaging works of humanist satire in recent memory.

"If Salman Rushdie had Morrow's light-handed sense of satire, he would be in demand for all the right reasons."
—*Chicago Tribune*

THIS IS THE WAY THE WORLD ENDS

Content in his life as a tombstone carver and family man, George Paxton lacks only one thing: a fashionable "scopas" survival suit to protect his daughter in the event of thermonuclear war. Then, through a twist of fate, George secures the coveted garment for the price of a mere signature. Unfortunately, what he signs is a confession of his complicity in the arms race, and as the war that could never happen happens, George is whisked into the past and the future to face the consequences of his guilt.

"Astute, highly engaging, and finally moving."
—*Los Angeles Times*

Have You Read? *(continued)*

ONLY BEGOTTEN DAUGHTER

Call it a miracle. Call it an accident at the sperm bank. But Murray Katz, the celibate keeper of an abandoned lighthouse near Atlantic City, has been blessed with a daughter conceived from the union of his own seed and a holy ovum. Like her half brother Jesus, Julie Katz can walk on water, heal the blind, and raise the dead. But then her life gets really complicated, as God's daughter undertakes a fantastic odyssey through hell, a seceded New Jersey, and her own confused soul.

"Morrow unerringly targets the nerve endings most readers won't know they have until he zaps them."—*Washington Post*

CITY OF TRUTH

Jack Sperry spends his days diligently destroying "mendacious" works of art in Veritas, a city where people have been brutally conditioned to always tell the truth. But then one day Jack's beloved son, Toby, is bitten by a rabbit at Camp Ditch-the-Kids and contracts a rare illness. Suddenly our hero must somehow learn to lie—the only way, he believes, to give Toby sufficient hope to conquer his fatal disease.

"A quick and delightful read, with a sharp, unmerciful edge that would have pleased old Jonathan Swift."
                    —*Minneapolis Star Tribune*

Job's back on the old dung heap, and he wants a rematch with God. A Series-700 computer successfully reconstructs the tablets with the Ten Commandments from a million indecipherable shards— only to have second thoughts. Sheila, the lascivious sinner fished from the Flood by the captain of the Ark, has an agenda all her own. A congregation of sexless androids believes that Darwin's theory of evolution applies to them and awaits the Great Genital Coming. And God justifies once besetting mankind with an unusual plague. Why? Spare the rod, spoil the species, He says. (And He's always right. That's why He's got the job.)

"At his best, Morrow is brilliant. 'The Covenant' offers a wonderfully warped view of the supposedly pernicious influence of the Ten Commandments on human history, and 'Spelling God with the Wrong Blocks' is the cleverest satire of the evolution/creation squabble that I've ever read."   —*Philadelphia Inquirer*

Read on

Have You Read? *(continued)*

THE CAT'S PAJAMAS AND OTHER STORIES

"Arguably science fiction's reigning master of satire, Morrow has already blessed the genre with two previous volumes of short fiction and the monumental Godhead Trilogy, in which a deceased Jehovah literally falls to Earth. His latest collection demonstrates that his rapier wit has lost none of its edge as it encompasses twisted scenarios ranging from Martians invading Central Park to having the fates of other worlds rest upon the scores of American football games. In 'Auspicious Eggs,' global warming forces the Catholic Church to enact rites of 'terminal baptism,' in which the souls of infants deemed infertile are immediately sent heavenward. In a shorter tale, King Kong and Godzilla pay their respects to September 11 victims. During the title story, a crazed genetic scientist kidnaps a hapless do-gooder and harvests his altruism genes. All the stories manifest Morrow's penchant for exploring the dark underbelly of technological promise and extracting quirky moral conundrums. Morrow's fans will revel, and first-time readers may find his grim humor making fans of them too."
—*Booklist*

Don't miss the next book by your favorite author. Sign up now for AuthorTracker by visiting www.AuthorTracker.com.